GOLDEN HOUR OF YOU AND ME

By

K. JAMILA

Dedication

To Kennedy — for believing in this story every step of the way and more importantly, for being my friend. I hope everyone is lucky enough to have a friend like you.

To Liya — you are my angel for life.

To Esther — never change, you are pure gold.

To You

For those who have ever felt too much or have been made to feel like they are not enough, for those who have made mistakes, for those who have made hard decisions even when they hurt, and for those who keep climbing even when the battle feels endless, this is for you.

I hope you grant yourself the kindness and the space to find what sets your heart on fire, to love what you love and to love it boldly — I hope you never let it go.

Playlist

"Wild Horses" – Natasha Bedingfield

"This Is Me Trying" – Taylor Swift

"Heavy" – Kiana Ledé

"Dynamite" – Sigrid

"Safety Net" – Ariana Grande

"Time and Time Again" – Counting Crows

"Again Today / Hiding My Heart" – Brandi Carlile

"Naked" – Avril Lavigne

"Crazier" – Taylor Swift

"The Climb" – Miley Cyrus

"The Safest Place" – Sade

"Pretty Places" – Aly & AJ

"More Than Enough" – Alina Baraz

"Everywhere" – Michelle Branch

"Till There's Nothing Left" – Cam

"You Got What I Need" – Joshua Radin

"Under My Skin" – Nate Smith

"Location Unknown" – HONNE

"Awe of Her" – Joshua Henry

"Share My Life" – Kem

"Cliché" – James Vincent McMorrow

"Unless it's With You" – Christina Aguilera

"Golden Hour" – Kacey Musgraves

"New Year's Day" – Taylor Swift

Authors Note

Dear reader,

Thank you for choosing this book as your next read, it means the absolute world to me. As you begin *Golden Hour of You and Me*, I wanted to give a quick warning before you dive in to make the best decision for you and your mental health.

This book contains content recommended for those 18+, alludes to mental health struggles such as anxiety and possibly depression, discusses medication, tough parental relationships, and features a degenerative disease in one of the characters. If any of these are triggering for you, please pause and consider what is best for you.

Golden Hour of You and Me is a story extremely close to my heart in many ways. A love letter to a town I used to call home, a message for multiple versions of myself as I've walked through life, resulting in a story that fees like home. If you read on, I hope you find something for yourself within its pages. I hope you enjoy it.

Thank you.

From K. Jamila with love.

ONE

Sheyanne

There isn't a place on earth I despise more than Flagstaff, Arizona.

Except maybe this shitty gas station, which is taking forever and a day to fill up the old Bronco. I watch from a few feet away, blowing small puffs of cigarette smoke into the dry, dusty, Arizona air that's suffocating me with every breath.

The nicotine stinks, as always, but the small gas station offered none of my usual crutches, so for the first time in years, I bought fucking cigarettes.

Sue me.

As the stick of nicotine gets smaller and smaller in my hand, I toss it into the dirt and stomp it out, grinding it more than needed into the ground, like a little *fuck you* to Arizona. My phone buzzes in the back pocket of my jeans as I make my way to the car, which still isn't full, and I pull it out to see Shane's name flashing on the screen.

I don't even have time to get a snarky word out before his voice fills my ears.

"You're two hours late, Sheyanne," he grinds out, and I can picture him pacing back and forth around the living room that I'm sure looks unchanged.

"I'll get there when I get there." An empty, sarcastic smile forms on my lips, the red lipstick dry now, and I'm sure he can hear the disdain dripping off my words.

"It's been years, you know. Since you've been back. Since I've seen you."

Sighing, I place my phone between my ear and my shoulder as I remove the fuel nozzle to close the tank. "There's a reason for that, Shane."

He hesitates, a beat of silence passing over the phone, but I know he doesn't say what he wants to. "Whatever. Just get here," he mumbles.

"Yup." I hang up the phone before he can say anything else and throw my phone into the passenger seat before climbing up myself. The cracked leather seat molds around my body, and I lean back, my eyes fluttering closed as a breeze drifts through the open windows, ruffling the tight curls around my face. I exhale, start the car, and pull onto the street.

Music blares through the speakers as I drive towards the small town that used to be home. The cacti and dirt are no great sight. Not even the rock formations bring a smile to my face like they did when I was a kid, when I would imagine endless stories and people running through them into the forests. I try to distract myself in the sound around me, the beat of the song, the loud rush of the wind, but all I feel is the heavy dread balled up in the pit of my stomach.

The temperature gradually changes as I get closer to Flagstaff and the mountains, away from the desert that is southern Arizona, and the mid-October air creeps through my windows. Bright green pine trees start peeking through the sea of endless dust. The occasional deciduous tree dappled with orange, red, and brown leaves paint a picture of Flagstaff I haven't seen in so long.

Haven't wanted to see.

The two-hour drive from the gas station passes all too quickly with not nearly enough time to prepare for this—for seeing the stables again, my childhood house, my dad and Shane, or anything, really.

I avoid the small-town square, not wanting to accidently see anyone that doesn't want to see me as much as I don't want to see them. The tension in my body thrums through my blood and over my skin, pulled tighter with every mile I get closer to what used to be home, like I'm being stretched continuously.

The stable looks the same as it used to.

A rickety sign marks the long, gravel driveway, *The Shaw Ranch*, the white paint now cracked, and a gate—broken now—hangs open below it.

The tires of my Bronco crunch the gravel as I drive slowly down the long pathway. To my left, horse pastures are lined with brown fencing. Snowcapped mountains peak in the sky behind them. The white barn with faded maroon shutters appears like a beacon, acres of green and brown land to the right. And in the center of it all, the old ranch house.

I pull in slowly towards the simple, white ranch-style home. Dirt and dust stain the outside walls and the wraparound porch. Two rocking chairs sit near the front door, and the small front garden surrounds the walkway. I park in front of the shed to the right of the house, next to an old truck and a slightly newer one.

Shane, in his favorite hoodie that must be at least ten years old, leans against one of the pillars of the porch with his arms crossed. I can't see it, but I can imagine the line his lips are set into a mirror imitation of our dad's.

I take my time fixing my lipstick and adjusting my shirt, if only to piss him off further before jumping out of the car, landing on the dirt with a crunch. I leave my bags for later as I walk with my chin up towards the house. Above, the sky is gray, just a tad lighter than my mood.

Nyx, our golden retriever, comes bounding around the porch straight for me, ears perked and mouth open in his signature smile like I never left. My heart tugs in my chest, but I keep my face stoic in front of Shane as I lean down to pet him. His soft fur is warm under my palm, and I run my hand through it before standing.

"Hi, Shaney. Sorry I'm late." I grin.

His deep, brown eyes hold my stare for a moment before he gives the smallest shake of his head. "Please—you've never been sorry a day in your life."

My sarcastic grin dies as quickly as it came, my lips falling back into their usual semi-pout. "Someone's pissy."

Nyx barks at the two of us, his tail no longer swishing back and forth on the old wood porch. Shane and I continue the stare-off of two people who are interacting far more like rivals than siblings. His eyes glint with a coldness that wasn't there when I left, but right now, I don't care. I want to find out what was so important that I had to come home and then get out. As fast as I can.

"Sheyanne—"

"Let's get this over with, please." I exhale, not letting him finish, holding his gaze and taking in his defensive stance before pulling the leather jacket closer to my body and walking right past him. My fingers hesitate for half a second on the old doorknob before twisting it open. I can feel Shane's stare on my back and the swish of Nyx's tail as he moves past me.

The temperature is the same inside. I can feel the breeze coming through the open windows of the old familiar ranch. The small entryway is practically unchanged, the same faded doormat and rusting coat hooks on my right before it opens into the living area, which is also unchanged. A corner TV, small and old, probably only running on cable—if that— faces the same faded, dark green couch. The wooden coffee table on the patterned rug is scratched on the sides, the coasters and remote haphazardly spread on the glass surface.

The late afternoon sun shines through the back windows, illuminating the old hardwood floors and the kitchen to my right. The same old appliances and countertops and—for God sakes, literally everything is the same. The dog dish is in the same place, the coffee maker unmoved from its signature spot, and my stupid fifth grade artwork on the fridge.

The clearing of a throat brings me out of unnecessary feelings of nostalgia. I turn, my dark curls almost whipping me in the face as I do, immediately crossing my arms across my chest.

The only thing that's different about this place is him.

"Hi, Dad," I say, an accidental but not unwelcome bite to my words.

He's got more wrinkles on his face than I remember, and he walks with a limp as he makes his way to sit in one of the wooden dining chairs. I move deeper into the house, knowing when I look left, I'll see the hallway that leads to the bedrooms. I have no desire to walk down that memory lane this very second.

"May I ask why you've so lovingly requested my presence here?"

Shane snorts from his spot on the edge of the couch but otherwise keeps his mouth shut.

"Shane didn't tell you?" Dad's voice is as gruff as ever, the same deep tone to it as always.

I roll my eyes, squatting to pet Nyx, who hasn't left my side. "No, he told me I had to come. He *insisted* that if he told me over the phone, I would find a way to avoid it and not come back."

"Sounds like you." He doesn't smile. He just watches me from his seat at the table, his eyes unreadable as ever.

"Well, now that I'm here, per request," I motion to the house, trying not to focus on the chipped nail polish on my pointer finger I had picked at in the car. "Can one of you kindly spit it the fuck out?"

Dad's deep brown eyes darken, and instantly, I stiffen. It's been years since I've had to mind my tongue, and already, I'm falling back into my role as the disappointment to the family. The look he gives me brings me right back to the past. We all have the same eyes, except I can barely remember a time my dad's held anything but unfiltered disdain or disappointment for me.

"Sheyanne, language." His voice is stern, leaving no room for argument. I bite my tongue. "I need your help."

I furrow my brows. "What on earth could I do for you?"

His dark brown skin hardens, the evidence of the years of sun—even with sunscreen and being Black—showing on his face. All hard and deepening lines and dark spots spattering his forehead and nose. "I'm selling the ranch. And the house, too, I suppose."

My heart beats deeply twice in my chest. "What? Why?"

Shane snorts. "Oh, please, Sheyanne, don't act like you care."

I ignore him, eyes fixed on Dad's face, waiting for an answer that makes logical sense. I may hate it here, but he and Shane most definitely don't. Or maybe they do. I honestly wouldn't know.

"He's been diagnosed with Alzheimer's."

I blink once, twice, and completely forget the scolding I received moments ago. "You've got to be fucking kidding me." My voice rings through the silence. It seems to echo off the old kitchen and the walls where the paint cracks. Even Nyx's tail stops swishing next to me.

Dad ignores the curse word that slipped past my lips.

"It's early onset. We caught it early enough to manage it for now, but still. That's what it is." Dad runs a hand over his coarse, cropped black hair, now peppered with specks of gray, and I feel Shane's invasive gaze on my face. I keep it impassive, my lips set in a line, no flicker of emotion there even if it comes out in my words. "This folder has the diagnosis and recommended doctors and treatment plans."

For a moment, I look away from them both and stare at the plain manila folder on the old dining room table. My eyes flicker back and forth between that and my dad and my brother, ignoring all the questions bubbling up in my throat except one. "Okay, but why are you selling? Isn't it just going to Shane?"

Shane clears his throat, which I ignore, keeping my eyes on Dad, who just shrugs. "He doesn't want it, and I won't force it on him."

My brows furrow with disbelief. Last time I saw Dad, he barely cared about what *we*—or at least *I*—wanted, as long as the job or task was done. It didn't matter in his book as long as it was what *he* wanted. And now, he's just willing to sell everything? Just like that?

"Okay," I drawl out, "but what does that have to do with me?"

It seems heartless to not ask how he's doing or the details of what the doctors have said, or to even pick up the folder or ask how Shane is doing, but the part of myself I used to let care or get close to my dad is shoved deep, deep down in the trenches. While I can feel a small tug of it deep in my chest at the news, I don't pull on it.

I don't want to feel it. I don't want the thread to unravel.

His stare is cold as it meets mine, and I'm sure mine is the same. "You're both going to help me get things ready to go before I have to move into assisted living."

Dad in assisted living. That'll be a day for the record books.

I look between him and Shane, who still leans on the edge of the couch with his arms crossed. The sun is starting to set behind the clouds, the first few hues of orange lighting up the sky and filtering through the windows to splay across the floor. I stare at it for a few moments, not really knowing what to say to either of them.

All I know is that I don't want to fucking be here. In this house that isn't really a home.

The sound of gravel crunching causes me to whip my head up, my eyes narrowing as I look between the two of them. Nyx's tail starts wagging like it always used to when someone would drive up into the driveway.

"Who is that?" I mutter, turning on my heel and going back through the front door to see a sleek, black sedan pulling onto the dirty driveway, dust already staining the car.

Shane sighs behind me. "That would be the financial advisor he hired."

I stare at him incredulously. "You let him hire a financial advisor?" The breeze passes by me, blowing my curls around my face, and I pull them back in frustration.

"I didn't *let* him do anything, Sheyanne," he says roughly, shaking his head at me and leaning against the dirty, white siding of the house.

Dad has finally caught up, his limp slightly worse now, but he leans in the open doorway. His eyes are focused on the now parked car and the man who steps out of it.

The man is in pressed black slacks and a perfectly ironed, white button-up, a suit jacket hanging off his arm, with glossy black shoes on that are going to get dirty as soon as he takes two steps over the dusty gravel. I can see the glittering watch on his wrist from his rolled-up cuffs and the polished cufflinks to match. I watch, leaning against one of the pillars that hold up the porch covering as he grabs not only a briefcase but a suitcase.

"What is this? A live-in intervention for you?" I ask, turning to look at my dad. Every second I spend here somehow gets worse.

"That's exactly what this is."

The man now rolls two suitcases towards the front porch, his dark brown face unreadable behind the sunglasses covering his eyes.

I don't care if he can hear me or not as I stare at my dad for the hundredth time today. "He's living here?"

"Yes."

I look at Shane. "With Shane and I?"

"Yes."

"With you?"

"Yes," he says firmly, done with my questions by the tone of his voice, and I know better than to ask another one.

I turn to see whatever his name is standing at the foot of the steps, looking around at the grounds of the place. He takes his sunglasses off, hanging them off the white button-up shirt. His eyes flicker from the fenced-in acres, to the barn, to the house, and finally, to the three of us.

He makes eye contact with me, the obviously angry one, for a brief second. No clear emotion flickers in his deep brown eyes, and I keep my own face impassive as I silently study him before turning back around and walking straight past Dad and Shane and into the house.

I fucking *hate* Flagstaff, Arizona.

Two

Sheyanne

Liam Landon.

The name echoes in my head.

At least, that's what I thought I heard from leaning against my closed bedroom door. I haven't gone back out there yet, but I can hear their soft voices in the living room, discussing God knows what.

The room around me is the same ugly, purple-gray color I painted it all those years ago, illuminated by the setting sun and the bedside lamp. Under my feet, the hardwood floor is cold, cooling my heated skin. The espresso-colored furniture is all the same—my vanity, my dresser, and my nightstands. Each have a few pale scratches down the side or on the tabletop from overuse, and even now, all my posters hang on the wall. Some of the ends are curled in and ripped, but it seems as though once I left, no one ever stepped foot in here.

Which is fine with me.

I stare out the window where I can see straight to the barn and the few horses out in the pasture. After a few deep breaths, I turn around and wrap my hand around the knob, willing myself to get this over with. A financial advisor. A live-in intervention. Alzheimer's.

This is fucking absurd.

Nyx is waiting outside my door; his tail immediately starts wagging when I exit. The voices stop as if they can sense me, like I'm the Wicked Witch of the West. I pause in the hallway, leaning against the doorway with my arms crossed.

Shane, Dad, and Liam all sit at the old, wooden dining room table, and slowly, their eyes all turn to land on me.

"What's your name?" I direct to Liam, even though I know the answer.

He holds my gaze, lifting his chin a fraction of an inch. "Liam."

A smirk tugs at my lips. "Leo?"

"Liam."

I narrow my eyes slightly and tilt my head. "Oh, Leon, perfect. Nice to meet you."

"It's Liam," he says again, calmly, but his deep brown eyes, deeper than Shane's, darken further. He leans back in the chair, crossing a leg over the other in one smooth motion.

Shane glances between us, visibly agitated. "Don't worry; she's like that all the time."

Ah, yes, I do have that effect on people.

Striding across the floor, ignoring the glances trailing over me, I take a seat at the table right next to Shane. I glide my eyes up to Liam, not caring if he sees me looking over him.

Liam doesn't seem much older than me, maybe by a few years. His dark brown skin is flawless, both his face and his forearms where the sleeves of his white button-up have been rolled up. His eyes are big and searching, but there's something incisive about them—intelligent, sharp.

I flicker over his face, the sharp jawline, his full lips, and the clean cut of his black hair that suits him perfectly. The shirt hugs him, not too tight, but I can easily see the ripples of lean muscle underneath.

He's attractive, in an expensive kinda way.

I take one last sweeping glance, trying to get a read on him, before my eyes flick between my dad and Shane. "So, what exactly is the plan?"

Dad clears his throat, leaning back into his chair. "Mr. Landon is here to help me get everything in order financially, to sell or put away or divvy out everything where it needs to be. He'll also be working on a rebrand, re-designing the brochures, the sign, all of that. In the meantime, you and Shane are responsible for the grounds and the barn and any new customers. All of us will work together in researching possible buyers and seeing where we can improve in order to sell."

I tug at the ends of my curls until I feel it in my scalp, trying to distract myself before stealing a glance at Shane. "Just like old times, huh, Shaney?"

My mind runs back to being younger, waking up for chores and helping run the stables. The best part was the horses. I'm sure that hasn't changed.

Shane huffs, running his hand over his own shortly trimmed curls. His are lighter than mine, a warmer brunette unlike the black of my own, but his face is sharper than mine, especially as we've gotten older. Higher cheekbones and a more defined jaw compared to my softer, slightly rounder features. Nonetheless, the likeness is clear, especially when you stand us next to Dad. There's no hiding the family resemblance.

The only clear difference is Shane's and my skin tone, lighter, courtesy of our white mom.

"I don't think this is anything like old times, Sheyanne." There's a sarcastic bite to his words that I ignore.

"Well, I'd hope not. It's not like it was any better back then." I roll my eyes, looking back to Dad whose eyes are focused on me. "So, while Shane and I take over the ranch, Leon's here to sit inside, and what? Run numbers?"

Liam looks straight at me, not saying a word, but I refuse to break eye contact. I feign innocence, waiting for him to say anything.

"I'm here to help your dad get things in order wherever he needs, so this can be a smooth process."

I snort. "If you think anything about this is going to be smooth, you need a fu—" I swallow the curse word after a sharp glance from Dad, "Reality check."

"And you will be expected to help him if he needs anything as well. If I am ever unable to answer or help him, you both will step in. We will all be working together," Dad adds, looking pointedly at me.

I ignore him, my eyes locked with Liam's. "How much is he paying you?"

"Sheyanne Meli Shaw."

My eyes flicker to my dad, the tone of voice stopping me for a brief second. "What? It's gotta be hefty since he's coming to *live* here."

"It's none of your business—"

"I'm sitting right here, you know—"

I continue, ignoring the lecture about etiquette. "And by the way, where exactly is he sleeping? Is he gonna cook for himself? I'm just not understanding."

Shane and Dad stare at me, unblinking and unamused. "The guest room has been cleared out," Shane fills the silence.

I nod, pursing my lips, throwing a smile to Liam, "Ah, good place, right next to me. And that's where all the deep dark family secrets are, mostly about me since Shane is the golden boy." My eyes flicker to Dad. "Guess we'll have to pull them out for old times' sake. A trip down memory lane one last time."

Shane shakes his head, letting it fall forward into his hands. "Jesus Christ."

I stand up, done with this conversation, done with the fact that I have to fall back into the same old shit my life used to be, and pat Shane on the back. "Don't worry, I'm sure this will be a blast."

With that, I turn on my heel to go retrieve my bags. Nyx follows me, his paws creating soft patters behind me until we step into the cool air. The sky is darker now, barely any sun left as I look over what's gonna be my life for the next few months, like a little dark cloud hanging over my head.

I bound off the steps, swinging open my car doors and dragging out the two large suitcases that have been in my car for almost a month, since I didn't renew my lease back in San Diego and I've had to bum it since. I never found a home there either, so I guess I'm just taking loss after loss.

Life there was as shitty as life here.

It's probably just me and my miserable attitude, but that's what keeps the world spinning.

A deep sigh escapes me, and I sit atop one of the suitcases for a moment, my eyes taking it all in. A low whinny from one of the horses echoes in the background as Nyx comes up to me, shoving his golden head into my hands. The soft fur surrounds my fingers, and I scratch his ears, taking deep breaths in the process.

"This is gonna be interesting, isn't it, buddy?" I murmur, kissing the top of his head, and he nuzzles my cheek in response. I shake my head with a sad smile. "One day at a time, right?" His tail wags a bit quicker now, and I lean my head against the car, staring at the sky above.

Nyx is the only bright light in this situation for me right now.

And the bright light is dimmed when I sense the presence of someone by the stairs. I glance over to see Liam's tall figure on the porch, car keys in hand.

My smile falls immediately, like it was never there, as he walks towards his own car.

He pauses when he reaches the back door, eyes coasting over me. "How difficult are you going to make this exactly?" His voice is smooth and resonant as it reaches me.

I shrug. "Depends on the day."

Liam reaches in and grabs another smaller bag from his car, slinging it onto his shoulder. "Great. Looking forward to it." The sarcasm drips from his words, so at least we're on the same page in that respect.

I look at him for a second, realizing how out of place we each look in opposite ways. Him because he's dressed like he's going to a business meeting, and me because I simply don't fit here anymore.

I did everything in my power to separate myself from this place after growing up. It's never been anything but a black hole in my life that sent me spiraling down many different paths—paths I never thought I'd have to walk again.

Liam's shoes crunch as he walks towards the steps, locking his car with a beep. He turns to look at me once more. "Wish I could say it was nice to meet you and that this will be easy, but I can't."

My lips quirk up as I look at him with a raised eyebrow, not bothering to answer. He holds my gaze for a second, unflinching, both of us unamused by the other's presence.

The screen door swings open with a loud creak, breaking the stare-off. My eyes flicker over to Shane, who stands in the doorway. "Mr. Landon, I can show you the guest room if you're ready?" he says, looking between the two of us.

"Please, call me Liam," he responds, his lips quirking up in a small smile.

Shane nods, holding the door open for Liam as he passes through before looking at me. The darkness settles in around us, and the constellations are starting to peek through. Little flickers of light in a sea of darkness.

He hesitates. "Are you coming in, Shey?" His words are soft, like when we were kids, but I shake my head, taking one last look at the house and my suitcases on the gravel.

"No." It's all I offer before hopping into my car and starting the engine, letting Nyx hop in with me. I ignore the flash of disappointment on his face, ignore the suitcases left on the driveway, and pull the fuck away from that house.

At least for a little while.

THREE
SHEYANNE

Alcohol was most definitely not the answer.

My head spins as I lean back against the fence of the front porch. Nyx's head rests on my lap. His quiet snores and the occasional cricket are the only sounds around me. The porch overhang blocks out the sky, which is fine since the last time I tried to look at the stars, my head spun.

I can't go inside because I don't have a fucking key.

Because when I left this place almost four years ago, I threw it out of the car window and never looked back.

I also refuse to call Shane at 1:30 A.M. to let me in like I'm sixteen years old again. If I have to sleep on this front porch with only Nyx and my leather jacket to keep me warm, then so be it.

After my trip to the liquor store, I was surprised to see that my suitcases were no longer in the driveway, but I didn't go inside to thank anyone. I just walked around the old farm with a bottle of whiskey until it was completely dark out and all the lights went out one by one. It never occurred to me to let anyone know I had no way of getting inside until it was too late.

The creaking of the old screen door fills the silence, and my eyes snap open. Too quickly, because instantly I'm hit with the spins, but I keep them open until the feeling fades as the porch light flickers on, buzzing overhead.

"Sheyanne, you need to come inside." Shane's voice is low and stern, and I look up at him. His eyes are hazy with sleep, but even then, and even drunk, I see the frustration floating in them.

I roll my eyes and pat Nyx's head, using the wall to stand up, unwilling to let Shane catch me off-balance, literally and figuratively. Bugs float towards the light, and I sigh, trying to focus on my steps.

Shane reaches out his hand, but I take a wobbly step back, catching my balance. "I don't need your help," I say with an overexaggerated shake of my head, trying not to cringe at the slurring of my words.

He sighs, stepping back and letting Nyx and me through the door. I stop to grab a glass of water in the dark kitchen. The door shuts and locks behind us, but I still feel Shane's presence as I down a glass before refilling it and turning around.

He opens his mouth, but I hold up my hand, leaning against the counter to steady myself. "I'm—I'm not doing this tonight." My tongue stumbles over the words as the world spins again. "Actually, I'm not doing this ever."

Shane's eyes harden, his face overtaken with disapproval so clear, it could rival Dad's.

"Whatever. Just get to sleep. We have to be up early."

With that, he turns to walk down the hallway to his own room, pausing to look back, eyes coasting over my face before he runs a hand over his curls and leaves me alone in the kitchen. I wait until his light flickers out to walk towards my own bedroom, happy to see Nyx resting at the foot of my bed where my suitcases have been placed. Slowly and dizzily, I pull my shoes off, tossing them in the corner before peeling my jeans and shirt off, replacing them with pajamas.

After a moment, I quietly make it to the Jack and Jill bathroom—the one that unfortunately connects Liam and me—to brush my teeth all the while avoiding looking myself in the mirror. The door to the connecting room is closed, and my gaze lingers on it before I shut off the light and head into my room.

When I shut my nightstand lamp off, I'm cast into darkness. I slam my eyes shut to block out the dizziness and the sheer fact that I have to be here at all.

A fact that not even alcohol could help me forget.

There's a pounding on my door and in my head, and it takes everything in me to stifle the groan building in my chest as I shove my head into my pillows.

"Get up, Sheyanne." Dad's gruff voice carries under the door before his footsteps fade away, and I inhale before pushing myself upward. It's still dark, only a glimpse of the dawn sky coming through the blinds, but even that sends my head pounding. Nyx eyes me from his space on the bed, and I pet him before swinging my legs out and landing firmly on the hardwood.

My phone informs me that it's 5:45 A.M. The blank screen with no notifications also reminds me of just how empty everything is. I didn't leave anyone behind in San Diego, and I sure as hell wasn't getting a welcome back here. I toss it on my pillows before getting dressed, having no use for it anyway.

Before I do anything, I head into the bathroom to splash my face with water and pop two ibuprofen. I finish the rest of my morning routine and gently adjust the wrap around the edges of my curls, making sure the rest is sufficiently pulled back for my chores.

I hear the muttering of voices as I open my door, holding my boots in my hand. Nyx bounds out, to go get his breakfast, I assume. With a heavy sigh, I will myself towards the smell of coffee that is thankfully filling the space and my head. I survey everyone in the kitchen with cautious eyes, forcing a sly smile on my lips, hoping to paint the same picture of the person they all saw yesterday.

There are already folders on the table in front of Dad and Liam, who looks surprisingly awake this early. He sends me an indifferent glance. Dad says nothing, so I look to Shane who's holding his own cup of coffee, dressed similarly to me in dark-wash jeans and a long-sleeve T-shirt with a hat tucked over his curls and settling on his forehead.

The silence sinks in uncomfortably. "Well, what a lovely morning this is," I mutter to myself.

"Let's go," Shane orders, taking another sip before setting his mug down. I bring mine with me, not ready to let go of the caffeine I know will get me through this. When he glances at me, his nose turns up. "You smell like whiskey."

"That's what I was drinking last night," I say, following Shane towards the front door, and this time, I feel the eyes on me. Turning quickly, I send a two-finger salute to where Liam and my dad sit, both of whom shoot their eyes downwards at my gesture. The screen door creaks shut behind me.

Shane sends me a glance. "And what? You drank so much you forgot how to get inside?"

"No, Shane. I don't have a key anymore." The familiar farm starts to come into view as we move along the connecting pathway between the house and the barn. To the right, another path breaks off, leading to the small greenhouse and the garden.

He says nothing about my key as we move closer, Nyx trailing behind us. "All right, so—" he starts, but I shake my head.

"I'll get a start on the horses. Start with the pastures, and we can meet in the middle to finish," I state firmly, leaving no room for an argument. Caring for the horses and taking care of the barn was my favorite before, and I'm sure that hasn't changed.

"Sounds good. Any special instructions are written on the stall card." He turns away, but I could've sworn hurt flashed in his eyes at my dismissal. For a moment, I watch him walk away, hands tucked in his pockets.

But I don't know what he expected. I've made it clear I don't want to be here and am doing the bare minimum to get through it.

The coffee slips past my lips again as I near the barn. The sun is peeking through the early morning clouds now, turning the sky a warm orange, but the chill of the night still seeps in past my clothes. I push the large barn doors open, letting the light stream in over the floors that are sprinkled with loose hay. The noses of some of the horses peek over their stalls at the intrusion, causing me to smile.

"Morning, everyone. Ready to eat?" A few of them neigh in response, and huffs of air from their noses puff clouds into the chilly morning air.

I look around at the cards on the stalls. Three of the horses are fully boarded, meaning it's our job to do all the heavy lifting. The stalls, the feed, and turning them out into the pasture and exercising them. Two of them are partially boarded, so most of the time, the owner will be about at some point during the day to exercise them, but the same requirements go for them as well. They pay us—or my dad—for the heavy lifting. More realistically, due to the limp, it probably means Shane has been doing most of it on his own. Until now.

There are a few empty stalls, but there are two more with name cards on them towards the back doors. I walk down the barn hall to read them, my heart beating at the possibility they might be the two horses Shane and I raised from when we were kids. They were our first big responsibility. However, Dad is not a sentimental man, so I force myself to accept that those two horses are probably long gone.

I step to the first one, not wanting to look over the stall and be disappointed when I don't see one of my old horses. The name card reading *Theodore* is faded and scraggly and looks a lot like my old handwriting. My eyes shoot up to see the big brown roan quarter horse staring at me with wide eyes and perked ears.

"Teddy," I say, grinning, opening the stall door and cautiously walking in, remembering he might not greet me as happily as Nyx did.

He lifts his head, reminding me just how tall he is as I step forward with my hand out. His warm, big eyes blink slowly for a moment before he pushes his nose into my hand and then into my chest, which expands. I pet his cheek before leaning up onto my tiptoes to wrap my arms around his tall neck, pulling him into a hug.

I lean back. "Is Rayne still here, too?" He blows air onto where my hand rests on the soft skin of his nose before he nudges me. I turn around, and on the stall across from him sits the same scraggly name card with a different name, but one just as familiar.

After kissing Teddy on the nose, I close his stall and approach Rayne's. Her appaloosa coloring is still as stunning as it was when I left. Immediately, her eyes focus on me, but her ears are flattened, and she doesn't move toward me at all like Teddy did. I stay on my side of the closed stall.

I nod, disappointment tingling my fingertips. "So, you're mad at me."

She blinks, before dipping her head to drink water. I watch her for a moment, my eyes lingering on her soft coat. Her head and neck are a warm brown before growing into a spotted, white color. She continues to avoid me, so after another moment, I pat the top of the stall door. "You'll come around," I murmur, turning around to get the feed ready.

As I move throughout the barn, with Nyx lazily watching me from his warm, sunny spot on the loose hay, the horses' munching soon starts to encroach on the silence. Once all the horses are fed, including a disgruntled Rayne, I fill their troughs with fresh water. I haven't done any of this in a while, but I fall back into the pattern quickly. One by one, as the horses finish eating, I attach a lead rope to their halters, leading the boarded horses first into their assigned pastures. Teddy snorts as I come back to his stall and attach his lead rope. He strides next to me, his hooves clicking on the barn floor until landing on the soft grass outside.

My hand rests on his neck, feeling each step of the tall, sturdy horse beneath my palm. As we approach the gate, he nudges my chest with his head. "I missed you, bud. I'm sorry I left you here." His ear flicks back in response.

At the time, leaving the animals was the hardest part of the whole thing. They were what kept me going back then. Whenever Dad and I would get into it or when Shane and I fought—no matter what, they were the grounding force for me. I never thought if I ever came back that Teddy and Rayne would still be here. I thought Dad would've sold them the day I left.

Teddy shoves his head into my chest again, and I scratch his neck before I unclip the lead rope and let him into the pasture he and Rayne will share, if I can even get Rayne to let me lead her. I walk back until I'm standing in front of her stall again. Her eyes are big and round and unblinking.

I open the door, and she steps back. "Rayne, come on." I hold my hand out, but she doesn't give an inch, and I huff, met head-on with a familiar stubbornness. "I get it, okay? I know you're mad, but I'm sorry." She stays unmoving, unflinching.

Shane appears, leaning against the wall of the stall next to me. His eyes flick between the two of us. "Is someone not happy to see you?"

Biting my tongue, I sigh and hand him the rope. "She'll come around. But can you do this? She won't let me, and I don't feel like getting my ass kicked."

Shane snorts, and it almost sounds like he might laugh, but he doesn't. "I don't know; I think getting your ass beat would be good for you."

I flip him off, crossing my arms in the process, but step back as he attaches the rope. Rayne pushes her nose softly into his hand, all the while staring at me.

Who knew a horse could hold such a grudge?

Turning away, I roll up my sleeves to get ready to complete the last task for the barn and muck the stalls. Behind me, the sound of her hooves and Shane's footsteps fade out. When he returns, I pause.

"Why didn't he sell them?" I ask quietly.

He shrugs. "You'll have to ask him." Shane moves to the ladder that leads towards the small storage space above the stalls. "I need to bring some hay down, and then I'll help. Everything else is done."

I open my mouth to object but don't. I don't want to be here any longer than I have to. The air is awkward now, and yes, I may have created that tension, but I never wanted to have to deal with it in person. My intention was never to leave Shane behind, but it wasn't enough for me to stay just for my brother whom I didn't think cared, so he ended up caught in the wreckage.

I love Shane. He's my older brother. He was my best friend once, but even he couldn't have fixed Dad and me, so I didn't feel guilty when I left. But now, I'm stuck here, forced to deal with the consequences of my own actions.

As much as I'd love to avoid that, I don't know if I'll be able to.

We work so quickly, I barely even realize when we finish the last stall. With the sun higher in the sky, the temperature has warmed up in typical Flagstaff fashion, so I slip my dark, long-sleeve button-up off, leaving myself in short sleeves as I tie it around my waist. We exit side by side, the barn doors open to let the sun flow in. There's dirt all over my jeans, and little beads of sweat line my face and my arms. All I want is more coffee, a shower, and to lock myself in my room. Inside, the house is quiet while the smell of bacon and eggs waft around us.

I look over at Shane, his eyes flicking to me every so often but never staying too long, like I might bite, and I feel that emotional part of me tug a bit harder. Before I say anything, I'm interrupted by the clearing of Dad's throat.

My eyes shoot to his, and all feelings of annoyance and disdain come rushing back. "Everything go okay out there?"

After a long sip of coffee, I nod. "Everything is fine."

Dad nods, pushing his reading glasses up the bridge of his nose. "I need a favor, Sheyanne." When I don't speak, he continues. "I need you to take Liam into town today."

Liam is leaning back against the island countertop in simple black slacks and a button-up. His arms are crossed, his face stoic except for the tiniest hints of smugness and amusement as his eyes flicker to mine.

I don't hesitate to throw Shane under the bus. "Why can't Shane?"

Shane rolls his eyes but just moves to the coffee maker. "I have plans in a few hours."

"What—with your imaginary girlfriend?"

"Yes, actually." My jaw pops open, and I watch satisfaction settle over his face, his brown eyes dancing with humor.

I blink, looking back at Dad.

"You'll be taking him because I asked. He needs to see some records, so just take him where he needs to go: the courthouse and the bank, I believe." He looks at Liam, who nods, before looking back to me. "Stop making this difficult."

My face scrunches, searching for a way out. "Why can't he drive himself?"

"He doesn't know where he's going–"

I interrupt. "It's a small town. I'm sure he can figure it out."

When Dad raises a hand and slides off his reading glasses, placing them on the table, I stiffen, swallowing back any further arguments. "It's easier for you to take him where he needs to go. You're doing it because I'm asking you to."

Looking downward, I cast my words towards the floor. "You're not asking anything. You're just telling me."

Dad exhales loudly, letting me know he heard my whispered words, and takes a sip of his coffee. "You're right. I am telling you. Now get ready and go."

Liam stays silent through the whole charade. The unreadable look on his face only frustrates me more, but his brown eyes are stuck on mine. I narrow my own when his quiet, smug words wash over me.

"Any day now, Miss Shaw."

Four

Liam

My grandparents taught me to trust my gut and never question my decisions. For the most part, I never have. Every decision, every job, every choice has always led me somewhere I needed to go, taught me something I needed to learn.

After a single day in Flagstaff, Arizona, I've begun questioning everything. All because of Sheyanne Shaw. I adjust the watch on my wrist, checking it for the fifth time in the last forty-five minutes.

The arrangement when I applied wasn't so strange. The only thing that made it any different from other freelance jobs I've taken was the fact that it was long-term and the live-in aspect. Of course, the circumstances were sadder than most, the diagnosis and the unfortunate selling of a long-term family business, but none of that affected my opinion. And really, the pay made it almost impossible to ignore.

Especially since I am saving for two reasons. One, to help my grandparents move into a new home. They aren't hurting for money, but they aren't as comfortable as I would like. My grandfather is a mechanic—which he loves—but it certainly isn't the most lucrative industry, and it also has caused multiple injuries with his hips and back. As for my grandma, she used to be a chef, but now, she just caters for special occasions. Time and time again, they've insisted they are fine, but fine isn't enough for the people that raised me. The second reason I'm saving is for me. My grandparents won't let me continue to live on and off with them. I told them it was to save, but they knew it was so I could help out and keep an eye on them. So, I need to figure out where to go, where I want to live, and set down some roots.

While the job mentioned the help of Mr. Shaw's two kids, it didn't detail just how difficult it may be. I have a feeling not even he knew the trials his daughter was going to put him through. Sheyanne seems quite determined to make it known she wants absolutely nothing to do with this place.

I stand, unable to control the situation by checking the time repeatedly, and instead grab the tablet and the folder I have placed on the dresser.

Leaning against the wardrobe, I leaf through the folder of the printed and signed contract. With a quick eye, I read over it once more, focusing more on the small details that I'd noted before rather than the larger, priority tasks. After a second read-through, a sigh escapes my lips.

I'm patient, but this is testing my last nerve.

With the ever-growing time on my hands, I survey the room I'll be staying in for the next few months. The walls are a blue-gray, and the hardwood is covered with a large rug that takes up a majority of the floorspace. A dark wood bedframe is situated between two windows on the wall opposite of me, facing the pastures and offering a glimpse of the mountains. The dresser I lean against matches the bedframe perfectly, as do the end tables on either side. Above, a ceiling fan spins on a low setting, just enough to circle the air that seeps in from the hallway through the door left ajar.

To the right of that is the closed door to the bathroom, the one I share with Sheyanne.

Instead of waiting in here any longer, I head back toward the kitchen. Mr. Shaw lifts his head at my appearance, and his eyes narrow at the lack of his daughter's. He's nice enough to me—kind, firm. But he's a boss. And there is obviously something off between his daughter and him, something I have no interest in diving into.

I dip my head at the man paying my salary for the time being. For now, personally, I have no qualms with him. "Mr. Shaw."

He folds the newspaper in front of him. The way he does it so diligently reminds me of how my grandfather does it after he's finished reading the comics. "Sorry to keep you waiting."

With a polite smile, I shake my head. "It's not a problem. Everything will get done. I'd like to go through the checklist with you later this afternoon if that's all right?"

"Absolutely. I want everything to run as smoothly as possible for you."

"That's my job, sir," I respond. He dips his head, turning his eyes back to the tabletop as silence descends.

Glancing around, I take in the house again. Based on the pay I was offered, I can't say this is what I was expecting. The house is dated—old appliances, creaky doors, and scratches in the hardwood. It's not bad; instead, it contains a strange sense of comfort and intimacy, at least in my eyes. But I certainly thought it would be bigger—updated. Mr. Shaw hired me not because he needed help making money or managing the everyday. Instead, he needed help investing some of it, allocating it to where it would need to go in the future, especially with costs related to his condition, and to make sure both of his kids had enough should they need it.

The door on the outer wall, situated halfway between the living room and the kitchen, is open. It leads onto a screened-in sunroom, and a bit of the cool air seeps through and into the house. Shane sits out there on one of the leather chairs, typing away on his laptop.

While it's not cold—yet—it's different from the dry heat of Vegas. I make a mental note to take a trip to whatever stores I can find to pick up some thicker layers. Not that I'll attempt that today. It's clear Sheyanne has no interest in driving me anywhere, not that I blame her. I fully expected to go alone. My best guess is it's just a power play by Mr. Shaw. My grandfather used to do it whenever I acted out growing up, made me do the most menial tasks just because he could. It worked because I was a kid. And because I adored him. I still do.

I'm not so sure this approach is going to work on Sheyanne.

But again, that is absolutely none of my business.

The appearance of dark curls in the hallway alerts me to her presence. Quickly, I trail my eyes over her. Skin peeks out of the large rips in jeans that hug her curves and the space between the band of her pants and the end of the cropped black long sleeve she has on. The long, tight curls of her hair fall to her midback, and she wears gold and silvery jewelry on her ears and a singular necklace around her collarbone.

When I meet her gaze, it's unflinching, the brown unreadable.

She stalks toward the front door without a word and grabs her keys from their spot on the wall. I tuck the folder under my arm and follow her out.

I wait for her to unlock the old Bronco, trying to ignore the fact that she climbs in, adjusts her seat, places her phone down, and turns the car on before leaning over with the smallest smirk on her lips to unlock my side.

She's a bit of an asshole, but it's more amusing than anything. Not that I'll let her know that.

She turns up the volume of her music when I climb in, her lips falling into their regular pout. Silently, she reverses and heads down the gravel driveway before turning onto the pavement. When I looked it up, the house is only twenty minutes away from the town square, which is one of the only truly populated areas of this place. After a few stoplights and silence, I feel her heavy gaze on me.

When it grows heavier, I break the silence. "Is there a reason you're staring at me?" Out of the corner of my eye, I see the edge of her mouth quirk before she erases it.

"Not particularly, no."

The next stoplight turns red, and the weight of her stare returns. "Well, could you not?"

The smugness drips off her words. "I think I'll do whatever I want."

I run a hand over my chin to keep the amusement from growing visible on my face. Not to say it's not annoying—it is. But it doesn't have the same effect on me that it might have on her dad or her brother. I don't know her. I don't care enough to be bothered by it.

Turning to face her, I adjust the cuff of my sleeves calmly. "You are ridiculous."

Her eyes are hidden behind her sunglasses, but I can tell she's searching for any emotion, any indication of what I'm feeling. Whether she finds it or not, I don't know. "What's ridiculous is that I'm driving you around like you aren't a grown man with a car. What's ridiculous, Leon, is that you're here at all."

I shrug. "It was a good offer. I wasn't going to turn it down."

She tugs her sunglasses off and places them on top of boisterous curls. "All about the money, are we? The other circumstances didn't make you second guess? A man with Alzheimer's, who owns a farm in Flagstaff Arizona, the middle of nowhere? None of that impacted your decision?"

"Nope." The town comes into view when she turns a corner.

She glances over, her eyebrows furrowing. I obviously don't know her enough to know what the deal is—whether she's just angry that she's here, angry that her dad is sick, angry that I'm here, or just angry about it all—but an emotion other than feigned indifference finally shows in her eyes.

"So, that's all you care about?"

I shake my head as she pulls into a parking spot in the square near the town hall. I meet her eyes for the first time as I sit up. "I don't really think you're in a position to judge me."

"I'm not judging. I'm just asking questions."

A small huff of air leaves my mouth, a sarcastic laugh escaping my lips. I open the door and step onto the sidewalk, tucking the folder under my arm. Her brown eyes are focused on me, waiting to see if I'll bite.

When I was younger, when I went to live with my grandparents, I was scrawny, short, and new. I got pushed around at that first school, picked on, until I figured out the only thing that pissed off the other kids in return was indifference. Whether it was genuine or whether it was feigned, which it often was, it worked. They got angrier; I got calmer. Learned to read people really well.

I'm not calling Sheyanne a bully; I don't think she is. But I'm not sure if she knows how to deal with it all—with whatever it is. So, I plan on taking the same approach I took with the bullies while figuring out how and when to fight back.

"I don't plan on answering them, so you may as well keep them to yourself." With that, I shut the door and bound up the steps to town hall.

Maybe I'm not getting paid enough for this after all.

Five

Sheyanne

I exhale when I'm finally alone in the car, leaning against the headrest.

The calm air dissipated when Liam left, and I'm still unsure whether he was truly that composed or whether he was only maintaining a façade. Either way, it was impressive. I know I was being unfair—I am more than well aware of that—but I don't care enough to stop attacking him. He's around, he's around my *family*, and therefore, in my mind, is not immune to my lashing out.

It's maddening, knowing my behavior is wrong and being unable to talk myself into stopping.

Disappointment and disgust crawl over my skin. Sighing, I place my sunglasses in the cupholder and glance around the square. I can hide away in my car, or I can man up, go grab a coffee, and hope to some higher power that no one will be around.

Although, that's almost impossible in a town where everyone knows everyone.

More specifically then, I hope no one I left behind is here today.

"Man up, Sheyanne." I turn off the ignition and hop out of the car.

Halloween isn't for almost three weeks, but the town square is already decked out in decorations. The old, cracked stone buildings have orange lights strung up over the four streets that make up the square. The little alleys that hold family-owned stores and restaurants have pumpkins—not yet carved—and ghost decorations and spiderwebs hanging above them.

Flyers tacked to posts and taped up in windows around the square advertise movie night. During the summer, movie nights happen every Friday, playing anything from Disney to rom-coms. When it gets colder, they obviously shut down, but they bring it back for any holidays where it's still semi-warm enough, and this year, Halloween is on a Friday, so it's a must. The flyer advertises that *Hocus Pocus* and other classics will be the movies of the night. Kids and families will come with their candy after trick or treating and set up blankets on the different levels of concrete and glue their eyes to the screen. And at intermission, before the next movie, there will be a line coming out of the Cold Stone Creamery so long, they'll wonder if they'll make it back, just like always.

I look away and tug on the end of my shirt, trying to make the sleeves longer, and tuck my arms in, trying to make myself small in this impossibly small town. The smell of coffee drifts through the air, drawing my attention. There aren't many people out, considering it's still early, and with a quick glance, I'm thankful to confirm that none of the faces I see mean anything to me.

In front of me, the sign lights up *Fire Creek Coffee,* and the bell jingles overhead when I pull open the door, instantly enveloped by the welcoming smell of mocha. The barista greets me with a smile, and the tension releases from my shoulders as I walk forward.

"Hi, what can I get you?" she says. Her hazel eyes are bright, and curls like mine frame her face perfectly, pulling off bangs in a way I never could.

"Just a café mocha with almond milk if you have it, please. Oh, and a chocolate chip muffin would be great," I say, smiling as I pull out my wallet.

"Sure thing," she responds, reading me my total, and I hand her cash, leaning against the counter to wait for my drink. I play with the muffin in my hands before tearing off the bottom and eating it in pieces, saving the top for last.

Outside, the sun beats down on the square that I used to love. I used to run around there with my two best friends when we were kids and do stupid shit like sneaking out or wreaking havoc, which turned into trying to get into the local bars when we got older. It wasn't all good back then, and I know that, know that most of those actions were desperate attempts to get the attention I wanted, but when the sun warms the familiar sand colored stone, the good's all I can see, and I choose not to focus on the bad. At least for this brief, fleeting moment.

The barista slides my coffee over the counter with a smile. "Thank you," I call as I make my exit, taking the first sip of my third coffee today. I anxiously play with my keys in my other hand. Liam is nowhere to be seen, so I assume he's still in the courthouse, and I head in that direction to wait on the stairs.

All my favorite stores are still in business, which is nice considering how often small businesses go down. The old candy store, the locally owned bookstore, the toy store I used to make Shane take me into, even though he's only a year and a half older than me. As I'm finishing the last sips of my coffee, the door behind me opens, and Liam appears. The sunlight reflects off the silver watch on his arm and illuminates his dark skin where his sleeves are rolled up.

He glances down at me when he lands on my step. "Are you finished?" I ask, breaking off the last few pieces of the muffin.

Liam shakes his head. "Not yet. I need to head to the bank, but that shouldn't take more than a minute."

"Okay, well, I'm going to the candy store before we go back to the house."

I stand, tossing my empty cup and wrapper into a nearby trash can. The bank and the store, aptly named *Candy Co*, are on the same side of the square. We fall into step with one another as we walk. I do my best to ignore him and the way he stands out in this town. Not by looks. Just by the way he is. The way he holds himself, the way he walks.

Growing up here is simple. It's not negative or positive. It's just a fact. There isn't much to do, so we adjust to a simple life. Hikes, sunsets, lakes, road trips. We find simple ways to make money, simple ways to stay happy. The people aren't hard to read or understand. They're straightforward, sometimes closed off because of how often newcomers don't last, but for the most part, easy going. I used to find beauty in the simplicity of it, but I haven't seen that since I was a kid, weighed down by too much of everything else.

Liam isn't simple. He's not easy to read. He walks around with a clandestine air around him, and I can't see anything other than what he decides to give to the world. Which isn't much. In fact, it annoys me to no end that I can't read him. It also makes me want to try harder, find what buttons to push, what buttons *not* to push.

It makes me feel weak when I don't know what bothers people.

It's one of my more negative traits, I admit, needing to know other people's weaknesses. I know it's a defense mechanism, but I don't care. I have an innate need to find out as much as I can about other people, and Liam Landon is now included on that list.

We reach the bank first, and I lean against the wall, making sure my mask of boredom is secure on my face as he heads inside. Out of the corner of my eye, I notice a familiar, dusty red Mustang driving around the square, and my breath catches at the sight. Only when it disappears from view do I exhale.

I need to get the hell out of here. Pushing off the wall, I decide to get my candy without Liam so we can leave as soon as he's done. The car has caused my anxiety to deepen tenfold as I walk away, unable to stop playing with one of the rips on my jeans, hoping like hell I'll avoid the car. I'm tempted to leave right now, but then I'd be scolded for leaving Liam in town.

I still can't believe I'm a glorified chauffer.

Only a few steps away from the bank, I'm unsurprised when Liam catches up to me. "Leaving me here, Shaw?"

"I wanted my sugar. You were taking too long."

Candy Co is only four stores down from the bank, and the smell of sugar greets me warmly. Liam eyes me when I open the door. "You realize it's only 10:30 A.M., right?"

"Do you have a problem with candy?" My feet carry me forward down the familiar aisles, passing shelves filled with artificial colors. Sour snakes, candy belts, sour cherries, and a whole wall of chocolate bring joy to my chest.

"Never said I did. Just pointing out that it's early." Liam trails after me.

I snort softly. "I didn't realize I was in the presence of the food police." Turning, I meet his eyes. He looks back with his arms crossed, unreadable as ever. "Maybe if you ate some sugar, you wouldn't be so dreary."

Liam's full lips quirk up on the side, just barely. "Well, that doesn't seem to work for you now, does it?"

I reach out, grab a plastic bag, and shrug. "Maybe it's because I haven't had my sugar yet," I counter, filling the bag with various candies, turning it into a rainbow.

"I doubt that's the issue." His words grate over my skin, irritation spreading out in tiny waves. It's also amusing how easily he throws it back. But I roll my eyes, refusing to show that he's getting under my skin—in any way—at all.

Even if just by an inch.

I pick out the rest of my candy in silence before creating another smaller bag for Shane, adding all his old favorites—war heads, gummy worms, and airheads. It's a very small, very miniscule step, but it will have to do for now.

Liam waits by the door, surveying the space like he does everything else. I suppose some people don't enjoy this much sugar early in the morning. To each their own. The cashier smiles and bids me goodbye after I pay, and I smile back as I make my way out.

"Come on," I say, my smile dropping as I direct my words to Liam.

The weight of his gaze lands on me as we walk, but I ignore it, making a beeline for my car.

"So," Liam starts, his deep voice filling the space between us on the sidewalk, but he's interrupted when I hear classic rock music coming up behind me.

I don't need to turn to know it's the Mustang or to know who's driving it, but I do anyway, dread filling my blood like lead. I keep my face as impassive as possible as it pulls up beside us.

Blake's coarse curls, tighter than mine, are dark, almost black, except for the ends, which are dyed blond, just like they were years ago. The car comes impossibly close to a stop, the wheels just barely turning. Light brown eyes, contrasting with the smooth dark brown of her skin, are on me with the focus of a snake chasing its prey, but I don't flinch. I grew up with those eyes, though the contempt is new.

Gaylee is in the passenger seat, her gleaming, straight black hair pinned back neatly as her foot taps on the dash, nervously if I had to guess considering she's staring at the street in front of her like her celebrity crush has suddenly appeared. Gaylee always hated confrontation, and I doubt that's changed, but it's hard to avoid when you're friends with Blake and used to be friends with me. Usually, she ended up being the peacekeeper, the middleman, always finding a way to diffuse whatever situation Blake and I set on fire.

It's funny, people used to think we were sisters, two of the only black girls in this town, our skin only a few shades apart. We used to act like it, but now, we've just ended up rivals, cold and resolute. Memories begin to flash in my mind, but I block them out, digging my nails into my palm to keep my calm and try to keep the adrenaline at bay.

"Sheyanne? What are you doing here?"

I straighten my shoulders. "Oh, you know, just doing some casual shopping, enjoying life. The usual."

Blake's gaze was cold. Now it's pure ice. "You won't fix anything."

"Didn't come back to try," I respond. It's true, I don't intend on fixing anything.

Blake adjusts the bangs she's cut her curls into. "Then you should leave."

"Yeah, no shit," I bite back, and finally, Gaylee looks at me.

Her deep gray eyes crinkle with awkwardness as she glances between Liam and I. Thankfully, she doesn't call attention to him, and if I had to guess, she wants nothing more than to leave. Gaylee, unlike the two of us, isn't one to hold a grudge. Beside me, I practically feel the questions emitting off Liam as this strange and uncomfortable scene unfolds.

"Let's just go," Gaylee mutters, and I watch, trying to feign amusement even though I feel anything but.

Blake's eyes flicker between Gaylee and me, and I wait. I know she wants to say something else, to lay into me with sharp words like I know she can. We used to go at it all the time despite being best friends. Neither of us were the type to bite our tongues. The difference is, back then, our fights only lasted for that singular moment. We'd make up almost instantly. That is no longer the case.

Blake opens her mouth and then closes it. The silence is louder and more telling than any words she could've tossed my way. When she's angry, she can't stop talking. When she is unforgiving, she is silent. Even so, her eyes say it all, giving me a searing glance that stings to the bone before she drives away, leaving me in the dust.

A full circle, I suppose.

I exhale as I turn back, gripping my keys in a shaking hand.

"Who was that?" Liam's words cut through the silence and the palpable tension in the air. I glance over at him, his hands in his pockets and his curious eyes on me.

"No one," I bite, unlocking the car.

I glance back to where the Mustang previously sat, the unwelcome memories flooding into my head, and look around the town that I have done everything in my power to avoid. My eyes flicker back to Liam in the passenger seat, and I sigh.

Nothing about being here, in this stupid fucking town, is going to be quick or easy.

There will be no quick escape, no easy exit. And I hate it.

I hate how it's crawled under my skin so easily in under a week. How much I can feel myself falling back into the drama, the life, and everything I left behind.

But I refuse to let Liam Landon see me break.

I refuse to let anyone see me break.

Especially this town.

Six

Sheyanne

Two weeks.

I've been back in this hellhole for almost two weeks. The morning sun beats down, but the early morning air sweeps around me, and I pull my sweatshirt closer to my skin. It's not quite cold enough for layers yet, but it won't be long. My legs swing as I sit on the old wooden fence of the pasture and watch the horses. Nyx sits patiently by my side like always.

The sun shines off their coats as they graze. Blue spruce trees line the far edge of the pasture. Other trees have just begun to lose their leaves and needles, starting to blanket the ground. In the background, the mountains peak, snow-capped and foggy. My eyes turn back to Teddy and Rayne. Teddy holds no grudges against me. Every morning at the break of dawn, he greets me with a chest nudge and a nuzzle.

Rayne, however, is a different story. And here I am, as I've been every morning for the past twelve days, holding her favorite treats, carrots, and sugar cubes, hoping she'll trot over and think about forgiving me. In the background, Shane's voice carries in the breeze, and I glance back to see him and Liam walking around the grounds, specifically towards the greenhouse. He's probably giving him a tour. I watch, unsure of the point of their developing friendship.

Whatever.

Secretly, I give Liam some credit. He hasn't brought up my little run in with Blake and Gaylee since it happened. No comments to my brother or my dad, whom I ignore as often as possible. So far, we've stayed out of each other's way to the best of our abilities. I've been sent on no more pointless errands with him, no more time spent in his presence than anyone else's. I let him do what he needs to do, and he leaves me alone.

Shaking my head, I turn back, looking at Rayne again. Her appaloosa coat looks beautiful in the sun as she lifts her head, turning her warm eyes straight to me, and I try not to smile. I hold out my hand, the sugar cubes visible. She blinks, moving a few feet closer before stopping again, and I let out a sigh.

We continue this game for what seems like hours, but I know that's me being dramatic. Finally, she's only two armlengths away. Teddy lazily grazes next to my seat on the fence as I hold my hand out again. She lifts her head, her eyes meeting mine, but she stays still.

"Rayne, come on," I plead, and she blinks slowly.

"Someone doesn't seem to wanna forgive you." Shane appears out of nowhere next to me, causing me to jump, my heart careening in my chest.

"Jesus, can you give a girl a warning?" I hit him on the shoulder with my other hand, and my eyes move past him to see Liam standing next to him.

He's lost some of the preppy clothes over the past few days. He's got on black jeans but still wears a crisp button-up rolled up to his elbows. The watch remains, the silver contrasting the single gold earring and the thin chain around his neck peeking through the top of the shirt that's unbuttoned. The sun casts a warm glow over his dark skin, and I think there's a residual hint of a smile on his face from talking with Shane, but I can't be sure. It disappears as soon as he steps closer to me anyway.

I turn away before he notices my prying eyes and focus on Rayne again. "Rayne, please?" I hold out a sugar cube, and her nose twitches. But she swishes her tail and goes back to lazily grazing grass.

"What did you do to her?" Liam asks, leaning down and petting Nyx. Traitor.

"I didn't do anything."

"Except leave her in the dust like you left the rest of us," Shane chimes in, but he's smiling, and I narrow my eyes, ignoring the hurt in my chest. Someone took a page out of the sarcasm handbook it seems.

Just because something's true doesn't mean it doesn't hurt to hear it.

"Aw, Shaney, was that a joke?" I respond, burying my feelings. I pop a sugar cube in my mouth, letting it dissolve as I swing one leg over the fence so I'm straddling it and facing both boys.

Shane turns to him, eyes flicking between me and the horse. He may not be looking at me, but his words are directed right at me. "She knows how to hold a grudge, just like someone else."

I shake my head, pointedly ignoring my brother's statement, and tug at a few curls. Shane silently plucks a cube from my hand and holds it out in his palm.

Rayne doesn't hesitate to step forward and take it from his outstretched palm, and Liam lets out a breath of air as my brother chuckles. My lips fall into a straight line as Rayne turns her eyes on me again, and I know she's doing it out of spite, damnit. I kick my other leg over and hop down, landing quietly on the grass and loose hay under my feet.

"Oh, shut up, both of you," I mutter to them, both still laughing, and

I flick sugar cubes right at their foreheads. I hit both of them right on target and give a sarcastic grin as I begin to back away.

"Don't forget we have that new horse coming in later. If you need help, I wouldn't mind," Shane calls after me, extending an invisible olive branch. I leave it hanging there, choosing to just wave my hand in the air, indicating that I heard him.

Nyx trots by my side with his ears perked, and my boots crunch the gravel until I reach the porch steps. I sit down and start untying them, glancing back towards the pasture. The sun climbs higher in the sky, hidden behind stray clouds, and I wouldn't be surprised if we got snow soon.

Shane and Liam are still by the pasture, leaning over the fence. I've not been blind to their quick bonding, despite Liam being here on a job. They talk to each other like old friends, about any topic. Shane answers willingly whenever Liam has any extra questions or certain contacts he may need to get in touch with. Then the conversation will flow into casual topics, and I've eavesdropped enough to hear little bits and pieces about Liam's life in Vegas. Sometimes, I'll even hear Shane share how life has been here in the past few years, and that's usually when I walk away. I don't deserve that information if I'm not willing to start fixing our relationship.

I shake my head and turn, trekking into the house that still smells like coffee. I grab another cup of it, turning around to head into my room and hide before I see Dad at the kitchen table. His eyes are already on me, and I hold his stare. There are papers spread somehow messily but still put together in piles around him.

Slowly, I take a sip of coffee. "What?"

He stares back at me with apathetic eyes, different from how he looks at Shane, how he's always looked at Shane, even before I started acting out, and the old familiar feeling of frustration sinks into my skin, reminding me why I've kept the mental wall up between us for so long. It took me years to build it, brick by brick, patching up every crack he made in the surface. Every side eye glance, every cutting comment, every comparison to Shane, every dismissal, all patched up carefully over the years. I refuse to let it fall even as I wait, somehow, still always on his terms.

"Where's Shane?"

"Showing his new best friend around the grounds."

He nods and leans back in his chair. Dad looks old, to put it simply. Which he is, but when we were younger, he never looked it. Days spent on the farm kept him in shape, and he always looked young for his age, until he didn't. Until now.

"Well then, can you sit?"

My brows shoot up. "Sit?"

"Yes." His eyes flicker up and meet mine. "I'd like to show you something."

I take another sip of hot liquid even though I'm warm from frustration and annoyance and feeling like the lost nuisance of a daughter I used to be. "What is it?"

Now, I can see the frustration growing on his features at my incessant questions that would be answered if I just sat down. When he meets my gaze, the firmness in them pushes my next argument back, and I swallow it down.

"Just sit, Sheyanne."

I blink, dragging my eyes over the man sitting in front of me who is supposed to be my father but never really acted like one and now is almost a shell of the man he used to be. Another slow sip as I let the request—or demand—linger in the air like the smell of burnt popcorn. Something that could've been good but went wrong in the blink of an eye, reminiscent of my entire childhood here.

I figure whatever he needs can't be too bad. Whatever it is, I'll figure it out and cut this conversation short.

So, I nod. "Fine." I sit uncomfortably at the table, waiting for his next move.

Dad just sits there, with his arms crossed, wrinkles and sunspots freckled over his dark brown skin. My eyes flicker up over the same features that make up much of my face, but I don't dwell on that as I turn back to the papers he's pushed in front of me. Nyx lays at my feet, his head alternating between resting on the floor and my sock covered feet, as if he knows I'm anxious just spending this much time in my dad's presence.

I look at the images printed in front of me, but they don't make much sense. "Okay, but what's the point of these?" They're collections of photos stapled together. The first is of a labeled box, and the rest, I assume, are items within those boxes.

"Before you came home, Shane and I went into the attic and shed, took pictures of everything. It's hard for me to go in those tight spaces." He says that like it pains him to admit he can't do something as well as he used to. "If we sell, this stuff will have to go somewhere. It's mostly from when you both were younger. Figured you'd want to look over it. Decide what happens."

I stare at him. "*If* we sell?"

His gaze is steady. "I'm hoping one of you decides you don't want it gone. So, until that's final, if."

"I won't. If you want anyone to stick around, better focus on Shane."

I push the photos to the center of the table, noticing his messy scrawl on each one that I didn't bother to read. I barely glance at the photos. It doesn't matter to me anyway. Dad leans back, eyes moving between the photos and me.

I don't know why I stay at the table. Why either of us do. Neither of us speaks, him probably waiting for me to care, and me, waiting for nothing. After long minutes of painful silence, I push away from the table.

He breaks the silence before I can escape. The words are nothing short of a shock to my system. "It was good of you to come back."

My head snaps up at the low sound of his voice, and my brain whirls. It wasn't a question, wasn't a thank you; it was just a statement. I look back down at the photos, my skin prickling. "I wasn't really given a choice."

He sighs, but he shouldn't have expected a different answer. "You had a choice."

"No, I didn't."

"You haven't been h–back in years." He coughs over the word, and though I don't bring it up, I'm aware of the unspoken term. *Home.*

"Yeah, because I always loved it here so much and was always so welcome." The sarcasm drips off my tongue, bitter and cold, and slices through the still air of the kitchen.

"Sheyanne—"

I roll my eyes, letting my curls fall in front of my face, but I swear I hear just a hint of desperation in the way my dad says my name, a hint of something brewing beneath the surface. I'm sure it's all in my head.

"Just let it go. Things aren't going to change, no matter how hard you try," I respond, an influx of emotions flooding my central nervous system.

Dad's face hardens, whatever desperation I imagined gone in an instant. Before he can respond, the voices of Shane and Liam sound from the front porch as the door swings open, letting in a burst of cooler air before it closes behind them.

They immediately quiet as they take in the sight of Dad and I at the table together. Even though we're seated together, I'm sure anyone could feel the distance between us.

"Everything okay in here?" Shane speaks quietly as if not to spook a wild animal. Meaning me.

I nod, downing my coffee, realizing it's now close to lunchtime. "Yup. Just dandy." I stand up, placing a few feet between Dad and me.

Liam watches, taking in everything with his brown eyes. It's almost terrifying, the intensity with which he observes, like he's trying to put the story together like a puzzle. His eyes linger on me for a moment, and I hold his gaze before averting my eyes to my brother, who watches nervously.

"I'm not going to explode," I mutter, slipping my phone into my back pocket and placing my mug in the sink, anxiety and frustration causing my hands to shake.

"One can never be too careful," Shane states hesitantly.

I can tell he's trying to joke again, testing the waters like he did outside by the pasture. The only difference is, I feel welcome out there. By the green—albeit browning—grass, by the familiar patterns of the animals. In here, near my dad, in a house that often felt more like a jail cell than it did a home, I don't even attempt to joke back.

But I don't want to sever the thread of sibling friendship that's attempting to grow back like a flower that's been plucked one too many times. I choose my words wisely, walking a line of civility. "I'll be in my room if you need anything, Shane."

Shane opens his mouth as he glances between Dad and me, like he wants to try and fix it, to mediate, like he used to, and I sigh, tensing my shoulders as if preparing for a fight. To my surprise, Liam clears his throat, breaking Shane's attention. My eyes flicker to his, and I swear Liam gives me the smallest of nods before walking towards the table.

It's so minuscule I think I might be imagining things, but he makes eye contact with me again and holds it as if to confirm what I thought I saw.

I roll my shoulders back and hold the look for a second before heading to my room. Nyx follows me down the hall and climbs onto my bed the instant he enters. After changing, I pop my headphones in and click play on a random movie to distract me. Weight rests heavy on my shoulders, my chest—my entire body feels heavy at this point. It could be an array of things.

Being here in general.

Being around my dad.

The fact that I'm fighting tooth and nail to not get close to my brother.

And the fact that I'm trying to avoid Liam as best I can, to convince him that I'm as bad as I've made myself seem. As bad as I paint myself for everyone else—in shades of black and white so they ignore that I'm completely made up of gray instead. Unsure of myself. Unsure of everything.

I'm aware that the way I struggle, the way I react, the way I manage situations isn't beneficial or healthy, but I lack the will to change. I want to be left alone, especially when I'm upset—which is my permanent state of mind since being back—and the best way to be left alone is to make sure no one wants to be around.

Seven

Sheyanne

A few days later, on Sunday, I watch the horses graze in their pastures, tails flicking in the slight breeze.

Teddy stands next to me, his large body brushing against mine. I open the gate and remove his halter and lead, watching as he trots over to Rayne before going towards the water bin. We just returned from a quick ride around the property, dipping under the shade of the trees to hide from the sun's rays. Doing something I used to love—and still do—has left me feeling nothing but peaceful, at least for the moment.

I leave the halter and the lead in the barn hanging near Teddy's stall and head towards the house. Shane is headed towards the greenhouse, but we meet in the middle when he stops me.

"My girlfriend is coming over tonight. I know you're cooking, but I wanted to make sure that was okay."

"The imaginary one?"

He runs a hand over the fluffy curls on the top of his head. "That's the one."

"Okay."

"I want you to meet her."

It sounds like my brother is nervous around me, which makes me feel terrible. I ignore it. "I figured that when you told me she was coming over," I say with a playful quirk of my lips.

He smiles. "Okay. If you need help with dinner before, I wouldn't mind."

"I think I can handle it, Shaney."

With a roll of his eyes, he continues towards the greenhouse, and I continue towards the house and a shower. It still smells like coffee; it always does since we all practically live off the stuff, and I grab another cup and fill it with almond milk which Shane bought, somehow noticing that's what I preferred. Dad is flipping through something on the dining table, and I pass him with a single nod, heading straight to my room to find Nyx passed out on the floor.

I bend down, patting him on the stomach before heading to the bathroom. Without thinking about why the door is closed or knocking, I enter, immediately confused by the steam clouds that surround me. Blinking, I look for the source, realizing too late the shower is on and the only other person that could be in here is Liam.

I slap my hand over my eyes a little too hard and accidentally let out a tiny squeak.

Shit.

After I'm unfrozen from my shock, I tiptoe out, praying he didn't hear anything as I shut the door behind me. Nyx looks at me inquisitively from his new position on my bed, wagging his tail. I'm glad one of us can find amusement in this stupid, ridiculous arrangement.

I look around my old room—the bookshelf and desk near the door, the dresser on the wall of the attached bathroom, and the windows situated right behind my bed. Collapsing in my desk chair, I kick back and forth until my eyes land on an old keepsake box situated between some books on my shelf. I grab it and unlock it, surprised to find a collection I don't quite remember.

It's filled with old polaroids. Gaylee got a camera one year for Christmas, I think our junior year of high school, and for the next two years, up until I left, we documented everything on that camera. I feel a strange emptiness in my chest at the sight, and my gaze doesn't linger long, finding an array of other things in here. Old notes we passed in school, old jewelry from when Gaylee was learning to make her own, and even old scraps of song ideas from Blake. The nostalgia that blankets my skin settles in uncomfortably. Mixed with the restlessness this place brings me is the awkwardness I feel at navigating a life I tried to avoid and the general feelings of unease I haven't been able to shake.

I can't help but pick at my lip, pulling the skin, trying to ignore the unsettling feelings.

Closing the box, I set it back on its shelf, tasting blood on my lip from where I've picked too hard. Sighing, I pull my hair into a high bun, a few tight curls escaping the hold, to keep them out of the water—whenever I can actually get into my own bathroom—and rest my head on the back of the chair.

At some point, my eyes flutter closed, my body still adjusting to the early wake-up calls every morning. In the haze, somewhere between being asleep and being awake, my mind stays blank, not attacking me with memories or unwanted thoughts.

A door opening and the creak of the old hinges jolt me awake. When I blink my eyes open, I'm met with the sight of Liam, leaning in the doorframe of the bathroom. Dark clothing drapes over his slightly damp skin. The simple and graceful gold chain around his neck is tucked into the

T-shirt, and he spins the small gold stud twice before dropping his hand.

"Did we forget how to knock, Shaw?"

I bite the inside of my cheek, meeting his eyes with boredom. "Not used to sharing a space. It won't happen again."

He nods slowly, his eyes light. "Let's hope not." Liam kicks off the doorway and taps the frame lightly. "Bathroom's all yours."

"Took you long enough." I stand with a slight eye roll. He shakes his head, clearly amused though his features maintain a coolness, and turns towards his room without another word. I stalk in directly after him and make sure the lock on his door is turned.

The steam still permeates the bathroom, only just fading off the mirror. Grabbing a fresh towel from the linen closet, I place it on the counter. Making sure my doors are locked, leaving the one to my room slightly ajar to avoid it getting too steamy, I strip out of my clothes and step into the water. I needn't have worried about the steam—since Liam decided not to save me a goddamn ounce of hot water. That's how I know he heard me enter. He wasted time in the shower and now this. If I weren't freezing, I might laugh. Perhaps it's payback for the snark I've given him from day one. If so, I guess I have to appreciate the silence pushback.

Mother fucker.

By the time I exit my room later, it's painted in shades of a deepening gold. I spent my time watching Netflix, binging almost an entire limited series, and avoiding going through anything else in my room. And I certainly didn't even consider going through those boxes Dad showed me pictures of—I'll be putting that off for a long time. But after a quick check of the time, I realize Shane's girlfriend will be here in less than an hour, and I have to cook.

I pad out of my room into the kitchen where Dad sits on the couch, watching the old grainy TV, and Shane sits at the island counter, doing a puzzle. He glances up as I pass by heading for the fridge to pull out some chicken and the ingredients for a honey marinade. Cooking isn't my favorite, but I don't hate it; a lot of times, it's a distraction. And if there is anyone here I want to extend my own olive branch to, it's my brother. The least I can do is attempt to make a good impression on his girlfriend.

God bless her for putting up with him.

With only the noise of the TV, I begin to mix everything together. I sip water as I go, chopping garlic and discovering everything in this kitchen is truly in the exact place I left it. Occasionally, my eyes flick up to my dad and my brother. Dad is watching the same old channel, the one that replays all the popular crime shows, and Shane's brows are furrowed in concentration. It strikes me that this is a new hobby for him.

He didn't do puzzles when I left.

I hate how much it hurts that I didn't know that small, simple detail about him. Swallowing, I concentrate on my task. Eventually, Liam makes his entrance, nodding to my dad. As he enters the open space, gold flickers on all the wood furnishings from the sun streaming in. He heads straight towards the fridge behind me, and I cast my eyes down.

I'm quite aware of Liam's proximity, still embarrassed about entering that godforsaken bathroom without checking first. Next to me, he puts ice in a small glass and pours a bit of whiskey over it. I lower my voice so only he can hear me.

"Thanks for the cold shower, Landon. That was quite kind of you."

He side-eyes me, his features giving nothing away, and keeps his own voice low. "Figured it might turn you down a notch." A pause. "I can see that it didn't."

I lift my head, giving him a pointed look, pausing the cutting I'm doing. Liam glances at the knife in my hand and eyes the look on my face, then raises his glass and hides the twitching of his lips by taking a sip of his drink.

He makes a soft tsking sound and takes his whisky to the dining table, confusing me further. One minute, he's giving all my attitude and all my—undeserved—insolence right back at me. The next, he's watchful and curious, taking notes and not saying anything at all. I'm not quite sure which version of him I prefer. He settles with a crossword puzzle in front of him, turning to talk to my dad every few minutes before focusing.

I sigh, pouring the marinade over the chicken and heating up the pan. When I look up, Shane has a puzzle piece in his hand, and he's looking over the parts of the puzzle he's already connected. It hasn't been as easy as I would've liked, trying to maintain the space between us. Shane was never supposed to get caught in the crosshairs of my dramatics, and I'd be lying if I said I didn't miss my brother. I don't like that I don't know things about him, and I'm not sure it's worth it to try to act like I don't care. Somehow, between Dad and I, he still stayed kind, always the quiet optimist. I lean up on my tiptoes, reaching across the island, and pick up a stray piece, placing it down correctly.

He raises a surprised brow. "Thanks." Then, he puts his own puzzle piece in the correct spot.

I lean forward on the counter, watching the sun begin to hide behind the clouds through the windows. Anger is easy when there's something to respond to, something to be angry about. Like the request to come home, like finding out my dad has Alzheimer's, like being a raging bitch to someone your family hired, or like running into the personification of a burned bridge in a place you have no desire to be in.

But it's a lot harder to *stay* angry than I thought. When it all fades to the background and the uncomfortable silence settles, I find myself more resigned than anything.

"Can you cut the potatoes for me?" I ask quietly, looking at Shane again. It's a very minuscule olive branch, asking for his help, but it's something.

"Sure." He smiles, just a little bit, and I roll my eyes. The puzzle forgotten, Shane grabs the potatoes and a cutting board, placing it on the freshly wiped counter as the chicken begins to sizzle in the pan. He motions to the pan and proves that we are in fact siblings. "You're not planning on poisoning us tonight, are you?"

"I'd never do that to your girlfriend. She already has to put up with you."

Shane raises an amused brow. "What about the rest of us?"

"Still deciding," I respond, and he flicks a tiny end of a potato at my head and then acts like he didn't do anything at all.

"Asshole," I mutter.

"Prick."

I stick my tongue out at him and turn to the fridge, grabbing the fresh green beans Shane grows in the garden. When I turn around and see the smile on his face as he cuts the potatoes, the hurt I felt earlier lessens just a little bit.

Shane, unlike me, though he may be hurt by my actions, doesn't seem to be harboring them against me. I think that maybe, he just misses his sister.

EIGHT

SHEYANNE

Shane's girlfriend is perfect.

Or as close as you can get to perfect. There's no reason for me to be surprised. While I may not admit it to his face, he's one of the best people I've ever met in my life. So, it shouldn't come as a surprise that his girlfriend is an absolute angel. Stunning, too.

Tight black curls frame her face with a few in the front in the way of bangs. She pulls them off perfectly. With a round face, both young and refined at once, full lips, and dark brown skin, she is absolutely stunning. Tonight, her eyes are lightly lined, and a simple gloss covers her lips, her nose ring reflecting off the light above.

They make a gorgeous couple. It's completely unfair.

We're all seated at the dining table, her and Shane next to one another, me on the other side of my absolutely-in-love brother, with a space between me and Dad, and Liam directly across from me. Liam and Dad are working quietly on other things, my dad reading an old book and Liam reading over a contract, I think. MJ is telling me about how she ended up in Flagstaff while my brother leans back in his chair, arm around the back of hers, with a watchful gaze.

She's animated and excited about seemingly everything in life, even living here, which she adores. The joy she radiates is infectious. She and Shane are two very sunshiny peas in a pod.

"So, you ended up staying here and going to school instead of going back to San Francisco?" I ask, petting the top of Nyx's head as he pushes his ears into my palm.

MJ tucks a curl behind her ear smiling. "Yup, that's how I met your brother."

Shane presses a kiss on the side of her head before standing. If it was anyone else, it'd be cute, but it's my brother, so I kind of want to gag. He notices my face. "Oh, grow up," he says, causing MJ to laugh. "I'm gonna make my dessert."

I'm not one to stop him because he makes this killer chocolate mug cake. As soon as he's away from the table, I lean towards MJ, lowering my voice on purpose. "You're sure he's not forcing you to date him against your will?"

She laughs, and if laughter could *twinkle*, hers would. With an amused shake of her head, she purses her lips, and her eyes brighten. "I swear," she mocks. It warms my heart when she says it because I can feel how much she likes—or loves—my brother. "Honestly, he couldn't force anyone to do anything anyway. He's too nice to people who don't deserve it."

Swallowing, I nod. "He absolutely is." I choose not to add that I'm probably one of those people. I'm enjoying the night and don't feel like ruining it with my own pity party, at least not in front of them, so I ignore the uncomfortable feeling blooming in my chest.

I glance back up to see Shane mixing ingredients. The smell of chocolate permeates the kitchen, and I'm taken back to when we were younger. Sometimes, when things were especially bad with Dad and me, whether it was me sneaking in past curfew, an argument, or a nasty fight, Shane would make me his special chocolate mug cake. Sometimes it was two A.M., and I had just walked in the door, or he'd bring it to my room when I refused to come out. He'd even make it for Blake and Gaylee if they happened to be with me. On days when things weren't awful and I wasn't getting into trouble and we actually came home from school together, he'd make it while we did our homework.

"So, Shane told me you're fighting with a horse."

I cough, trying not to choke on my water. To my left, I'm pretty sure Liam lets out a puff of air, his equivalent to a laugh. Even Dad's hand pauses from turning the page before continuing.

"He told you?"

MJ grins shamelessly, and I think I love her. She seems unfiltered and unapologetic in everything she does, which I think is good for Shane. Like she said, he's too nice. He's too good. Too focused on how he can help other people—whether they deserve it or not—or trying to make a situation easier for someone else. But MJ, she knows what she wants, means what she says, and is somehow still probably the nicest person I've met besides my brother.

"Shaney, are you telling the entire town I'm arguing with Rayne or just your girlfriend?"

He doesn't even hesitate. "Just MJ, for now."

I lean back in my seat. "That is so lovely to know."

MJ lifts her head from looking at her phone, eyes narrowing in amusement. "Wait, did you call him Shaney?" A wide grin starts to spread across her face, and Shane groans as he walks toward us with two mugs, setting them down in front of us.

Shrugging, I cup the warm mug in my hands. "I did. Have since we were kids."

"And every time she says it, a piece of me dies inside," my brother says dramatically as he returns to the kitchen to grab his own mug and a fresh water for Dad. Shane takes his seat next to MJ, his arm going right back around the back of her chair like it was before.

Looking away, I watch the mini marshmallows he put on top of the chocolate cake, tiny speckles of cinnamon and nutmeg dusting them and the surface of the dessert, melt with the chocolate underneath. I glance between the two of them as they talk quietly to one another for a moment, noticing the way he moves when she does and vice versa, even if just an inch.

Outside, the sun is mostly gone, the sky now a midnight blue. Nyx places his head on my leg as we sit, spooning the dessert. We talk a bit more—about MJ and how she wants to be an environmental scientist, about Shane and what he was like as a kid—carefully skirting anything that may include me. Sometimes, I just sit as Shane and MJ tell stories, about how they met and finishing up school together, and just watch as they enjoy each other's company, even in the presence of others.

When I was younger, I didn't pay much attention to his dating life, but I know it was nothing like this.

I realize that despite it all, Shane has found something that is all his own, not tainted by his attention-seeking younger sister or overbearing father. He has MJ. It is a beautiful thing to see and is something he so deserves, more than anyone I know. He deserves to love someone like it's clear he loves her and to be loved like that in return.

My heart grows and aches at the sight because I'm incapable of believing this place could foster anything beautiful, anything worthwhile.

For me, all this place is good for is pain.

But I'm not going to stay here and let my own issues, my own insecurities and anxieties that build every time I realize people that used to be close to me have moved on and grown up, affect everyone else.

Shane's voice interrupts my thoughts. "We were gonna watch a movie if you want to join," he says, training his hope-filled brown eyes on me.

My teeth pick at the inside of my lip like earlier, and I finish the rest of my cake. My hesitation must be longer than I think because when I look up, Liam is also looking at me—with curiosity more than anything.

I shake my head. "No, I'll let you guys do your thing. I'm gonna bring in the rest of the horses and head into town for a little bit." I stand and pat my brother's shoulder, silently letting him know I do appreciate the offer, more than he knows, even if I can't accept it right now.

"Into town this late? For what?" Dad interrupts, and I sigh, not wanting to say that I just need to escape and not wanting to talk to him at all.

"Just gotta pick up a few things," I mutter, placing my dish in the sink. I'm thankful when Dad says nothing else. I don't know why he cares or why he expected a real answer.

"Well, it was nice to meet you, Sheyanne. Shane is always talking about you," MJ says softly, standing as my brother does next to her. He collects the empty mugs and brushes past me, unaware that him talking about me while I'm away strikes an emotional chord.

I pull MJ in for a brief hug. "It was my pleasure. We'll have to get together and get drinks one night. Without Shane, so we can gossip."

Her light laugh echoes, and she nods. "I'd love that."

MJ and Shane move from the table to the living room, stopping only to filter through the collection of DVDs we have. Before heading out, I put away the leftovers, rinse the dishes, and place them in the old dishwasher, forcing myself to breathe. I don't say a word as

I head towards the door, slip on my leather jacket, and slip out the door. It's colder than I thought it would be, but I forgot how easily the temperature drops at night, even in late October. Above, the sky has faded from a midnight blue to almost black, the crescent moon taking its place among the stars as I head to the barn.

The cold air wraps around me as I enter the barn. Before dinner, I brought in the boarded horses, making sure they were taken care of, but instead of bringing Teddy and Rayne in, I let them enjoy the outside air a little bit longer. I grab the lead ropes and head towards the pasture, where luckily, they aren't far off. While Rayne hasn't shown me any more forgiveness, she has at least started to let me lead her to and from.

I clip the rope onto her halter first, and we walk side by side into the barn. Once we are in her stall, I remove both the halter and the rope. "I'm going to get you to forgive me soon, Rayne. You can't be mad forever." She flicks her ear at me before I turn to go get Teddy.

He greets me as always by pushing his head into my chest. The simple action takes away a bit of the unease I felt earlier. Not all of it, but for this moment, the anxiety running through my blood slows to a walk. Before leaving, I feed them all sugar cubes, leaving Rayne's with her feed since she still won't take it from me. And because I am showing favoritism, I give Teddy two. His head is hung over the stall door, and I roll my eyes at his antics, stumbling back a step when he pushes his head into my chest again in thanks. I pat his soft nose in goodbye.

Finally, I turn and leave, pulling the barn doors shut behind me as I head toward the Bronco. That's when I notice Liam. He leans on his sleek black vehicle, watching as I approach. Maybe he's finally going exploring on his own, though this late, the only things still open are the Walmart and the bars, which is exactly where I'm going. But I don't see keys anywhere, so maybe not. Who knows.

I leave some space between us and meet his eyes.

He clears his throat in the quiet of the night. "You good?"

My brows rise on their own accord, and I don't even have time to attempt to manage the shock that spreads over my features. I stare at him, uneasy with the way he seems to be able to read things. In this case, how easy it is for him to read me.

I nod slowly, pocketing my hands. "Yeah, I'm fine." I kick the gravel, moving it around with my boot as I attempt to train my face into neutrality after my initial surprise.

Liam studies me, eyes coasting all over my face, and I can't read him at all, especially in the darkness. He kicks off his car and moves away toward the house. "Okay, well if you need anything." I blink, taken aback, and force my lips into a typical smirk, even though I feel anything but poised. "Who am I kidding? I'm sure you don't need anything from me. Just wanted to check."

My heart beats in my chest at his words, so I just nod, trying to keep a frown from forming on my face as he walks away. Even though the words are something I've told myself every day for years, they're uncomfortable to hear and leave a bitter taste in my mouth. Especially hearing them from someone else. But he's right.

I don't need anything from him. Need is a word that doesn't really exist in my vocabulary. It's not something I do. I don't need anything or anybody, and nobody needs me.

It's been that way for so long, I've forgotten what it would even be like if that wasn't the case.

I huff as I climb into the car, turn the key in the ignition, and pull out of the long driveway. Without hesitation, I drive towards my old haunt, a towny bar that used to let me, Blake, and Gaylee—and others—in underage whenever we wanted.

But the driving doesn't take away the stains from tonight, the ache at dinner, Liam's lingering words.

I've only been here for two weeks, but it's all so much harder than I could've thought. Dealing with it all, with myself. Every day I'm around Shane, and he treats me just like he used to, when I was just his little sister, not the sister that left him behind, I'm reminded of how low I think of myself. Every time I'm around my dad, there's a part of me—a very small and quiet part of me—that's dying to see if there's any relationship to be salvaged after years of us destroying it.

And every day, the urge to scream at myself to be better, to do better, to at least try, scratches at my throat. But I don't because it's hard, and it's painful, and I'd have to open doors I don't want to open and relive memories I'd rather forget. I don't like hard.

I like running away.

Every minute, every second, I feel myself getting closer to letting it all out. All it's going to take is one single catalyst to set me off.

I wave the bartender down for another drink. Focusing my eyes on the old TV screen that hangs over the bar, I avoid looking towards the booth in the back—the booth that is occupied by Blake and Gaylee.

The bartender, Keith, the same one that's been here for years, gives me a smile and pats the bar twice as he slides over my drink. I take a sip, the liquid cool against my throat and warm as it settles, and pop another chip in my mouth, licking the salt off my lip before going in for another.

This old place is the same as ever; old, dark linoleum floors and black booths create the dim atmosphere, but the vintage neon signs and the TVs brighten it up.

"So, how you been?" Keith asks, crossing his arms across his chest and leaning back, an easy smile growing on his face.

He was twenty-one when he started letting us in here when we were seventeen, and he was cute then. He's still pretty cute now, with the same short brown hair and dark green eyes.

But he's still *Keith*, now twenty-six, and bartending at this hole in the wall. "Pretty good. Rather not be here, but duty calls," I chime.

He chuckles, rubbing a hand over the stubble on his chin. "Yeah, it's been a while for you. Can't imagine how that's going." His eyes flicker away from my face, and I know he's glancing at the two girls I used to be tied at the hip with.

My eyes roll before I can stop them. "It's been something."

He opens his mouth to respond but stops, his eyes falling on someone behind me as the bell above the door of the bar rings. I turn, hopeful that maybe Blake and Gaylee are leaving. Instead, I see Liam Landon walk through the door. Tipping my glass, I take another slow sip as he shrugs off his coat. Our eyes meet, and I watch him over the edge of my glass.

He nods, walking toward me. "What are you doing here, Landon?" I cock my head to the side, eyeing him carefully.

"Came to get a drink. That okay with you, your highness?" he bites back, the comment making my lips turn up. Even I, deep down, can appreciate how at times, he bites back.

He drapes his coat—new I think—over the back of the barstool, adjusting the dark hoodie underneath, and takes a seat two chairs away from my own.

"Please, by all means, enjoy."

Liam lets his gaze fall on my face, searching for something—maybe a heart—and the slow track of his eyes on me makes my skin prick with awareness and warmth. It lasts for only a moment, but it feels like a lifetime.

I turn back to Keith who's watching with inquiring eyes. "What's that about?"

"Go do your job." I wave him off, knowing how much he loves to gossip. I know he'll be back to ask.

Behind me, the music gets louder, someone adding songs up next on the jukebox, and my eyes find Liam, holding a glass in his hands. He watches the game on the TV and seems relaxed, a bit more at ease than he is at the house.

Keith returns after helping the other customers, pours me my third drink, and leans his forearms on the countertop. "So, you gonna tell me, or am I gonna have to beg?"

I swirl the liquid around and take a sip, smiling. "Begging sounds fun."

Keith opens his mouth to respond, his eyes twinkling. Then, they narrow again, and this time, I don't have a good feeling about it. Following his gaze, I twirl on my stool to see Blake's steely brown eyes right behind me. Her fingernails wrap around her glass tightly, and when I meet her eyes, I see the familiar haziness that always appears when she drinks.

"Lovely Blake. How can I help you?" Sarcasm falls out of my mouth like rain on a cloudy day. I rest my head in my hand, digging my fingers into my curls.

"I'm trying to figure out why you're really here."

"It's not any of your business, is it? We're not friends anymore. I don't have to tell you anything."

Keith sighs. "Please, just don't break anything," he says, and I turn to see him walking towards the other end of the bar. I turn back as Blake takes a sip of her drink and look past her to see Gaylee watching uncomfortably from the booth.

"We're not gonna break anything are we, Blake?"

I know I'm egging her on. I know exactly how to get to her, how to piss her off, but if she's gonna tell me that I'm unwanted in a town I grew up in—albeit in a town I left—she can at least have the balls to say it straight to my face. And not drive off.

She scoffs, swaying slightly. "Fuck off."

"You came up to me. I was minding my own business."

Anger and frustration start to filter in, heating my skin. I can feel eyes on me now, more than Blake's, Gaylee's, and Keith's. Liam watches as well.

There is a focus in his brown eyes I don't usually see unless he's working. They flicker between Blake and me cautiously as he leans back, turning himself towards us just a bit more as if he's preparing to step in and mediate.

I'm so close to losing it, to snapping, to screaming in this bar that I just want it to stop. Instead of saying anything, I spin away from her. It's pointless. Blake grabs the stool and spins it right back.

I sigh, focusing on the girl who used to be one of my best friends.

Her eyes narrow, still hazy, but the focus in them reminds me of when we used to fight. I know she won't let it go. Because she's drunk or sick of me or both, this won't be going my way. When the low chuckle builds in her throat, I down the rest of my drink.

"God, you think you run the world, don't you?" She hiccups, and exhaustion erases anything else I feel. "You leave everyone behind without a second glance and then walk back in here like nothing is changed. Walk back in like it doesn't matter."

My chest burns with the hurtful yet truthful claim she throws at me, and it takes every stubborn bone in my body not to avert my eyes. I watch her with a pit burning in my stomach.

I see Gaylee stand up from the corner of my eye, concern written all over her face, and I realize the bar is mostly silent except for the occasional commentary from the TV.

Blake continues. "I hate to fucking tell you, Sheyanne, but everything has changed. We're not the same people you left behind. So, you should just go. Just leave again. This time, we won't give a shit."

Blake exhales, and I think she's at least done yelling, but instead of walking away, she tosses the rest of her drink right at my face. The liquid, her typical fucking vodka sprites, sticks to my skin and drenches my hair, like the shame that has blanketed me thicker and thicker every day.

Time slows as the liquid drips down my skin. I am searching for words, actions, my pride.

My heart pounds in my chest painfully as I'm struck by her words. They were a slap to the face, way more than the liquid she threw at me. Now, the silence of the bar is palpable as we stare at each other for a moment, neither of us moving.

"Blake, stop it." Gaylee comes up and grabs her arm, pulling her towards the booth again. Blake looks at me without a word as she lets herself get pulled away. "Sheyanne, I'm—"

I hold up my hand. "Save it." And that's as many words as I can muster before the bow breaks, and I start crying, whether that's out of frustration or every other emotion I've bottled down until now.

My shirt sticks to my arms, to my chest, to my stomach. Every part of me smells like vodka and soda. It even drips off my hair and onto my shoulders, leaving marks on the leather jacket. On shaky legs, I stand, feeling the eyes of every single person in the bar focused on me. I want to tell them all to fuck off, but I don't. Instead, I throw cash down on the bar, doing my best to avoid the pity in Keith's eyes, and walk out into the cool air.

It wraps around me, but instead of it cooling me off, I feel more suffocated, more surrounded by everything I hate. My jacket smells, and

I rip it off and toss it in the backseat. I lean against my car, facing away from the bar and looking out into the enveloping darkness, trying to breathe. Trying not to let what Blake said get to me.

It's hard when I agree. No one would care if I left again, and why should they? I've never given them a reason.

"Sheyanne."

I whip my head around, meeting Liam's gaze in the darkness a few feet away.

"What?" I bite out, for once not meaning to but snapping anyway because I can't help it right now. Liam looks on unphased. I stand there shivering.

"You didn't deserve that."

My heart tightens, and I squeeze my hands together, digging my nails into my palm until it stings. "I don't—"

"Need me to tell you that? Need anything? I'm well aware you don't. But that doesn't mean I'm not going to say it. Because you didn't deserve that at all." He shakes his head, and I want him to stop talking because I'm scared of what he's going to say next. "We're not friends; I know that. I'm not saying we need to be. I'm here for a job, and you don't want to be here at all. But you need to take a good look in the mirror before you let this place destroy you."

I hold his gaze as best I can until the tightness constricting my throat makes me look away. His footsteps sound on the gravel of the parking lot as he moves closer. The jacket in his hands suddenly appears in front of my eyes, and I look up.

"You shouldn't give anyone or anything that power. No matter what you may have done."

I finally find some bite, some life in my blood. "Why do you care, Landon?"

His lips pull up at the sides, just slightly in the dim glow of the lights near the bar. "Believe it or not, Shaw, I don't think you're as bad as you believe you are."

I furrow my brows. "As I believe I am?"

Liam nods. "I think you view yourself in a darker light than anyone else here does."

Before I can say anything, he drapes his jacket over my shoulders and turns back around, walking back towards the bar. I'm left standing outside my old haunt, questioning how exactly I ended up here, dejected, emotional, and alone in a town that was never my home but has somehow affected me more than I ever could've thought.

Feeling more exhausted than I ever have in my life.

Questioning why it's so easy for Liam to see what I can't.

Nine

Liam

I step back into the bar without a second glance.

As soon as I'm back on the barstool, I run my hands over my face and exhale. A few deep breaths later, I reach for the neat whiskey I left behind and gulp it down. Sparing a glance to the right, in the back, I watch just for a moment as the two girls argue in the booth. The one with blond tipped curls and dark brown skin has her fingers threaded through the coils while the other talks quickly with her hands.

With another sigh, I turn forward, finding the bartender right across from me. He's got an intrigued smile on his face, and I lean back, picking up my glass and raising it. Like he was expecting it, he grabs the whiskey and pours it instantly.

"You're new here." It's a statement.

"Yeah." I nod, sipping the whiskey. "What gave it away?"

He chuckles, leaning on the counter behind him. "Just a hunch." He reaches his hand across the bar, and I reach up to meet it in a swift handshake. "Keith."

"Liam."

A beat passes, and the question I was waiting for finally comes. "So, Sheyanne?"

A small laugh passes my lips. "What about her?"

Keith narrows his eyes but grins. "Considering she hasn't been home in almost five years and then walks in like it's nothing and you come in shortly after? And you know her?"

Sheyanne and I may have our issues and a strange relationship that has had a varying degree of conversations from spiteful, to somewhat calm, to nothing at all, but I highly doubt she's told anyone about her father—considering they barely speak to each other and seeing that, apparently, she hasn't been home in almost five years. This information isn't mine to share.

"Who said I know her?"

"She addressed you by name."

"And?" He raises a brow, and I chuckle. "Listen, I'm just here for a job."

Keith nods, unbelieving. "That happens to involve her."

I raise my hands in surrender. "Maybe, maybe not. It's not anyone's business but hers. If you want to know, you can ask Sheyanne."

Admiration appears on his features, and he nods slowly. "I like you. You seem like a good man. I know she isn't, but I'm happy she's home, even if others might not feel the same." Keith looks towards the booth in the back. I follow his gaze, once more eyeing the two girls before turning back and leaning back on the barstool.

"Well, she seems to like you," I say, aware of how she seemed genuine with him. More open.

Keith laughs. "That's 'cause I helped her get in underage years ago."

I shrug. "Could be."

Truthfully, I don't think that's the case. She's not superficial; that much I know. The only other person she'd talked to so freely was MJ and, on occasion, her brother. Maybe it was the fact that he did that all those years ago, but maybe it was the fact that he was simply nice and didn't seem to hold a grudge like others had.

Keith's response is interrupted by a few patrons further down calling his name. "Duty calls. I hope I see you around, Liam. It was nice to meet you."

"You, too, man." I down the rest of my drink and place two twenties on the bar top.

Plucking my keys from my pockets, I head out and slide into the leather seats of my car. Bags are on the back seats from my trip to Walmart. It was the only place open so late. With the dropping temperatures, I figured it was better to buy thicker clothes now than later. And then, I'd ended up here, only realizing Sheyanne was here as well when I saw her car in the small parking lot. I'd certainly not been expecting the night to go how it had. I assume she hadn't either. With a sigh, I run a hand over my hair towards my forehead. I start the ignition and begin heading back to the stables. A short drive later, the broken gate comes into view, and gravel crunches under the tires of my car as I park near the shed next to Sheyanne's car.

When I step out, the first thing I notice, the thing I always notice at night here, is the sky—not infiltrated by city lights but instead dotted with stars. It's peaceful, in a strange way, being in a place so small and secluded. Quite different from Vegas. One thing I appreciate is the quiet. It's never truly quiet back home in the city. Bright lights, planes coming and going, the sheer amount of people always around—it's never quiet.

I never imagined I'd find something enjoyable about such a small town, but I have found I enjoy the silence, being allowed to choose how to fill it.

The house is silent when I enter, the darkness only broken by the light above the stove. Usually, I'm greeted by Nyx—everyone who enters is—unless he's with Sheyanne, which is where I'm assuming he is now. After grabbing water, I head down the hallway where a soft illumination escapes past Sheyanne's closed door. Without even realizing it, I pause, only for a step, outside her door.

Sheyanne is freer in her emotions than I've experienced. When she feels something, no matter how hard she tries to hide it, she feels it all the way. It becomes written on her face, in her mannerisms. It's interesting to watch, interesting to be around. Sheyanne doesn't fight for control; she adapts to what the situation calls for, even if that's anger. She doesn't appease people; she doesn't let herself get walked all over. While it may not always be advantageous, I admire the way she is so open with it all, that she doesn't tuck it away and hide it like others do, like I usually do.

While I haven't been here long, I have also realized that most of the anger and the spite that escapes Sheyanne comes from a place of hurt and a deep desire to tuck it all away.

There's no use in crowding her, so I don't.

It would be pointless, and it would only be a hinderance, causing her to retreat even further, and quite frankly, it *isn't* any of my business. So, just like I told Keith, that's what I tell myself, and I keep walking.

The next morning is quiet as usual.

Mr. Shaw and I sit at the dining table with two cups of coffee while his kids go about their work. On the tablet in front of me, I'm sketching design ideas for the rebrand he requested—a new sign, new logo, and name marker for brochures for the stables, all simple stuff—while he looks at some of his earlier accounts and some statements for us to go over later.

The door to the sunroom is open, the sounds of birds chirping the only noise in the early morning. My phone ringing is the second sound that breaks the quiet.

When I see it's my grandfather, I stand. "Excuse me, Mr. Shaw."

He waves a hand, not even looking up from the papers. "Take your time."

With my coffee in hand, I answer the call, stepping into the sunroom. For late October, it's colder than I expected.

"Liam?" My grandfather's voice comes through the speakers.

I sit on one of the chairs near the screens. "Hi, Pop, I'm here."

"How's it going, son?" he asks, and I hear the smile in his voice and the sound of him settling into his favorite leather chair. It's so old that you can't even count the cracks in it, but he refuses to let anyone buy him a new one and wouldn't dream of getting rid of it.

Glancing around, I take in the views that are visible from this tiny ranch house, the mountains in the back with the fading snow caps. "It's going all right. Still getting into the swing of things for this type of job, but good. How are things at home? Did you get the roof patched? The leak fixed?"

"Will you stop worrying about us and the damned house?" he scoffs, and I run a hand down my face.

The house is old—too old. It had problems when they bought it, way before I was even alive, and now, those problems are being repeated nuisances. Something is always breaking; something always needs fixing. And they refuse to leave. If they won't buy one for themselves, I've decided I'll buy one for them—without letting them know. Hopefully, that is something they can't refuse.

"I'll stop worrying when you get out of there."

With the sigh he lets out, I imagine he's rolling his eyes. "Well, it's useless. It's not your job to worry about us."

"And it's not your job to live in some old broken house when you don't need to, Pop," I argue, exhausted because we've had this conversation a million times.

"Watch the tone, young man," he says firmly. "Now, what's that place like? We tried looking it up, but the internet was being difficult."

I grin to myself, leaning my head back on the chair and cracking my neck. "I'll send a few pictures to your email." Every time I send a picture straight to his phone, he can't figure out how to look at it and save it.

"Good, good. I didn't wanna bother you; just wanted to say hi."

"Is Grandma there?"

"No, she's out dropping off some food. I'll tell her you said hi and to give you a call." He clears his throat, and even over the phone, I can hear the creaking of the chair as it rocks ever so slightly back and forth.

"All right, thanks, Pop. Love you."

"Love you, too, kid. Stop worrying about us. I mean it."

"I'll do my best," I respond before saying goodbye and ending the call. With a sigh, I head back into the kitchen.

As I sit, the front door creaks open. Nyx bounds in first, tail wagging, trailed by Sheyanne and Shane. As always, Shane's smiling, and Sheyanne—well, given last night, I don't expect anything different—she strides past everyone with her eyes cast to the floor and heads straight down the hall, Nyx hesitating only seconds before following her.

Mr. Shaw turns back to the work in front of him with a small shake of his head as the coffee pot clicks to a start in the kitchen for a second time that morning. I stand again and grab Mr. Shaw's empty mug along with my own. He dips his head in thanks as I place them on the counter and wait for the coffee to finish.

"Last night was that bad?" Shane asks quietly, taking a long drink of water. Earlier, before anyone else woke up, he told me he was here when Sheyanne came in last night, and I told him where we had both ended up and that I'd catch him up on it later.

"I certainly wouldn't call it good," I retort, and he chuckles. I don't feel as apprehensive talking to her brother. "She got a drink thrown on her."

Shane groans. "Lemme guess. Curls?"

I nod. "Curls."

"That would be Blake. I assume Gaylee was there, too, probably trying to stay out if it." He runs a hand through his curls. I gather that Gaylee is the dark-haired girl—Japanese, I believe—that I've seen twice now, once in the car and now in the bar.

"She was. She tried to intervene, though it came a few seconds too late."

Shane looks at me knowingly. "Gaylee hates confrontation. To this day, I don't understand how she ended up friends with them. But she's never left their side since like second or third grade, I think." He moves to the fridge, grabbing an apple and peeling the sticker off of it. "Should I be worried? About Sheyanne?"

Rolling my neck in a stretch for a second, I finally shrug my shoulders. "Not sure. I don't know her like you do, obviously, but I think just give her some space."

Shane smiles at that. "Well, whether you like it or not, you'll probably get to know her just like we do. You're kinda stuck here."

I pour the coffee. "I imagine so."

"Dad and I are going into the town square a bit later, run a few errands. Would you like to join? I know you mentioned grabbing some winter clothes." Shane pours his own cup of coffee, and a second, I assume, is for his sister.

"I grabbed most of what I needed last night before the bar. But I need to look into some things for your dad, so that'd be good."

Shane nods, patting me on the back as he exits the kitchen, Sheyanne's mug in hand, "Sounds good. I'll let you two get some work done and find you when it's time to leave."

I watch him walk down the hall towards his sister's room. Her door opens, only for a second, long enough for the mug to be passed over and maybe a word or two exchanged, but that's it. I set Mr. Shaw's mug down in front of him and take my seat. He slides me the papers he was reading, highlighted, and we begin to go over his financial records together. He has kept a careful account of expenses from as far back as when he bought the farm to the last few weeks, along with loans, loan payments, bank statements, and the like. It's all extremely detailed, which makes my job that much easier.

Shane returns, taking his seat at the counter, still working on that puzzle. Even though I'm supposed to be working, my thoughts return to his sister.

I don't have any siblings. The only family I have is my grandparents and a semi-distant relationship with my dad. Sure, I also have my best friend, Wyatt, who is practically my brother, but it's different. Maybe these two are different, under other circumstances. I imagine other siblings might not bounce back—or even attempt to—but that doesn't seem to be the case here. Watching Shane with Sheyanne, despite the tension that hums like a live wire in this house some days, it's nice to see a bond like that in person. A bond that, so far, hasn't been broken just because life gets in the way.

It's nice to know that Sheyanne has someone to always be there for her, even if she doesn't think so.

Ten

Sheyanne

The early dawn light breaks through my curtains as I roll over. My eyes latch onto the glimpses of the sky I can see, watching as it begins to change from midnight blue to shades of orange and pink.

Physically, it feels like I can't get out of bed. Like even placing my feet on the rug is too much effort. And a part of me deeply wants to cry. I've wanted to cry for five days straight since I walked away from that bar drenched in alcohol with Liam Landon's jacket draped over my shoulders. The harsh—but true—words from Blake follow me everywhere I go and burrow into my thoughts. I want to cry. But for some reason, I can't.

I haven't cried in years.

"Where did I put my keys?" The voice is low, but it cuts through the heavy silence like a knife.

Furrowing my brows, I force myself to sit up, wiping the sleep away from my eyes.

"God damnit."

It's louder this time, and I'd recognize that voice anywhere. It's Dad. Nyx whines beside me as I shoot up and out my bedroom door. No one else is up, surprisingly, and the only sounds are the mumbled curses coming from my dad.

I rub my eye with the back of my hand as I stand a few feet away. "Dad?"

He looks over at me, looking tired and old and confused. Wrinkles deepen as he squints at me, and his once dark hair is peppered with gray. But his voice, his tone, reminds me of before when I was in high school. Back when I was just . . . never enough.

"Sheyanne, help me find my keys. They aren't here, and I need to get to the shed and get my work done."

The words send chills down my spine as I try to stop reliving my own memories. I keep my distance, but this is the first time I've seen the disease in action. I have no idea if he's had an incident before since Shane hasn't mentioned them, but I assume he has. For me, this is just reality starting to sink in.

With a sigh, I walk forward until I'm lightly touching his arm. "Here, come sit down. I'll look and make some coffee."

He doesn't argue. It feels weird to be this close to my dad. I don't know the last time we physically touched. A hug, a kiss on the cheek? None of it rings a bell. Leading him to the dining table, I let my eyes linger for just a second. A strange sensation builds as I do, unsure of how to manage what I'm feeling, sadness at the confusion he's feeling but still a desire to distance myself so I don't get hurt.

Nyx heads over to his side and sits at his feet while I start the coffee as quickly as I can without leaving him alone too long. I knock on Shane's door, knowing he's probably awake since we need to get going on our usual stable chores.

"Dad's having an . . ." I pause, not knowing what to say, rocking uncomfortably on the balls of my feet. "He's confused. I don't know, looking for his keys and . . ."

Shane sighs and heads to the kitchen. I don't go back out right away, not before getting dressed for the barn, pulling on my old blue jeans and a turtleneck under the crewneck that falls to my thigh. When I exit, Liam is standing in the doorway a few feet away from my own. I pause because I haven't spoken to him since outside the bar. His jacket is still draped over my desk chair because I refuse to acknowledge anything happened. I haven't wanted to look at his face or his eyes, afraid of finding pity there.

But after a second, I look up to those brown eyes and find nothing but a hint of kindness. An unexpected warmth spreads over the surface of my skin.

It's like he's seeing everything, even in the early dawn light when the sun has barely come up. It's prickly and unfamiliar and strange and addicting all at once, and as quickly as I looked up, I look back down at the old hardwood floors.

I dig my nails into my palm, pulling at the skin of my lip with my teeth, and head towards the kitchen without a word. I say nothing, not to Shane, not to Dad, who still has a confused look on his face, which makes my chest hurt, and certainly not to Liam who pads in behind me. In silence, I pour my coffee and head straight to the barn.

My breath comes out in puffs, the beginning of November entering with a chill. The cold has come to stay, fully settling into Flagstaff just as all the emotions I buried over the years start to resurface. I'm thankful for the chill; it cools my hot skin and my running thoughts. The horses neigh when I approach the barn, and my lip curls up slightly as the tiniest bit of life returns my blood. I go about my routine as normal, saving Teddy and Rayne for last.

Rayne and I have improved. She doesn't back away when it's her turn anymore; instead, she actually takes a few steps toward me. And today, on a day when I need it, on a week where I need it, she nuzzles me ever so lightly, and the heavy pressure on my chest dissipates for a brief moment. I unclip the lead rope and the halter as I let her into the pasture, her heavy body next to mine until she joins Teddy to graze. I lean over the fence and breathe in the cold air, my curls flowing around my face in the breeze as I sip my coffee.

"Hey."

I whip my head around. Liam stands a few feet away, hands tucked into his pockets. My hands squeeze my mug as I hold his gaze. The colors that began earlier have disappeared as a hazy gray settles into the sky—a blanket of clouds.

"What's up?" My fingers are freezing, and I adjust my weight from foot to foot to keep the blood flowing.

Liam nods his head toward the house. "Shane asked me to come get you. Your dad has an appointment later today, but Shane wants you to drive them there now."

I furrow my brows, taking a slow step towards him. "Why?"

"He said your dad's still a bit confused, and he wants to sit with him. I'm coming, too, to keep track of the paperwork. Shane says we should get there soon."

Pressure intensifies on my chest, my shoulders, everywhere. At the same time, I'm irritated and frustrated. There's no way for me to release this energy, all my pent-up feelings. I don't even know how, not when I've spent years pushing them down. Instead of letting me deal with things gradually, it's as if the world said, *Hey, here's something else you need to deal with.*

I can't. I *can't.*

But I have to. Whether I know how to or not.

Liam watches me carefully, like he did outside the bar. Gently. So gently that it makes me feel exposed.

Swallowing, I start walking, and when he turns to walk with me, I accidentally brush his shoulder as I pass. I try to ignore the warmth that seeps past the layer of cold the air drapes us in, past the layers of clothing I have on, and keep walking.

"Well then, let's get this over with," I murmur. The grass, covered with a slowly melting frost, crunches underfoot. From his spot next to me, I feel Liam's eyes land on the side of my face, and I steel myself to keep looking forward and push ahead of him.

If he looks too long, he'll start to see the cracks I've worked so hard to hide.

The drive is quick and quiet, only about fifteen minutes. Shane says they haven't switched doctors yet because the disease hasn't progressed to that point, but as it gets worse, we'll probably have to start driving him to Phoenix to get better all-around care for this kind of thing. The car is stifling with the nerves and anxiety rolling off my brother in waves as I pull into the parking lot.

Shane leans forward, between the two front seats, a tight curl falling over his forehead. "You wanna come in?" He's hesitant, and my heart pounds. But I know I can't, won't be able to bring myself to walk in those doors.

I meet his gaze and shake my head. "Not this time. Just text me if you need something."

To my surprise, he's not disappointed. He just nods and pats me on the head like he used to when we were little before climbing out of the car. He helps Dad out, and they disappear into the building. I look over at Liam who has his hand on the handle.

He nods at me. "I'm going to go help with the paperwork and get the information I need."

I don't say anything because I'm not positive it won't be something rude, and I don't have the energy for that. I don't want to do that. Liam trails his eyes over my face before pushing open the car door and following my brother. I turn the music up and lean back into the old seats of my car. Part of me wishes I could turn it up loud enough to ignore the thoughts thundering in my head, ignore the exhaustion that has battered me all week.

My phone vibrates in the cupholder, which surprises me because there's no one that contacts me on the regular. I pick it up and blink at the name on the screen—Gaylee—and a text asking if we can meet up in a few days and talk. I huff out a breath because, unlike before, whatever version of myself I am right now has no desire for confrontation, no desire to deal with them. I place my phone back down, leaning my forehead on the steering wheel and letting my heavy curls shield me. After a few deep breaths, I turn my head to stare out the window at the distant mountains capped with snow.

I wonder if the thoughts that pound my head every day would be quieter or louder up there.

"Everything okay?" The softness of his voice creeps into the car.

I turn to see Liam climb back into the truck, the cold air that enters the car with him causing goosebumps to pop up on my skin.

"Why wouldn't it be?"

Liam sighs, leans back in the seat, and lets his eyes flutter closed. I take the moment to notice his hair is longer than when he got here, not a far cry from the nicely trimmed cut, but it's getting there. His sharp cheekbones and angular face are . . . pretty, if I'm speaking objectively. A few scattered scars on his chin and near his eyebrow are much lighter than his otherwise flawless skin. He's almost always just in jeans or sweats and a hoodie now. It suits him.

But I've noticed that pretty much anything he wears suits him.

"If you take a picture, it'll last longer." His voice is a low hum, and he opens his eyes, humor dancing in them like firelight. I fight the warmth that contests to color my cheeks and stare out the front window.

"I don't know what you're talking about. Why are you back? Don't you have work to take care of?"

Liam stretches his legs out in front of him. "Already got everything I needed."

I pull my legs up and lean them against the steering wheel. "Well, didn't mean you needed to come sit in here with poor old Sheyanne."

He snorts in a sort of laughter. "It was either you or the doctor's waiting room."

I furrow my brows, finally looking at his face again, only to see his full lips fighting his own smile. "So, I'm barely better than a doctor's waiting room. That's comforting."

Liam shrugs with a cool nonchalance, one hand playing with the simple chain around his neck. "You said it, not me. And it's not like you've really given me a reason to think otherwise."

"Don't be an asshole."

He pulls his phone out of his back pocket, a full-on smirk on his lips now. "I'll stop if you stop, Sheyanne." I roll my eyes at the use of my name, ignoring that I like the way it sounds, and realize that in that moment I can breathe a bit.

"All right, Leon, let's not get ahead of ourselves."

He grins, a full smile this time, and it lights up his whole face. I can't help but stare again, just for a second, at the beautiful picture. "Don't make me pick the doctor's office; it's probably not too good for your image."

I hit his shoulder with the back of my hand and cross my arms, feeling like a child with a big pout on my face. But there's a warmth blooming in my chest that wasn't there before.

"You don't know anything about me or my image, pretty boy."

Liam leans in just slightly, resting his elbow on the center console with a smug smirk on his face. I can smell him, like winter and fresh air, and it's distracting. So is the way his brown eyes look, dancing as if they have a secret. "Oh, but I am learning. And quickly, too."

As quickly as that warm feeling was born, it dies.

Apprehension slams into me at his words, and the smile that was forming on my lips falls away. I don't want him to learn anything about me. Not who I was when I was younger or who I am right now because I'm not even sure I like her. So, how could he? How could anyone? And what does it matter? In a few months, I'll be out of here, and everything will go back to the way it was.

I don't say anything in response, just bite the inside of my cheek as my thoughts run wildly back down to the dark. He sighs and leans back, the old leather creaking as he does.

"I didn't mean anything by that, Shaw. Not in the way you think." His words are cradled by the soft tone he speaks in.

I shrug, tapping my fingers on my knee. "Doesn't matter."

"Yes, it does. If it bothers you, it does."

He says that as if it's as simple as that. As if that's all it takes. If something bothers me, then it matters. Easy. Maybe easy for him. I glance away, feeling my guard come back up.

I didn't even notice that it had fallen down.

"It doesn't. It doesn't matter. It doesn't bother me. My dad is sick; I think my brother probably secretly hates me, my old friends, this town… none of it matters. You don't know me, and you don't want to."

My chest is heaving by the time I'm done, and I realize what I've said, which is a whole lot of too much. I can't bear to look Liam in the face as silence fills the car—fills it to the very top. Every inch, every crevice is crammed with the painful silence that surrounds us. I can't bear it.

Can't bear the self-pitying cloud that I created.

I open my door, grabbing my phone and my wallet. "I'm walking home. Shane will show you how to get back."

"Sheyanne," Liam says, a roughness, a firmness to his voice as I kick my feet out, but I don't turn around, scared this will be the time I remember how to cry. "It's freezing outside, and it's too long of a walk."

"I'll call an Uber if I get cold."

My feet hit the gravel, and my chest tightens. My blood feels heavy and so do my feet, but I'm not going to sit in that car after saying all that shit out loud to someone I barely know and deal with the consequences.

"You can't run away from everything," he mumbles softly behind me, and I look up, staring at the endless gray sky above me.

"Just stop. Stop acting like you care," I spit out the words even though I don't want to.

I need him off my back. Need him to stop . . . whatever this is. To stop trying, to stop being nice to me, to stop these small gestures. Because I don't deserve it. I turn to look back, and his brown eyes meet mine. All notes of the lightness that had creeped into the car when he did have been suffocated by the dark I can't keep from sneaking in. I look away before he can say anything else and start walking.

I feel his gaze on my back as I stride away from the car and the doctor's office, away from my problems like I always do. Disappointment in myself weighs me down.

It sinks in with every step I take as I run away yet again.

I wish I could find all the puzzle pieces of myself and put them back together. But I worry that I wouldn't remember how. What I said to Liam was true. He doesn't know me.

But at this point, I don't think I know me either.

ELEVEN

Sheyanne

"Sheyanne, hey, it's Blake. I'm sure you knew that from caller ID." The voicemail pauses, and I listen, waiting. "I'm rambling, sorry. I just called to say that I shouldn't have thrown my drink on you. I probably shouldn't have said what I said either, or I at least shouldn't have said it how I did, but I'm especially sorry about throwing my drink. I really did just want to talk to you, and I went about it all wrong."

I shake my head. This is the most Blake Kelly apology I've ever heard. But it's an honest one. Even though her words hurt, she meant them. At least she has the guts to know that. It's why we were such good friends— we never pulled any punches, and we always got over it. But that was then, and this is us now—with four years of silence between us. When the message concludes, I tuck my phone into my jeans and continue throwing hay down from the hayloft in heaps as if nothing's changed. I'm not sure it has.

Both Blake and I skirt around apologies. I'm not sure if either of us has ever given a full apology in our lives. She doesn't say things she doesn't mean, so I appreciate the apology. I just don't know what to do about it. It's not like she doesn't have a right to be mad at me. I let her take the fall for the night that caused the rift in our friendship. I never apologized for it.

And then, I left.

We, just the two of us, had decided to get back at the girls who bullied Gaylee in high school. Living in a town that was predominantly white wasn't easy on any of us. Gaylee was just an easier target; she was sweeter, and she saw the best in everyone whether they deserved it or not. I loved that she was like that, that she was kind even when the world didn't earn her kindness. Blake and I weren't mean, per se; we just fought back.

So that night, not that Gaylee would've ever wanted us to do it, we fought back for her. We keyed the bullies' cars, slashed a tire or two, poured milk in their trunks and the vents—and God knows what else. It was, I think, the worst thing we ever did. Not that those girls didn't deserve it. They used to treat Gaylee like shit, tearing her down verbally, always breaking the jewelry she made or pointing out a loose stitch and pulling it, destroying whatever she'd spent hours making—with her own money, on her own time. It was our senior year, and we were fed up. Gaylee always stood on the side of being the bigger person, which she always was, but we were not afraid to stoop. So, stoop we did.

The next day when the police came, I was already on strike ten— more likely far beyond that—with my dad, who was one mishap from kicking me out. All I had to do was make it until graduation, and I could leave for college.

We'd been careful, worn gloves and done everything we could to take precautions. But we were chaotic; we were teenagers who should've known better but didn't. Somehow, Blake's prints got on the car, and of course, because we were two peas in a pod, they brought me in, too. Shane lied, said I was with him that entire night and gave me a look that made me shut my mouth to agree with him. I wanted to argue, to tell the truth, if only so Blake wouldn't catch all the blame.

Banner was willing to let her off with a fine, which was what happened, but her parents were livid. They grounded her for a month, I think. Even worse, they made her miss her second audition at one of the highest rated music schools on the west coast. Blake's parents had always argued that pursuing music was a waste of education. Instead of making the audition, she spent the entire day with her parents, figuring out ways to pay them back. Of course, we deserved consequences, but this, her future, it wasn't fair. We were stupid, we knew that, knew it was our decision that landed us in trouble. But somehow, she got stuck, and I walked away.

I had begged my dad to let me go vouch, to take the blame so she could go. Begged Shane to let me tell the truth, to do something to help her, anything. They didn't let me. Said it was another consequence of our actions. I knew that, but it didn't change the fact that I was just being scolded at home while her dreams were being hindered.

That was only the start of our downfall. Things escalated from there.

Knowing graduation was coming up, I couldn't bring myself to face my friend. Even though it wasn't just my fault, I felt like it was. So freshly eighteen-year-old Sheyanne did what she knew best. She avoided. Avoided both Blake's and Gaylee's calls, avoided them in the hallways during the last days of school, and avoided saying goodbye before I left. Looking back, it was all immature, a stupid fight that's led to all this. But that's what we were.

Immature.

My eyes flutter closed as I lean against the wall next to the ladder, just for a moment.

"Hey."

I jump and look around frantically to see MJ leaning against the barn doors with a soft smile on her face.

"Hey." I give her a small smile back, the best I can muster. "What's up?"

She shrugs and enters the barn, walking away from the cold air blowing outside. She has a thick sweater dress on and stockings with a big jacket that I recognize as my brother's over top.

"Shane is making lasagna. Wanted me to come tell you it was almost ready."

I nod and push the hay to its rightful spot.

MJ's shoes scuff over the floor. She reaches her hand over one of the stalls to pet the nose of one of the brown horses being boarded here. "He's worried about you. Ever since you walked home," she says, and my brows shoot up. "He told me. I'm sorry; I'm nosy."

At her honesty, I laugh—a small laugh—tucking my hands into my pockets. "It's okay. I'm happy he has you to talk to."

MJ grins again, a smile filled with warmth and pure, unfiltered joy. "He wants to talk to you, you know." The horse nuzzles her, and she coos. "Come on; I'm not letting you sit out here and hide in the barn."

"I have to finish a few things," I argue as gently as I can.

"Shane said you've been out here since the sun came up. I don't know much about barns and farm work, but even I know you have nothing left to do, Sheyanne." She crosses her arms, watching me with a knowing gaze. She's Shane's age, so only a bit older than me, but she acts like an older sister I never had. I like MJ, and for once, I don't want to push her away. I really don't want to push anyone away anymore.

Heat spreads up my neck and onto my cheeks despite the cold, and I hold up my hands in defeat. "Fine, fine, you win."

MJ winks, her eyes twinkling. "I always do." She steps forward and loops her arm through mine. "Now, come on. I'm starved, and your brother is a great cook, as you know, and I'm sure you're hungry. Hmm, you smell like hay."

I laugh, loudly this time, and it reverberates through my chest as we walk through the cold. The sun is still up, just beginning its descent as we head to the house.

"It does tend to come with the job," I say. I open the front door, kicking off my boots and leaving them on the porch, Nyx following along with a wagging tail. "Tell Shane I'll be right out. I'm gonna rinse off."

"Will do," MJ responds but then pauses, grabbing my arm gently. "Hey, if you ever want to talk, I'll always listen. I'm here for you if you need anything."

Overtaken by emotion, I swallow. "Thank you." I squeeze her hand before she goes, making a beeline for the kitchen.

I head straight past everyone and into my room, closing the door behind me, grabbing what I need, and stepping into the bathroom. Turning the water as hot as it'll go, I leave the door to my room ajar for the steam to escape. Stepping into the shower, I let the scalding water wash over my skin until all the dirt of the day is gone. I lean against the wall, taking deep breaths and trying to get into a better headspace, only shutting off the water when it runs cold. After slathering on some moisturizer, I dress quickly, throwing on a crewneck and some sweats, sitting down to pull on some socks.

I fall back, resting my arm over my eyes as my phone vibrates yet again. I ignore it, sliding on *do not disturb,* and leave it resting on the mattress.

The creaking of my door causes my head to snap up, watching Shane close it quietly.

He smiles, but it doesn't reach his eyes. "Can we talk?"

"Well, you're already in my room. Kinda beats the point of asking, doesn't it?" I attempt to say it playfully, but it comes out monotoned. I look up, meeting his eyes and immediately feeling guilty. "Sorry, yes, we can."

Shane grabs my desk chair, dragging it closer to me before sitting down. Only a foot away, he rests his elbows on his legs and looks at me with warm eyes.

"I don't hate you, Sheyanne."

"What?"

He raises a brow in a move that reminds me how alike we can be and runs a hand over his curls. "I don't hate you. I never have."

I tuck my hands under my thighs. "I highly doubt that, Shaney."

He chuckles. "Oh, no, believe me, I tried. After you left, I tried to hate you. I wanted to, for getting out, for leaving. You know, a good dose of brotherly angst? But I couldn't then, and I don't now." I meet his eyes, and there's nothing but warmth in them, nothing but honesty glinting back at me. "You're my sister. And a pain in the ass, sure. But I will never hate you."

I ignore the words for a moment and try not to drown in the feeling of the weight dissipating off my shoulders and chest. "So, Liam told you what I said?"

Shane laughs and shakes his head. "That is so not the point of this conversation."

I'm inhaling deeply, feeling my chest rise and fall as I let Shane's words wash over me, let the silence sit there for a moment. It's delicate, and I'm scared to mess it up.

"You don't hate me?" I ask after a moment.

He smiles, and the tiny excuse for a dimple in his left cheek, one I never got, pops through. "I don't hate you."

I nod, more to myself than anything, and fully digest the words.

Shane doesn't hate me. And says he never will. Deep down, I knew that. The feeling that he did was just the overwhelming amount of discomfort I felt in the situation, that self-pity I had been determined to drown in. But that doesn't take away from the fact that it's nice to hear. Finally, I look up and give him a sheepish smile, nodding as we both stand. He slides my chair back under my desk and steps towards the door. Before he can open it, I wrap my arms around him and squeeze. I don't even remember the last time I hugged my brother. After the shock passes, he hugs me back.

This doesn't fix everything or erase all the damage, but it makes me feel hopeful. I have a chance to get to know my brother again.

He pulls away, abruptly flicking me on the forehead.

"Ow, what was that for?" I rub the heel of my hand over the skin, frowning at him.

"You owe me."

"Oh, come on, you're gonna do this after that cute moment?"

"Hell yes, I am. You owe me big time."

I push him back. "I'm your little sister. You're supposed to let me off easy." He doesn't flinch. "Come on, let's go. I'm starving." Again, he doesn't budge. Just waits. I huff. "Fine, fine! I owe you." Shane grins, pulling open my door. The smell of lasagna hits me instantly. We start walking slowly down the hallway.

"You can start by being nicer."

"To who?" If he means Dad, well, that's just too much right now. Too soon.

"I'm not saying forgive Dad, but can you talk to him? Just a little. But especially, you could be nicer to Liam," Shane pleads, blinking puppy dog eyes at me. I raise a brow until he drops the look and rolls his eyes, once again reminding me how alike we are.

I scowl at his request, knowing it's really not asking much at all. "Why?"

"Because I'm asking. Nicely." He drawls out the word and gives me a pointed look.

I stare at him. "But I don't know him."

"Then how do you know you dislike him?" I open my mouth to argue, but Shane flicks me on the forehead again. "Anyway, you're gonna do it because I, you're amazingly loving big brother, am asking you to. And because he's not so bad. He's here for a job, yeah, but may as well make it easy for him. So, just be nice."

We pause at the end of the hallway, and I cross my arms. "Fine. Even though he spilled my secret meltdown."

"Well, can you blame him? You have a lot of those." He says it playfully and bumps my shoulder a few times until I shake my head.

"Shame on you." I walk into the kitchen, and Shane follows with a laugh.

MJ watches with a smug smile from her seat at the table and gives me a cute wave. Shane pauses his walk to the kitchen and presses a kiss against her temple. Avoiding *that*, I turn and crouch in front of the old bookshelves that stand on either side of the TV. Without looking too hard, I find one of my old favorites and take my own seat at the dining table. I leave the seat next to MJ, who is scrolling on her phone, open for Shane, which leaves me next to Liam. Turning, I rest my foot on the piece of wood connecting the legs of the chair and draw my other leg up.

I don't say anything to Liam, and he doesn't say anything to me as I open the book, leaning back in the chair. Shane plays an old CD, and Dad and Liam talk quietly to one another as Liam pinches and points at a design on his tablet, their voices fading into the background as I read.

But every now and then, I feel a slightly familiar gaze land on my skin, my cheeks, my nose, my entire face. A searching one that warms my skin whenever it passes over. It never lingers long, and I never look up to make eye contact, but I know it's there.

"Oh, Liam," Shane says from the kitchen as he pulls out what smells like garlic bread and then the lasagna. "I know you wanted to go into town and get your hair cut soon. They're calling for a blizzard late this weekend and into next week, so might want to do it sooner rather than later."

Liam looks up, letting Dad study the tablet more in depth, and nods. "It'll be nice to see snow; I certainly don't get it back home." Liam pauses, and I notice just how long his usually short hair has grown. The edges are even a little frizzy, grown out. "Do you know a place I could go? I'll drive myself in."

"I can take you," I say quietly, ignoring how Shane's eyebrows shoot up when I say it. It's a small act of kindness I can show in return to what he's shown me. Standing to go help Shane, I continue. "I was planning on going to town soon anyway, so I can take you. If you want."

Liam's eyes follow me as I walk away, grabbing plates and silverware, putting them on the table. His eyes meet mine when I set a plate down in front of him. "I appreciate that. You don't mind?"

I shrug, ignoring the way my skin pricks under his gaze. "Yeah, no big deal."

"Well, well, well," Shane mumbles under his breath as he passes me. Out of view of everyone else, I pinch his lower back.

"Shut up," I mumble just as MJ smiles at me.

"Sheyanne, can you pass me a drink from the fridge?" she asks, and I nod.

"Would you grab a beer for each of us please? There are seltzers in there for MJ. And you, if you want one," Shane notes as he sets the huge tray of lasagna on the dining table. I nod, grabbing three beers and a seltzer out of the fridge, sticking with water for myself.

"Thanks," Liam and MJ say at the same time as I set their drinks on the table and take my seat.

Shane serves the lasagna and passes the salad he made around to each of us. It's silent for a moment, and I accidentally meet Dad's eyes from across the table. I don't know what I expect to see in them, but they're unreadable.

"Since you're going into town, can you go tomorrow, Sheyanne? And stock up for the storm?" he grumbles before shoving a bite into his mouth. "Shane needs to take me to a follow up appointment. I figure you won't want to come to that unless we want a repeat of last time."

I tense my jaw, ignoring the dig at me. I don't feel like fighting with him in front of MJ, or anyone, at the moment.

"Sure." I'm pretty sure I hear Shane's exhale from next to me, so I kick his leg under the table in annoyance.

Liam glances around until his eyes land on me. "I'll come. We can just get everything done in one day."

I glance over at him.

"That's fine. You're carrying the bags though."

Liam chuckles, and I don't like the way it sends a chill through my blood—one that heats as it flows through my veins, too, leaving a residual warmth behind. I take a bite of lasagna and tell myself it's from the food instead.

"Wouldn't have it any other way, Shaw."

I shake my head and force my eyes down, trying to hide the smile growing on my face, and continue eating. Dinner finishes shortly after that. The old CD playing in the background, melodic voices, and the rumbling of an old dishwasher are the only sounds in an otherwise quiet house.

Shane comes up next to me as I wash the rest of the dishes. "I'm gonna take MJ home. You good to finish up?"

I nod, and MJ comes up, pushing my brother out of the way, and gives me a quick hug. I stick my tongue out at him over her shoulder. "You're okay?" Her words are quiet, and I nod. "Call me if you need anything, and next time for real, we're getting away from them."

"Of course."

They head out, and by the time the counters are wiped, the dishes are drying, and everything is put away, the room is completely cleared out. Dad and Liam are gone from the dining table; the only thing sitting on it is a tablet, a folder of papers, and my book. I turn off all the lights except for one and switch out the CD, enjoying the peace and quiet. For once, it's not so loud in my head, and my thoughts aren't pounding relentlessly. I think Shane's forgiveness and admittance to never hating me took a bigger weight off me than I'd thought.

It's one thing to tell yourself something, but it's another to hear it from the person you needed it from.

Nyx stays as I sit at the table, flipping through the book and popping a piece of chocolate in my mouth every few pages, thumbing over the old, folded corners of my favorite parts. A shadow appears in front of my light, and I look up to see Liam.

"What time do you want to leave tomorrow?" he asks, and I close my book, stretching out my legs.

I burrow into my sweatshirt and lean back in my chair, patting the top of Nyx's head when he rests it on my thigh. "Around ten, if that's okay."

"Sounds good to me," he responds, grabbing himself some water. Before he can see me watching him, I pick my book up again, drawing my knees up and leaning it on my thighs.

After a moment, he sits at the table across from me and neither of us speaks. But in this case, the silence is loud. I feel like he's studying me and trying to figure me out. It's not uncomfortable, it's just . . . different.

When I look up at him again, he's tapping along to the beat of the song playing in the background, and there's a phantom smile on his face as he pulls his tablet closer to him. When he first arrived, I pushed all my anger on him, like I pushed it on my brother. All of my frustration and irritation toward my dad and my disdain at being here and being stuck needed a target.

I painted him as a villain in my head instantly.

Someone new, someone easy to take it all out on.

But every time we interact, I fear that my paint never settled, never dried, and is chipping away piece by piece, peeling off the canvas as a new image takes its place.

One of the real Liam, not the one I created.

"What are you reading?" He breaks the silence, and I exhale, thankful for it.

I look at the book and back up at him. My lip curls, but I fight it. "Nothing, just a book."

"Do you make everything so difficult?" His tone is playful, humor dancing along his words.

"I did warn you when you first came I wouldn't make anything easy, you know." I shrug, keeping my eyes trained on the paper in front of me, not reading anything at all.

Liam snorts out a breath of air. "Oh, I remember."

I purse my lips and hide the grin that threatens to grow on my face. He takes another sip, his hands wrapped around the glass, fingers moving around in the condensation.

"Sure you wanna spend all day with me?" I ask, enjoying the back and forth.

He grins. "Well, if anything goes south, I'll just walk home." My eyes narrow, and I throw a piece of chocolate at his face. Liam catches it easily and pops it in his mouth. "Too soon?"

I give him the finger, and he chuckles, filling the space with it. The sound of his laugh crawls over my skin, leaving me warm and aware of him. He stands and heads toward the hallway, patting the doorway before he does.

"Goodnight, Landon." I wave him off. "I'll see you in the morning."

He turns back to glance at me, his own small smile fighting to appear. "Looking forward to it, Sheyanne." He raises his glass in the air before disappearing into the darkness.

I watch the space where he once stood for a moment. The new image forming as the old one disappears seems to be one of someone who is inviting, who brings a feeling of ease, a calmness wherever he goes. I get why my dad hired him. I get why Shane likes him. I get it, and I don't know if I want to. It's easier being spiteful and rude and maintaining the reputation I left behind.

Except, it's like it doesn't bother him—like he doesn't care about the walls I've put in place.

Maybe I should care less, too. Because I'm not so sure I'm the same person I was those years ago. I'm still struggling—with a multitude of things—but I don't feel like that girl anymore. And I don't really want to be her again.

I can't change the past, but maybe I can paint a better image of myself as I try to learn from it instead of running away from it. Maybe I can let myself grow into a better version of me.

TWELVE

SHEYANNE

I knock on Liam's door, rolling up the sleeves of the oversized gray corduroy button-up I have on and pulling at the hem of my turtleneck.

Dad and Shane already left for his doctor's appointment to get new scans before the storm, so it's just us. Liam's door opens. I look up from my phone just as he pulls his black hoodie down, but I don't miss the sliver of dark skin that flashes as he does. I avert my eyes, making sure my face gives nothing away as he makes eye contact with me.

"Ready?" I ask, twirling the end of a frizzy curl.

"Ready as you are."

We head down the hallway, Nyx following behind as I slip my warm boots on over my leggings and fuzzy socks. I lean down and gently tug his ears. "You can't come today, but we'll play when I get back." He wags his tail, and I grin.

"You smile around him more than anyone else, you know that?" Liam comments, amusement all over his face.

I shrug my coat on over my layers. "He's nice and sweet and perfect. And he loves me. Can you blame me?" Liam shakes his head, eyes warm. "Exactly. While we're out, I was gonna stop at the bookstore. Is that okay?"

"I'm just here to carry the bags, remember?" He pulls open the front door dramatically, motioning for me to walk through. I bite the inside of my cheek to keep from smiling as I walk out into the cold.

The sun is hidden behind a sky full of heavy clouds, and the wind whips around us as we step outside, the otherwise quiet world hinting at the impending snowstorm. I unlock my car, and we climb in as I blast the heat. My phone connects to the stereo, and I turn it up to kill the silence. After a moment of driving, as I get closer to the local grocery, I break it.

"You've never seen snow?" I ask, glancing over before looking at the road again.

His hood is pulled up partway, covering the back of his head and his ears, disguising his hair growing out. "I've seen it; just not like this."

I tap my fingers on the steering wheel. "Flagstaff must be a mighty big shock. Small town, nothing ever happening, and a lot of snow."

Liam stretches, resting his elbow on the window. "It's different, but I like it. I miss home, but it's not so bad a place to be."

I don't argue even though I don't agree. I'm a bit biased towards how I feel about this town, but I won't ruin Liam's newfound appreciation for this little dot on a very big map. We fall back into silence, and I notice how the town still looks different right when it's about to snow. It's gray, the mountains brighter and bigger in the background. It's colder, too, but it seems more alive somehow. The packed grocery store parking lot only confirms that.

Even though I ran away before and plan to leave again, there's a part of me—a very miniscule part of me—that's excited for this. To see it again.

Almost an hour later, we're checking out and bracing for the cold again. I carry three bags in one hand and my key in the other. Liam grabs the remaining five, doing so with ease. He tugs his hood up as we exit, a small smirk on his face.

"I thought I was carrying all the bags." Liam passes me with his long, strong legs, and I narrow my eyes at his back.

"Well, I'm not a monster."

He leans against the Bronco as I hit the unlock button so he can start unloading. "That's yet to be seen."

"Oh, fuck you," I mumble, the cold creeping through my inefficient layers and making my lips feel numb. I pull the bags off my arm and put them in the trunk.

I climb into the car, fully appreciative of the heat coming through the vents. When I turn to Liam, his eyes are already on me, gentler than I expect them to be, which catches me off guard. My heart pounds, unsure of what this moment is. I watch him watch me, watch his eyes flicker over my features, pause on my lips, and trail up to my eyes.

Clearing my throat, I look away, but the feel of his gaze remains. "Now, you just need a haircut, I need books, and then, we're outta here."

As I pull out of the parking lot, I remember that there is only one barbershop in town—at least close by. I used to cut both Shane's and my dad's hair. It got awkward as I got older doing Dad's, so eventually, he started buzzing the coarse hair off. Shane learned because he was terrified I would purposely mess up his hairline as a prank. Asshole. I had learned because the barbershop was almost always fully booked or there was always a painfully long wait. There is also a very good chance they're already closed ahead of the storm. I drive around the small town towards the barbershop as the clouds paint the sky in different shades of gray.

I am not the least bit surprised when I see a line out the door of the shop. Liam sighs and runs a hand over his hair towards his forehead.

"Well, there goes that." He purses his lips, then shrugs and leans back. Resting his head on the seat, he turns to look at me. "To the bookstore then."

I hesitate. "I can give you a haircut." His gaze meets mine; his warm brown eyes widen in surprise. "I used to cut my dad's hair and Shane's all the time. I'm sure I still remember."

The edge of his mouth twitches, and I know he's got something smart to say. "You're not going to accidentally kill me?"

"What by nicking your throat with a razor?" I shake my head, but there's a laugh building in my chest, a lightness to the conversation, a lightness I almost never feel.

Liam grins, and it lights up his whole face. "Yes, exactly like that."

"If I wanted to kill you, Liam, I probably would've done it already." For some reason, he smiles wider, and humor dances in his eyes like those little figurines in a music box. "Why are you smiling?"

"That's the first time you've ever said my name."

I furrow my brows as I put the car into reverse. "That's not true."

He chuckles, looking at me. "Yes, it is. Every other time it's Landon, or Leon, or Leo."

I feel my cheeks burn because I realize he's right. I was so insistent on not naming him to his face because I wanted to keep a distance, a space from anyone and anything.

"Don't sweat it. I'm not mad." He draws his finger through the condensation on the window. "I just think it's funny."

The bookstore appears down the street as I stop at the red light. "I'm sorry for doing that." My eyes stay focused on the light, waiting until it turns green, and then the road— anything but Liam as I pull into the parking lot. Even so, I feel Liam's eyes latch onto my face, and it warms under his unwavering gaze as I park the car. "Really, that was beyond immature of me, and you didn't deserve it."

His lips quirk up. "Thank you. I forgive you, all right? Let's go get your books so I can get a haircut and hopefully live to see another day." I finally look over to see him with an expectant look and hand on the door, ready to go. "Besides, I'm interested to see what books you like to read."

I exhale, laughing as I do, taking the keys out of the ignition, and we hop out of the car and push through the wind to the store, walking side by side, our shoulders just inches from brushing.

Only time will tell, and the picture is still being painted, but for once, I'm excited to see what takes shape on the canvas. Maybe, just maybe, it wouldn't be so bad to have someone understand and choose to see me and not all the mistakes I've made.

"Did you really need that many?" Liam says as we unload the car and he watches me swing my extremely heavy bag of books over my shoulder, stumbling only a step or two on the gravel.

"One can never have too many books."

He shakes his head, grabbing the bags of groceries and hauling them on his arms. Whatever's left, I pull onto my own arm, trying to balance out the weight of books that are dragging me down. The rocking chairs on the porch sway in the wind as we walk up, and the windchimes jingle with every swoosh of wind. The cracked paint looks bright against the gray sky and the evergreen trees in the background. With Thanksgiving approaching, it'll be time to put the Christmas lights up soon.

"Sheyanne, can you come here?" Dad's voice rings out as soon as I step inside.

I sigh and walk inside the house after kicking off my shoes, placing the bags on the counter. Shane comes to the kitchen, pats me on the shoulder as I pass, and helps Liam unload.

I pad to the table where Dad sits, reading glasses on the bridge of his nose as he looks at some paper. "Yes?"

"I need you to help me this week." He doesn't look up, and I cross my arms.

Quickly, I look behind me to see Shane and Liam both watching, hands halfway in the grocery bags that they should be unloading. I raise a brow. They both cough and continue, unashamed of their eavesdropping.

"With what?"

Dad looks up at me. His dark eyes are clear today. He almost looks like the dad I grew up with. "I would like you to come with me to meet with the owners of the horses that board with us."

"Why me?" I fidget uncomfortably.

"You're the one that takes care of them. You're the one that knows them best. Figured it'd be best if you came with me to explain that while the ownership is changing, the plans in place will go on as usual."

"Changing to who? I thought you were selling?"

Dad looks up at me, eyes flickering between Shane and me. "I'm still considering the idea of selling. But in the meantime, ownership will go to one of you two. I'm going to put it in both your names, and the two of you can work it out."

"You don't have to put my name on it if you don't want. I know you probably don't want my name anywhere near it."

He stares at me, the only gaze that still makes me nervous, still makes me want to look away after only a few seconds. The statement wasn't meant for pity. I said it because, for me, in my world, it's true. Nothing I ever did was good enough. Especially as a kid, when the only way I felt like I could get his attention was by getting into trouble. Of course, all that did was further the endless disappointment he had for me and that I had for myself.

"You're still my daughter, Sheyanne. Your name is going on it. If you want to remove it, you can. But it's up to you two. We'll be meeting the owners sometime after the storm passes." His eyes flicker downward, back to what's in front of him.

And that's the end of that.

I walk away, not bothering to look at Shane or Liam, take my bag of books to my room, and sit on the floor, leaning against the bed. Nyx barks for my attention and crawls across the mattress towards me. He nudges me with his nose, and I reach up to scratch his favorite spot. I hate that such a quick conversation with my dad has me feeling like a kid again. Even in that short conversation, I reverted to feeling like the disappointment even though he really didn't do anything to make me feel that way. It's just what I'm used to.

When I was a kid, it wasn't as bad. Some days were good days, and some days were bad. I just always wanted Dad's attention, since it was just the three of us. But when I got older, when I became a teenager, it got worse. Shane was always a good kid, played sports, got good grades, and never complained—at least to Dad's face—about our chores. Yeah, he got into trouble occasionally, but he was golden. I always felt like I lived in his shadow. As I got older, none of that went away. It all just heightened with the pressure of growing up.

When I was sad, I had nothing to be upset over, and crying was a waste of time.

When I was angry, it was my own fault that I'd made myself feel like that, even if I explained why I felt that way.

And when Dad was angry, he turned quiet, would ignore me and state that he wasn't angry—just disappointed. When I was a kid, I did everything I could to apologize, thinking it really was my fault. But when I got older, I just did everything I could to get his attention—even if it was him yelling at me. I wanted to be seen and heard, and I made it impossible to ignore me.

According to Dad, everything I did—if I got hurt, if I felt sick, if I was struggling—was faked for attention. I couldn't take a joke, I was overdramatic, and I was too sensitive.

So, when I wasn't that, when I wasn't *too* much, where did that leave me? What was I?

I was too everything, and in turn, I felt like I was never enough.

I exhale, not wanting to feel like this. Because I had a good day.

Unlike before, I don't want to wallow in these pitying feelings towards Dad—towards myself. I take a few deep breaths, trying to settle the emotions running through my brain and under my skin, trying to get rid every negative thought, even if it's just for a moment, so I can breathe without feeling layers of doubt and disappointment pulling me into the darkness.

After a few seconds, there's a knock on the wall next to my door, which I left ajar.

"Come in," I say and look up, bringing my legs up to sit cross-legged on the floor as my room takes on a gray hue from the light outside.

Liam pushes the door open, leaning against the frame, so casual and so sure of himself in everything he does. I watch as his eyes move around my room—a picture of who I was when I was here before—until they land on me. Two different versions of the same girl in an old bedroom.

He cocks his head to the side, studying me. "So, how about that haircut?"

I shake my head. I'm smiling whether I want to or not because every time I'm teetering on falling over the edge or walking away from it, Liam shows up.

Whether he knows it or not, he shows up. It's not obvious. He never explicitly offers to help me because I'd never accept it if he did, but he appears like a beacon reminding me that drowning in my thoughts isn't my only option, that I can always turn away from the dark skies that threaten to pull me in.

Either I sit in here alone, stuck in my head, or I go out with him.

Today, I choose Liam.

THIRTEEN

SHEYANNE

The barn is warmer than it should be thanks to the space heaters I put near the doors, away from anything flammable. Liam watches as I grab a chair and put it in the center of the barn, dropping the electric clipper, comb, and alcohol on a small table I drag next to it.

He crosses his arms. "Are you sure you should be drinking when you're going to have a sharp tool near my head?"

I look him dead in the eye and begin pouring myself a drink. The dark amber liquid turns molten in the soft, yellow lights. "If you'd like to cut your own hair, be my guest. I'm fine." My hands motion to the table of supplies.

He steps forward, further into the barn. The horses are all peeking their heads over their stalls, interested in the late-night intrusion. He pauses a few feet away, grabs the back of his hoodie, and tugs it over his head. Then, he eyes my set up and me again.

"I'm not scared you'll mess up my hair."

Sighing, I look up to the ceiling before circling around to meet his eyes. "I'm not going to kill you, Landon. Now sit down." I point to the chair, and he chuckles, sliding into the chair. Grabbing an old blanket, I drape it around his shoulders, tucking it into his T-shirt. Nothing fancy, but it will do. "Now do you want a drink or are you gonna be a baby?"

"Someone is feeling a little—"

"I will hit you." My eyes bore into his. Amusement dances in the deep browns as he looks back, a smirk playing on his lips.

"I don't think you will." He tips his head back to look up at me, the dynamics changed for once.

"We can find out."

I finish making the drink, mixing the whiskey with the ginger ale over the ice I brought, and I make Liam one, too, holding it out. He watches amusedly for a moment before reaching up and wrapping his fingers around the cup, brushing the tips of my fingers just so. I try to ignore the goosebumps that pop up on my skin from the contact.

As I plug in the clippers, I glance back at the horses who watch with lazy eyes. Nyx pads around the barn, stopping to sniff each nose that hangs over the stall door. I turn music on the old stereo I always kept in the barn, happy to see that no one ever removed it. The CD I made myself years ago is still in there and starts flawlessly.

When I turn around, Liam is watching me. My heartbeat quickens in my chest. "What?" I ask quietly, turning the clippers on and off to check them before I start.

He shrugs his shoulders under the blanket. "Thank you."

I meet his eyes, and the sincerity shining in them makes me nervous, so I just nod and turn on the clippers. I start behind him by taking off the extra fuzz, partly so I don't have to make eye contact with him and so I can regain some control. I don't necessarily enjoy how frazzled I become around him.

He doesn't say anything as I begin, and I let my thoughts wander. Why does Dad want to put my name on anything when our relationship has not improved one bit? Both of us are to blame, I presume. Why does it seem like Shane doesn't want the farm as much as I thought he would? While I'm here, will I make any amends with the other people I hurt besides Shane? Like Blake—if I return that voicemail she left? Even deeper, I wonder if she'll let me.

Liam lifts his glass to his lips, bringing my attention back to him and the feeling of his skin beneath my fingertips. Deep down, I'm wondering why he let me do this, why he's been nice to me after I was awful to him, why he seems to care at all.

The clippers' buzzing is calming as it plays almost perfectly in tune with the music. I try to stop my thoughts from spiraling about Liam, knowing it's a pointless endeavor. I pause for a second as I finish the back of his head, everything much shorter and more faded out now, and reach for my own glass.

"The music isn't surprising, but it's still not what I expected." Liam's words break the silence between us.

I hide my grin as I sip my drink. "What did you expect?" The CD has gone from the Rolling Stones to Elton John to Jagged Edge to Bryan Adams to Prince, variations of what Dad and Shane used to play when we were growing up.

He eyes me as I lean against the side table, crossing my ankles together. "Well, I couldn't decide between heavy metal or straight pop."

"Those are vastly different genres of music." I furrow my brows. "And why pop? Heavy metal, fine, but pop?"

Liam's features tighten like he's got a really funny inside joke with himself.

"Spit it out. Why pop?"

"Have you ever heard a pop song?" He starts ticking off fingers. "Melodramatic, moody, sad, sometimes even angry—"

Before he can finish, I have an ice cube from my drink, and I'm moving fast. He doesn't realize what I'm doing until the ice cube is sliding down his back. He shivers as it does, rolling his shoulders and giving me a look. That single look sends an equal chill down my back.

"See what I mean? Melodramatic." He grins beautifully, and I roll my eyes, covering my smile with my hand. A moment passes, and I again grab the clippers and move to the front of his hair. He puffs out a breath. "Maybe I shouldn't have made those comments before you finished."

My lips curl into a smirk. "Do you want me to clean this up, too?" I tap his chin and cheeks where there is stubble growing on his usually smooth face. The stubble scratches the sensitive skin of my fingertips.

His eyes meet mine. "If you don't mind."

I nod in response, the soft smile remaining on my lips. The clippers buzz as I clean up his hairline first, keeping my hand steady as I make sure it's all the same length and make the sharp lines fade out, how his hair was when he first arrived. Liam barely moves as I go, but I feel his eyes on every movement I take, every step to get a better angle or the way my arm positions itself.

A curl pops free from the loose bun I put it in before this, and I watch his eyes latch onto it as it brushes his skin. I reach up with a swallow, tucking it back behind my ear to continue.

I finish his hair and move to his chin. Everything becomes more intimate the moment I tip his face back with a finger under his chin. Our eyes connect briefly, the deep brown of his eyes seeming even darker, more beautiful, and it almost pains me to force my eyes away. My heart careens in my chest, and I'm almost positive he can feel my pulse through my fingers on his skin. I bend forward to get a better angle, and my knee brushes his, sending little sparks through my body.

I force myself to inhale.

Which turns out to be a horrible, horrible, idea—because all I breathe in is Liam.

We're so close, I can smell the whiskey on his breath and the faint scent of the cologne he wears. He smells like winter—fresh and cool with hints of sandalwood and some lighter undertones. I turn all my focus on my hands, making sure they don't tremble, and he doesn't notice that I am clearly more affected by him than I ever wanted to be.

But when I place my hand more firmly on his neck to turn his head, just for a second, I feel his pulse and discover it's beating almost as fast as mine.

When I tilt his head back down, turning the clippers off, I don't remove my hand right away, and he wastes no time in connecting his eyes with my own. Emotions swirl in the endless brown as they look at me, holding me in place. He doesn't move a muscle, like he knows I would spook if he did; he just watches me.

It's more intimate than anything else I have ever felt in my life.

"Stop looking at me like that, Liam," I breathe out, unable to look away. He cocks his head.

"Like what?"

"Like you're trying to figure me out."

There's a pause, different from hesitation. I've come to discover that Liam doesn't really hesitate. He says everything with purpose. I think the pause is more for my benefit, so when he does say the words, they sink in through my thick skull. He blinks, his dark lashes touching his cheeks quickly before his eyes pierce me again, and I feel my heartbeat in the tips of my fingers and everywhere else.

His lips begin to tug upward. "That's exactly what I'm trying to do, Sheyanne."

My name rolls off his tongue softly, and I swallow, trying to bring moisture to my throat, trying to focus on anything that isn't him, the smell of whiskey, the smell of his skin, the way his eyes watch me all the time.

"Liam."

My throat constricts because no one has ever looked at me like this in my life. I drop his chin and step back so I can breathe. Immediately, I miss the contact and the warmth of his skin.

His eyes never leave mine, and it terrifies me how deeply he looks at me—as if he could see everything I am, everything I have, and not run away from it. He places his glass on the table and stands up, and I just watch him. He pulls off the blanket that was draped over his shoulders and moves in my direction. My feet are frozen to the ground.

Just as he stops in front of me, his phone rings, echoing in the barn and breaking the tension that was growing so quickly in the room. He glances away for the briefest of moments to check who it is before bringing his gaze back to me.

"I'm sorry," he says, raising the phone.

I blink, bringing myself back, and my hand grips the end of my sweatshirt. "It's okay. Take it." I move past him like nothing happened, which technically, is the truth. Nothing happened. It just felt like it was about to, and I'm not sure if I would've stopped it or welcomed it.

I grab my drink and go sit on the floor next to Nyx, putting space between us so Liam can have some privacy. Nyx places his head in my lap with his ears perked and a knowing look as I scratch his head gently.

"Don't look at me like that," I whisper. "It was nothing."

At that, Rayne lets out a soft whinny, and I give her a look. She flicks her ear at me and blinks her big eyes. I'm being ganged up on by my pets, which is just rude. Nyx licks my leg and rolls over, putting his legs in the air, and I pat his belly.

I try not to strain my ears and listen to Liam's conversation, which is hard to hear anyway with the music playing, and his voice low. He smiles as he talks, walking in slow circles and sipping from the glass in his hand every few seconds. Briefly, he looks over at me, and I avert my eyes even though it's too late to act like I wasn't watching him. I keep my eyes trained on Nyx for the next few minutes, not looking when Liam sits next to me, our outstretched legs barely touching as he places the bottle between us.

He clears his throat, but before he can speak, I do. "Are you close with your family?" I finally look up as Liam leans his head back against the wooden wall.

He nods, starting to smile. "Yeah, I am. Well, my grandparents at least."

"Siblings?"

"Nope, only child."

I leave my lip on the rim of my cup, still looking at him. "Makes sense," I joke, and Liam doesn't hesitate to pinch my leg and grab the bottle from my hand. I hesitate, not wanting to overstep my boundaries. "Parents?"

There's a pause again, like he's gauging how much he wants to tell me, wondering if I've earned this information from him at all. "No—yes. I mean, they exist. I don't know anything about my mom, and my dad, well, his parents—my grandparents—took me in when I was five. I keep in touch with him over the phone and with letters, but that's it. I used to see him once or twice a year, but it's been almost two years. We got in an argument last time."

I nod. "Is that the reason you haven't gone back?"

"Not necessarily. We talked it out, but it almost felt like opening an old would. He'd already left me once, you know? I'm older now, and it's not like he could leave me again, but it just felt like that."

His vulnerability with me makes me appreciate him far more than I can express.

Liam shrugs. "We got over it, and I'll probably visit soon, but to me, my grandparents are my parents. They never left me wondering whether I mattered to them. Never made me feel anything less than loved."

My heart breaks and swells in my chest all at once. Nyx crawls over to sit between us, resting his head on Liam's leg this time. "You don't like being away from them, do you?" I question, leaning my head back, and adjust so I'm looking at him. When his eyes close, my nerves intensify. "You don't have to answer that if you don't want."

His eyes stay closed, so I study his face in the silence that stretches. It's rude how long his eyelashes are and how they fan out over his cheeks. I'm unable to stop myself from counting the dark spots that sporadically dot his smooth brown skin, and I have to actively stop myself from reaching out to touch them.

"No, I don't." Liam's low voice breaks the silence, and I look up, finding his eyes open again. "But it's not like I leave often, and even when I do, it's for a good reason." He looks at me pointedly when he says that.

A part of me is happy that he feels like being here and helping my dad isn't a waste of his time. "I'm sure they'll be happy when you get back."

Liam blows out air in a half laugh. "Actually, they want me to back off, to leave. They think I worry about them too much."

"Do you?"

"Probably. They never tell me when they need something; I always have to figure it out on my own. They always refuse my help and are determined to live in the same tiny house I grew up in. Which would be fine if it wasn't falling apart. They're not that old for grandparents, but they're what I have." He brings up his own glass, taking a long sip of the whiskey.

I pat his leg. "I think they just want you to have a life, you know? One that doesn't revolve around worrying about them." I say it softly, but I'm worried it came out too harsh. I don't really know what it's like to have a family that cares so deeply. At least, aside from Shane. "Sorry, that probably sounded ridiculous and stupid. Especially from me."

I pull my hand back, but he stops me, giving it a squeeze, and I look up at him. "It wasn't stupid." In the background, the next song begins, and his eyes light up, an idea sparking. He stands, hand still on mine. "Come on."

I furrow my brows. "What?"

He gives me a look. "Come on," he mumbles and pulls me up. I'm careful to balance my drink.

"What are we doing?" I ask.

Liam grins, and my heartbeat spikes. "We're dancing."

I cross my arms and furrow my brows. "I don't dance." Liam takes the drink out of my hand and sets it down with his. "I'm serious. I'm not dancing."

Instead of being deterred, Liam places his hands on my shoulders and starts moving me in time with the music. He steps around me, forcing me to take a few steps in time with the beat of the song. I fight to keep my face in a straight line, but with his exaggerated steps, I fail pretty quickly, and a smile spreads on my face.

His eyes light up. "Look at that. A full smile from Sheyanne that isn't directed at an animal."

I uncross my arms and hit him on the chest with the back of my hand. "Don't ruin it."

Liam grabs my hands again, now that I've uncrossed them, and grips them in his own, pulling me closer. There is still an appropriate amount of space between us, a gap I'm not willing to close yet, and he seems happy to be doing this at all. He's stopped his exaggerated movements and is swaying more like a normal human being now, and I guess it's not so bad.

"Why are we doing this?" I mumble over the soft music. The sporadic but calming strums of the guitar beat in time with my heart.

He looks down at me, his features soft and open. "To celebrate."

"Celebrate what?" I ask as he turns us in a circle, keeping me steady.

"I think that we just became friends."

I laugh. "You're celebrating becoming friends with me?"

Liam dips his head, his eyes playful. "So, you admit we're friends?"

I think over his words. From me telling him I was going to make his job as difficult as possible to giving him a haircut and dancing with him in a barn, I suppose I can't deny it.

"I suppose," I drawl out the words. He grins. "I don't know if that's something to really celebrate, Landon."

He shrugs his shoulders and squeezes my hands again, sending a wave of butterflies straight to my stomach. "I think it is."

My heart lightens at the words, and I decide it's nice. It's nice to have a friend here. After Blake and Gaylee, I can't remember the last one I had. Certainly, no one in the years I was gone. If Liam wants to take that spot, I'm not going to run away from it.

"Fine, friends then." I fight my smile as he sways us back and forth again.

His eyes meet mine, sparkling. "Friends."

We both smile, and I let him finish the dance as the song continues. While I don't think friends send butterflies to another's stomach or look at someone with an intimacy that sets their blood on fire, I don't dwell on those thoughts.

For the first time in years, I have a friend. Even better, it's Liam Landon.

Fourteen

Liam

The snow came down just as they predicted it would and blanketed the entire world.

At least, that's how it seems when I wake up. Even within the house, the silence is resounding. I have never experienced a peacefulness such as this, where the whole word is at rest. The sheer brightness of everything reflecting off the snow, even in the dawn and with a gray sky, woke me up through the curtains.

I check the time on my phone—barely six A.M.—and listen for the sounds of anyone else. When silence returns, I settle, resting my feet on the lip of the bed frame and place my elbows on my thighs as I look through the window.

In the distance, the mountains—almost camouflaged with the sky— have brighter snow caps. The evergreen trees are all outlined in thick, white snow on each of their branches. Behind the clouds, the sun rises, the light reflecting across the calm surface of the snow. I rub my hands on my thighs before pulling on a pair of sweats over my briefs and head into the bathroom.

Only to find Sheyanne standing at the counter with her toothbrush in her hand.

"Can I come in?" I ask, clearing my throat, pausing in the doorway.

Her brown eyes are hazy with sleep and her curls unruly as they fall down her back, the satin scarf she had them wrapped in tossed haphazardly on the counter. "Mhm," she hums, leaning on the wall next to her sink like she's still asleep.

I grab my own toothbrush, wet it, and apply the toothpaste. Then she holds out her own, "Would you be so kind?" Her eyes close, and I can't help but let out a soft laugh, putting toothpaste on her brush as well.

We brush our teeth next to one another, and the entire time she keeps her eyes closed. I trail my eyes over her warm brown skin peeking out of the flower-printed sleep shorts that form to the curves of her hips and legs and are almost completely covered by the oversized T-shirt hanging off her shoulders. Her long, dark lashes fan out over her cheeks, and I trail my eyes over the speckling of dark spots that dance on the tip of her nose. I can smell the lingering scent of coconut and rose water from her hair.

I was indifferent about Sheyanne when I first arrived.

But the warmth that sinks into my skin and the heat burning through my blood do not feel like indifference, especially after last night. I can still feel the brush of her curl on my neck when she bent down to get rid of the stubble on my chin, the feel of the pads of her fingers lingering on my skin when she adjusted my face, and her hands when I forced her to dance. Looking at her now, sleepy and quiet, it all comes rushing back. There's also a level of calmness that comes over me when she's near. Ironic, since she's more of a spitfire than anything. We're different in many ways—she's excitable, emotional, audacious—and I'm not. I like maintaining control over things.

She shakes that control, and I'm growing addicted to it.

I turn on the faucet, pulling my eyes away from her, and finish brushing my teeth. In the mirror, her eyes have opened, and I find them watching me. She doesn't look away as I grab my facewash and start circling the suds on my face, resulting in her lips twitching up in the smallest of smiles. Her eyes follow the slow motion of my hands, only pausing to finish her own brushing, but they come right back to me when she straightens. It's a strange game we're playing, and I'm not sure either of us knows the endgame yet.

But I'm a patient man. I have no trouble figuring it out.

"Coffee?" She breaks the silence, gently pulling her hair up and out of her face.

"Please."

Her footsteps land softly on the tile. She pauses in the doorway, her lips twitching again. "Morning, Liam."

"Good morning, Sheyanne." I watch her eyes flicker up as I untie the durag from my head, tracing the motions of my hands. A smirk grows on my face.

With a quick eye roll, she closes the door behind her, aware of my routine by now, and I jump into the shower for a quick body rinse. As soon as I'm finished, I run a flat brush over my hair towards my forehead, slather on some lotion, and get dressed. The babbling of the coffee maker slices through the otherwise silent space.

"Morning, Mr. Shaw." The dining chair creaks as I pull it back and sit.

He smiles a bit, the wrinkles in his skin deepening. "Figured we can take a half day today."

I nod as he slides the thin stack of papers over to me. "Sounds good to me, sir."

On the papers are all his expenses. Weekly, monthly, yearly. In different colored highlighters, he notes what's a usual expense and what's not, details what he considers a splurge, and what's necessary. At the end is how much he averages yearly and what he'd ideally like to put away. He's mentioned putting some aside for care in the future, to keep the weight from landing on his kids, and I assume that's what we'll be trying to work out here—just how much he can.

Seconds later, two mugs with tendrils of steam appear on the hardwood table. Mr. Shaw looks up to find his daughter sliding him a mug with a small nod of her head. Neither of them says anything, but when Mr. Shaw faces forward again, the surprise still lingers in his eyes. I dip my chin in a silent thanks before she turns and heads out the door, Nyx padding behind her like usual. By the coat rack, Shane watches with a smug grin. She flicks him on the forehead and strides past him and out into the snow.

Turning my eyes to the paper, I grab a blank sheet so I can make notes if needed. I rewrite the number he's circled. "This is the goal?"

He nods. "I overshot a bit, but as close as I can get to that. I would do this on my own, but—" Mr. Shaw waves his hands and looks away.

This is the only indication I've noticed of the disease, though I know it's in its early stages. He often has trouble with the numbers, judging certain things right. Little things for now, but those are only indications of what's to come. From my own research, what Shane's told me, and the doctor's notes he asked me to keep and add to his file, he's still a mild case. There's just no telling how long that stage will last. While I'm here to help financially, he's also asked me to help him find someone to help deal with the future—his will, end-of-life care whenever that need should arise—because he wants to have a say, and right now, he can.

It's certainly a more depressing job than I'd first thought, but I enjoy being able to help him. Mr. Shaw is a guarded man and, aside from his familial issues, a kind one.

"No worries; we'll get it done." I start looking over his highlights.

On the left in his usual scrawl, he's detailed a few care facilities and their average prices. Time passes as I sip the coffee, adding and subtracting as I go. Mr. Shaw offers insight to some of the purchases that stray from the norm and helps whenever able. After an hour, I've split all of the figures into categories, placing each care facility in a column based on their average, with a detailed plan for each one and how best to reach the goal number.

He looks over my notes and the plans I've detailed. "I'll type them up and print them out so we have both electronic and physical copies," I say, "but we'll need to make a new account for you and get this put away. Whenever you'd like."

Mr. Shaw nods in agreement. "Sounds good. We'll have to keep this in the folder for Shane and Sheyanne. They'll most likely be making the decision so, as long as it's in safe keeping." He taps all the papers together on the table to even the edges. "Is everything okay so far? Your stay, all of that?"

"It's been wonderful, Mr. Shaw. I've enjoyed it a lot. It's different here, but it's a nice change."

Mr. Shaw runs a hand over his face, looking only slightly exasperated. "Please, Liam, call me Jones."

I smile. "I appreciate it, but I'm probably going to keep calling you Mr. Shaw, sir."

"I figured. I'm glad to hear it, though. You're a guest as long as you're here, so never hesitate to ask if you need anything."

"Thank you, sir." A burst of cold air arrives when Shane appears in the door, snow dusting the top of his coat.

Mr. Shaw glances at his son and then back to me. "That's enough for the day. May as well enjoy the peace while we can." He stands and pats my shoulder. "Thank you for all the help."

He strides towards the kitchen, pausing to speak to Shane, who pats his father on the back as he pulls some food out of the fridge. After a moment, Mr. Shaw heads to the living room, relaxing into the couch in front of the old TV. I stand, taking my mug to the sink.

Shane eyes me, cracking eggs into a bowl. "Hungry?"

I shake my head. "I was actually gonna head outside, see the snow. There's quite a bit of it."

Shane chuckles, taking a sip of coffee. A pause. Then he lowers his voice, his face smug. "Sheyanne's near the pasture." Deadpan, I stare at him. He grins. "What? Just thought you'd like to know."

I shake my head, turn away and head down the hall to find the boots I'd bought for the winter. I never would've explicitly asked Shane for his sister's whereabouts. One, because I could've figured out where she was on my own. Two, because that just seems to be toying with a fine line—not that Shane seems to care. I slip my arms into the black winter jacket, over the thick black sweater, and pull on a hat over my short hair, covering my ears.

Shane waves his spatula as I stride out the front door. The quiet settles once again as I step into a blurry haze of white and gray. A golden blur is the first thing I see, Nyx pouncing in and out of the deep snow, and I head towards him. He perks up when I approach, floppy ears and tail wagging, and bounds straight for me. I crouch down and scratch his ears, snowflakes dusting his golden fur. When I stand, he heads straight towards the pasture, and I follow.

Teddy and Rayne stand at the fence, snowflakes speckling their coats, and Sheyanne leans against it, reaching a hand out to Rayne. Apparently, they've made up because Rayne shoves her nose into her palm. Even from here, I see how excited that makes Sheyanne.

"Do you love me again?" Sheyanne coos, and Rayne flicks an ear, blowing out a breath that crystalizes in the cold air. "I love you, too."

My eyebrows shoot up, only a foot away now. "Sorry, can you run that back? Was that baby talk?"

Sheyanne whips around, her wide-eyed gaze landing on me immediately. Her light brown cheeks are already flushed from the cold, but I swear the pink deepens.

"No," she lies, continuing to pet Rayne's nose.

I lean on the fence, raising a brow. "Now you're lying. I had you pegged as a better person than that." She rolls her eyes. Teddy shoves his head into my forearms on the fence. Taken by surprise, I meet his big eyes and reach out to pet his nose.

"You can't be mean to me, or Teddy will come after you. He's protective."

I reach up to pat the horse's cheek, his tail swishing. "I can see that."

Sheyanne eyes me. "Aren't you supposed to be working?"

"Your dad said we did enough. I think he just wasn't feeling it this morning, but we got some done."

She pulls herself onto the fence, sitting now and avoiding my eyes. "Was he all right?"

"I think he was just tired."

Rayne places her heavy head over Sheyanne's shoulder, and she leans into it, petting her opposite cheek with her hand. She doesn't admit it or say anything else, but I think a part of her is worried about him. Given the nature of their relationship, I understand why she might be hesitant in admitting that, but I think anyone would be hard-pressed not to care.

"All right," she sighs. For a moment, we just let the still falling snowflakes lightly land on our shoulders, and I watch as they float through the air. Teddy moves towards Sheyanne, nudging Rayne out of the way, and she softens. "I know, bud. We'll go riding again soon."

It's endearing to me that she actually lets herself be when she's around the animals. She's not calculating whether or not she should smile or how anything else makes her feel. When she's around them, Sheyanne lights up. It's beautiful to see.

"When was the last time you rode?"

"I took Teddy out a week or two ago, but before that, the last time was before I left. So, four years? A bit longer."

I let out a low whistle. "That's a long time. Did you miss it?"

Her eyes brighten, but she shrugs. "Yeah, I did. Still do. It was—is— my favorite thing to do. Have you ever ridden?"

Blankly, I blink at her. "I've never even sat on a horse."

"Let's change that." She jumps down, landing in the snow, and starts heading towards the pasture gate, a rope in her hand and mischief in her eyes.

"Right now?" Hesitation floods me as I watch her stride straight towards Teddy. I knew she was crazy, but now I'm leaning towards insane.

"Right now. Why not? What else are we gonna do?"

"I don't know, build a snow fort?"

She blinks, and then laughter bursts from her chest as I stand there with a blank stare. Her laughter comes out in spurts, like she's having trouble breathing, but it's a beautiful laugh, and instantly, I know I'd like to hear it again and again and *again*. It takes her a few minutes to catch her breath, but her cheeks are bright and her eyes warm, golden under the gray sky.

"You know, friends don't laugh at other friends' requests," I grumble just as Rayne nudges me from over the fence.

Sheyanne's face softens, but it's still amused. "If you sit on Teddy, we can build a snow fort."

I meet her eyes. "Fine."

Teddy whinnies as she attaches the rope to the halter on his face. I watch, quite hesitant about the whole thing considering how large he is. But he walks gently next to her, making her look even shorter than she already is and flicking his ear every so often. I follow as she closes the gate behind them and leads the way into the barn. She hooks him up with a tie on each side of the halter, keeping him in place. She grabs an old stool and moves it to Teddy's left side.

"You're sure about this?" I ask.

"Teddy is the best; you'll be fine." She grabs my arm and pulls me forward, heat fanning even through my layers when she does. "All you're gonna do is step up, hold his mane, and swing your leg over. It would be different if he had a saddle on, but we'll do that another day."

"That's it?"

Sheyanne nods, a few curls loose from where she put it up earlier. "Yes, it's that simple, and I'll hold him. I promise." If she didn't look so excited, I don't think I would be so willing to give in, but I won't be the reason for that light in her eyes to dim. She moves around me and stands next to Teddy, his shoulder above her head, and runs a hand down his neck. "Come on."

I roll my eyes and step forward. Gently, I hold onto his long mane and swing my leg over easily until I'm sitting squarely on his back. Adjusting, I move around until it feels more comfortable, trying to find the correct seat. Teddy lifts a leg, throwing me off balance, but I stay still until he places it back down, feeling the steady movements of the horse until they feel less foreign.

When I feel comfortable enough, I grin, looking down at Sheyanne. "That wasn't so bad." I reach forward, petting Teddy's neck. "I think he likes me." Teddy flicks his ear at me, and I meet her eyes again, her amusement clear. "He totally does."

Her fingers pull at the neck of her turtleneck underneath her thick sweater. I see the smile she tries to hide as Teddy rocks under me every few seconds. It gives me a strange sense of pride, doing something I'd never thought I'd do and not being completely fucking afraid of it.

"See? You're a natural. Next time I ride, you can come with." She glances up. "If you want."

"Sounds good to me." I pat the horse's shoulder again. "How long have you had them?"

Sheyanne stands there, her hand still on one of the ropes tied to Teddy, chewing on her bottom lip for a moment, and I can't help but latch onto the sight. "Since we were eleven or twelve, I think. It's my—it's one of the good moments I had with my dad. Shane and I were sitting on the porch, playing UNO, which is interesting with only two people but whatever, and Dad pulls in with his truck and his trailer attached to it— which was normal then, so we didn't bat an eye. Not until he walked out with a young quarter horse," she motions to Teddy, "and an appaloosa." She points outside to Rayne. "I'd never smiled so hard in my life."

The same smile pulls at her lips, the edges fighting to turn up, and I keep my eyes solely on her. "I remember he said as long as we took care of them, they were ours. Teddy was originally Shane's, but as we got older, I ended up taking care of both of them more. As a joke for my birthday a year or two later, he gave me a certificate that he made and printed out himself that I was the sole owner of both Teddy and Rayne. Don't tell him, but I still have that piece of paper locked in another keepsake box under my bed." Sheyanne pats Teddy's cheek again before connecting her eyes with mine.

I barely move when they do. Seeing her—hearing her—talk about something she actually loves, that makes her happy, is a vision like no other. There's nothing on earth that could hold a candle to the sight.

"Wouldn't dream of spilling your secrets." I find my voice, clearing my throat. "He made a good decision. You love them, and they love you." This time, the pink color of her cheeks does deepen, and she finally pulls her eyes away from mine. I already miss looking at them.

"Do you have any pets back home?" she says, then motions to me. "You can get down whenever by the way. Just swing your leg back over and slide down. Don't be afraid to hold him—gently—as you do."

I nod, replicating the instructions she gave me until I'm back on the floor. "Nope. Never had any." I eye Nyx and the horse next to me. "But I might have to change that."

Sheyanne disconnects the ropes from the halter and begins to lead Teddy back out, me following behind. "I think you'd like it. It's the best, in my opinion."

I watch from the barn doors as she leads him back to the pasture. The other horses are scattered in their own pastures, playing in the snow or grazing on the grass they find below. Rayne waits for her friend at the fence. Sheyanne unclips Teddy after they enter the gate, and he strides right for the appaloosa horse. I can't help myself as I bend down, forming a ball with the snow and waiting for the perfect moment. As soon as Sheyanne turns, I launch it and watch as it hits her square in the chest. She blinks and looks down, finding the snow all over her sweater. I couldn't keep myself from grinning if I tried.

She puts her hands on her hips. "Are you serious, Landon?"

I shrug, bending down to pet Nyx, who stands next to me with a wagging tail. "Couldn't help myself. I've never seen snow like this, so can you really blame me for giving in to temptation?"

"The temptation to hit me with a snowball?"

My cheek twitches. "Yeah, I mean, come on. You kinda deserve it."

"You're never gonna let it go, are you?"

"Nope."

Instead of answering, she bends down and forms her own snowball. "You sure you wanna pick this fight?"

"It's a fight I'm going to win, so sure."

"In your dreams," she mumbles, forming the snowball perfectly, and she stands as I finish packing my own. It's not as good as hers, but it'll get the job done. I throw mine first, and she narrowly avoids it. She then tosses her own, hitting me square in the chest as I stumble through the thick snow.

"You don't know anything about my dreams, Shaw." Probably a good thing, too; she's been in quite a few of them. I push the thought out of my head and work on making another snowball.

When I look over, she's pushing snow into a wall, a makeshift fort I suppose, so I take the chance while I have it and aim. The snowball rushes right past her face, which I was *not* aiming for, and she hits me with a look that turns my skin hot.

"If you hit me in the face, I will not hesitate to run you over with my car," she bites out, still building her shield, which is now just big enough to duck under.

If she wasn't so pretty when she was mad, I might be scared. Instead, I'm just momentarily distracted.

"You're all bark and no bite," I call back, and she rolls her eyes but gives in to a small smile. Crouching, with Nyx barking away at us, I quickly build up my own snow wall, just enough to hide behind, and start making another snowball.

She launches one, and I duck, narrowly avoiding it. We both pause for a moment. I peek up to see her still bent over, not paying any attention. I throw one to keep her distracted and quietly, with a large amount of snow cupped in my hands, head straight towards her. I'm standing almost directly above her, and before she can look up, I drop it right on her head. Snow coats her curls and lands on her cheeks. She shivers and glares up at me.

"I hate you," she says, but there isn't even a bite to the words this time. I hold out a hand and help her up, not bothering to hide my grin.

"Thought you weren't a liar, Sheyanne." Reaching up, I brush the snow off her hair and then slowly, brush away what's on her cheeks. This close, I can see the snowflakes coating her eyelashes. She blinks up at me, and I watch as the snowflakes slowly melt away into water droplets on her cheeks.

"Hey!" A shout breaks the silence, and we turn to see Shane on the porch. "I made mug cakes!" It echoes over the snow, and the excitement from Sheyanne is palpable.

She wraps her hand around my wrist and pulls me forward through the snow, practically dragging me to the house. About halfway there, she realizes what she's doing and drops her hand. I miss the warmth of it instantly. "Sorry, I got excited."

"Why are you apologizing?"

"Well, I didn't mean to drag you like a ragdoll is all."

I raise a brow, and she flicks out her tongue, catching a snowflake on her lip. "I promise you I'm tougher than a ragdoll, Sheyanne. Don't worry about me."

She shivers again, but instead of taking my arm back, she nudges my shoulder. "Come on."

We walk side by side, Nyx bounding ahead of us until we reach the porch. We kick off our boots and hang the jackets on the hooks inside. The smell of chocolate from Shane's dessert is overwhelming, almost completely masking the smell of burning wood. Sheyanne looks around before finding her brother decorating the cakes with whipped cream.

"Do we still have the woodburning stove?" she asks, peeking through the door that leads to the sunroom.

"Yeah, it's pretty warm in there if you wanna sit. Could always take the heated blanket with you." Shane dusts the whipped cream with cinnamon and nutmeg and grabs spoons out of the drawer.

Sheyanne nods, heading down the hall, reappearing minutes later in oversized sweats, a sweatshirt, and fuzzy socks. From the living room, she finds the heated blanket and holds in in her arms.

"Dad?"

Shane looks up. "Taking a nap."

I lean on the counter, taking a minute before I head in to change and get these cold clothes off. Sheyenne steps out to the sunroom, plugging in the blanket and draping it over a chair before stepping back inside. Shane slides the mugs over, topped to the brim with the chocolate cake and whipped cream.

"Thanks," I mumble, dipping my spoon into the topping.

He holds his in his hands, eyes flickering between the two of us. "I'm gonna check on Dad and then call MJ."

Picking up her own mug, Sheyanne nods. "Okay, thank you." Shane smiles and heads down the hall, leaving us alone again. "I'm gonna sit out there and read. You're welcome to join if you want," she says. Her voice is quiet, but I love that she tossed out the invitation regardless.

"I'm gonna call home real quick and change," I say, taking a bite of the whipped cream, trailing my eyes over her face. "Then I might." I give her an easy smile, and she tucks a curl, now set free from the hair tie, behind her ear.

I watch from the counter as she strides out to the sunroom. Nyx takes up a spot near the chair as she sits, tucking her legs under the blanket and grabbing a book she'd placed on the table next to it. She yawns as she settles in, her curls framing her face and the falling snow in the background. If she notices me watching, she gives no indication of it. Eventually, I drag myself away.

Once again, I'm beginning to question everything about my decision to come here—in a whole different way—because of Sheyanne Shaw.

Fifteen

Sheyanne

I wake up with a start when Nyx barks from the other side of the glass door where he wags his tail.

I rub the sleep out of my eyes and sit up, furrowing my brows in confusion. I don't remember setting my book on the table or setting my mug down. And I sure as hell don't remember wearing a hat out here. But my ears are covered and so is the top of my forehead, and the blanket is on a different heat setting than I left it on and is thoroughly tucked into the sides of the chair like a cocoon.

It's also darkened outside, the light gray slowly turning dusky as the sun sets behind the clouds. The snow has stopped, but any tracks from earlier have been freshly covered since the time I must've fallen asleep.

Shane slides the door open. "Hey, you coming in soon? Dinner's almost ready, and I figured we could watch a movie."

"Yeah, that sounds good," I say, and a smile forms on my brother's face. "Is this your hat?"

That smile quickly turns into a smirk. "Nope." He starts to close the door but then pauses. "And I didn't tuck you in either."

Inside my chest, my heart starts pumping at the other possibilities, but outwardly, I glare at my brother. He chuckles, and if I had a snowball, I would chuck it at him. Nyx waits for me as I unplug the blanket, gather up my things, and head inside. Actual heat surrounds me, chasing away any of the chill from outside, though I was rather warm in that cocoon.

"Go ask Liam if he's ready for dinner." Shane's voice sounds as I enter, sliding the door closed. When I turn to look at him, he's grinning.

"Stop making that face, Shane."

"What face?" I open my mouth to argue, but he holds up his hand. "Just go."

I flip him off and pad down the hallway. Liam's door is ajar, and I knock. A muffled "come in" follows. He's sitting in the old desk chair with his feet up on the bed, a hoodie pulled over his head, and a book in his hands. He pushes the hood down, and his eyes soften when he takes me in as I lean against the door frame.

"Dinner's almost ready, and we're gonna watch a movie, I think. If you'd like to come out." I kick the carpet with my sock. Liam nods and closes his book, placing it on the desk behind him. "Is that one of my books?"

He stretches, and I ignore how the sweatshirt moves with him, exposing the bottom of his stomach, and keep my eyes on his face. "Saw it on the bookshelf, and it looked good. You don't mind, do you?"

I hide my smile. "Nope." I remember the hat on my head and pull it off, not caring if my curls might be frizzy from the cotton. "Is this your hat?" He nods. "Where did it come from?"

"Well, I think you pulled it off your head."

"How did it get there?"

Liam fixes his gaze on me, and heat crawls up my spine.

"I put it there. Your ears looked cold."

I tell myself that the reason my skin feels like there are a million little butterflies on it is because I'm still warming up. That it's not from the fact that at some point, Liam came on the back porch when I was asleep and tugged his hat down over my hair because my ears looked cold.

"I'm keeping it."

His eyes meet mine, a flicker of something I can't decipher within them, and I force myself to inhale when he quietly says, "It's all yours."

I look down, playing with the bottom of my sweatshirt.

"I believe you still have my jacket, don't you?" Amusement coats his words, and there's a smile on his full lips. There is nothing I can do about the flush on my cheeks.

"What jacket?"

Liam laughs, the sound filling the room, wrapping around me like an embrace. I look down grinning to myself until he's right in front of me. Liam taps the hat that I've slid back on. "Don't worry, you can keep both. They look better on you anyway."

Liam looks down at me, and I am hyper-aware of the proximity between us, but he doesn't seem to notice. We stand there for a moment, me trying to figure out when I became so easily affected by someone else merely standing near me. By Liam. It's like a current between us was suddenly zapped alive. After another moment, mischief glints in his eyes, and I narrow mine.

He leans down. "You snore, by the way."

My mouth drops open as I reach up and pinch the back of his arm, ignoring the pace at which my heart beats in my chest. "I do not snore, Liam Landon."

"Jesus Christ that hurt," he mumbles, rubbing his arm through his sweatshirt. I pat him on the shoulder as I turn to walk away down the hallway.

"I can't let you have all the fun."

"You could let me have a little though. It is my birthday."

"You'll have to earn that—" I pause in the hallway, his words registering. "Your birthday?" He nods. I furrow my brows. "Today? Today is your birthday?"

"It is."

I hit him on the chest, crossing my arms as I look up at him. "Why didn't you say anything earlier?"

Liam tucks his hands in his pockets and leans against the wall. "I was having a pretty good time. Didn't feel the need to." He purposely looks at me when he says it, his gaze flickering over my face. While his face stays almost stoic, it's not void of emotion. It's not void of emotion *at all*.

Instead of being painted on all his features, it sticks to one place and one place only, his brown eyes—which are seemingly intent on driving me absolutely insane.

"I'm going to tell Shane."

He takes a step toward me with a shake of his head. "Don't. My birthday—it's not my favorite day. I don't like to make a big deal of it." My heart pings in my chest because I feel the same way about mine. But I never liked finding out others did.

But he told me. Maybe he doesn't want to do anything, and that's fine. I can respect that. "All right, I won't say anything."

A barely there smile takes over his face. "Thank you." He motions to the hallway. "Now let's go; you're holding up my dinner."

Liam gives me a nudge. I roll my eyes and adjust the hat on my ears, my curls escaping from the edge as I do, and ignore the warmth that's been running around in my chest all day, a warmth that's starting to become normal.

Comfortable.

My lips fall into a frown as I enter the kitchen because I have a feeling this is a dangerous line I'm walking—this line of supposed friendship between Liam and I that is starting to feel like anything but. I take a deep breath and ignore the uncomfortable sensation that starts to unfurl. Right now, this line we're dancing on is easy, it's light, and I like it.

But I'm scared of being comfortable or used to something or coming to lean on something—or someone—because that's dangerous. Not because I'm scared of getting hurt, but because that's when I hurt others. I know already that I don't want to hurt Liam. Whether that's on purpose or accident, it's not something I want to do to him.

If the line gets crossed, that'd be a risk I'd have to take, and I'm not sure it's worth it.

I can't remember the last time I spent any time alone with my dad and enjoyed it. Most of the time—or really—all of the time, it was rife with brewing arguments, comments of disappointment or dismissal on his end and rebuttals of anger on mine. The moments where we weren't at each other's throats were few and far between.

Today—two days since the serene days of the snowstorm—does not seem to be the day that is going to change.

The tension between us as we sit in the car is so thick, I have my window cracked open so I can breathe in the evergreen and cool winter air. Neither of us has spoken a word to each other aside from what's been necessary. We've visited all of those currently contracted with us and those who have reached out about boarding with the stable in the future—all except for one. The one I've been absolutely dreading.

All the previous owners had never met me, so they didn't know how

I left or anything about me. I wasn't nervous.

But this house, the house of the former police chief and his wife, is not a house I look forward to. Chief Banner picked me up off the street multiple times. For little things, like smoking pot or drinking underage, and often he would just take me home or give me a lecture while I sat in the back of a cop car, ignoring every word. But as I got older, I pushed the limits of what I could get away with and our semi-civil relationship deteriorated. Back then, I showed no remorse, no responsibility—I was a rebellious, angry, and maybe even a slightly depressed kid. Not that those were valid excuses; back then, I just didn't care. I never thought I'd have to face the consequences. I doubt Banner has forgotten any of the trouble I caused or the number of times he put me in a jail cell for a night.

Everyone we've talked to up to now has had no problems with my dad retiring—since that was his story—and either Shane or I taking control of the farm afterward. He never mentioned selling, so I suppose that was something Shane and I could figure out later. It didn't bother them that I had been taking care of the horses since October because they didn't know any better. I had felt confident going in with my dad and laying out the plans.

But as I drive up the long driveway and see the small but nice single-level home looming in front of me, there is no part of me that thinks this will be easy. Trees line the drive, intermittent with the greenness of the pine and the bare branches of others.

I park the car. "Do you really need me for this one? It's the last house anyway."

Dad doesn't even glance my direction as he adjusts his thick winter coat. "You're coming in." He steps out before I even have words to argue.

The car shuts off, and I sit there in the cocoon of heat for a moment more, watching as my dad begins his slow walk towards the house before I trudge after him with my head down. The house is stunning in its simplicity. Crisp white walls, triangular slanted roofs, and the yellow lights on the porch make it clean yet warm and inviting. With dark brick accents and the long gravel driveway, it looks classic, and I have no doubt it's just as beautiful on the inside. However, it feels like I'm descending right back into the past.

As we near the door, I catch up to Dad who gazes at me, no readable emotion in his eyes as he knocks. In my hand, I hold the folder of all the papers we've shown to the others boarding with the Shaw Ranch. The door opens, and when I look back up, Chief Banner is already looking at me, a cold, cautious glint in his eyes. He's still as tall, lean, and intimidating as he ever was. He holds the door open.

"Mr. Shaw," he says, pausing. "Sheyanne. Please come in."

Steeling myself, I tuck a curl behind my ear, ready to step forward, but it's Dad's hand, cautiously placed on the middle of my back that shocks me. Gently, he pushes me forward, guiding me inside as he whispers, "Come on. Sooner we're in, the sooner we're out."

I blink as I spare a glance towards him, meeting his eyes, which are not as harsh as they were moments ago. Nodding, I take a step into Banner's house. The police chief watches with emotions that I can't uncover.

"So, Sheyanne, what brings you back?" Chief Banner's cold voice snaps me out of my thoughts as we take a seat at the dark wood dining table.

I place the papers on the surface and slide them to my dad. "I don't believe we're here to talk about me, Banner."

Dad clears his throat, but Banner watches me like a hawk, and I pull my jacket closer around my shoulders, trying to shield myself. I look up, giving him a steely look of my own, even though I feel anything but. "I'm aware," he replies, "but it truly piqued my interest when your father told me you'd be coming along."

Absentmindedly, I survey my nails. "I'm sure it must've been a great surprise for you considering we had such great times together." I place my hands on the table. "Let's talk about the ranch, please. The sooner we do that, the sooner I'm out of your hair."

"Yes, let's." Dad's voice cuts through the tension, and I straighten, but for once, that intimidating tone is not addressed to me. Instead, it's directed towards Banner, who seems to notice it as well, but just nods, drawing his gaze away from mine. I exhale and settle in.

The chief's wife is nowhere to be seen, and I'm sure she's done that on purpose. I tune out the sound of Dad's and Banner's voices as they go over the beginning of the changes until I come in. I was a menace to the chief—the problems I caused and the grief I gave him—but I was a different type of rude to his wife, Clara. She only ever met me or interacted with me in the kindest of ways. Offering me gentle words whenever I saw her, she invited me over for dinner countless times—I think for both my sake and her husband's—and was generally the only positive female influence that I'd ever known. I think she saw me struggling with my dad, with life, with everything at the time. But I didn't care. I wish I hadn't been so disrespectful to her when she only wanted to help me.

The ashamed part of me is happy she isn't here so I don't have to face her and the disappointment sure to be swimming in her eyes. It both resolves me and adds guilt to my already heavy shoulders.

"Sheyanne, why don't you tell Chief Banner about the plans," Dad says, and I notice his choice of words this time, before he's said *my plans* but here, he is pointedly not.

"The horses will, of course, continue to be cared for either by Shane," I hesitate, but I'm tired of hiding and refuse to give Banner any control over me, "or myself, as they have been. Protocols will stay the same. Owners still may come and go as they please to care for and see their horses, but I will continue to give them the same quality of care that has been provided for years."

Banner sits back in his seat, crossing his arms, and my dad sighs. "So, you've been helping around?"

It takes everything in me to not roll my eyes. "Yes. In the sake of honesty, Chief, since I've returned, I've been the primary caretaker for the horses, not my brother or my dad. And that would include your own."

His cold eyes glint at me, and he scratches his chin. "You're demonstrating responsibility; how wonderful of you, Sheyanne. Just years too late."

I grit my teeth, but Dad speaks before I can. "Banner, I'd appreciate it if you would talk to my daughter with a hint of respect if you'd like to continue your boarding services while I still have a say."

Both Banner and my own eyes shoot to my dad. He sits calm and collected next to me, as if this whole thing is a bore. Which it is, but this meeting has for sure taken a turn.

"Your daughter who caused me the utmost of problems for years? That daughter?" Banner snaps.

"Yes, that daughter. The one sitting right in front of you that you're berating. She made mistakes; I get that. But you're the one acting like a child."

I would speak up for myself if I wasn't in shock at Dad defending me and doing so like it's second nature. Even Banner looks surprised because, in the past, my dad often agreed with him. Never once did he defend me.

"She made so many *mistakes*, one would think they were no longer mistakes, Mr. Shaw."

Annoyance sparks in my dad's eyes, the first show of emotion. "Regardless, how is one to grow or move on if never given the chance?"

At that, Banner stays silent. "Now, as long as you don't have a problem with Sheyanne taking care of the horses as she has been, we are done here. If you do, you can take your business elsewhere because my daughter is the best handler I've ever seen. Any objections?"

Banner gazes at me, and I meet it steadfastly, backed by the support of my dad, which is something I could've never predicted. "Not that I owe you anything, but I promise I'm not here to cause trouble," I add. "I have no desire to return to the person I was. And I enjoy working with the horses."

It's true. Slowly, piece by piece, I've started finding joy in being here again. Not always, and mostly when I'm in the safety of the stables and doing what I love. It's as though I'm seeing Flagstaff in a different light this time around. When I arrived, I was so determined to walk in and walk out. To be the same girl I had been. Not everything's changed; I'm still apprehensive about a lot—especially my father and dealing with other consequences. Slowly, however, that outer shell of indifference and anger has started to chip and break off, and I don't have a desire to glue those pieces back on. I just want to let myself be and see what appears.

Banner clears his throat and stands as we do. "No. I have no objections. I will continue with the Shaws, regardless of ownership." He then grabs a plate of chocolate chip cookies covered in Saran Wrap and hands it to me. "From my wife. She sends her best."

My heart pounds as I take it. "Please tell her I say thank you."

Banner and my dad shake hands at the door. "Thank you, Mr. Shaw." He gazes at me. "Sheyanne."

"Chief," I say, maintaining eye contact. It's a moment before he gives me the slightest nod. The pressure that fell on my shoulders as soon as I entered lightens just a bit.

"Have a good day, Banner," Dad calls as he walks back to the truck.

The gray midday sky hangs overhead as I fall into step with him. I unlock the old truck, and we climb in.

We're both quiet, the silence uncomfortable. As I turn onto the road, I glance over. "Thank you." My throat feels scratchy. "Thank you for saying all that."

"Sheyanne, I know that we've had our issues, and I want to apologize—"

I shake my head. "No, please don't. It's not like I was the easiest daughter or even a good one. Please don't apologize to me." I can't take the guilt of having to live up to an apology and expectations I doubt I'll ever meet.

He sighs and leans his head back against the seat. "Sheyanne, you weren't a bad daughter. You've never been a bad daughter. I—"

"Dad, I'm serious. I just don't want to do this right now. I appreciate what you did inside, more than you know, but can we just leave it at that for now, please?" My grip tightens on the steering wheel as I continue driving us home.

It's quiet for a moment, my heart frantic as he takes in my words. It's not that I don't want to have this talk with him or try and understand what about the two us just couldn't make it work as parent and child back then. I just don't want to have it right now. Him defending me inside was a step in the right direction, but I'm at my limit. I appreciate it, but I'm still hesitant, and I need more time. Need to be in a better place for that conversation. I know that it will be anything but easy.

But I'm sure he can't understand that from my vague words, so I take one more step and hope that it's enough for now. "I'm happy I came home," I murmur, looking at the gray sky that seems less unfriendly and more like a welcoming blanket now.

Luckily, Dad seems to take it for what it is. He nods and clears his throat. "Yeah, I'm happy you came home, too."

We stay silent the entire rest of the ride, but it's not heavy; it's just quiet. And in that moment, I try to forget about the diagnosis and the fact that this feels like a last ditch effort before it's too late and instead focus on the fact that we still do have time and on the tiny blossom of hope in my chest.

Later that day, I'm waiting for the perfect time to take Liam to the surprise I have planned. I didn't tell anyone it was his birthday a few days ago like he asked. But ever since the night he draped his jacket over me outside the bar, I've had a growing urge to do something for *him.* So, I've decided to take him to a place that used to mean the world to me, where I'd go on my birthdays.

MJ and Shane are in the living room with Dad. I'd really like to sneak out and past them without raising any questions, but considering they just started binging some new TV show, I doubt that I will be that lucky. It's not that I want to hide anything; I just want to keep it private— whatever *it* is—for now.

But I also really want us to have something to bring along. With a sigh, I roll over on my bed and grab my phone from the nightstand and send a reluctant text, asking for Shane to make two mug cakes and put them in a thermos for me to take. Less than a minute later, there's a knock at my door.

I let my head fall onto my pillow. "Come in."

Shane appears at my door with a grin so wide I think it might fall off his face. Sometimes, I think we're the exact same and then sometimes, I think were the exact opposite. He's the optimist, and I'm the pessimist.

The man can't stay angry for longer than a minute without smiling.

He leans on the closed door. "What's this message?"

"What does it say?" I counter.

"What do you need two for? What are you doing? Where are you going?"

"Shane, can you please just make them?"

He sits in the desk chair and spins happily. "If you tell me who the second one is for."

"You know who it's for," I mumble, feeling embarrassed now. I should've made them my damn self. "Please."

Shane rolls his eyes, but before he can respond, there's another knock on my door. He answers for me. "Come in." I glare at him, the look only softening when MJ enters.

"What's going on? I wanna be included," she whispers and looks between us. It only takes her a moment to find a place to sit, and she does so by sitting on my brother's lap.

I fake gag.

They both just laugh, Shane wrapping his hand around her hip. "I have to make Sheyanne two mug cakes because she is taking a certain someone somewhere and doesn't want to tell me."

My face is hot, but I glare at him, nonetheless. "You are an asshole."

MJ grins almost as widely as my brother. A match made in heaven. "Is it Liam? It's Liam, isn't it?" I don't bother with a response. Since MJ is fully taking on the role of joining this family, she can get regular old Sheyanne now, too. "Okay, okay, I won't say anything else. My lips are sealed." She motions to her mouth like a zipper.

All this from one stupid text message.

Shane stands, taking MJ with him. "I'll have them ready in twenty; is that okay?"

"That's fine, Shane, thank you." My voice is muffled from the pillow I've buried my face into, only glancing up to see them exit with smug smiles.

As soon as they're gone, I stand and pat Nyx on the head. "Thank you for being the only normal one here." I plant a kiss on his head and then open my door so he can go since I'm leaving. I change before slipping through the open bathroom doors, stopping on the precipice of Liam's room. I knock twice, and he looks up.

"Come on in," he says, placing his tablet and stylus on the bed. Stepping in, I lean against the wall. His eyes trail over me, warmly enough for the look to linger everywhere it lands.

"I have something to show you. But you have to get dressed and be ready to go in twenty minutes." I pause, lifting a shoulder. "Please."

Liam let's out a low chuckle. "All right, just give me a minute. I'll meet you in the hall." Wordlessly, I return to my room, hoping he likes this place as much as I do.

Shortly, he opens his door. His lips quirk up, and he motions to the hall. "After you, Shaw." I roll my eyes, fighting against the smile that wants to form. We head down side by side and are greeted at the dining table by Shane holding two thermoses.

To my left on the couch, both MJ and Dad are staring. I ignore them and grab the packed desserts from my brother. "Thank you." He crosses his arms and just looks on happily at the sight. I head towards the front door where Liam waits.

His eyes flicker with amusement when he glances behind me, and when I turn, I find everyone still watching. "You all have a staring problem, you know that?"

Shane chuckles unabashedly as he takes a seat at the table. "Just go, would you? Wouldn't want to miss whatever you have planned for your—"

"Shut up or I will throw my shoe at your face," I threaten and pull on my coat, patting my legs so Nyx comes to me and Liam, who stands beside me. He coughs, badly disguising a laugh. "And you stay quiet," I say under my breath. "MJ, if you ever want to murder your boyfriend, please make sure I am the first person you call."

MJ grins, her curls bouncing around as she laughs. "You'd be the first person on my list."

"Murderers and matchmakers it seems I have for kids now," Dad mumbles, shaking his head, taking a bite of whatever he's eating, and all of our eyes collectively land on him, a quick silence settling before every single one of us starts laughing except for him. "I wasn't joking; I was serious."

His final comment makes the whole thing ten times better, even if I'm still slightly embarrassed by whatever conclusions they're coming to on their own. "We're leaving now." I nudge Liam with my shoulder, holding the desserts in one hand and spinning my keys on the other.

I close the front door behind us as we enter the cold, mid-November air. Liam falls into step beside me, and I feel his presence immediately. I check that everything I placed in the car earlier is still in the back and let Nyx jump up into the back seat. When I turn around, Liam is looking at me, hands tucked into his pockets.

"So, where are we going?"

I exhale, my breath materializing in the cold air. "Just shut up and get in the car, Landon." I open the passenger side.

Liam raises a brow. "Isn't it my surprise? Aren't you supposed to be nice?"

"Do you want me to be nice or to be myself?"

He steps closer. "I don't know; recently, you've been pretty nice to me. I think you're just faking this tough act."

I cross my arms, eyeing him. "I'm not faking. I don't fake anything for anyone."

Now, he's right in front of me, and if I were to move, we'd be touching. My breath hitches, and suddenly, I don't even realize it's cold or that we're running late. The cheekiest of grins comes over Liam's face, eyes lighting up with mischief as he bends down just a little.

"You don't have to fake anything with me, Sheyanne."

It's useless to fight the flush coming up my cheeks, the heat sinking into my skin. "Please just get in the car or we're going to be late."

He reaches up and tugs a curl that lays over the collar of my coat, twisting the frizzy end around his finger, meeting my eyes with warm brown ones. "Whatever you say, boss."

Liam brushes past me, touching our shoulders together as he climbs into the passenger seat with a big, satisfied smile and looks down at me.

I give him one last look before shutting his door and letting the cool air whip away the heat he left surrounding me. Whenever he looks at me or lowers his voice or honestly just exists in the same stratosphere as me—well, it all just takes my breath away. Like my brain short circuits and has to remember how to inhale again, only to experience it all over again.

Whether he's aware or not, he is scorching me, setting my skin on fire with the smallest of matches.

The passenger door opens with a snap, and it hits my butt since I haven't moved an inch. I turn around to meet Liam's amused eyes again. "Well, come on now, move it. Or we're going to be late." His words drip with self-satisfaction, and a fresh wave of heat flushes over my skin.

"Oh, fuck you, Liam."

I change my mind as I walk around to the driver's side.

Liam Landon knows exactly what he's doing, trying to get me out of being the angry—or hurt—and closed-off person I was when we first met and trying to burn me into being alive, creating a place for me where I can do just that. In this moment, I know it's working because that heat, that burn—I crave it now. It's starting to become the only thing I want to feel anymore.

That and the feeling of being alive.

152

Sixteen

Sheyanne

"So, where are we going?"

I spare a quick glance to passenger side before turning back to the road. We're right on time—the sun is just starting to lower in the sky, hinting at the approaching golden hour. The lone peak in the distance gets closer with every mile I drive on the small-town roads.

"It's called a surprise for a reason," I mutter.

"And if I don't like surprises?" Liam adjusts in the passenger seat so he's facing me more, his full lips tugging up into a smirk.

"Guess you're shit out of luck then, huh?"

He chuckles. The sound echoes in the car and settles over my skin like a blanket.

Reaching forward, I adjust the dial, turning up the music a bit as we approach the off-road that leads up to the lookout. Up here, the snow on the ground is still fresh and bright, the sky strewn with thick clouds. Soon, we're surrounded by a deep forest green as the trees grow taller and we enter the shadow of the peak. Liam stays quiet as we ascend the long winding road, just watching it all pass by. Every so often the sun peeks through the gaps before disappearing again behind the sea of trees. Snow dusts the thick branches and reflects the light as we climb higher.

We approach the top of the drive, the sun reappearing. The sky has just begun to turn orange as I reverse into the small gravel parking lot so we can see the view from the back. I look over to see Liam looking out the window before looking back at me, an endless number of emotions pooling in his deep brown eyes.

I open my door and hop out, turning the car off before pulling the back of the Bronco open and pushing the back seats up to make room. Nyx bounds out and lands on the ground, collapsing as he looks out over the peak. After a moment, Liam appears, leaning against the side of the car as I unpack everything I brought. Two blankets, the thermoses of the dessert, and a small portable speaker.

There is a small smile on Liam's face as he takes it in. "This is one hell of a surprise, Shaw."

Satisfaction pumps through my blood, and I look down to hide the smile I feel growing in response. You can see everything from up here— the other peaks, the small town, the endless clusters of trees and pastures that dot the town in different colors. In the spring, at the right time, you can find spots of brighter colors when flowers start to bloom.

"It's nothing." I stare out, watching the sun paint the town gold. I climb into the Bronco, leaning against the back seat.

He looks at me directly. "It's not nothing. Not if you brought me here."

I don't respond, taken aback by his words and the sincerity in them. I pat the spot beside me, and he climbs in, taking a seat. Only his thigh rests against mine, but I feel him everywhere, through the layers of clothes and the thick wool blanket I have draped over my legs. He picks it up, draping it over his own.

"I brought two, you know. One for each of us."

He leans his head back against the seat, turning to me, his hood pooling behind him. "I thought we could share. More warmth that way."

"Mhm. I'm sure." I unfold the second blanket and drape that over the first one to fight the cool air. I hand him his own thermos and a spoon as I connect the speaker to my phone.

We soak it in for a second, the beginning of the sunset. Above, the sun rays paint the sky orange and red in streaks through the clouds, tainting the blue and turning it violet. It's my favorite time of day. Golden hour into the sunset into the night sky that'll be speckled with stars soon.

I take a bite and look over at the man next to me, the dark singular freckles that are scattered sporadically around his dark skin—his full lips and the warm eyes and the sharp jawline—and wonder how the hell he has somehow wiggled his way in through the cloud of darkness I think follows me everywhere.

Liam turns, as if he knows I am unabashedly staring at him, and I don't look away. In awe of how, in just a glance, my skin warms from waves of heat. His eyes don't waver, and I take another bite, licking away the stray crumb of chocolate, and watch as his eyes catch the movement.

"Happy belated birthday," I say softly. "I know you're not a fan; I'm not either. But I used to come here on mine by myself. It's not a gift, but it's something."

He presses his thigh against mine, and my heart pounds. Liam shakes his head. "I've never needed gifts, Sheyanne." His eyes flicker back to the sky briefly. "Whatever this spot is to you, whatever it means to you—you brought me here; you've let me in just a little bit." He looks at me, smiling, and holds up his fingers, leaving a small space between them. "It's better than any gift I ever could've gotten."

I flush. "It's just a lookout." That's a lie, and he knows it, but feeling vulnerable isn't something I'm used to. Doesn't change the fact that I can't stop replaying his words in my mind like a broken record.

He exhales. "You have to stop doing that."

"Doing what?"

"Pushing things off like they don't mean anything to you. It's okay to admit that things, that people matter to you." Liam pops another bite into his mouth. God, it's frustrating how fucking easily he does this, how easily he sees through me.

"You're annoying." I lean back and pull the blanket up a bit higher, watching the sun continue to set, shades of purple beginning to show as the blue mixes with the red of the sky.

"Yet, you continue to spend time with me."

At the smugness in his tone, I reach over, determined to pinch him again, but his hand flies out, wrapping around my wrist. "None of that. That hurt last time."

I stick my tongue out at him, and he chuckles, the sound turning up the heat dancing over my skin, pressure building low and immediately between my legs, stealing my breath for a moment.

"Anyways," I breathe out, trying to distract myself, "will you tell me something?"

He turns to me, the lowering sun casting a warm light on his face. "What do you want to know?"

"I don't know. Something about the illusive Liam Landon."

He sets his half-eaten cake to the side. "I'm not very interesting."

This time, I meet his gaze, and I watch his pulse in the crook of his neck increase for just a second. My heart pumps at that, at knowing it's not just me. "I very highly doubt that, Liam."

"Grew up in Vegas, but you knew that. I ran track until my third year in college. When I was younger, didn't do much till I got smart enough to sneak out with my best friend."

"A secret troublemaker?"

Liam snorts softly. "It's no secret. My grandparents, especially my Pop, always knew, and when I'd sneak back in, one of them would be waiting in the living room every time. The next morning, when I was hungover and tired, they'd wake me up early and have a list of chores for me to do, most of which involved me being outside in the heat all day. They made my friend, Wyatt, do the same if he was with me."

"I like them. They sound like my kind of people." I adjust my legs, pulling them up and turning to the side, tucking my sock covered toes under Liam's thigh and leaning back so I can look at him.

After a second, like he's waiting to see if I do anything further, he reaches under the blanket, wrapping his hand around my legging covered ankle, and moves his thumb in slow little circles.

It's dangerous how good that small movement feels, but I continue. "I never imagined you getting into trouble."

"Why is that?"

Sparks dance under his fingertips as he taps the back of my calf. "You're just always so in control, put together. It's like nothing really phases you." It's one thing I quite admire about him, something I wish I could learn from him.

He squeezes my lower leg and gives me a playfully sharp look. "Things phase me, believe me. Maybe you'll figure them out, maybe you won't."

My lip quirks up. "I do like pushing people's buttons." I take a spoonful of cake to play it off.

"You? Push someone's buttons?" He places his free hand on his chest, giving me a blank look. "I never would've guessed."

I purse my lips spiritedly. "I guess that's fair." A small laugh bubbles out, pulling my lips into a smile.

Liam stares at me, that look that he always gives me that makes me feel like I can't do anything wrong. It's such an intense gaze, I swear it's like he can see every dark place I go to hide, every shadow, and it doesn't even matter.

"I wish you would do that more often."

"Do what?"

"Smile more. Laugh more. Either of the two." He's so sure of himself all the time, even when he's talking about me, and I don't ever know how to respond. "Your whole face lights up. Like it takes a weight off you."

My breath catches. "You are ridiculous."

"No, I'm honest."

My head falls forward, my curls shielding me for a moment. "Please just tell me more about you."

He sighs dramatically, picking up his dessert and taking a bite. "When I got injured from track, that's when I started doing graphic design. I always needed something to do. Sometimes, I have trouble slowing down. I got a job right after graduation, didn't take a vacation for the first two years, and immediately started saving up to give my grandparents something for everything they did for me. I still am. I want to buy them a house if they'll let me." His hand trails higher until it's fully on my calf, and his fingers circle and press in no particular rhythm.

I rest my head in my palm. "You want to buy your grandparents a new house?" Liam shrugs. "You want to buy them a house, and you expect me to believe you ever caused any real trouble in your life?"

That draws a smile out of him, and I inhale, taking it all in. Taking him all in. To my left, the sunset deepens into a darker haze, and right in front of me is a whole different sight, one I'm really starting to like.

"Enough about me." Liam breaks the momentary silence. "Will you tell me something?"

I hesitate, feeling the wall start to come back up, because talking about my past after listening to his just feels wrong. I don't want to talk about any part of myself I still don't like to look at.

As if he can sense it, Liam tightens his grip on my leg, pulling my gaze back to him.

He speaks softly. "I'm not asking you to tell me anything you don't want to. Even if you did, I'm not going to look at you any differently, Sheyanne. Just tell me something I don't know."

Half of me wants him to stop saying my name because it's addicting; it's hazy and sweet, and the other half doesn't want to hear him say anything else but my name.

I pause, looking out to the now midnight blue sky. The sun is barely a blip on the horizon, but the glow still lights the sky. It'll be a bit until the stars appear, but shadows start to wrap around the single mountain peak and us as well.

Maybe it's the softness in his voice or his eyes, the way he always notices when I feel like retreating, but it's the little things. He treats me carefully when I need it, but he also treats me like a human being when I don't, throwing attitude right back. He makes me feel human, worthy, and not like someone who has trouble looking in the mirror some days.

I'm not sure what does it, but I know I'm utterly fucking screwed because I don't know how to get out from under whatever spell he's cast over me.

Turning back, I meet his watchful eyes, his hand still on my leg as a warm reminder. I motion to the sky. "This is my favorite time of day," I start, telling him what I thought earlier. "Golden hour and sunset and when the stars finally come out. Everything seems better, quieter, and warmer all at once. All the colors and the transition of the sky." He taps my leg, and I feel insecure. "I'm not sure if that's what you meant though."

"It's perfect." He's firm and demanding. "Keep going."

"I don't know, it just feels like in that moment, no matter how shitty a day is or how bad of a person you might be, golden hour always comes. No matter who or where they are, it wraps everyone in the same hue of light. It's like a goodnight kiss from the sun. If I could wrap that color up in a bottle, I would never need anything else."

Liam stays quiet for a moment, but his eyes never stray from my face, and I feel his sure and steady hand wrapped around my calf, heat spreading from his palm to my skin to my blood to my heart beating wildly in my chest. The cold air doesn't even begin to break the warm bubble he's created.

After another moment, he sits up straighter and gently, but confidently, grabs my other leg. With a slow tug, he pulls it towards him, over him, until I'm straddling his hips. He lets go, but only to pull the blankets up to my shoulders until they're well draped over both of us. I don't know where my heartbeat begins or ends because it's everywhere, pulsing in my fingertips and in the palms of my hands as blood rushes past my ears. One hand returns to my thigh, sending small waves of heat that sink in and wrap around me, while the other hand comes up to my face. His thumb brushes over my cheek, back and forth in smooth steady motions.

"That was enough?" I ask, my words quiet because I'm scared to break this moment.

Liam nods, his hand tightening, like he's trying to hold it together. I like knowing that whatever I feel, he feels it, too.

"Wanna know something else?"

He meets my eyes in the settling darkness. "I want to know whatever you want to tell me."

A small smile grows at that because I believe him. "I like the way you say my name."

Whatever control he was holding on to, I watch it—I feel it—snap. Liam sits up and pulls me impossibly closer with the hand on my thigh, suddenly pressing it on my lower back until we're practically molded together. It's the hand that goes from my cheek to the nape of my neck, burying itself tightly into my curls that I feel the most. He tugs my hair as he brings my face closer to his, tightly, a bite of pain intermixed with the wave of pleasure that washes all over me and settles deep in my core. Breathless already, I rest my hands on his chest, feeling his heartbeat under my palm, but I am not in control here; Liam is.

He leans forward, his hand finding my thigh again, his fingertips pressing into the sensitive muscle, like he's never going to let go. A second later, I have to bite my lip when his lips lightly land on my skin, just brushing the spot where my jaw meets my neck. Finding air is impossible with him placing soft whispers of kisses on my skin, all over my jawline as he tugs my head back. My hands tighten on his sweatshirt, gripping it as he goes, heat pooling between my legs and my skin turning more sensitive by the second as he builds the pressure with every touch.

He hasn't even really kissed me yet, and I know I would do anything and everything he asked me to do. Whatever power he holds, I decide he can have mine, too. If he asked me, I would place all my broken puzzle pieces in his palm without hesitation.

His hand leaves my thigh, and I can't stop the groan that escapes me at the loss. Instantly, I feel the smirk on his lips as they brush my cheek, and that free hand lands on my lower back, massaging the muscles right above the band of my leggings, imprinting their rhythm on my skin.

Liam slowly places a kiss on either side of my mouth, barely touching the corner of my lips, and I huff impatiently. His response is to tighten his grip on my hair until my breath hitches. I tighten my grip on his sweatshirt, curling one hand on the neck of the hoodie, and finally, *finally*, I feel his lips right over mine. And I don't even remember my eyes closing. I open them to see him watching me intensely, brown eyes incredibly dark but expressing a million things at once. The phantom feeling of his lips on my skin brings forth a wave of goosebumps.

For a second, we just study one another, not saying anything, and his fingertips tug at the roots of my hair as he tips my chin up. My eyes flutter closed when he *finally* leans forward and presses his lips to mine. It's softer than I expect from how tight and sure his hands are. But it's this act, kissing, *us kissing*, that slows everything down. The press of his lips against mine, the slow movements they make are so gentle I want to cry. I can even feel the telltale prick of tears pooling in my eyes—something I haven't felt in years—and I have to squeeze my eyes for it to dissipate. But I know that even if I were to cry, it's not because I'm sad; it's because I never would've expected this from Liam.

He treats me gently, carefully, soothingly, while setting me on fire everywhere else. He's created a place of safety for me, one that only exists with him. Our lips move together in a careful dance of a first kiss, and I smile when I realize that's what this is. Our first kiss.

Liam pulls back not even an inch, his lips brushing mine when he says, "You can't smile when I can't see it. That's not fair."

My chest aches at his words, and I part my lips to respond, but he presses forward, his tongue carefully slipping inside my mouth, and a part of me simultaneously dies and reawakens when he does. The undertone of gentleness is still there, but he knows what he's doing as he kisses me, our tongues moving together, sure and steady. Liam is everywhere. His hand spreads on my back, enveloping my body. His other hand is in my hair and brushing against my skin, and the heavy smell of him—it's everywhere. One of my own hands leaves his sweatshirt, moving to cup his jaw, feeling the smooth skin under my thumb, holding him to me.

And we kiss and kiss, and I never want to stop.

I never want to feel any other type of heat in my life. Not a warm breeze in the fall when the leaves start to descend, not the warmth of a blanket in the dead of winter, not the first rays of sun in spring, and not the heavy heat of summer. If it's not the heat of Liam and his hands tugging me where he wants or his lips on mine, then I don't ever want to be warm again.

Everything would pale in comparison to him.

After a few more moments, or hours, of kissing, of Liam nipping at my bottom lip, of me trying to take the upper hand and him never letting me, which only builds the pressure that feels like the catalyst for something bigger than this moment, he pulls back, leaving me breathless and speechless.

My lips feel heavy in the best way, and he uncurls his hand from my hair, gently untangling his fingers and brushing the curls back from my flushed cheeks. I open my eyes to see his. They glimmer with mischief and lust, and they're on me, looking at the deepest parts of me like he always does. With flushed cheeks, I let myself smile gently, and this time, he sees it.

Liam's eyes soften. "If I could wrap that up in a bottle," he traces my smile, presses his thumb against my lips, "that would be all I need."

And again, for some reason, the tenderness, the sincerity, everything, brings the tears forward. This time, a single teardrop escapes, and I sputter out a breath as it trails down my cheek, embarrassed, and move my hands to cover my face. Liam stops them, grabbing both my hands and holding them between our bodies until he lets go with one and wipes the tear away delicately without a second thought.

Our eyes meet. "I need you to stop being nice to me. I don't like crying. And I don't like that you're seeing it."

"And I need you to understand there is no part of you I don't want to see. I want to see everything, Sheyanne."

Stupid Liam. Of course, he'd be the one to make me cry after all this time.

And stupid heart, for latching onto everything he says and tucking it away like precious gold.

I reach up and brush my thumb over his cheek, finding his skin just as hot as mine and feeling the smoothness of his face under my fingers. My eyes wander over his face, the heat between us still crackling in the cool air, and I study him under the stars and the light glow of the half moon. He lets me trace my finger around and around, over his lips and his neck, until I have the feel and shape of him committed to memory and can breathe again.

He just watches me in that quiet way of his. Like always.

Before I can do anything else, Nyx hops up next to us, tail wagging and ears perked. Liam grins, and I shake my head. I adjust, moving off him and taking up the space next to him this time. Our thighs and sides are pressed together, barely a silver of space between us as his hand finds my leg under the blanket. Nyx curls into place beside me, resting his head on his paws.

Darkness has fallen, and the stars blink in the dark of the night sky, the constellations shining above us.

I glance over, still feeling the effects of his kiss and his hands. "Thank you."

Liam looks amused. "For kissing you?" On instinct, I hit his chest. He smirks at me. "There she is."

"I never left. You just distracted me," I respond, rolling my eyes as I tuck both my hands between my thighs, for warmth and to keep from touching him again.

"Well, what exactly were you thanking me for then?"

Leaning my head back, I turn to look at him, and he does the same. But I can't elaborate. I don't know how to explain it to him. While I'm thankful—for how he sees me, for not rushing to conclusions, for it all really—it also scares me. Terrifies me at just how easily he does it. I've ruined a lot of the relationships in my life, and I haven't gotten close to anyone in years, so the idea is daunting. Liam makes the idea of it feel easier, more manageable, even if I'm still scared. So that's what I'm thanking him for, but I can't say it out loud.

I shrug, meeting his eyes. Like I hoped he would, he nods, like he gets it. Gets what I can't say. We sit there in that bubble, and for the moment, I push away anything else.

Choosing for a moment to let it all be.

Seventeen

Sheyanne

"Landon, get up."

I knock again on his door. The sun hasn't risen yet, and the house is quiet, except for my knocking and the noise of Shane starting the coffee. Dad's been sleeping more, sleeping later. I try to ignore the worry settling in, but it's there to stay.

The door creaks open before me, and a tired Liam takes its place. I'm used to seeing him in his T-shirt and sweats in the bathroom, where we almost always end up brushing our teeth at the same time. Since the first time, it's become a routine. I stand there half-asleep, and he puts toothpaste on my brush without a word. But today, there is no T-shirt. There's just Liam with low-hanging sweats on his hips.

My throat goes dry, and I swallow as my eyes trail over his dark skin, the slope of his shoulders as he crosses his arms and leans on the door frame, and the muscles they cover on his chest as it all tapers off into a leanly muscled stomach. There isn't enough time to take it all in, but now

I'm wishing when we kissed five days ago that I had snuck my hands under his sweatshirt and traced it all myself.

"Morning, princess." He gives me a small smirk with sleepy eyes, which is a sight in and of itself. "Can I help you with something?"

"Come on."

Liam stretches with a yawn, his arms going above his head. "It's the crack of dawn. On Thanksgiving."

"Yes and?"

"I wanted to sleep."

"I used to go riding every Thanksgiving. Figured it could be your introductory course. But if you'd rather sleep, I guess I can go alone."

He brightens a little at that, some of the tiredness fading away, and the smell of coffee fills the air. "Never mind; sounds great." He enters the hallway with me, forgetting he's shirtless for a second, while I have most certainly not. "Wait, let me put on something other than sweats."

A soft laugh builds in my throat, but I just purse my lips as he pushes back into his room. "I'll be in the kitchen," I call before heading that way.

Shane already has all the thermoses pulled out and on the counter, holding his own in his hand. The smell of coffee fills the quiet morning air, and even Nyx is feeling lazy because he's sprawled out on the couch instead of padding by my feet, ready to head to the barn.

"You going riding?" Shane leans against the countertop as he runs a hand over the fluffy curls on the top of his head.

Grabbing the thermoses, I pour almond milk in mine and leave Liam's black. "Yeah."

"With Liam." He grins, raising a brow, and I'm tempted to punch him in the face. With one hand, he pulls the hood up and over his head as he straightens. I grill him with a glare.

"Stop it."

Shane moves towards me, pressing his shoulder against mine. "What you staring at? Waiting for him to walk down the hallway?"

I attempt to shove him away. "I hate you."

Instead, he throws an arm over my shoulder. "No, you don't. I'm your favorite brother."

"You're my only brother, you dipshit."

"Exactly, hence being the favorite." He pats the top of my head. "Cute hat. Wonder who gave it to you."

I reach around quickly to pinch him, but he knows the move and avoids it just as quickly. I dodge his own hand when it reaches towards me, slapping it away. With a deadpan stare, I pull my hat—Liam's hat—down to cover my ears, not caring if the cotton will make my four-day-old curls frizzy.

"I'm gonna shove you into a pile of horse shit if you keep this up."

Sneakily, Shane pulls me in for a hug, squeezing me as my hands hang limply by his side, refusing to give in. "I'm just teasing, you know that?" When I don't answer he squeezes harder. "You know I'm just playing around, right? I just want you to be happy," he sings, lifting me off the ground.

A flood of emotions comes over me. "Put me down." When my feet hit the ground, I loosely hug him back. "I'm trying," I mumble into his chest, pinching his arm successfully to get him off me.

"All right, I'm gonna go get my work done, and I'll start the food when I get back. MJ is coming over later since we already did Thanksgiving with her family."

"Perfect." I take a slow sip, looking down the hallway again to see if Liam is planning on making his appearance anytime soon. "She's really great, you know."

Shane smirks, pulling on his heavy winter coat. "Yeah, I know."

"All right, get out. It's too early for me to deal with you."

He laughs and heads out the front door, letting a blast of cold air into the house. I'm about to go knock on Liam's door again when he comes out of his room.

"Took you long enough." I hand him his coffee, our fingers brushing as I do.

"My sincerest apologies, Shaw," he says dryly as we slip on our shoes, but his eyes are playful.

I pull on my coat. "You're not sorry at all."

He shakes his head, his cheek twitching. "Not even a little bit."

I nudge him toward the front door. "All right, all right, let's go, Landon." He pauses in the doorway, looking me over, his eyes resting on his hat currently situated on my head. I shrug with an innocent blink.

With a shake of his head, he pulls the door open, and we head out together, walking side by side towards the barn. Streaks of orange have broken up the dark sky, and our breath crystalizes in the air. Our arms brush with every step over the gravel and the frosted grass, but it's a comfortable silence. I think about what Shane said, how he just wants me to be happy. I want the same thing; I do. Some moments, I genuinely think I can find it here. Having made up with my brother, having him back. My dad defending me and the possibility of that being the start. And Liam. Sometimes when I spend time in the stables or reading in the serene house, seeing the mountains with a passing glance, I think I could be astonishingly happy here. The problem is, it's not the same when I'm alone, with nothing to distract me. No fictional world, no larger-than-life mountains. When it's just me, and it's just . . . silent, my anxiety spikes, and my thoughts spin. Some moments, I find myself just waiting for the bad and end up missing the good.

For now, I'm going to focus on the small moments I do have and enjoy finding the beauty again, even knowing there's still work to be done.

As we approach the barn, Liam gently shoves his shoulder against mine, and I push him back. The barn doors slide open, and I shut them behind us to keep the cold out as best I can. A few noses peek over the stall doors, ears perked.

I take a sip. "I just have to turn the horses out, and then we can go."

Liam nods, glancing around. "Do you want any help?"

Looking around at the place where I can always find one moment that makes me feel good, I shake my head. For once, this isn't me pushing away; I'm just being honest. "No, I did everything else, and I like doing it alone. But thank you."

He smiles softly, his lips barely moving, and takes my coffee from my hand. With a tap on my hat, he lowers his voice. "It's your world, Shaw. You do whatever you want to do."

Liam goes to sit on the bales of hay placed against the wall as I complete my final chore. It's just me and the horses that I get to take care of. Horses greet me with big, warm eyes and perked ears every single morning. That's when I feel a sense of belonging.

As I place blankets over some of their backs, snapping them closed around their chests, I brush my hand over their short coats, feeling the muscles beneath and the strength they have even as they stand in stillness. I've always been convinced horses know everything, like dogs. They can sense a person and who they are inside and out. As stupid as it seems, the fact that I've always felt at home here, with them, is the one reminder I hold onto. They still love me despite all my faults.

The best part is they can't speak on it, can't guide me in a direction or give me advice that I may or may not take. They just give me a quiet place where I can exist.

I lead all but Teddy and Rayne into the pasture, and when I return,

I crosstie both of them, their hooves clicking on the barn floor. Rayne is surprisingly loving today, and I can't help but smile as I pat her cheek, meeting big bright eyes. Looking over my shoulder, I find Liam watching me with an unreadable gaze. Swallowing, I motion for him to come over.

Standing, he strides to the horses and me. A loud stomp from Teddy echoes through the barn, excitement I presume, and I smile again. Although now, every time I smile anywhere near Liam, I hear his words from the weekend that have been on a constant loop in my head. As weird as it sounds, he makes smiling feel . . . illicit and has turned it into this thing that means more than it should.

Smiling around someone shouldn't make a smooth warmth spread all over the surface of my skin. It shouldn't make me feel like I can do no wrong or send a wave of butterflies to land comfortably in the bottom of my stomach. But the way Liam looks at me when I smile, when my lips are barely even beginning to form one, it's like he can sense it, and his eyes latch on with unwavering focus. Like he wants to see it happen from beginning to end, like he cannot bear to miss it.

I absolutely hate it.

I'm also absolutely addicted to it.

To Liam and his stupid, beautiful brown eyes.

"You're on Teddy again," I say as he approaches me, the smile still on my lips, his eyes latching onto it. We haven't kissed since the weekend or talked about it, but half the time, all I can think about is kissing him again.

I'd die before I'd say that out loud at the risk of inflating his ego and ruining my pride.

He hands me my coffee, and I place it in the little attachment on the saddle my dad made for this reason alone. I show Liam the spot for his, too.

"Where are we going?"

I grab the step stool and place it next to Teddy again. "You ask a lot of questions."

"I like to be informed."

"Do you not trust me or something?"

"No, I do." Liam leans down a bit, closer to eye level, and my heart speeds up in my chest as I fight to maintain my composure and try to ignore how easily flustered I am just by him entering my space. "I just like pushing your buttons."

With ease, he steps back and onto the stool, swinging his leg over Teddy's back, looking at home almost instantly. I stand there watching him and trying not to prove him right that I am, in fact, easily riled up by him. He's already learned exactly how to push my buttons.

"It's just a trail on our property. But we should be able to see the mountains from a little spot." I move the stool away and stand beside him and Teddy, making sure the saddle is on tight enough and everything is as it should be.

Before he can say anything, I give him a brief overview of instruction—how to tug the reins and ask Teddy to move and how to sit to make sure he doesn't end up falling off and hurting himself. I make him go through the motions inside the barn before opening the barn doors. I lead Rayne out and watch him walk with Teddy before shutting the doors behind us.

"Got it?"

He smiles. "Got it."

I swing myself up onto Rayne, patting her neck, and move closer to him and Teddy. "We honestly won't have to do much; they know their way around."

"After you, Shaw."

We begin walking, and I lead us toward the path into the forest on the backend of our property. The horses' hooves crunch the ground beneath us, avoiding larger branches or any large rocks on the path as we walk. I glance over at Liam to make sure he's doing okay, only to see a huge smile on his face. Despite the cold weather and the unfamiliar task, pure joy radiates off him. I wish I could reach up and grab it so I could tuck it in my pocket for a rainy day.

We head deeper into the woods, the pine trees sparse but still green, and the baby blue sky peeking through the branches. The sun brushes each of us gently with its early rays, not providing much warmth but dotting the ground golden beneath us. Teddy and Rayne walk side by side towards the old spot, heads moving back and forth with every step.

Every now and again, Liam reaches down to pet Teddy's neck, looking comfortable and at ease. No learning curve or anything; he jumped right in and took it by the reins—literally—and made it look easy.

I think Liam makes everything look easy, and I'm eternally in awe of it.

Shortly, the clearing starts to come into view. It's small, on the edge of the forest, and we can just see the peaks of the distant mountains and Buffalo State Park with its wheatgrass glory from here. The early sun reflects off the snow caps, and the blue sky is bright.

I glance over, seeing wonder bloom in Liam's brown eyes, and in turn, I feel a bit grow in my own chest. I forgot how beautiful it was here. It's nice to be able to see it again.

"We're here." I climb off Rayne and wait for Liam to dismount before I grab both the reins and tie them loosely to a tree with enough room for the horses to graze.

I hold the blanket close to my chest as Liam walks toward me. It's cold, but the air is still. There's no wind whipping against our skin. Liam looks at me, sticking his hands in the pockets of his black sweats. He wears a thick jacket around the hoodie underneath and a hat—similar to the one on my head—rests over his ears, the golden earring just peeking out. Even in the layers, I can see the leanness of his muscle that I saw earlier today, and I remember briefly how the skin I brushed over felt in the car at the lookout and how strong and sure he was holding me there.

"When I took the job and heard the name of the town, I knew nothing about it. I never expected any of this." His words cut through the silence, eyes taking it all in. I sit down, and he follows, lowering himself next to me. I drape the thick blanket over top of us.

"It's beautiful." I look it over. "I told myself it wasn't for years. But it is."

His shoulder touches mine. "It's a hidden gem. Surrounded by deserts and then you get this."

"Have you ever been to Arizona?" Liam shakes his head, his eyes still on the rising sun. "So, no Grand Canyon? Sedona?" Again, he shakes his head. "What a shame."

Liam draws his knees up and rests his forearms on top, his eyes flicking to me. They're a million times warmer than the sun that touches my skin. "What, no offer to take me?"

"Do I look like a tour guide?" He moves suddenly, pushing me over with a quick hand on my shoulder as I struggle to hold my coffee upright. "That was so rude." I push myself back up into a seated position. "I'm definitely not taking you now."

"What if I ask nicely?" Liam's voice is low, and his eyes roam my face.

"I think you missed that opportunity."

His lips quirk. "I'll make it up to you."

"And how would you do that?" I adjust the hat on my head, pulling on a curl that's intertwined itself with another.

"Make a list." He leans closer. "Or I'll just have to figure it out on my own."

My heartbeat quickens in my chest. "I'd like to see you try."

Liam just grins mischievously. I break away from his eyes, attempting to distract myself. I'm almost surprised at my lack of fight, my lack of resistance to his persistent personality, but even when I try to keep my guard up, he just finds another way in. Not in a way that's obtrusive or unwanted. Instead, there's a softness to it, a gentleness that I'm not sure I've ever experienced.

After a moment of silence, a phone begins to buzz, and Liam pulls his out of his pocket, surprise on his face as he looks at the facetime request from someone named Wyatt.

"Sorry, I wasn't expecting this. Do you mind?" I shake my head, rolling my warm thermos between my palms. He swipes his thumb, and a man appears with a smile. I realize we're both on the screen.

"What's up, man? How are you?" Wyatt's voice comes through, and it's warm even through the phone. His skin is lighter than Liam's but not by much, a warm brown to match the bright smile. Seeing him and looking at Liam, I believe Liam when he said he got into trouble. I could easily see the two of them running around town together.

Liam smiles. "I'm good; what's up with you? Why are you up this early?"

"I'm headed to your grandparents house, dropping off a pie for them since I can't spend the actual meal with them today," Wyatt says, and even though they aren't my grandparents, my heart warms at the sentiment. "But who is this?"

Liam adjusts the phone, so I'm more fully in the screen. "Wyatt, this is Sheyanne. Sheyanne, this is Wyatt, my idiot best friend."

"Nice to meet you." I wave over the small screen. Wyatt smiles, showcasing double dimples, and I raise a brow, amused.

"You too, Sheyanne. May I ask what you're doing with this fool?"

That causes a small chuckle to escape. "I'm kind of stuck with him."

Wyatt nods, walking along the street. "I know the feeling."

Liam rolls his eyes and pushes me away again. "Fuck you guys." I smile into my arm as I lean forward on my knees again, resting my head and letting the two of them catch up.

The sun is higher now, the sky a brighter and deeper blue. Clouds dot the sky in white fluff, and the kid in me still wonders what it would be like to jump on one even though I know it's impossible. On long car rides in the backseat with my CD player, I used to imagine jumping from cloud to cloud with the canyons below, just being free. That was back before life took a sharp left turn, when I didn't hate it here so much. I wonder if it's possible to get back to that feeling. I hope it is.

Liam and Wyatt's voices have faded into to the background, the cold air finally letting up as the sun grows higher and the heat from the blanket finally settles in. But a second later, Wyatt's questions rings loud in the chill of the air.

"So, when are you coming back? We gotta get up when you do. I miss tearing up the strip."

Liam responds with sarcasm. "I'm sure my being gone has not kept you far from the strip."

"That's true."

But the question that hasn't been answered yet is ringing in my bones and snapping me back to reality. None of this—this arrangement, Liam's job, my being here—is permanent. It's all temporary. Even if I do discover that beauty again and the things I used to love, I'm not sure if it's enough for me to stay. For a moment, I swear I feel Liam's gaze on me as if he knows exactly where my mind has gone, but I keep my eyes trained on the sky.

I ignore the anxiety crawling at my spine, hoping it won't take over.

"The contract was for three months. Should be back around the end of January."

I rest my head on my forearms, the clouds passing by as I reel. He's been here a little over a month, but it feels like it's been forever, like I've been back in this place forever. And at some point, things will all go back to how they were. I'll leave again, Shane will resume regular life, and Liam will go home. When I first arrived, I thought I'd be happy about the idea of leaving.

Now, all I feel is confused.

The call ends before I even realize it, and Liam's hand landing on my arm makes me whip my head around. His eyes are cautious but calculating as he watches me watch him. There's only one kiss between us, a single kiss that feels like so much more, and already, I'm aware that we're both going to walk away. I hate the way it makes me feel. Maybe it'd be easier if we just cut the thread that's begun to grow now instead of waiting until we're fully intwined.

"Sheyanne," he rumbles, his hand like a brand on my sweatshirt-covered arm.

I lean back, brushing his arm off as I rest on my palms. If he notices the strategic move, he doesn't say anything. "I like Wyatt; he seems funny."

He stills before nodding, like he's okay to go along with whatever tactics I have in mind to avoid talking about anything deeper. "He's a good guy. Been around as long as I can remember."

Liam still watches me, but my eyes are trained on his jawline. I focus on everything but his face—the small earring glinting in his ear from the sun, the thin chain around his neck tucked under his sweatshirt, the dark freckle on his nose. I stay away from looking at his lips because they make me want to touch him, make me want to kiss him again and feel the heat on my skin. The heat that burns away all my anxiety and all my doubts. It feels wrong to depend on that heat, to crave it.

I have to want to be better, not just depend on what makes me feel better in the moment.

"Well, good; you need as many friends as you can get. Give your grandparents a break," I say, meaning it as a joke, but it comes out flat, and Liam sees right through me.

This time, he turns to face me. "Tell me something, like you did before." Like I did this weekend, like a distraction.

My teeth pick at the skin of my lip until I force myself to talk. "Like what?"

"Don't care. Just want to hear you talk."

When he asks to hear about me, it has the opposite effect than if it were to come from someone else. He makes me want to tell him, even if it's just to get something off my chest. I still get nervous that he'll look at me in a different light or change his mind about me, but so far, it seems the opposite is true. Every time I let him in a little bit, he just wants in further. He never retreats.

"I used to love Thanksgiving. When I was kid, before Dad and I completely stopped getting along, Shane and I always watched cartoons in the morning, played board games, and went riding until the food was ready. Before the fighting started, I loved it. But after I while, I just started spending Thanksgiving alone, and then when I left, I was always alone."

"You're not alone this year." Liam's fingers tap on his leg, like he wants to reach out and grab me, to reassure me. But he doesn't.

I shrug. "I probably will be next year." I stand up, stretching and folding the blanket.

The rustle of the grass lets me know he has stood, too, and is following me towards the horses, the sun at our backs. I tuck the blanket away and crack my neck, trying to release the tension, but the anxiety just crawls higher up my spine, taking over more of me than I'd like.

"You don't have to go back to that."

I turn and find he's closer than I realized. "But I will. We all will."

Liam steps forward, capturing me in his unflinching gaze. "You're not listening to me. Just because you think that's what will happen, you think that's what needs to happen, doesn't mean it does. You don't have to fall back into what you've become used to because that's the only option. It's not. You can choose."

I want to believe him, that I can choose. That things don't have to return to how they were. But I don't know how. "It doesn't matter. I didn't mind being alone." The lie slips out, and I move to turn away, but this time, he grabs my wrist tightly and pulls me back.

Whatever fight he had in him that kept him from touching me dies as he gently grips my face. "It does matter. I don't get why you fight the things you feel or the things you care about, but you're allowed to feel however you want. You're allowed to care. I'll remind you of that until you believe me, Sheyanne."

I don't tell him that everything I've cared about, I always ruined. Now, I stop myself from caring because I'll just end up sabotaging myself.

I don't tell him, but I don't want to feel that way either.

Instead, I let myself revel in the feel of his one hand wrapped around my wrist and the other that curls around my neck, his thumb moving softly over the side of my cheek, and I let myself lean into his palm. I want to chase whatever belief system he has, whatever optimism flows through his blood, but I can't. Not until I believe it myself.

"Okay," I mutter in response. I don't have the heart to tell him that it doesn't matter how many times he tells me—because he's going to leave, and that too will end.

Liam sighs but says nothing else. He just pulls me into his steady chest and wraps his arms around me with the same gentleness in which he kissed me, but he doesn't touch his lips to mine today. He just holds me tight, one hand on the back of my head, his fingers in my curls. After a moment, he pulls back and brushes his lips against the side of my head, and I feel hints of that warmth that he carries reach me, but it only brushes the surface today.

I lean back and force my lips upward. "Well, let's get back and help Shane with the food."

Liam nods, but instead of letting me go right away, he brushes another soft kiss to the top of my head and rests his chin there, just holding me.

Despite everything else I feel, it feels nice, really nice, to just let myself be held.

The way back to the barn is quiet. I don't feel terrible, but I don't feel better either. I'm just somewhere in between, trying to find a balance. I appreciate Liam just letting me be silent; somehow that makes me feel far more seen than if he had tried to force an explanation out of me. The horses are unsaddled, given fresh water, and led into their pasture as the sun approaches midday. Liam and I leave the barn side by side, our feet in sync as they crunch the ground.

I break the silence this time, trying not to let the whole day go to waste and wanting him to know as best I can that I'm thankful for what he did. "Thanks for coming with me this morning."

Liam looks down at me and bumps my shoulder with his. "Of course." We step up onto the porch and begin to slip our shoes off before we enter. "Listen, I—"

The door swings open, and MJ steps out, a smile on her face, but one that doesn't reach her eyes. "Hey, you guys are back. Shane sent me out to ask a favor before you got all settled."

"What's he need?" She hesitates, and I hear something crash from inside the house. "MJ, what's wrong?"

Her smile falls. "I don't really know. Something with your dad."

Liam mumbles under his breath, and the pit inside me just deepens. This day is not at all turning out how I wanted it to. MJ holds the door open and drops the ruse of Shane needing an errand as we enter the house. Nyx is laying down in the middle of the hallway, watching with his ears perked. My eyes go right to Shane and my dad.

Dad is pacing around the table, frustration written all over his face and in the tense set of his shoulders. I'm taken right back to being a teenager and getting scolded by that look on his face. I stop where I am, a decent distance away. Shane looks at me, distraught as MJ approaches him and wraps her arms around him. Liam steps closer to me, and I step away.

"What's going on?" I ask, my voice breaking the silence.

My father whips his head around, piercing me with his dark eyes, and they narrow. "What the hell are you doing here?"

My heart drops in my chest as I gather we're in the midst of an episode, a progression in the disease. I have a feeling this is different than him losing his keys or forgetting a simple task.

"Dad, she's been here. You asked her to come home." Shane's voice is soothing, but it does nothing.

He's never hit me; that's not why I keep the distance. In my mind, if I put enough space between us, I think maybe none of his words or whatever feelings he may have can reach me.

"Why on earth would I do that? I would never ask her to come back here." The words are cold.

"Dad," Shane says, trying to calm him down to no avail.

"She made it clear how much she despised this place. Despised me." He turns his gaze on me again, and this is not the dad that defended me last week to Chief Banner. This is the dad from before. "Get out."

"No," I spit out, my chest growing tight.

He steps toward me, everyone watching us. And I fucking hate it. "I don't understand why you're here."

"You asked me to come."

He scoffs, running a hand over his short hair, and I can see the confusion mixed with the anger. But he doesn't stop. "You hated it here. We all knew it, so even if I did ask you, you would've never come back."

I shake my head, the anger and frustration clawing at my skin, hating that everyone is seeing this, that Liam hasn't taken his eyes off me, that MJ is visibly trying not to cry, and that Shane won't even look at me. And that my dad, after we finally took one step forward, is being forced into the past by a fucking disease. Hating that he doesn't see the me I've slowly been trying to be and instead sees only the me that fought with him at every step. I can't even be mad at him because it isn't his fault.

Dad looks to Shane this time, frustrated. "Why is she here?" It almost sounds desperate this time coming from his lips. I can't take it.

I don't wait to hear Shane's response. I can't stand to see their faces anymore, so I stride down the hallway towards my room. Nyx pads after me, following me into my room before I shut my door behind me and lock it, making sure to shut the door to the bathroom too, just in case. I lean my back against my bedroom door until I'm sitting on the floor.

I know I can't be mad, so I'm trying not to be. It's not Dad's fault; it's not even mine. More than anything, I feel frustrated, tired. I wanted so badly for today to be a good day, and it was, *it was*, for a little bit. But after that stupid question Wyatt asked and now this, I just wish the day would end. Nyx scoots closer, resting his head on my knee, and I pat his fur, hiding my fingers in the softness as he settles next to me. Through the door, I can hear Shane doing his best to calm down Dad, and I try my best to block it out.

A knock on my door makes me sigh. I don't move to answer it.

"Sheyanne." It's Liam. I lean my head against the door. "Can I come in?"

I want to. I want to let him in. But I can't bring myself to do it, so I don't say anything in hopes that he will walk away. I should've known better than to think that's what he would do. From the rustling and the slight pressure on the old door, I'm almost positive he's sitting against it.

"Please don't spend today alone. You don't have to be alone."

My jaw clenches and unclenches, tension running through my body because I can still hear my dad and Shane, and I wonder how we'll handle this. What this means. I also hear Liam's calm and steady words, but I can't bring myself to follow them out of the hole I've crawled into.

"I'm going to sit out here all day; I hope you know that." He's not joking; I hear that in his tone.

I swallow, finally bringing myself to speak. "Liam, just don't. Just go."

"Nope."

"I'm not coming out," I say and pluck the hat off my head and toss it, digging my fingers into my curls.

"Well then, I'll be outside your door."

I want to cry. Which makes me angry, too. I used to just get mad and run away, but now, I'm being reduced to tears too often for my liking.

I want to tell him that I'm thankful that he's not giving up on me.

But I also know that he will save us both a lot of pain if he does.

Everything would be a lot simpler if he just walked away and left me alone, like he will inevitably do in a few months.

Eighteen

Sheyanne

It's as if eggshells line every inch of this house.

It's been six days since Thanksgiving, and the outburst has sent us into silence. That day, Liam stayed by my door almost the entire time, only leaving to grab water and food, and when he finally did walk away, there was a wrapped plate of food for me left on the hardwood. But since then, I have avoided everyone, including him.

Today hasn't been awful. I was outside doing my job like usual and back inside in my room for a bit. The past few days, Dad and Liam have been busy, dedicating more time to getting as much sorted as possible and setting up any necessary appointments. Through the door, I heard Shane made an appointment with the doctors in Phoenix since the disease seems to be progressing. They've all tried to talk to me over the last six days with no success. Dad has tried harder than anyone.

I want to talk to him, but I'm scared it wasn't just an episode. I'm scared he meant every word.

I turn off my car, shaking my thoughts away, and begin to unload the bags of groceries I went out to get. When I turn around, Shane is standing on the porch, and if his face is any indication of his mood, he's pissed. I sigh, weighed down by much more than just the heavy bags on my arms and walk up as the sun begins its descent.

"Sheyanne."

I ignore him, pushing through the door and straight to the kitchen, which thankfully, is empty.

"Would you please stop acting like I don't exist?"

The bags land with a thud on the counter, and I grip the edge of it. "Shane, I really don't want to do this right now."

He steps towards me. "I don't care. You can't just avoid everything, you can't just—" He stops himself from whatever he was about to say.

I meet his eyes, ignoring the prick I feel behind my own. "Can't what, Shane? Can't just run away?" He says nothing. "Well, newsflash, I'm still here. After being scolded by Dad yet again, I'm still here. I haven't left."

My voice cracks, and I look away, peeling my fingers away from the counter, ignoring the red marks on them from holding on so tightly.

"Yet. You haven't left yet."

"If I wanted to leave, I'd be gone by now." I try to breathe, try to keep my voice level.

"But isn't that what you're going to do? When everything is done and sorted and Liam is gone?" That statement sends another knife to my gut, but Shane doesn't stop. "Aren't you just going to leave all over again?" Hurt bleeds from his statement, but I can't focus on it.

I'm shaking now, overwhelmed with a boatload of emotions, and I rest my head in my palms, trying to shut him out. I know he's just hurt, but I can't deal with his hurt and my own right now. "Shane, please."

Even though he doesn't show it as much, he has the same temper that

I do, the same stubbornness, and today is the day he decides to let it show. "No. I get it; I get that this place had become anything but a home for you. But what about me? I'm your brother, and you left without a goddamn goodbye. And somehow, I just know that you would do it again."

But I wouldn't.

It hurts more than I'd like to admit that Shane thinks that I would. I'm hoping, wishing, that he's saying it out of anger and not a place of honesty.

"If you think I would leave without a word again, then maybe nothing has changed like I thought it had."

He runs his hands over his face, frustrated. "If things have changed, then why are you ignoring me? Why won't you talk to me?

I swallow the yell I feel. "I got yelled at like I was fifteen all over again in front of people that I care about. He told me to fucking leave, Shane, told me he didn't want me here. I'm sorry if my unhappy walk down memory lane is making you upset." I breathe. "I'm ignoring everyone, not just you. And it's because I have nothing to say right now because every time I look at any of you, all I see is pity or disappointment, so excuse me for wanting some time to myself."

Shane deflates. "Sheyanne, you know he didn't mean it."

He may have let the anger go, but I haven't. "You don't think I know that? That doesn't make it hurt any less. I told you I didn't want to do this right now, and you just wouldn't let it fucking go. I get that you're mad, mad at me for more things than just ignoring you for a week, but you were not the one reduced to nothing. I just needed some fucking space." My voice cracks again, tears fighting to spill, and I stop myself before anything else comes out.

The anger feels like a pot of water filled too full about to boil. Like its bubbling up and up and eventually will overflow. And for once in my life, for *once*, I don't want to burn anyone else.

"None of us pity you. None of us are disappointed," he says, trying to diffuse the situation that's already been lit.

"I don't believe that. I can't speak for MJ or Liam because they never knew me before. But you and Dad? I see you both watching me, glancing at me like I'm just a façade hiding that distressed teenager. I'm not. Did it occur to you that I hated that girl as much as you both did? I don't want to be like that again, and it sucks that you're both just waiting for it to happen."

Shane steps forward, and I shake my head, moving away. "I told you I don't hate you, Sheyanne. I never did."

"Then please act like it and just have a little faith in me."

I walk away, leaving the groceries on the countertop and Shane standing there, proud that I didn't lash out like I used to and also depleted at feeling like the walls are caving in. The house is quiet, and I'm thankful that at least Dad and Liam are nowhere to be found, even though I'm sure they heard everything from wherever they are. I enter my room and collapse on the bed, watching my ceiling fan go around and around, hoping it'll take my emotions with it on a rotation so that I can breathe. I just lay there.

Feeling everything fall out of my control.

Turning my head, I watch the sunset through my window, watch the sky change yet again, like it does every night and yet is still somehow beautiful, still calming. In the distance, I hear the front door shut and a car start. I assume it's Shane going to MJ's. I turn over on to my side and breathe. I start to worry that maybe they're right to assume that nothing's changed, that I'm no different than I was.

No. I push those thoughts away as quickly as they come because I don't think they're true.

"Sheyanne."

I roll over to see Liam standing in my doorway, and I sigh, looking back to the ceiling. "What?"

"Are you okay?" His voice is soft, and I realize he's the first person to ask that.

Liam's given me the most space all week. Didn't try to talk to me because I clearly didn't want it, but he made sure to check on me in small ways. We kept our morning routine; I just didn't speak. He'd bring me extra coffee and leave it on my desk without a word. Dad and Shane wanted me to talk about everything all at once. But Liam never once tried to force me to break my silence.

But right now, I can still feel the residual anger in my veins, and that's probably not a good sign.

"Everything is fine."

I look over to see his brow raised at my response. His hands are tucked into his pockets. "I didn't ask about everything. I asked about you."

Me. He asked about me.

I sit up. "I'm fine."

"You're not a liar. Don't start now." His words are firm, but I just shrug. "We don't have to talk about it. I just want a yes or a no."

Liam knows the answer, he just wants me to say it. To let it out.

"No."

He's silent for a moment, and a part of me thinks he was expecting me to lie, to not admit that I am still upset over it all. Liam steps inside and takes a seat at my old desk chair as I wrap my arms around my folded legs.

"Do you want to talk about it?" he asks gently.

"Not really." I rest my head on my knee.

"Do you want to talk about anything?"

I press my palm against my legging. "I thought you wanted a yes or no answer."

He leans forward, resting his elbows on his knees. "I did."

"Well, you got one. And I don't really feel like talking. To anyone."

When Shane and I argued, there was nothing I couldn't read by his features. He's always been an open book. The hurt and the anger, I could see it, so I understood it. And I knew once he got it off his chest, he'd calm down. But looking at Liam, I can't read him right now, and I have no idea if he's so inclined to let me wallow in silence.

"So, you're just going to go on like this?"

 "Like what?"

"Not talking to any of us. One day, you'll just snap out of it and expect us all to go back to normal? And to be okay with it?" Liam is stern, not harsh, but the words still sink in.

I'm taken aback by the call out. Realistically, because that's probably exactly what I would've done. "Why is it so wrong of me to want to just ignore everything right now? I just need some silence."

"That's not what I asked you."

I look away from him, feeling the anger crawl at my skin again. "What difference does it make?"

Liam leans back, cool and collected. I see his own frustration reflect in his eyes, but he holds it together. "You can't run away from everything."

At that, something snaps. No one gets it. I know what running away is. It's me leaving and throwing away the key to my childhood house and not coming back for four years. It was me running so far away from all my problems that I destroyed any relationship I ever had, with my friends, with my brother, and I'm still dealing with those consequences.

It's not me wanting space for a week. It's not me just wanting to be left the hell alone in my own room with my own thoughts.

I shake my head, my skin burning. "This isn't me running away. I know what running away is, Landon." If one more person accuses me of it, I'm going to go insane.

"Then what is this?" He motions to me. "The silence, shutting everyone out and avoiding it. Is that not running away?"

"No, it's not. Not to me. I just wanted some space, and no one seems to get that."

His frustration shows. "You've had space. For a week, you've been given space."

I laugh without humor. "Newsflash, you don't get to decide how much space someone else needs. You can control a lot of things, Liam, but you can't control that."

Silence fills the space as we stare at each other, and I'm so angry I can barely catch my breath. I'm sure he is just as frustrated with me, if not more. Restlessness floods me, an urge to run. To leave, to walk, to drink—I don't give a shit, but I don't want to sit in this house. Liam runs his hands over his face, leaving them there for a moment before looking back at me.

"You said you weren't okay," he begins, and I narrow my eyes. "And all I want is for you to be okay, Sheyanne, so is doing this making it any better?"

I swallow at his honesty. My heart beats loudly in my chest, and my blood rushes, anger and sadness mixing together, more at myself than anyone else now. At this point I think it might physically manifest somehow, take up the shape of a dark cloud.

"Do you think this," I point between us, "is making it any better?"

Liam sighs. "I just wanted to see if I could help. I don't know what you want me to do."

I stand up, planting my feet firmly on the ground. "That's the thing. I didn't ask you to do anything. I don't need you to do anything." I grab a hoodie and tug it on, ruffling my hair in the process.

He stands too, somehow holding his composure, but his emotions dance in his eyes. "I didn't ask you what you needed. What do you want?"

I blink back the tears.

I *want* a lot of things. I want to not be the person I was when I was younger. I want people to believe me when I say I'm not going to run. I want my dad to be okay. I want to admit to myself how much I care about Liam and how bothered I am by the fact that he's here for a fucking job, but I can't—I won't. I want him not to leave. I want to not care that he's going to. I want to fix my friendships with Gaylee and Blake, but I don't know how.

I want to forgive myself, but I don't know how to do that either.

But instead, I say, "I don't want anything."

Liam steps forward, but I move quickly and slip through my open bedroom door. His footsteps follow me down the hall until I'm standing at the front door and pulling my coat and shoes on. I don't bother with my car keys as I head out the door.

"Sheyanne," Liam says my name again, and I ignore the chills it sends straight down my spine. I turn over my shoulder and shake my head at him before the front door swings shut behind me and begin my long, cold walk to the bar.

Keith is leaning on the bar top when I pull open the door, darkness settled in the sky behind me. He smiles when I enter, but it falls immediately after a quick glance, and he grabs a glass and starts pouring.

I stride past the other patrons and take a seat, drawing my coat off and letting my head fall into my hands. I know that drinking isn't the answer, and I don't give a shit. A glass slides across the bar in front of me, and I smell the whiskey. It's cool in my hand, and I take a big swig, meeting Keith's watching gaze as he leans back against the bar.

"Rough day?"

I down the rest and slide the glass back to him. "Rough week." He pours it full.

"Aw, and you came to see me? I'm honored," Keith teases, and it brings the smallest, saddest chuckle out of me.

"Shut up. Are you taking one with me or no?" I point to the alcohol, and he doesn't hesitate, pouring himself a single shot to my double. We clink glasses and down the drinks. Already, I feel the heat of it in my stomach and my skin, drowning out the anger, I hope.

"Wanna talk about it?"

"Nope. I do wanna keep drinking though."

Keith laughs and nods. This time, he only pours a single and slides me a water as well. "You want chips?" I can't even answer before he moves and yells to the small kitchen in the back. "Stupid question," he mumbles. They have killer homemade potato chips. I've been addicted for years, so I'm grateful.

"Thank you."

He pats my head, like a kid. "Anything for my favorite customer."

"Flattery will get you nowhere, Keith."

His lips quirk. "I think flattery has gotten me plenty of places so far."

I purse my lips in disgust. "Ew, keep all of that," I motion to him, "to yourself." He laughs again but walks away, going to check on the other customers. It's a decent crowd for the old haunt, all regulars and locals. I tap my fingers on the bar, anxious and frustrated and mad all at the same time. And guilty too.

I have nowhere to put all those emotions right now. I can't yell and don't want to anymore because I said things I shouldn't have. I don't want to be home because I can't deal with another confrontation. So instead,

I just sit in the deep, endless pool of vicious emotions that are clawing at my skin to be let out.

"Sheyanne," Keith's voice makes me look up, "please tell me your bad week has nothing to do with those two?" He nods behind him, and I don't even need to look to know who it'll be.

But I do anyway as the door swings shut behind Gaylee and Blake. I start to wonder if tonight could possibly get any worse.

Nineteen

Sheyanne

I've lost count of how many drinks I've had, but my head is dizzier than I'd like to admit. With every passing second, I swear I hear the invisible clock ticking down to the inevitable confrontation that will happen. The tension is like a tightrope that's unraveling and shouldn't be used because with too much weight, it will snap.

Keith watches with careful eyes, more cautious than I've ever seen him, probably a result of last time, and I don't blame him. I down my drink as the barstool next to mine scratches the floor. I turn to see Gaylee sitting next to me. Blake is still in the corner booth.

"Hey," she says softly, tucking her pin-straight black hair behind her ear.

She's mostly unchanged, maybe a little older around the edges like we all are. She still carries the same soft features she gets from her Japanese mother, who is a spitfire of a woman I always loved, and the stillness, the calmness of her dad. Her eyes are warm like always, and her style is the same, vintage and girly, while still somehow looking seamless. The reclaimed long-sleeve lace blouse and the old denim jeans embroidered with little pearls on the pockets and matching earrings look timeless on her.

I meet her gaze. "Hi."

Gaylee and I didn't really end on bad terms like Blake and me. We just ended. Mostly because I avoided Blake after everything went down, never apologized, and on our last interaction, we were two steps away from physically fighting. And then I left.

"We've been wanting to talk to you." She leans her elbow on the countertop, taking a sip of the drink in her own hand. Her usual whiskey sour, I'd bet money on it.

I nod, not really looking at her as Keith watches with his arms crossed, eyes lingering on Gaylee a second longer.

"Sheyanne."

Turning in my seat, I meet her eyes. Kindness swims there, like it always does. I've always admired her ability to stay calm and true to herself even in a difficult or hostile situation. Gaylee is sweet, and some might call her too soft, but she stands her ground and has always been sure of who she is. Otherwise, she wouldn't have been friends with us.

"What?" I sigh, feeling dizzy from my movement, and I take a sip of water.

"I'm sorry for that day in the square. What Blake said in the car, and then last time at the bar, and for not doing anything." She shakes her head. "It was uncalled for."

I blink the blur out of my eyes. "Yeah, just a little." I glance over to Blake who is watching like a hawk. "Did she send you over to apologize for her?"

"No, I came over because I thought you might be more willing to listen to me. Considering you two probably can't interact without attempting murder."

Our eyes meet, and she raises a perfect brow. I sigh. "It's not a good night for this, Gaylee."

"Is there ever going to be a good night for it?"

"Ever since the square, it's been one thing after another, like a dramatic coming of age movie, Gaylee. And now you want to talk? I'm sorry if I'm not interested."

"She left you a message."

I spin to look at Blake before turning back to Gaylee. "And I listened."

"She apologized." Gaylee straightens when I stay quiet. "Even after years of radio silence from you. You could at least act like you care."

I rest my head in my hands yet again because I can't seem to gather a moment of peace anywhere. Not at my house, not in my bedroom, and not even at the bar. I rub my fingers in what I hope are calming circles against my scalp and the back of my neck, but it doesn't work. It's not that I don't want to have this conversation. I do. I just don't want to do it tonight. There's been enough arguing, enough yelling, and I just need a fucking break.

"I do care, but Gaylee, I cannot do this right now." I don't look up when I say it, and of course, *of course*, it's not Gaylee who answers.

"What, still just avoiding it all?" The chill in Blake's voice is enough to start cutting the last thread of patience I have.

The alcohol I down only fuels the red-hot anger simmering underneath my skin as I turn to face Blake.

I meet her icy brown eyes. "No, Blake. I'm not." Even I hear the slight slur to my words. "I'm not in the right headspace for this right now, and I'm trying to make that clear."

Her curls are slicked back, making her features sharper, highlighting her face. "I've been trying to talk to you."

"You called me one time and left one voicemail. Sorry if I didn't take that as a sign to try to make amends."

"It's more than you've done. You were gone for four years." She tenses her jaw, and for the first time, there is something other than anger on her face. Hurt breaks through the façade she tries to maintain.

Part of me wants to toss my drink in her face like she did to me. Most of me wants to shake her and tell her that I'm sorry for everything, that I'm sorry I couldn't stay here, that I'm sorry for just walking away.

"I couldn't face you; I couldn't stay. Don't you get that?" I look between the two of them, my two former partners in crimes, my best friends.

"No, I don't get it. That's the problem." Gaylee speaks this time, gentle but frustrated.

None of us are getting anywhere in this conversation. We're just running around in circles, chasing each other for answers that we can't give right now.

"Listen, I'm not lying to you but I—I can't do this right now. It's been a bad week, and I can't deal with this, too," I mumble. "We can—"

"Come on. I'm so tired of you getting to decide when we can talk about something, when to deal with something. It's always on your terms."

Gaylee sighs, playing with the pearl on her sleeve as our voices rise.

I stand up, ignoring the dizzy spell that hits me. "No, Blake, you're mad because it's not on your terms. You're mad that I didn't accept your apology."

"Well, at least I gave you one!" Other patrons are now looking at us. I make sure to leave extra cash on the bar for Keith. "You never gave me one. You never—we never even tried to work things out. You shut us out and left. And you didn't even look back."

The hurt comes off her in waves, and it suffocates me.

I'm barely afloat on my own, and now I'm trying to fight the heavy current of her emotions.

"I was drowning here. It was more than just about you, and I didn't do it to hurt you." I'm angry, but I'm also pleading with her at the same time. The bar starts to crowd me, closing in on me, and I push past Blake and Gaylee and stride outside into the cold.

The door jingles, and I know they've followed me. I keep my eyes trained on the dark sky, stars glittering against the black. After a moment of painfully loud silence, I turn to see them both watching me. Gaylee looks apologetic, and Blake looks like a mirror of my own emotions. Every single emotion is skating the surface, and my eyes prick. The tears are closer than I'd like.

"I am asking, begging you to just let me have tonight. I cannot handle anything else tonight." The desperation in my voice is pathetic.

Blake softens a fraction of an inch, her jaw unclenching, and her eyes dropping to the ground where she kicks at the gravel. Gaylee steps toward me, and I move back, keeping the distance between us. I shake my head, and I barely realize my arms are wrapped around my torso.

"Just give me some time. I promise I'll reach out in a week or so. Please."

Before they can answer, a car—Liam's car—pulls into the small parking lot. The door opens, and Liam steps out, his face a blank canvas as he leans against the black sedan. I look back to the girls, who watch with confusion.

They meet my eyes and nod, agreeing to my desperate plead. Gaylee turns to head inside, but Blake watches me for a second longer. "I miss you, Shaw," she says and turns, heading back into the bar. I'm left in the dark, watching her go.

TWENTY

Liam

Standing there, Sheyanne's back to me, her friends walking away, I realize just how loud silence can be.

Quietly, I walk toward her. She makes no move to turn around or to move at all, even as I move closer. I step in front of her, only to see tear tracks on her cheeks, her face turned toward the ground. She steps back, but I grab onto her wrist as gently as I can.

"Sheyanne," I say, but she shakes her head, trying to pull away. After a moment, she glances up. The dim lights from the old neon sign of the bar makes her wet eyes glisten. My chest tightens at the sight, at seeing her this run down and knowing I can't do anything about it.

I try again. "Come on." She tries to step back, but she stumbles—from the crying or the alcohol, I don't know.

"I'm fine. I'll walk." She wipes at her tears.

"You're not walking home in the dark when you're drunk." My voice is firm, and it finally gets her attention. "Get in the car, Sheyanne."

"Why are you here?" she asks, ignoring my request, another few tears falling.

"What do you think?"

Sheyanne huffs in frustration and clears her throat, but even I can hear the crack when she begins to talk. "I don't know, Landon. I don't know anything. I thought I was doing better; I thought things were getting better, but they aren't. Everyone is always mad at me or disappointed in me, including myself. And I'm sorry if I can't handle you feeling that way either."

The confession, drunken or not, feels so vulnerable—like glass about to break. I step forward, moving my hand from her wrist, up her arm, and holding her there. "I'm not having this conversation when you're drunk." With my other hand, I wipe away the tears with my thumb, ignoring the pain visible in her brown eyes. "Come on."

"No. It's not your job to take care of me."

Sheyanne Shaw most certainly takes the cake for the most stubborn person I've ever met. It's practically endearing at this point. I take a deep breath before I say anything. "This isn't a job. I'm not doing this for any other reason than I was worried. I was worried about you."

Her teeth gnaw at her lip, like they always do when she's upset or anxious. It's her nervous tick, and I'm pretty sure she thinks she hides it, but she doesn't. "I can handle myself. Now let me go." She tries to pull away again, but it's a weak attempt. Even her words don't have the usual bite to them.

"Get in the car."

When she shakes her head, I just nod, and before she can stop it, I'm scooping my arms around her, one under her knees and the other supporting her back. She's given me no other choice.

"Put me down."

"I gave you the option to walk yourself, and you didn't take it."

We're only a few feet away, but in that short time, she lets her head fall on my chest despite all her protests. Her curls tickle the bottom of my chin, and they smell sweet like they always do. Like Sheyanne. She's warm in my arms despite the cool temperature, and I wish this was under a very different circumstance, wish I didn't come here to find her standing by herself crying. Wish she wasn't crying at all. I wish there was something else I could do besides just being there for her, even when she tries to act like she doesn't need it.

Carefully, I open the passenger door and set her down into the car. I stay crouched down. "Stop fighting the people who care about you, Sheyanne. No one said everything was going to be easy, but you've got to try to stop making it harder for yourself."

She puts her head back, training her eyes on the roof of the car as another tear falls. I don't say anything about how she wrings her hands together or the slight shake in them or how her lips quiver. Briefly, her eyes fall to me, and I hold the gaze before grabbing the seatbelt. My hand brushes her stomach as I pull it across her body, her eyes watching the entire time.

I won't force her to talk. I didn't get it earlier. Usually, in my life when people retreat, it's because they want someone to come find them and work it out. But Sheyanne genuinely just wanted to be alone. I brush away a few more stray tears before reaching for the water I brought just in case.

"Here." I place it in her lap and wait until her hands untwine themselves and hold the bottle. "Let's get you home."

I pull back and stand, shutting the door and moving around to the driver's side. As I circle the car, I take three quick, deep breaths. I wait till the air in the vent turns warm, taking a quick look at the girl in the passenger seat. She's pulled her legs up to her chest and rested her cheek on her knee.

I felt guilty for earlier, for crowding her; my intention was only to check on her, not force her to talk. I needed to feel like she wasn't running from me. But I realized quickly that was the wrong approach. At first, I'd gotten angry. I didn't get it, wasn't used to it. But just because I'm not used to something doesn't mean the other person is wrong. People process things differently; I should've known that or at least backed off when she asked me to before she walked out of the door.

I can't change that, but I can make sure she's okay now.

I'd be lying if I said that I didn't have doubts, more self-doubts than anything. I've been left before, been abandoned by the people who were never supposed to do such a thing. Luckily, I was caught by my grandparents, and they did everything they could to make sure those emotions didn't last, didn't stick around like poison.

Sheyanne's reaction should scare me more, but it doesn't. This is something I'll have to learn, and I like learning about Sheyanne.

But I have to acknowledge that the distance she puts between us prods at that old wound, pokes at the bruise. What if her need for space puts me on edge, and my need to talk threatens the fragile thing we do have? It makes me worry that I'm not the right person to help her, worry that I'm nothing like my grandparents and that I won't be a good enough, strong enough, support system for her. Logically, I know that it's just something we'd have to talk about, to manage, but the thought lingers whether I want it to or not. And of course, I know that at some point, she has to want to do better for herself, but I couldn't have done it alone, and I think it's ridiculous we expect people to go through hard things on their own all the time.

I guess while I learn about Sheyanne, I'll have to learn about myself in the process.

Finally, I put the car in drive, dragging my eyes away from her and not bothering with the music. It's a short drive, over in fifteen minutes, and in the drive, I picture her walking down the streets to get here. The broken gate comes into view, and I slow, pulling into my spot next to the old Bronco. Silence descends when the engine stops, and when Sheyanne doesn't move, I'm convinced she somehow feel asleep in that short time. Not that I blame her.

I'm at her door in an instant. Her eyes are closed and her lips slightly parted as she breathes with her knees still tucked into her chest. She doesn't look as sad in her sleep, though there are still tear stains on her skin. Her curls frame her face messily now, but they're still beautiful.

No matter what, she'd be beautiful.

I pick up her up, cradling her to my chest. A quiet murmur escapes her lips, but her eyes stay closed, and she curls into me, still holding onto the bottle of water. All the heat in her body sinks into mine as I head towards the house, unlocking it with the key Mr. Shaw had made for me. Nyx greets us at the door, sniffing Sheyanne's sleeping body, and I find Shane pacing in the dimly lit kitchen by his still unfinished puzzle.

He stops when he sees us. "Is she okay?"

I adjust her, her head cradled between my neck and my shoulder. "I think so. Just a little drunk. Exhausted."

Shane runs a hand over his face. "Thank you."

"It's not a problem. It's not my place, but we may have pushed too hard. It didn't help that when I got there, she was arguing with Gaylee and Blake."

"Yeah, that probably didn't help. And you care about her, Liam; I think you're allowed an opinion on the situation," Shane says matter-of-factly.

A quick rush of air escapes me as I chuckle. I glance down at Sheyanne and then back up to her brother. "This wasn't in the plan."

"Are these things ever?" He leans on the counter. "We'll figure it out. I'll talk to her in a few days again, see where she's at. I'm gonna have a drink myself if you'd like to join."

"Yeah, just give me a minute." I head down the hallway to her room and close the door behind me after Nyx trots in. "Sheyanne," I mumble by her ear, my lips just brushing her skin. "Come on; you have to get changed." When she doesn't stir, I whisper her name a few more times until she groans unhappily.

Her tired eyes blink open, the brown almost as dark as her room.

"I'm going to put you down just for a minute, okay?" She nods and lands on her feet, only stumbling once.

I find her pajamas folded on her dresser and grab them, just a long-sleeve and soft shorts but better than what she has on now. Approaching her again, I slip her jacket off, placing it on her desk chair and reach for the bottom of the crewneck. I pause and meet her eyes, all the sadness rushing back now that she's awake, but she just nods. Lifting it gently, I keep my eyes on her face the entire time, only catching glimpses of her skin as I remove the sweatshirt.

I want to see all of Sheyanne when she wants me to and not a minute sooner.

Before I even have time to look, I'm sliding the shirt over her head and helping her push her arms through. She reaches up and pulls her hair through and exhales, holding out her hands. I hand her the shorts and turn around. Moments later, she speaks. "Okay."

I drop the worn clothes in the hamper near the bathroom door and turn back to her. Sheyanne just stands there, unsure of herself in her own room. "Let's go," I say softly and nod to the bed. I pull the covers back and wait until she climbs in to bring the sheets up around her shoulders.

Nyx crawls up to her side, and she doesn't hesitate in throwing an arm over him. I step away only to grab a glass of water from the bathroom to place on her nightstand with the bottle. Then, I sit on the edge. I wait a moment, watching her closed eyes and tiny movements of her body as she breathes in and out.

"I may have been a little angry, but I wasn't—I'm not disappointed in you."

Her hand tightens on her sheet, but she turns over to face me better. "You should be. I am." Sheyanne's voice is soft in the cool darkness.

I reach up, fixing the edge of the blanket, and leave my hand near her shoulder. "Why would I be?"

She rubs her eyes before burrowing further into her pillow. "You expect too much. You expect me to be better than I am."

Sheyanne meets my eyes cautiously.

"You're drowning in your own disappointment and expectations," I say softly. "Not anyone else's. I don't expect you to be anything but who you are—which is someone I happen to like very much."

Her lips close after my words sink in. The comforter is still around her legs, so I stand and reach for it. As I draw it up, my knuckles brush against her just so, her hip, and her arm, until I drop it over her shoulders and towards her chin. I crouch down, eye level with her face on the satin pillowcase, and she just watches me.

Reaching up, I run my finger over the back of her hand that's holding the comforter. "You don't have to try to be anyone else, Sheyanne. I just wish you weren't so hard on yourself."

I brush a curl behind her ear and watch her eyes close as I do. Sheyanne exhales and seems to sink into the mattress. I stand and pull the door closed behind me. I find Shane at the dining room table and take a seat with him, exhaling as I lean back, stretching. The tension in the entire house has been high for all of us since Thanksgiving; I should've known it was a million times worse for her.

A glass slides across the table, and I mumble my thanks to Shane before taking a sip. "You okay?" I ask him.

"Regarding my sister or regarding everything else?" He huffs out a sad excuse for a laugh.

"Both."

"I'm worried about both of them. Worried that asking her to come back was a mistake. I didn't really think about what it might be like for her, didn't expect that to happen," he says, alluding to Thanksgiving. "It wasn't easy for me, but I'm sure it was worse for her. It always was with the two of them. I love them, and then I get angry at them for being so hurtful to each other. Now and then. It just sucked to see; didn't think I'd have to see it again."

The similarities between him and Sheyanne never appear when I expect, but they both avoid answering questions like it's a gameshow and a million dollars is on the line. "I get that, but Shane, what about you? Aside from being worried about them. Are you okay?" I've easily come to care for everyone in this house along with Sheyanne. Even her dad. Especially her brother, who reminds me of Wyatt. And I'm sure this is hard on him in different ways.

Shane smiles like he knows exactly what he did. "I'm all right. I'm happy I have MJ. I think it'd be very different if I didn't. I was there when he got diagnosed, so I knew this would happen. I just didn't think it'd be like that."

"Understandable. Can't say I did either." I take another sip.

"You ever have to deal with anything like this?"

"Family wise?" He nods. "Not really. An old friend in college dealt with this with his grandparents, but we weren't that close. I wasn't around it. My grandparents are healthy, so I'm lucky."

"And your parents? If you don't mind me asking, I consider us friends at this point, but if you're not comfortable—" He rambles and then inhales.

"No, it's okay. We are friends." The question doesn't bother me. It's not my favorite thing, but I was expecting it, so I don't mind. "I don't have a relationship with them. At least, not with my mom. My dad and I, well, it's a little complicated. I don't know anything about my mom. She left me with my dad right after I was born. He didn't know what to do, wasn't in a good place himself mentally and physically, so he moved back in with his parents—my grandparents. He stuck around until I was five, then he gave custody to my grandparents and went and got help. He wrote letters, and that was how we communicated; I saw him maybe twice a year."

I take another sip, thinking about how when I got older, I felt how it seems Sheyanne feels. Angry, hurt. For me, it felt as if I had no control over anything. Not my parents, not my life. None of it. The difference between me and Sheyanne is I had my grandparents. They helped me through it, and as strange as it is, I was removed from my situation. My dad didn't struggle right in front of me, and my grandparents made sure to manage every nuance of it all the best they could.

"When I got older, I got angry about Dad leaving because I didn't get it. Then, I realized I was happier with my grandparents anyway and content to spend limited time with my dad. I still make an effort to see him once a year, but it's been harder since we've gotten older. He still writes the letters though. And I'm thankful for that."

"I know you're older than us, but you're very mature. You get that, right?" Shane asks, breaking the silence that followed my quick story.

I laugh. "It took years, believe me."

Both of our glasses are empty now and the exhaustion hits when everything settles. Shane yawns. "Well, I know that my sister is not what you expected when you came here, and I know she's not easiest, per-se, but thank you. For everything."

Sheyanne isn't easy; she's not simple. But just because she's got a few more walls in place doesn't mean she doesn't deserve to be understood.

Standing, I grin, trying to lighten it just a little. "She's not so bad."

Shane lets out his own laugh, shaking his head. "No, she's not." He pulls me in for a quick hug, patting my back. "Still, thank you, Liam."

When he pulls back, I tell him to go get some rest and that I'll clean up. I don't mind the silence or the dark. I rinse and wash the glasses and wipe off the counters before shutting off the light above the stove. Quickly, I brush my teeth and wash my face and spare one last glance into Sheyanne's room.

Nyx ears perk when I lean in the doorway connecting the bathroom, his head resting on her hip as she's curled up on her side.

I think about how when I was younger, I was able to confide in my friends and in my grandparents. When I learned about my parents, I was angry sure—*very*—felt unwanted by them for a long time. But my grandparents never let me feel that way. Sheyanne wasn't able or didn't want to lean on anyone. Whatever she's struggling with will take time.

Everyone's needs are different from one another, so I'll just make sure I'm there for her in a way that fits.

One that she understands.

TWENTY-ONE

SHEYANNE

The next two days pass quietly. Everyone gives me the space I both wanted and needed.

Even with the space, I wasn't really alone.

When I woke up late after my night out, there was a note from Shane saying he took care of the stables that morning. There was a fresh cup of coffee on my nightstand and fresh water. Just like there was yesterday and today. Liam, I assume. Even now, I struggle to stop replaying the arguments and the words tossed around. So currently, I'm deep cleaning my room to avoid being out in the kitchen with the three of them. My phone has been turned off since seeing Gaylee and Blake at the bar.

Despite the things that shouldn't have been said in all those arguments, I meant what I said about needing my space.

As I go through all my old belongings, sorting them into piles of Goodwill, memory box, and just a regular old keep pile, I realize that Liam is right. Unfortunately. That out of everyone, I am the one most disappointed in myself. I'm the one who's harboring all the anger and not letting it go anywhere. Shane, at least, could admit his feelings and tell me to my face. Even Blake and Gaylee, in our argument, made points. I never apologized to Blake. For anything. I never gave us any chance to work on things, never even had the guts to admit to my wrongdoings. I need the space to work through all of *that*.

I take a sip of the water on my desk, folding yet another sweatshirt into my keep pile. There's a knock on my door, and it opens. Nyx lifts his head from my bed as Dad enters, which was not what I was expecting.

He stands at my door. "Can I come in?"

I'm taken aback because he never used to ask. I nod, and he takes a seat at the desk chair. There's a picture there of the day he brought Teddy and Rayne home. It's one of the only pictures with the two of us. We're standing between the horses, holding the lead ropes, and I have the dopiest smile on my face as I look up at my dad and at the best gift that ever existed.

"I remember that day," he says roughly. "It was a good day. I didn't even know you had this picture."

I fold my hands in my lap, leaning against the foot of my bed where my floor is littered with stuff. "I'm happy I do. Not like we had many good days after that."

Dad sets the frame down exactly where it was and leans back, assessing me. I sit there, breath held, unsure of what this conversation will turn into.

"I'm sorry, Sheyanne," he sighs, and I look down, "for Thanksgiving. Shane told me what happened. I'm sorry that those episodes will most likely happen again. And I'm sorry for everything before that."

"I know I wasn't the easiest daughter, but can I ask why?"

Why everything I did was never good enough? Why every time I tried to get his attention, it only got me the opposite? Everything Shane did as a kid, as a teenager, was practically perfect. He almost never got scolded. Whenever I was excited about something, I could always do better, I could always *be* better. As if I could get higher than straight A's. Sure, I occasionally got in trouble, I liked talking back and arguing, I asked too many questions and was never satisfied with the answers, but I never let my grades falter, took every test, passed every requirement, and still did what I was supposed to around the house. When even that wasn't enough, I gave up and started causing real trouble.

I was tired of trying to be perfect yet still being ignored.

"I wish I had a valid answer to give you, but I don't. You didn't deserve my anger or my frustration—well, maybe when you started getting arrested." He smiles—my dad smiles—at *me,* and even I can't fault him at the attempt at a joke. "But before that, it was never you. It was always me. Nothing you did warranted my behavior. I was disappointed in who I had become."

"What about Shane? You were never mad at him. Granted he was a perfect kid, but still."

"He was, yeah." He hesitates, looking around the room, but I know.

"Mom was around with him. However brief, you had help," I say for him, and he nods.

"Not that we had the easiest relationship, but she was here. He has little memory of it, but I do. A little more than a year shouldn't have made a difference. But when she left after you were born, it's like even then, you knew, and everything seemed to get harder. You cried all the time, and nothing I did worked. You were only happy around the animals and around Shane. I was angry at your mom, and I know it was wrong and I shouldn't have, but I took it out on you.

"I tried to raise you so that you would be tough, able to deal with anything so that when you learned about your mom, it wouldn't hurt you, so you couldn't be disappointed. But by then, I wasn't a great dad, which you realized. I wasn't really a dad at all. I pushed too hard, and it all just backfired on me. It probably felt like you had no parents instead of one."

I look anywhere but at my dad and his confessions. I focus on the single drop of condensation sliding down my water glass and not the hole in my chest.

He continues, "When you were old enough, you started pushing back, and we fought over everything. Dinner, table settings, how to care for the horses. I'm sure you remember. So, in turn, instead of yelling or pushing you every time, I stopped fighting back. Which meant you fought harder. I don't blame you. I'm not mad at you. I thought you were ungrateful, that you hated me without reason. I told myself I was doing right by you when I was actually doing everything wrong. And you reminded me so much of her that I didn't know how to change, and I thought that if I spoke with you other than to scold, I'd blame you for things out of your control. So, I just didn't speak at all."

For the first time, I speak. "Your silence made it all worse. I thought you were always disappointed in me. Always angry. I get the jail stuff; letting me sit in there was probably a good choice. But I mean everything else. Nothing on the stables, nothing in general was good enough. It's like you trained Shane to take over when I was the one who loved it. I wanted you to love me, and instead, you pushed me away." I meet his eyes. "I would've rather you blamed me for everything than act like I didn't exist."

"I've always loved you, Sheyanne. I'm sorry it ever felt like I didn't."

If shame was a real tangible entity, I was sure it would be sitting next to my dad.

He continues, "I assumed you'd always want more than this. I wanted you to have more than this. So, I pushed and pushed and kept you away. But this ranch, whether you can see it or not, is fueled by the ideas you used to toss out. The ones that I would ignore." He leans forward, and I meet his eyes this time. "I'm sure there is more we could talk about, dissect every single incident, but I just want you to know I'm sorry. I am sorry for not being the dad you deserved, the one that Shane got."

His voice shakes, and it's the most emotion I've ever heard from my dad in my entire life. "And I'm sorry that in the future, we will have moments like Thanksgiving when I revert into that person. And I'm sorry I only asked you to come home now, with things declining, and not when I had the chance, when I had more time."

I let silence fill the space as I drink in his words and try to absorb them. I get it; I get why my dad was the way he was. It doesn't mean I'm not still hurt by his actions but having them out in the open and acknowledged instead of tucked away in a dusty drawer takes away a lot the unknown.

Makes my pain feel real instead of something I made up.

I nod, my eyes landing on my dad's face again. I see myself there, too. In our eyes, in some of his features. "I would like to try, while I'm here. I'm not—I don't want to be—that girl anymore."

Sadness arrives in his eyes. "Sheyanne, there was, *is*, nothing wrong with that girl. Maybe a little misguided and confused, at times angry, but not by your own hand. By mine. You're just you. And I would like to get a chance to know you if you'll give it to me."

I intertwine my fingers in my lap, feeling overwhelmed by this new information overload. "I think I would like that."

Dad nods and looks away, but I see the smile on his lips, and it lightens the air around us, takes away some of tension that is usually present when we're in a room together. He stands, tucking his weathered hands into his pockets. "I'll leave you to it."

I pick up another sweatshirt, holding it on my lap. "Thank you."

"Don't thank me." He pats the doorframe as he begins to exit. "It was long overdue."

He pulls my door closed, leaving it ajar like it was before, and I lean back among my piles of clothes and take a few deep breaths. That went better than I ever expected. Maybe it's because we're all yelled out. We've been angry for years, and now, it's like we had a choice: either continue that or try and work on things while we still could.

He's right; I'm sure there is more we could talk about, but right now, I can breathe, feeling welcome in a place I thought never wanted me, that I thought I didn't want to be a part of. *You're just you.* There aren't two of me, not a past me or a current me or a future me. There is just *me*.

I slide the letter under Shane's door when I finally venture out of my room later that Sunday afternoon. It's what I used to do when we would fight. Neither of us wanted to talk, so we'd write it all down. Granted, back then, we were kids, and most of the letters were filled with us telling each other how annoying we were, but the concept is the same, and it's the thought that counts.

When I exit, I don't expect to see Christmas decorations in the living room. There isn't a tree yet, mostly because I'm assuming they keep the tradition of going to get a real one, but there are lights along the walls and tiny, handmade decorations on the hearth.

It smells like chocolate when I enter the kitchen. I find a note on the fridge addressed to me from Shane, informing me that he left a mug of cake for me to heat up, and a modicum of tension lifts off my shoulders.

I heat it up, leaning against the counter and enjoying the silence until the cake is hot enough, and I top it with whipped cream.

I pad into the sunroom and turn on the space heater and the heated blanket. Nyx curls up on the floor near the loveseat as I curl into the warmth. There are Christmas lights out here as well, and they create a calming light as early evening sets in.

The door opens, and I look over to see Liam, who takes a seat beside me on the small couch.

At his appearance, his words ring in my ear: *Which is someone I happen to like very much.* It's disgusting how much I've replayed that statement and pretty much everything else he said that night. I fiddle with the blanket I have draped over my legs, suddenly aware of how frizzy my hair is and how I'm three days past when it needed to be conditioned again. Liam doesn't seem to notice.

"Thank you for coming to get me," I begin, taking a small bite. "You didn't have to do that."

He stretches out his legs on the ottoman before looking at me. "I did. And I would do it again."

"I'm sorry for how I acted. I was drunk, and that's no excuse. I was just—"

"Shey, stop, it's okay."

My heart beats quickly at his nickname. "It's not okay."

Liam rolls his eyes. "I'm not excusing the actions. I'm letting you know I'm not mad. I pushed too hard when you made it clear what you needed. I overstepped a boundary, so stop apologizing." Amusement flickers in his eyes. "I just didn't think it would drive you to walk to a bar."

My lips quirk over my spoon. "I'm dramatic. And a little stubborn."

"I think *a little* is an understatement."

I kick him lightly under the blanket, and he chuckles. Just like that, another weight off my shoulders. "I appreciate what you tried to do now that I look back. I just couldn't see it in the moment."

"I assumed you wanted to talk even when you said you didn't. It's okay that you needed space." Liam glances at me. "Can I ask you a question?" I nod. "Can you tell me what it's like when you get inside your head?"

My heart tightens in my chest as I ring my fingers together around the mug. If anyone else had asked me, I wouldn't have even considered answering. "Sometimes, I guess it just gets loud. Too loud. It's like I don't even feel like myself because not only am I combating whatever happened, all my thoughts try to fight me, too." I look up to see him watching me, patience in his eyes. "The only way for me to make it stop has always been to retreat. And when I can't, when people want answers or want to talk, that's not how it feels. It feels like I have to fight them, too. I know that's not true, that they just want me to be all right, but I can barely process my own feelings, so how can I be expected to explain them out loud?"

I exhale. "Then, I end up feeling guilty for turning all my anger on them, for not being able to just say I need space. And it all just feels deafening." I feel vulnerable and exposed, but it doesn't feel so terrible with him.

Liam's eyes soften. "Okay. That makes sense."

"It does?"

"I mean, I'll never understand it like you do, but now I understand that's how it feels for you. Like I said, you set a boundary when I asked you that day, and I ignored it. But now I know what it's like from your perspective. That helps me make sense of it all."

Liam caught my vulnerability and didn't laugh at it. The relief I feel is almost overwhelming.

"Can I be honest for a moment?" he asks, and I nod. "The reason I crowded you was because I didn't want that space between us. I didn't want you to push me away. I know now that's not what you intended; it's just hard for me to process. If something happens in the future, I don't need you to talk it out right away, but—" he hesitates, and I swallow, understanding what he's having trouble saying.

"I can try," I say, hoping to remove some of the pressure he feels. He's done so much for me; the least I can do is try. "For you, I'll do my best, okay?" I watch as he exhales, some of the tension evaporating from his shoulders. There are some things left for another day, but it's a start.

Chocolate melts on my tongue as I find my next words, trying to find an easy shift in the conversation. "You know you're a fixer?"

He furrows his brows, placing his hands in the pocket of his hoodie and leaning his head on the back of the couch, looking at me. "Meaning?"

"Meaning you see a problem, and you try to fix it."

His lips twitch. "And?"

I hesitate because I don't want to be harsh or say the wrong thing. Universe knows I've done plenty of that. "Not all problems have easy solutions. You can't fix everything and everyone. You can't fix me, Liam."

He strikes me with a sure and steady gaze. My leg is still outstretched and brushing against his thigh. The tension pulls tight like a guitar string, and I wait to see how he'll play it. My grip tightens around the mug, willing the warmth to surround me.

"Maybe I am a fixer, sure. But you're not broken, Sheyanne. I'm not trying to put you back together or save you. You don't need saving. I just want you to know that you aren't alone."

Warmth pools in my stomach and spreads till I feel my cheeks heat up under his eyes and the certainty in his tone. As if he believes that with every bone in his body. As I study him, I realize that initial picture I painted of him is completely gone; I don't even remember what it looked like. Instead, there is only one of a man who is kind and supportive, and quiet and gentle and funny, and one who only wants the best for the people he cares about. It's almost funny how wrong I was about him when he first stepped out of his car. But I'm thankful that he did, and I'm thankful that he's here, no matter how brief.

I'm thankful that right now, with him, I don't feel alone.

I'm kind of speechless though, and I'm not sure there's anything good enough to follow that statement up with. "Wanna bite?" I ask, meeting his eyes, and he starts to smile, nodding. Our fingers brush as I hand him the still warm mug.

"Have enough whipped cream on there?"

"No."

He chuckles, and I lean my head against the side of the couch, still looking at him.

He hands me back the mug as his hand snakes under the blanket to land on my knee. I revel in the small touch and how the tension has dissolved. I still have amends to make and conversations to have, but right now, I'm just happy to be sitting here with Liam. He leans his head back, his eyes fluttering closed. His thumb moves in circles on my knee, each rotation sending a flurry of mini shockwaves over my skin. I try not to think how I want to know what his hands feel like in other places, so I can memorize how they feel there, too.

"Can I ask you a question?"

Liam blinks his eyes open, squeezing my leg in reply.

"How are you so good at this?"

"At what?"

"Knowing what to say and what to do all the time."

He squeezes my knee again and continues his circles. I'm distracted by it until he speaks. "I struggled when I was younger, with my parents." I blink, hoping he'll go on. "When my dad gave custody to my grandparents when I was little, I didn't know any better. I was upset—often. Between our limited contact and learning my mom never once reached out, it was a lot to handle. My grandparents never once left me to struggle on my own. When I wanted space, I got it, but they always allowed me to talk about it and did the best they could. Even Wyatt, the same age, never failed to be good at getting me out of a mood."

Liam pauses, tapping his feet together on the ottoman. After a moment, he turns to look at me with his brown eyes again. "I still struggle sometimes. After that, I turned into a bit of control freak and still am most days. It's not that I'm good at this, Sheyanne. But I never knew what it was like to not have a support system. I don't know what kind of system you had when you were younger. I wasn't around, but I'm around now. So why wouldn't I be there for you?"

Liam's words are liquid gold to me at this point, better than anything else on Earth, better than chocolate, better than most of my books, better than any song, any movie, and anything else I've ever experienced in my life.

I didn't know how much I needed them, needed words in general. But I guess after getting ignored for so long, words carry just as much weight as actions do when they're coming from the right person.

Since I'm pretty sure I'll start crying if I speak, I just grab his hand under the blanket and squeeze it. I'm hoping it's enough that he understands. Liam's full lips curve, and I know he does when he squeezes back. We go on like that, in the silence that I don't find uncomfortable at all—the exact opposite. We share the heat from the blanket and pass the chocolate cake back and forth until it's gone.

Later, with the sun lower in the sky, a car on the gravel interrupts the silence, and minutes after, I hear the front door swing open. Liam's hand uncurls from mine, and he pats my knee before moving to stand up.

"They went to get food, so I'm going to see if they need anything. You okay?" he asks, and I nod, meaning it for the first time in days. He opens the door and heads inside. Even out here, I can smell the familiar scent of grease filling the air.

Through the window, I watch as Shane carries two boxes of pizza and a bag, Dad trailing inside after him. Liam falls in beside him, pulling out plates and setting them on the counter. He and Shane seem to be joking about something, both with smiles on their faces, and Dad takes a seat in the armchair in front of the TV. He turns and looks through the window at me, giving me a soft look, and I return a small smile.

Shane hands a plate to my dad as he searches for a movie. Liam takes a seat on the couch, throwing me a glance. When the door opens again, I hear the familiar sounds of a movie playing as Shane takes up space in the doorway. He has a plate in his hands with two slices of pepperoni and mushroom pizza and French fries piled high.

He steps forward and hands it to me with a napkin. "Here, if you're hungry." I take the outstretched plate and set it on my lap.

"Thank you," I say softly.

He taps the doorway. "We put on a movie if you want to join. You don't have to, but . . ." he trails off.

"Okay." I pop a fry in my mouth.

"Okay." My brother gives me a small smile before shutting the door behind him and returning inside.

He settles in the chair opposite of Dad. After a few bites of pizza and sitting out here watching them, I realize that they have given me space. Respected it. It didn't come easily, but they adjusted, realized that sometimes it's too much for me and that this process is more of a marathon than a sprint.

Right now, I don't want to distance myself; I don't want to be alone. I don't have to talk, but I can at least be near them. I shut off the space heater and the blanket, and with my plate in hand, I head inside. Liam's eyes flicker to me as I shut the door, and I swear he fights a smirk, turning quickly back to the TV.

I collapse next to him on the couch, leaving a healthy space between us as I throw a regular blanket over my legs. The bottom half of my legs brush against Liam's thigh under the softness of the blanket, but my eyes stay on the screen. Shane and Dad give me one glance filled with warmth but don't say anything, just let me make my decision to be in here without giving it some deeper meaning. Liam's hand snakes under the blanket and gently wraps around my ankle, and I take a bite of pizza, ignoring the warmth that singes my skin at the touch.

For the first time in a long time, I feel welcome.

TWENTY-TWO

SHEYANNE

I stare at the note on my door for a second like it's in another language before peeling it off and pushing inside my bedroom.

Meet me outside in fifteen – Liam

It doesn't say anything other than that—no instructions, no indication of what we might be doing, and that causes my blood to rush quickly past my ears. Because *we* are doing something. Instead of panicking, I take a deep breath, pull my curls out of the messy bun I'd put it in for my shower, and start searching for something to wear.

It's afternoon, right around three. The sun has looked deceptively warm all day when I know it's much colder. I force myself to take another deep breath, ignoring the nerves budding all over my body and pull on a pair of thick leggings, a long sleeve turtleneck, and an old black and maroon crewneck that I used to love. Quickly, I pull the loose curls by my face back into a half up half down mess, with the rest of my curls down my back. I'm just about to pull on my boots when there's a knock on my door, and Shane pushes it open after I respond.

"Got your letter." He leans against the doorframe.

I nod, unsure of myself. "Uh, okay."

Shane blinks. "You couldn't have just told me that?" I lean on my desk.

"It was easier to write it. No room for mistakes that way." I told him everything I could manage. Why I left, why I didn't say goodbye, and how sorry I was. And why I was so affected by Thanksgiving and said the things I did.

"I'm sorry I yelled. And I'm sorry I was angry."

"I understand."

"Just because you understand why I did it doesn't mean I handled that well. And I don't—I don't mean to look at you in any way that makes you feel lesser, Sheyanne. And I'm sorry. I really don't think you're going to leave again, at least not like you did, and I shouldn't have said that. I was just upset and scared." He studies the ground, his hands in his pockets, before looking back up. "I just missed my sister, for a long time."

I meet his gaze. "I didn't think about my actions then, Shane. Didn't really think you cared, which isn't your problem so don't say anything. And I'm sorry for leaving you." He shrugs now. "I missed you, too, even though you annoy me."

Standing, I move towards my brother and reach up on my tiptoes and pat his fluffy curls before wrapping my arms around him, hugging him like I did a few weeks ago.

"Love you, Shaney," I mutter before I can stop myself.

He groans and pushes me away. "You just had to ruin the moment, didn't you?"

I smile. "What else am I good for?"

"For plenty. I'm sure you'll learn something new someday," he jokes, and I flick him on the forehead. He turns to leave and gives me a passing glance, a serious, heartfelt one. "Have fun today. You deserve it."

My heart swells, and he doesn't give me any time to respond as I stand there and watch him go. I give him the space and take the offering, mentally wrapping it up and tucking it away so that I can pull on it when I need it. I exit, pulling my door halfway shut and leave Nyx passed out on my bed. Dad is nowhere to be seen when I pass through the house, but I notice another car in the driveway as I step onto the porch, throwing my winter coat over my arm.

I'm distracted by all of that when my eyes land on Liam standing near his black car, phone in hand. I fight back the smile, saving that for later, and start walking towards him. He's in black jeans and a thick knit sweater with a winter coat over top, simple but effective in stopping my heart for a second or two.

Liam looks up just as I get closer, turning those unwavering brown eyes on me.

I'm about to say hi when I hear voices getting closer from the barn. Furrowing my brows, I turn to see Chief Banner, his wife Clara, and my dad. They stop a few feet away, and Dad sighs when he picks up on the tension. Chief Banner gives me a once over, but it's much less intense than the meeting at his own home, like we've come to an unspoken agreement to coexist, but Clara's eyes are watching me like a hawk. Not unkind, just guarded.

"Sheyanne." Chief Banner dips his head in a nod towards me.

Liam takes the smallest step closer to my side as he watches the interaction. Even though it shouldn't, the movement to be closer to me makes me breathe a bit easier.

"Hi, Mrs. Banner," I say, meeting her gaze despite the nerves.

My dad clears his throat, adjusting his coat. "They came to see their horse, Lu, just to check in on him, and I went over how you've been caring for them. Just routine stuff."

I swallow. "Everything okay? If there's anything you need adjusted for Lu, just let me know, and I'll make the changes."

Surprise flickers in both Banners' eyes before it's replaced with gratitude. The Chief places his hand on the small of his wife's back, making brief eye contact with her, and she's the one who speaks. "Lu seems great, Sheyanne. You're doing brilliant, not that we've come to expect anything else from here."

"Okay, good. That's great."

Clara steps forward with a careful smile. "You look good, Sheyanne. You seem . . . good."

Every eye is on me as I look back at the woman whose every kindness I once threw dirt on. "Thank you, Mrs. Banner; I feel good. I'm happy to be here."

Her eyes soften, and a silent message is conveyed between us, or at least I hope it is. I hope she can read the sorry in my eyes, the apology I should've given years ago. She gives me the smallest nod, and I exhale in relief.

"I'm glad to hear it." Clara leans into her husband, and they both shake Dad's hand. "I'll send some goods over for Christmas."

"You don't have to do that, really," I say.

She pats my shoulder as they move to leave. "I want to, Sheyanne. It was good to see you."

Dad turns, his attention on Liam and me now, and if I hadn't been watching so closely, I wouldn't have noticed the slight narrowing of his dark eyes. Liam is still just a step away, and neither of us says anything. Even though Dad and I may be better than we were, we are not close enough that I wouldn't stand up for this—whatever it is. I care about repairing our relationship in the time we have left, but he hasn't really earned the place to give me advice about certain aspects of my life. So, I meet his gaze, surprised to find only kindness there. He just gives me a nod and turns away to head inside. After watching him go, I exhale and face Liam.

His face is stoic, but humor dances in his eyes. "That was fun."

"I think you and I have different ideas of fun," I mutter with a small shake of my head.

Liam raises a brow, a smirk growing on his lips. "You show me yours, and I'll show you mine."

Despite the instant pool of heat that forms at the words, like a match, I step forward, tipping my head up. "If that was your idea of fun, Liam, you won't like mine very much." I step around him, brushing against his body. "Where are we going?"

He blinks a few times, eyes trailing over every part of me, slowly, studiously, before returning to my own, setting me on fire. The car unlocks. "Get in."

"How the tables have turned. Now you're the bossy one." I cross my arms, cocking my head playfully, taking in the man who has made this place infinitely easier to be in. "I'm not sure if I like it."

Liam walks casually around to the driver's side and looks at me from over the car. "I'm not sure you have a choice."

I climb in, enjoying the thrill of every sentence he speaks. Probably more than I should. He starts the car without a word, adjusting the heat setting quickly and turning on music.

"So, where are we going?" I ask again, adjusting so I can see him more clearly as he pulls out of the driveway.

"The Grand Canyon."

I furrow my brows. "Today? Right now?"

"No; tomorrow at six A.M." He shoots me a look before turning onto the street. "This is my way of forcing you to give me a tour. And we'll get there just in time for sunset."

I get comfortable knowing we've got at least an hour drive ahead of us. "Fine, but can we stop somewhere first? I'm hungry, and you'll like this place."

"Just tell me where to go." His face glows under the afternoon sunlight streaming through the window. I pull my legs up onto the seat as I point him in the direction of my old favorite smoothie spot, Wicked AZ.

Familiar pine trees shadow the road, the sun peeking out of the sky that is full of thick, gray clouds. Looks like snow again in the next few days. Somehow, the green trees make the dead grass look not so bad, adding to the strange beauty this place maintains, even in the winter.

"It's right up here on the left." I point to a little building in the center of a parking lot with one single sign that blinks neon blue and purple.

"The hut?" He looks over at me, blinking.

"Oh, knock it off. You're being judgey." I'm facing him almost completely in my seat at this point. With a cautious look, he turns into the lot. "Have I led you wrong yet? Just trust me."

"Whatever you say, boss."

"Shut up and drive." His lips twitch, but he follows the sign of the drive thru. When we pull up closer, the menu appears with an array of smoothies and coffee drinks listed. I look over at Liam. "What do you want?"

"What do you get?"

"Usually strawberry banana or peanut butter banana. If not those two, anything with strawberries or raspberries."

His eyes light up with amusement as he drives forward, one car away from the ordering screen. "You choose."

"What?"

Liam shrugs, leaning back and running a hand forward over his textured hair, which has grown a bit again and could probably go for another cut soon. "You choose for me. I'm sure I'll like it." He pins me with a look that should be innocent but sets my skin on fire, like little zaps of lightening, hitting the same pool of heat growing in my stomach.

I swallow as we pull up, unable to look away from his beautiful, steady eyes. I unbuckle and lean over as he rolls down the window. I'm careful to avoid touching him at first, but I feel him in the air, and it's like those days where you can smell the rain, but it just hasn't fallen yet, and you're waiting for the first drop. I know he's there, and I know what I want, but I want to enjoy it, drown in the smooth cologne he wears, drown in the feeling his mere presence brings me.

Stopping just in front of him, I block the heat pouring from the vents, which only makes the proximity a million times worse—in an intoxicating way. When the voice comes through the speaker, I order one strawberry banana and one raspberry smoothie. As I fall back to my seat, I lightly drag my hand over his thigh, pushing myself off the window and landing back where I started.

When I try to take my hand back, he stops me, driving forward as the next car receives their order, and wraps his long fingers around my palm. He doesn't intertwine them, just holds it loosely in his. Heat pulses between them.

"You're a tease." The rough tone of his voice sends shivers down my spine, sparks shooting between our hands when he squeezes.

"Couldn't miss the opportunity, could I?"

Liam squeezes my hand again and continues to hold it as we pull up to the window. I smile to myself and only pull away to grab my wallet. By the time I have cash and a tip, Liam is already handing them a credit card.

I purse my lips but put my money away as he watches with amused eyes. "Thank you."

He reaches over and squeezes the spot above my knee. "You're welcome."

We're interrupted when we're handed two smoothies and straws. Liam grabs them, placing them in the cupholders between us. He plugs directions into his GPS as he pulls out of the drive thru, and I unwrap the straws. Leaning back in my seat, I rub my palms against my pants, unsure of what to do with them now that he isn't holding one.

Who'd of thought I would ever want to hold someone's hand so fucking badly?

He drives out of the small town and onto the highway. "Which one is mine?"

I shrug, grasping my hands together. "Figured you could try both. We can share."

He takes a sip of the raspberry first, his tongue flicking out to gather the fallen drop as I sip the strawberry, and then we switch. They're just smoothies, but they've always made the best smoothies, and I watch as unfiltered surprise comes over his face.

He meets my eyes. "It's good."

"It's a smoothie, not poison."

Liam chuckles, and I look down, hiding the smile I feel growing on my own face.

I'm about to ask him something when his hand reaches over and plucks my hand from where it rests on my thigh. This time, he intertwines his hand with mine, his fingers threading through my own. The pads of his fingertips brush the sensitive skin on top of my hand, pushing us palm to palm.

He looks at me briefly before back to the road. "This okay?"

This, all of this, makes me nervous. The light touches, the handholding, the careful looks. It's all much more intimidating than I expected.

Physical intimacy is one thing. It's there, and it's useful, but it's never something I needed. It filled the space, filled an occasionally shallow ache for the time being. No one I'd ever slept with or been with made me have a second thought about something *more*. But this, this need I have for Liam, is not just physical. It never has been. It is unending, and I'm not sure I'll ever get enough of it.

The simple act of him holding my hand, his thumb brushing over the thin skin of my knuckles, is enough to chip away at the walls I've had up for years and release this unfulfilled need and wanting in waves that wash over me in a continuous pattern.

"Yes," I murmur. "Yes, it's okay."

He squeezes again, and a thrill shoots through me from the tips of my toes to the top of my head. It melts me from the inside out. I glance up, meeting his eyes in the rearview mirror, feeling my heartbeat pick up all over again when he smiles.

On the way to the canyon, I changed our course, setting us to Horseshoe bend, the best spot in my opinion for sunset in this part of Arizona. Liam didn't put up a fight to my decision, especially not after I promised to take him again another day, and we pull into the parking lot just as the sky starts to show signs of a deepening gold, excitement blooming when I see it.

Liam parks the car, taking a sip of the smoothie that is mostly gone.

"Ready?" I ask.

He nods, and we step out of the car. I reach up and adjust my turtleneck, pulling the sleeves of my crewneck down. Liam comes around the car with a blanket in one hand, and he reaches out with the other, intertwining our fingers again without a second thought.

I've decided handholding, or at least holding Liam's hand, has brought more life to me than anything else. I step closer to him as I lead him in the direction of the curve of the bend to give us the best view. My shoulder brushes his upper arm, his warmth seeping through all the layers as our hands rest between our bodies.

The red dirt is damp from previous rain, thank God, because otherwise it sticks to you like a second skin. We head towards the spot I know of, a cliff kind of, but it's flat on the top so we can watch the sun descend in the sky. When we reach it, the entire bend is visible, the curve around the rock formation in the center and the water that runs through it.

I move to sit, but Liam stays standing, his hand tightening on mine as his eyes roam over the canyon. "This is beautiful."

My eyes move away from him and focus on the canyon, which I haven't seen in years. All the grooves and the indents, the shades of red and brown, the formidable formation in the middle. It's peaceful, even with a few other people around taking in the view. Birds fly overhead, blending into the sky as they become tiny specks on the horizon. The clouds are turning colors now, a breeze blowing past us, but even this high up, it doesn't feel too bad.

"I forgot how much I love it here," I mumble, leaning into his shoulder and resting my head on it.

"It suits you." When he says it, I feel his lips brush the top of my head, and I smile against his arm.

"Are you smiling?"

I hide it, forcing my lips into a frown, but they fight to go back. "Maybe."

I lean back so I can look at him, the sun hitting his dark skin, making it glow warmly in the light. Liam rolls his eyes at my answer, and before I know it, let's go of my hand and the blanket to twist me into his arms, his front to my back, and squeezes while he cages me in, my heart careening in my chest.

He leans down and presses his lips to my cheek. "Always when I can't see it. That's not fair, and you know it."

I shrug, but the corner of my lips turn up anyway, and he chuckles against my cheek. Liam lets go of me and grabs the blanket, wrapping it around my shoulders before pulling us down to sit, me in the cocoon of his legs. I lean back into him and rest my head on the bent knee that traps me in. He wraps his arms around me, and I reach for his left hand, the one with the simple gold pinky ring.

"Do you always wear this?" I ask, looking over my shoulder at him before turning back. I spin it around and thumb my finger over the smooth gold.

"Yeah, when I was thirteen, my dad sent it in one of his letters. I've worn it ever since." He reaches around and slides it off, showing me the inside. "It's got our last name on the inside."

"That's really sweet," I murmur, and he gently drops it in my hand, allowing me to run my finger over the engraving on the inside. After I'm done, I slide it back on his pinky. He flexes his hand as I do and then holds mine briefly before he leans back.

Above, the sky is painted orange, hues of deep red starting to bloom and stain the clouds. One of his hands twirls the curls that rest on my back, and he tugs lightly on the ends.

"Can I ask you something?" he says. He leans forward, his breath hitting the skin of my neck, and I inhale, nodding. "Do you still hate it here?"

I focus on the sky in front of me as his hand continues to play with my hair, heat pooling in my blood and running under my skin, thinking about the question.

"No. I'm not sure if I ever hated Flagstaff itself, but more what it reminded me of."

Liam wraps his other arm around me, his hand resting on my forearm, tapping his thumb to an invisible beat. "What do you mean?"

I sigh, swallowing the fear that rises at the question. The uncomfortableness of addressing all those things. I lean back into him, grounding myself.

"For a long time, and still sometimes, it's just been a reminder of every bad or stupid thing I did. Of how I made people feel, of how I felt. It reminded me that if I ever came back that I would have to deal with all those things. Like I have. I'm not sure I ever hated Flagstaff. I hated that it held all the consequences I'd have to deal with one day."

Silence stretches between us as my words hang in the air. It's not everything, not like I bared my soul to him, but saying it aloud is weird.

"I don't know if my opinion matters," he starts lowly, and I don't bother interrupting to tell him that it does. Probably more than he realizes. "As an outsider, aside from the things you've dealt with since you've been back, I think you flourish here. That sounds stupid considering I didn't know you before, but the person I've gotten to know, I can't imagine anywhere else."

I hold my breath.

"You just seem peaceful here." He shrugs, unaware that his words have reached a part of me that used to dream about this place. About what it was in my head, how it used to make me feel as a child.

I grab the arm that's in front of me, wrapping my fingers around it. "Thank you."

His fingers brush against my neck, underneath my hair. "You're welcome. Do you think you'll ever stay?"

"I don't know. It's still a lot for me to carry, and it's not a decision I would rush. I'll have to see how things go with Dad and the stables," I respond, and he nods, brushing his nose against my cheek.

"You know yourself best. You'll do what you know is right. Just make sure you do it for you," he says quietly, his lips brushing my skin.

I shiver as the sun dips lower, but I don't know if it's from the cold or from Liam touching me. The sky is mostly purple now, dipping into the midnight blue it will become, only hints of red lingering. He continues tapping my arm, and I let everything else fall away. Thoughts of the future, of what is going to happen, and of what has happened.

I used to know what I wanted constantly. Knew I wanted to leave and get away. But recently, I don't know what I want from the future or what I want to do when it arrives. Recently, I have only been sure of one thing.

I know I want Liam in whatever capacity I can have him.

He's not this overwhelmingly bright force, and I don't mean that in the sense that he isn't brilliant or warm or beautiful. That's just not what comes to mind when I first think of him. Instead, he's steady and sure of himself, like an anchor—the kind that holds you in place, even when you feel lost.

There are people that remind me of the sun. The first thing you look at when you enter a room, super bright and all encompassing. And some people need the sun, crave the constant rays and a bigger picture.

Liam reminds me of the person I would look at if I was giving a big speech on stage and got overwhelmed with nerves. I wouldn't look at the sun because it would blind me, make me stumble and fall. Looking at Liam would make me feel like I had an anchor to hold on to. Someone to remind me that shit happens, but I'm still standing, and he'd be there to make sure of it.

Liam isn't my sun. Liam is my safe place.

Darkness has settled in now, and my realization about Liam, even though I'm not going to say it to him, has built this endless yearning in me.

For him. It's growing like a river in a big storm, digging a well deeper and deeper inside of me, and only Liam can stop it. These small touches over the past few weeks have only tortured me. I don't want just the brush of his fingers or a whisper of a kiss on my cheek or my temple. I want more.

His voice surprises me when it cuts through the silence. "You ready? I was thinking we can get food on the way back."

I nod, and he pulls us up. The blanket stays draped over my shoulders as we walk back to the car. There is only one other car in the parking lot, but I don't see anyone around. I assume they're waiting to see the stars come out.

Liam walks around to the passenger side and looks at me, his hand on the door. "Why are you so quiet?"

I smile this time, letting it happen, and his eyes light up in the dark. "No reason."

His eyes linger on my lips. "You're smiling like that, and you expect me to believe you?"

My smile grows, and I lean against the hood. "Well, don't be rude." Liam blinks. "It's nothing important." Wrong. It's very important because it's Liam.

"If it's nothing important, then tell me."

"Can you just come here?"

His lips curl just briefly as he trails his eyes around my face. After a pause, he takes his hand off the door handle and steps towards me.

I rock up on my tiptoes and quickly place my hands on his neck, my thumbs on his jaw, and pull his lips down to mine. I don't know if I've taken him by surprise or what, but he barely reacts when I press my lips to his. It's just a peck, just a hint of what I want, of the pure *desire* burning under my skin, before I pull back and drop my hands.

"That was it," I breathe out.

Liam stands so still for a moment that I'm scared he stopped breathing. I'm about to reach over and push him or punch him or *something* when he pushes closer, backing me against the car and cupping my cheeks with both his hands.

There is only a beat before his lips are on mine, and any tension that existed in my body evaporates in an instant. One hand leaves my cheek and cups the back of my neck, his fingers burying themselves in my curls and tugging my head back. It sends an illicit thrill over my skin as heat pools in a split second. His lips move against mine with a surety I've never felt in my entire life.

Assuring me that this fragile, new thing growing between us exists.

It washes over me, and I reach forward, tugging his body closer to mine until he's flush against me, not an inch of space between us.

"Sheyanne," he mutters roughly against my lips, and my entire body flushes as he pushes me back against the car roughly. Liam doesn't say anything else, just nips and tugs at my lips with his teeth until his tongue slips through, and any coldness left fades away at the wave of heat flickering over every single cell of my body.

It's a push and pull between the two of us. He has control physically, his hand on my neck and in my hair, but I know how to play. I pull back slightly, tugging his lip with my teeth, feeling a soft groan escape from his body as I slip a hand beneath the layers and splay it on his side, feeling the warmth of his skin. His other hand that had stayed on my cheek is now buried into the strands of hair around my ear, his fingertips brushing the sensitive spot beneath, back and forth, making me short circuit.

Then holding back, like he did that night in my car, I kiss everywhere but his mouth. The side of his lips, his check, until his hand forces my chin up to look at him. Liam's breathless like I am, and I feel him like a brand against my thigh, making me forget how to speak for a moment as my eyes watch his lips before meeting his own.

The look he gives me reminds me of the look he gave me when I was cutting his hair, like he could figure me out all with a single look. I want to let him. "Don't look at me like that."

His eyes darken, and I move the fingers that are still on his side up and down on skin. "I'll look at you however I want."

My heart skips a beat at his tone, and I force myself to breathe, but I don't even want to breathe. I just want him to keep kissing me, to keep touching me, to look at me however the hell he wants. I lean up to bring our lips closer together, but he pulls back, leaving the space between us. Even apart, I remember the shape of them, the lingering taste of raspberries, how he's invaded my entire life, and how I am beautifully helpless to it.

"Liam."

"Sheyanne." He leans closer, his lips barely touching mine with a smile. "Say please."

I shiver when he says my name, making it sound forbidden, and I feel it all the way to my toes. Liam waits, keeping me on edge as I narrow my eyes at his request. When I try to push closer without doing it, he tugs my hair, keeping us apart. Liam continues his torture of not kissing me by kissing everywhere else, trailing his lips along my jaw, on the underside of my neck, and when they land on the sensitive spot under my ear my breath hitches, my eyes fluttering closed when he nips at the spot with his teeth. He whispers my name again until the sound is branded on my skin, and it's like he's desperate to kiss me as badly as I want him to, except he's determined to make me ask for it.

"Please."

He smiles against my neck before he finally finds my lips again. This time, there is no push and pull; I relinquish whatever control I did have—whatever control I was fighting for—and gift wrap it in a box and give it to Liam. Slanting his head, he leads the kiss, and I follow, letting his lips press and tug and move however he wants them to.

One hand stays buried in my hair at my neck, making sure I stay where he wants me, and he settles his fingers further into my curls. I never used to like anyone touching my hair, but even now, Liam does it gently, careful to avoid knotting the strands. His fingers brush my scalp, and a shiver runs down my back as he tugs my head back and tips my chin towards him. His other hand drags along my side, sending a burst of directed heat in each spot until it stops at my hip, and he bypasses the layers I have on, his palm landing on my skin.

His thumb brushes back and forth under the band of my leggings, a slow burn growing with every touch until I'm practically on fire. When we both need air, his lips leave my mouth and land on the spot near my ear again, and I can't keep in the soft moan that escapes me when his tongue touches it. His hand dips lower, brushing the spot where my hip creases, and I'm concerned I might actually fall to the ground if he goes any further. Even so, I don't want to stop.

Liam continues placing kisses on my neck, hard and soft, driving me up and up until my head spins, and his fucking hand tortures the sensitive skin of my leg and hip. I reach up, gently gripping the back of his neck, and bring his lips back to mine, thumbing the thin chain on his neck as I do. The feel of him, the taste of his lips, the fresh, intoxicating smell of him—it drowns me; every one of my senses are directed to him.

The tips of his fingers brush the band of lace on my skin, and I groan again, gripping onto his jacket, and just when I think he'll finally push past that barrier, the sound of tires in the dark break it, and my eyes fly open as we pull apart.

It's dark except for the headlights of that lone car pulling out of the parking lot and rolling past us. Liam lets out a deep sigh, his forehead resting on mine at the interruption. A little smile comes over my face despite how heavily I'm breathing and how hot my cheeks feel. Liam untangles his hand from my hair and reaches up, pulling the blanket between me and the car back around my shoulders. We're still close; if I leaned up, I could kiss him again and act like nothing interrupted us.

"Good thing we'll never see them again," I joke as I try to catch my breath, noticing I still have a hold on his jacket.

He pulls back, a sly smile on his lips as he looks at me. Even in the dark, I'm sure he can see how thoroughly flushed my cheeks are, and his eyes are swirling under the stars that have appeared above our heads. He shakes his head.

"Why are you shaking your head?"

Liam leans forward, kissing me again, softer this time, but when he pulls back, he takes all my air with him. "It wouldn't have mattered."

I'm confused. "What wouldn't have mattered?"

Liam grins because he knows what he's doing to me. "If we ever saw them again."

"Why?"

"Nothing else matters when you're around. I only see you."

Liam's eyes never leave mine, and the words settle around me, like the stars settled into the sky after sunset, making it come alive in a whole different way. The way he kisses me, the way he touches me, reminds me of the sunset, the different shades and levels of heat from the final rays that all come together to paint a different picture every single time.

Then his words, the way he talks to me and makes me *feel*, his words are the endless midnight sky decorated with stars and constellations. It's fuller and calmer, but it surrounds me even more. The way he says things, the meaning he puts behind them, makes me feel like he plucked a star from the sky and put it in my hands, like my own personal night sky, and I know without a doubt, I've never felt like this before and won't ever again if it's not with Liam.

I don't say anything. I just rock up my tiptoes and kiss him again. Gently this time like I'm trying to tell him something through my kisses.

That even with golden hour and sunsets and the star filled sky above us, I only ever see him, too.

TWENTY-THREE

Sheyanne

The diner is bustling as I pull into the parking lot. Cars fill most of the spots, and steam escapes the building into the cold December air. As I find my own spot, I eye Blake's car a few spots down and take a deep breath, leaning my head back.

Maybe I should've taken Liam or Shane's offer to drive me here and forced them to wait in the parking lot. Instead, I wanted to be a grown up and do this on my own. I wipe my sweaty palms on my thighs and ignore the heavy beating of my heart as I enter the diner.

Instinctively, I look to my left at our old corner booth we always used to sit at, and to no surprise, that's exactly where I find Gaylee and Blake. Three waters and three large silver milkshake tumblers sit on the table. Hesitant, I pause at the end of the table before sliding in on my own side, leaving some space between us.

Blake meets my eyes first. "I ordered your usual—or your old usual." A black and white shake with Oreos on top. "If that's still your favorite."

"It is. Thank you."

Gaylee's eyes flicker between μs, and she sighs, taking it upon herself to push each milkshake to their rightful owners. I point to G. "Strawberry vanilla still?" She smiles, and I look to Blake. "Coffee with chocolate chip?"

Her lips turn up, just slightly. "Yup."

I nod again, hiding my own smile. "Good to know some things haven't changed."

Gaylee opens her mouth to say something when a server walks up. I glance up to see Mrs. Dune, well into her late sixties or early seventies now. She has the same old smirk on her face, surprise dancing in her eyes as she approaches.

She wipes her hands on her apron and places them on her hips. "Never thought I'd see you three in this booth together again."

"Evening, Mrs. Dune," we all chime in sync. Her eyebrows quirk, and the three of us share an amused glance.

"You girls want the old favorites?" We nod in response this time, and she smiles, tapping the table twice. "Sounds good." She turns to walk away before throwing a look over her shoulder, her eyes alight. "No trouble tonight, understood?"

Each of us smile this time and call back our classic response that became a ritual for us. "No promises."

Silence falls again briefly, each of us sipping our milkshakes before Blake's steely, light brown eyes land on mine. "I meant what I said before you left that night."

I focus on an old groove in the table. The night itself got a little jagged in my memory, but I remember that—her saying that she missed me. "So, right on into it then?" I comment, avoiding it for a moment longer. I sigh. "I miss you, too. I missed—miss—both of you."

Gaylee takes a big sip and shoots me a knowing look.

I know the easiest thing is to just apologize, to start a long line and open the communication, but the words are stuck on my tongue, so I settle for the next best thing: a short explanation. Even though I did—do—miss them, I don't have to explain everything I've ever done to be worthy of their forgiveness or redemption. Yes, I've made mistakes, but so have they; so does everyone. And it's not the explanation or the words that should prove me or anyone worthy, but the actions behind them, the willingness to move forward.

"I shouldn't have left the way I did. I shouldn't have just disappeared without saying anything; I get that now. But I mean this when I say it wasn't about you, at least not all of it. Things with Dad weren't good and hadn't been, and I just had to go." I pause and finally say the words I know Blake and Gaylee are waiting for. "But I am sorry for not saying sorry, for not reaching out again, for not even trying."

"I'm sorry, too," Blake blurts out, her eyes warming. "For a lot of things."

"Probably too many to count," Gaylee chimes in, but the joke is clear in her voice, and Blake and I share a look before laughing.

"I mean it. I'm sorry for our fights before you left. I'm sorry for not considering how things were between you and your dad."

I shrug, taking a sip. "I think we can both admit we did things we aren't proud of then, Blake. I don't need an apology for that."

She shrugs, her lips tugging into a quick grin before she takes a sip of the milkshake. "Yeah, fair. We were all kind of assholes." We glance to Gaylee and both smile, speaking in sync, "Except G."

Gaylee smiles innocently and sips her milkshake. I'm surprised at how well this is going, at how light I feel having this awkward yet somehow not awkward conversation. Blake meets my eyes again. "I'm serious though. I'm sorry for what I said in town square and the bar and everything in between. I didn't know how else to react."

The apology floats over my skin, and I let the genuine statement settle in as I lightly kick her leg under the table. "You always did want to throw a drink on someone at least once. Can't say I'm surprised it ended up being me." Blake grins widely, tucking her curls hair behind her ear.

It seems almost like old times again. If we ever get back there, hopefully there's less trouble involved.

Gaylee speaks this time. "I'm sorry, too. For not trying to reach out or have a conversation."

I shake my head. "I wouldn't have answered or responded if you did. It's okay, G."

She nods and tucks a piece of black hair behind her ear just as Mrs. Dune comes back with three hot plates of food. The steam rises off the plates between us, and she smiles before placing down ketchup and other condiments and walking away.

Gaylee glances between us. "Does this mean were friends again now?"

I can't help the laugh that escapes me, and despite the nerves I feel at opening myself up again, even to my two former best friends, I answer honestly. "I'd like that."

Blake nods. "Me, too."

It seems easy, too easy almost, but it's as if what we all really wanted dug itself out from the dirt of those intense, angry encounters and made itself known. All we wanted was to find our way back to each other.

"So, how is everything?" I ask, taking a bite of a chicken tender.

Blake leans back, setting her burger down. "Good for the most part. Writing is going well, and I've been playing a few gigs here and there. No luck with anything bigger than that."

She was always an amazing songwriter and an even better singer, so I'm happy to know that hasn't changed. But we both know that if she wants to pursue it seriously, she's gonna have to leave this small town.

"Same with me. I've been making a few pieces here and there for a few of the boutiques in town, and they sell well. It's just a matter of if I want to go back to school for it or keep doing my own thing." Gaylee shrugs, smiling as if she doesn't have incredible talent when it comes to fashion.

She has her own unique style, but the pieces she used to draw up and stitch together were amazing, always stitched with care, whether that was delicate lace tops, glittering jewelry, or her beautifully embroidered sweatshirts. Even Blake's guitar strap is embroidered, thanks to Gaylee. Realistically, she should probably leave, too. She's got a real shot, and I want to see her flourish.

"Well, let me know about your next gig. I'd like to come," I say to Blake and then point to Gaylee. "And you'll have to take me shopping."

They both smile, Gaylee's dimples popping out and the old wrinkle Blake used to get on her nose reappearing. Things are different, but things are also the same. It's a weird paradox I thought I would hate, but it gives me a sense of comfort, of familiarity.

Blake takes a sip, and then her eyes widen, landing on me. "Okay, well enough about us; what about you? Who was that guy that picked you up? What is going on?"

I lean back, sitting cross-legged on the booth seat. "That's Liam. He's here to help my dad."

"What's wrong with your dad?"

I sigh, realizing I was wrong for assuming they knew when no one would've told them besides me. "He has Alzheimer's. That's why I came back."

"I'm sorry, Sheyanne. I'm so sorry," Gaylee says, meeting my eyes.

Shrugging, I take another bite. "It's okay. I mean, it's not. But he and Shane asked me to come home to help around the stables until he figured it out. That's why Liam is here. I don't know exactly what he is, either an accountant or financial adviser, but he's good, and he's from Vegas, and Dad hired him to come help with money and rebranding. At least until the end of January, I think."

"Well, if you need anything, you or Shane just let us know, okay?" Blake says, and I nod, thankful for the offer. "Not to switch the subject."

"Please switch it; I don't like to talk about Dad that much anyway. We're still working on things."

Blake nods and smiles, popping a French fry in her mouth. "If he's here to help your dad, why did he come to pick you up?"

"Not to mention he looked good while doing it," Gaylee adds with a harmless smile.

For a moment, I play stupid, eating another tender, until Blake kicks me under the table. "I don't know what's going on exactly. We didn't get along at first—"

"You not get along with someone? Shocking," Gaylee chimes in.

"Anyways," I try not to smile, "I don't know what it is. It just happened."

I leave it at that for two reasons. One, it's the truth. We haven't talked about it, not that I've felt pressured, and I'm just taking it a day at time. Two, I like keeping it to myself. Keeping Liam to myself. I feel like if I open my mouth and talk about it, it'll become something bigger and less private. And I'm selfish. I want to keep it to close, between us. Not because I'm ashamed of it or scared; I just like that it's this new, small thing that mostly exists between the two of us.

Shane knows; I know that because he can't help but shoot me a knowing wink or a smirk every time he sees us interact, and by association, MJ knows, but it doesn't bother me. And Dad, well, I think he does, too, but he never says anything, which I'm grateful for.

Blake and Gaylee have soft smiles on their faces, and I realize they probably still know me better than anyone. They know exactly what I'm doing by giving them bare minimum details.

"Cool."

"Yeah, I think it's wonderful, actually."

The three of us laugh and fall into an easy conversation. Small updates about both of their lives aside from music and fashion. Not to my surprise, Gaylee and Keith are hooking up on and off. She always had a crush on him growing up, so I kind of love it. Blake tells me about the music shop she works at, both as a sales associate and a teacher, giving lessons to anyone who signs up. The rest of her time is spent fixing up her Mustang like she used to in high school right before she got her license. We sit in the diner for an hour or two until it's dark out, drinking another milkshake and smiling at Mrs. Dune whenever she comes and chats with us.

It's easy falling back into this old routine that we always did on Friday nights before going out and getting into something stupid. It hits me how much I missed it, missed them, missed having friends. People who know me, and people I know that can share jokes and laughs and talk about stupid shit. I missed so much the past years, running away from this place and these people. We walk out of the diner side by side, hesitating for a second before pulling each other into one big hug. A pressure I didn't even recognize was there lifts from my chest, making room for this—for forgiveness, friendship.

"Don't forget to text me the details of your next gig, okay?" I say walking towards my car.

Blake smiles, pulling her coat tight. "'Course. We should get drinks soon, do something fun."

Gaylee rocks on her toes, her cheeks pink from the cold. "Yes, please. A girl's night. It's been a long time."

"I'd like that," I call back, unlocking my car with a beep. "Okay, get home safe. I'll see you later."

They both wave and climb into the old Mustang we all used to drive around in. Blake was so proud and is still proud of that car. I miss those days, too.

I smile as I hop into my own car, thrilled with how today went. Music floats through the speakers, and the heat blasts as I rub my hands together before pulling out of the old parking lot. As great as that went, I can't wait to get back home. MJ and Shane were doing some puzzles and baking when I left, and Liam and I planned on stealing some of the goodies and watching a movie.

The drive home passes quickly, and soon enough, the gravel of the familiar driveway crunches under the tires. Christmas lights line the driveway and are wound up the porch pillars and the roof, twinkling in the darkness. Christmas is only two weeks away, and we're supposed to go cut down a tree tomorrow or Sunday. I haven't had a real Christmas in years, probably since I was a kid. For the first time in years, being back here, with my family, I'm excited about what this Christmas might bring.

When I put the car in park, I see Liam sitting on the porch rocking chair, wrapped in his coat, and confusion floods me.

I walk up to the porch slowly, and his eyes land on me. "Hey, why are you out here? It's freezing." I reach for the front door, but he stands and pulls me towards him. Dread hits me like a brick. "What's wrong, Liam?"

"Not a good time." He pulls me back towards the rocking chair and sits down, forcing me to sit on the edge of his leg.

"Just tell me; what's going on?"

Before he can answer, I hear a shout from inside. It's Dad. Though I can't make out the words, the anger, the frustration, in his voice is clear, and so is Shane's calm response. I move to stand, to go inside anyway because Shane has dealt with this on his own enough. I'm frustrated, so fucking frustrated. Today was going well, and now, it's going to shit.

"Get off me, Liam. I'm going inside." I attempt to pull out of his grip, but his arm wraps around my waist and holds me tightly, the other coming to land on the top of my knees to keep me seated.

"No. Shane said to keep you out here."

Both angry and sad, I meet his gaze, and his face is calm, too calm, throwing me off. "I don't care what Shane said. Please let me go. You can't make decisions for me."

He forces me to look at him, turning my chin with his other hand, and his eyes flicker with something that makes me listen. "I don't want to control you, Sheyanne, but I can't see you walk inside right now and get hurt. You may not care about yourself enough to avoid it, but I do."

I'm taken aback by the words, by how they calm the emotions running wild under my skin. Liam spreads his fingers out over my thigh, wrapping around it.

"You had a good day. I can tell, and I'm not letting this ruin it. So, please, just sit."

He reaches to the side table between the two chairs and grabs his glass of water, handing it to me.

"Just let it pass," he says, his fingertips brushing mine as he reaches over again for a blanket folded up on the other rocking chair.

I wrap my hands around the glass, not feeling the cold as much anymore and barely at all when he drapes the thick blanket over our legs. Before, I would've kept fighting, would've kept picking and eventually won and walked inside. Part of me still wants to, wants to not let Liam keep me distracted or take care of me or *care* about me.

But a larger part of me wants to let it happen. So, I do.

I sigh and relax into his touch, and he exhales when I do. We share the water, passing it back and forth, ignoring the occasional shout that comes from the house, even though it picks away at me like an axe at ice.

Turning toward him, I see him watching me with his deep brown eyes, and all my emotions swell. I'm filled with a deep sadness at the idea that my dad is declining faster than I thought, right after we start working on having a relationship again, and a deep gratitude that Liam exists as a part of my life.

"Hey," Liam says, pulling my gaze back to him. "Stop thinking so hard. You are going to be okay." His fingers make small circles on the top of my knee. "You are okay."

I want to tell him thank you. For many things. For being here, for knowing when I probably shouldn't rush into something. But I'm scared if I open my mouth, I'm either going to cry or ask him how much time he's got left here or ask him to stay. None of which are things I want to do. At least, not right now.

So instead, I just grip the glass in my hands and lean forward, pressing my lips to his softly in the cold. It's soft and warm and doesn't turn into anything else but what it is. A silent thank you, a warm, steady comfort that grounds me just a little bit. His hand tightens on my leg, and my heartrate picks up in my chest as I pull back.

Somehow, everything is falling apart, and everything is coming together.

I don't know how to deal with any of it. But I know I at least have Blake and Gaylee back. I have Shane and MJ.

And for right now, I have Liam.

TWENTY-FOUR

SHEYANNE

It's not exactly warm as Liam and I sit on the porch. Even wrapped in the blanket, I have to stop myself from burrowing into his chest. I still haven't moved from his lap, and he hasn't said anything, so I don't plan on it.

I like the feel of his hand where it rests on my upper thigh, and every time he moves, sparks shoot up my spine, and I have to remind myself to breathe. The voices and occasional shouts have lessened but still happen inside the house. I've pushed them to the background, drowned them out. Nyx sits outside with us at the edge of the stairs. He nudged the door until we let him out, and now his breath sends little white clouds into the cold.

"Do you—" I start to say when the front door swings open aggressively.

"Dad, stop." Shane's voice floats into the air as my dad steps onto the porch. I inhale as my hands tighten on the glass in my hands, and the air sits in my chest like a heavy weight.

"There you are." Dad doesn't sound like Dad, at least not the one I've come to know. He sounds like the one from before, from when I was younger. "Always running away, getting into some damn trouble. That was the third call this month from Banner."

I can't pinpoint the memory he's stuck in, because there were multiple times when Banner called my dad more than once or twice or however many times in a month. But I can feel the small little cracks in my façade, little fissures, beginning to tear open. Liam's arm tightens around me, and I refuse to look at him, to see whatever pity might be floating in his brown eyes. Instead, I train my eyes on the glass in my hand and the old wooden deck.

But Dad's cold voice demands I look at him, and when I do, his eyes are blank. "This has to stop. I will not keep bailing you out and making excuses for you. I don't have any excuses left, Sheyanne." His eyes flicker to Liam and confusion floods them, his face dropping, until they land back on me. I can almost see the internal battle he's having. So, I keep my mouth shut and turn my eyes down.

"Dad, stop it. You don't know what's going on." Shane steps up and grabs him gently, trying to pull him back. His face contorts again in confusion.

"Don't talk to me like I'm stupid, son." He glances at me again, and his eyes harden. "You need to get your shit together. All you do is disappointment me, and I'm done. I'm done watching you throw your entire life away. I'm done fixing your problems when you don't care about anyone but yourself. You're just too much. It's all too much."

"Shane," Liam speaks for the first time, a deep baritone in his voice. "Enough."

My skin burns with embarrassment that licks up my arms and my legs like a flame when Shane meets my gaze. The sharp burn of tears pricks behind my eyes, and I lean my head back, staring at the old porch ceiling, willing the tears not to fall.

"Dad, inside. Now," Shane demands and all but pushes Dad inside. "Sheyanne," he starts, but I shake my head, internally begging him not to say anything. He hesitates but nods once before heading inside. Nyx pads behind him after giving my hand a lick.

It's this moment that breaks me. Every emotion from today, the high I felt earlier after Blake and Gaylee, after forging a path to fix our broken friendship to the low of being scolded by a father who remembers me some days and forgets me on others. Wetness pools in my eyes, and I am helpless to do anything to stop it.

"Hey," Liam whispers softly. He attempts to tug my face towards his, but I fight it. I don't want him to look at me like this. "Sheyanne, you know it's not true. He didn't mean that."

I shake my head. "I know, I know." My voice breaks on a quiet sob in my throat.

Despite knowing that, the words ring in my head. So often, my dad had to talk to Banner to get me out of shit. How selfish I was, for *years*. It was all about me. My problems with Dad, my stupid decisions to get attention, *my* everything. All about me.

I hate it. I hate that's who my dad remembers when he has an episode. A selfish girl.

"Except, it is true. He's right."

Liam turns my head, his fingers gripping my chin as a few slow tears roll down my cheeks. "Look at me Sheyanne. None of it's true." His eyes roam over my face, and I'm scared to open my mouth in case I start crying harder. He exhales. "What do you need?"

The tears just keep on creeping out, stinging my eyes and staining my skin. I blink, trying to look away from him, but he holds me there. "I don't know. I don't want to go inside. I can't." I wipe the tears with the back of my hand, but it does nothing. "Just distract me. Please."

Liam nods, his brown eyes radiating warmth, and places both hands on my hips and lifts me off his leg, leaving them there as he stands. I grab the blanket to keep it from falling off my legs, neither of us speaking as he pulls his keys out of his back pocket.

"Come on," he says lowly, his breath hitting my neck. He leads me from behind, walking in step with me and holding both of my hands as he guides me towards his car. He opens the back door. "Get in."

I don't fight him and climb in the backseat. The car starts, and music starts playing as he climbs in the back with me. I press my palms against my eyes and begin to curl my knees up, but Liam doesn't let me. He grabs my hand and pulls me towards him, kicking one leg up onto the seat and the other on the floor of the car, pulling my back against his chest.

He leans down, and I feel his breath on my neck. Despite the overwhelming emotions, goosebumps spread all over my skin. Liam places a soft kiss on my skin, and I lean back, wanting to be impossibly closer to him despite the trouble I'm having catching my breath.

One hand is on my thigh, circling slowly. "You're okay. I promise."

For a while, he just lets me cry. I pull my knees up to my chest as best I can and rest my forehead on them while his hands rest on my skin, one on my side, moving in tiny, rhythmic circles, and the other on my back. I have no idea how long I cry; I just know the entire time, Liam whispers his words over and over again as my chest burns. Telling me that I'm okay or that I'll be okay. When my eyes practically run dry, puffy and red I'm sure, I sit up and notice the tightness in my chest has lessened, so I force myself to take a few deep breaths.

Liam exhales behind me, his lips brushing my cheek. "What can I do?"

I pause, focusing on everything he's already doing—already done. And I feel him everywhere, the rise and fall of his chest that I lean on, the hands on my body and his body heat surrounding me so fully. The sheer weight of him. Feeling him on my skin grounds me, makes me focus on something other than everything else. I'm not even sure I need the blankets anymore.

At this point, I don't know if I need anything but Liam.

I turn, facing him, his legs on either side of me. My eyes roam over his face, the watchful eyes, and the steady feel of his hands still on me. The tears have stopped. I can still feel the tracks they left on my skin, but at least I'm not actively crying. Liam reaches up and traces a line down my cheek.

"I don't like seeing you cry. I wish you never had to again." He looks up at me, pushing my hair behind my ear.

"It's not your fault."

His lips tilt. "I know that. I hope I never make you cry, but if I ever do, I swear I'll spend however long you need making up for it. Hours, days, weeks, any amount of time you need is mine to give."

My heart breaks open, but in a good way. "Promise?"

"Promise."

It shouldn't surprise me when that causes more tears to fall. He pulls me into him, and I let my head fall onto his chest, unable to stop the tears or the way my chest heaves. I bring my arms up and press my palms against my eyes, hoping to stop the flow, but the anxiety has a tight grip on me, like a sickness that won't let go. When I breathe, it grabs the air away, and when I try to talk, it takes my words and turns them into tears. I don't know how to make it stop, so I don't.

Liam holds me like it doesn't matter how long I cry, like it makes no difference to him. Like he'd sit here for as long as I needed with no qualms about it. I've never had this, never had someone so willing to just be there for me when I'm messy and falling apart. I've also never let myself fall apart like this in front of anyone else. It's a type of vulnerability I never thought I'd experience.

"I'm sorry," I mumble into his chest when I catch my breath for a second.

He exhales beneath me. "What are you apologizing for?"

I pause, pulling in air and breathing in him. His sweatshirt is a bit damp from all my tears, and I push up, using the sleeve to wipe at my eyes. "For crying all over you."

Liam squeezes my sides. "You should be. I asked for you to laugh more, and instead, you cry all over me? How dare you," he says softly. I roll my eyes, but another tear falls when I find only empathy in his own. Not pity, not annoyance, just a softness I wasn't expecting. "I don't care what you do, Sheyanne. Cry for another hour if you want, two if it helps. It doesn't bother me. It never will."

I will the tears to stay in my eyes this time, but barely. The words piece together a part of me slowly, like a stitch.

"Now, what do you want to do? We can stay in the car, but it's gonna get cold, and you're shaking." He runs his hands up and down my arms twice before I notice the shivers racking my body.

"You're from Vegas. You should be the one that's cold," I bite out, and he smiles. "I'm just not sure I can go inside yet."

Liam cups my cheeks and wipes his thumb under my eyes. "What about the sunroom?"

With a still slightly shaky hand, I check the time. It's much later than it was when I first arrived. I look past Liam and toward the house, which is dark.

"I can check to see if they're asleep, if that helps," Liam offers, and I bring my eyes back to him. Without a word, he nods and gently sets me off him. "I'll be right back."

When he goes, I take a few deep breaths and notice he's right. It's already cold in the car, the chill seeping in even though the heat blows through the vents. I sniff, hoping I'm all cried out for now, and take in as much air as I can. Liam returns quickly and shuts off the car before opening the back door.

"All clear; come on." He holds out a hand, and I grab it, walking side by side with him towards the house, heading straight for the sunroom.

He takes a seat on the roomy love seat and takes me with him. The heated blanket is already turned on, and even with the crappy insulation, it's already infinitely warmer in here. Liam makes no hesitation in drawing me over him. There is plenty of room for both of us on the couch, so I feel guilty sitting on top of him again, his legs stretched out under me. When I finally still, he slides his hands under the blankets to land on my lower back, pressing me closer when I try to give him space.

"You can't be comfortable, Liam."

"Says who?" We're so close, I feel the breath from his words on my skin. His lips brush my cheek. "I'm perfectly fine." A hand slides over my hip and down to my thigh, forcing it down until I'm fully straddling him. My already hot cheeks warm even more. "See? Perfect."

Liam rests his head on a pillow near the arm of the couch, and I stop fighting how comfortable I am. I curl into the space between his shoulder and his neck, breathing him in. He reaches over, adjusting the blanket. Though I'm not sure why, the shivers continue to wrack my body despite the warmth. With slow but reassuring touches, he rubs his palms over my back and my hips, brushing them down my calves and back up. They roam up to my waist, slipping under the blanket and my sweatshirt until I feel his skin on mine. The shivers begin to slow, but he continues drawing circles up and down my spine and along my neck. The feel and the heat from his palms ground me, bring me back.

"I've got you, Shey, I promise. Whatever you need from me, I'm right here." The quiet words brush past my ears, and more tears trickle out. It's so goddamn annoying. Between his body and mine, I snake my arms up to press my palms to my eyes again to staunch the tears. "Is there anything else I can do?"

I shake my head against his chest. "No," I sniff. "You're perfect, Liam."

His fingers find the curls resting down my back, and with a gentle hand, he tugs on the ends, one by one. It's such a small motion, but I feel it in my scalp, and it feels so nice, I focus all my attention on that. Blinking my eyes clear, I notice the paper next to his computer, his crossword puzzle. Reaching over, I grab it.

"You didn't finish?"

"Just didn't get around to it; why? Wanna help me?" He yawns, and I take in how beautiful he looks, even tired, even in the dark.

"I probably won't be much use."

Liam doesn't say anything, just grabs a pencil and adjusts me in his hold, so I'm sitting up a bit more. "You write; I'll read," he instructs. Behind me, his fingers find my curls. "Eight letter word for a shade of purple."

I blink and his lips twitch. "Lavender." I say, and when he nods, I write it in.

"Word meaning Spanish palace or fortress?"

My brows furrow. "There is no way you know—"

"Alcazar." He's got a smile on his lips when I look at him.

Despite my puffy eyes and tear-stained cheeks, I smile. "Smart-ass."

We go back and forth like that, me turning the paper around so he can read the questions and then using his chest to write on it. Some are easy, like the Egyptian word for king, or names of the Greek gods—those are the ones I get—but some are harder, like the longest river in France or more weird terms which are all the ones Liam gets. As we go, his hands tugging and separating my curls, my anxiety cools, no longer at the forefront of my thoughts. Instead, it is replaced by exhaustion. By my tenth yawn, most of the puzzle is filled in, and with Liam playing with my hair and holding me carefully, I was able to breathe again, able to not fall into that pit where anxiety waited to strike.

"Tired?" he asks, gently taking the paper and pencil out of my hand and setting it down.

I nod, studying him, realizing how thankful I am to have him here, more so than I could ever explain. It's partly because he makes me forget my anxiety, but it's also partly because he makes me feel everything else. Everything good. I don't know if it's a culmination of everything from the day or how delicately he treated me, but vulnerable words lay on my tongue, and I don't want to keep them from him.

Like always, he notices. "What's on your mind?" He brushes my cheek with his thumb, running it over my lips, waiting for me to speak.

"I don't want to be selfish with you, and I know you have your own life, but I don't want you to leave." I look away, scared to meet his eyes, my heart beating in my chest at the admittance.

Liam taps my chin, forcing my gaze upwards. "I'm not leaving yet. And when the time comes, Sheyanne, we'll figure it out. I'm not going anywhere. At least, not without you."

I know I shouldn't ask, but I do. Promises can hurt in the end because life is full of surprises, but I can't help it. "Promise?"

He holds up a pinky, and I wrap mine with his. "Promise."

My heart swells, knowing that I'm not alone in all these feelings. I reach up and cup his face, feeling the slight stubble under my fingertips since he hasn't shaved in a few days, and kiss him softly, pressing all my feelings for him into a single kiss. His arms wrap around me and tighten, holding me like he never wants to let me go.

And I don't want him to.

When all I can do is breathe, he doesn't expect anything else. When all I can do is kiss him instead of finding the words to tell him something, he accepts that, too. When all I can do is cry, he just wipes the tears. He's my safe place to land. He just lets me be and lets me exist when that's all I can bring myself to do.

I am only who he's always seen me as and no one else.

Liam kisses me back for a moment before leaning into the couch and settling us there again. He pulls the blanket back up and over us, keeping us wrapped in the moment that belongs to us. I curl back into the space between his shoulder and his neck, breathing him in. In slow, soothing motions, Liam draws circles on the back of my neck. I didn't realize just how tired I was from it all until that moment, struggling to keep my eyes open in the dark and realizing I don't have to. Not with Liam here.

The last thing I remember before falling asleep is the soft press of Liam's lips on my cheek.

And the last thing I remember thinking is, I don't want to belong anywhere where Liam isn't.

Twenty-Five

Sheyanne

The coffee shop's heat surrounds Shane and I as we sit at one of the small tables inside, tucked into the corner. MJ is working the counter, although currently, she's playing on her phone since we're her only customers.

The smell of mocha fills my senses, and I rest against the wall where I'm sitting. There are five pamphlets laid out in front of us. I break off a piece of my chocolate chip muffin as my eyes coast over them. Shane runs a hand over his curls, recently shaped up on the sides but still growing out on top like usual. We just got back from Phoenix after talking to the doctor. When we left, we were handed informational pamphlets about care facilities since that's the track we seem to be on. We knew the disease would progress, but it's … different seeing it happen right in front of us. They told us it would be better to decide now so that when the time came, it wouldn't be such a shock.

"So, what are you thinking?" I ask.

He pushes two pamphlets towards me, one located in Phoenix, two hours away and another in Tuscan. "These are my top picks. I've heard nothing but good things about these."

"How much?"

Shane sighs. "Not cheap; none of them are. We'll need to talk to Liam and Dad, see if Dad has said anything to him about putting aside some money. When he was diagnosed, we'd guessed this might happen, but I have no idea if he remembers that conversation."

He's been forgetting small things recently. There hasn't been a huge fall out since a few days ago when it happened on the porch, but he forgets where his limp came from, forgets things we told him a few days ago, and he's fatigued all the time. Dad's best in the morning, so usually he works with Liam while he can. Some days, he's all right all day; some days, he isn't.

MJ appears, her bouncy curls pulled back in the cutest ponytail, and she sets down the two drinks on the table. "Here you guys go," she says, before bending down and placing a kiss on Shane's forehead.

I take a sip of the mocha, a small smiling gracing my lips at them. Since there's no one else in here on this rainy day, she stays by us, leaning on Shane's chair. I hold up the muffin. "Wanna piece?

"You're my favorite," MJ grins, and Shane shoots her a look as I laugh, breaking her off some. "You guys okay?" She motions to the booklets in front of us.

I look them over, the information, the taglines, the promises of good care. "I think we will be."

Eventually, at least.

"I vote Tuscan," Shane says, leaning into MJ's touch on his arm. "It's closer, easier to visit."

"There were none here?" I ask again, just to clarify.

Shane flips through them. "Here. This one. It's small and harder to get in, but we could try. I think we should talk to Liam and look at the cost."

"Sounds good to me." I lean back, taking a long sip and relaxing into my seat. A slow smile spreads across MJ's face.

"So, how is Liam?"

My stupid heart flutters at the mention of his name. "He's good."

"What is going on exactly?"

"Are you playing protective brother or happy-for-you brother?" I cock my head.

"Both. I just need to know if I *should* be playing happy-for-you brother."

"Well, you were playing matchmaker before, so can you make up your mind?" I rest my chin in my hands innocently, and he kicks my ankle. "Ow, you're such a fuck—"

"Please, back to the point," MJ interrupts with an expectant gaze, tugging on Shane's ear until he grimaces. When he shoots her a look, she just blinks.

"We haven't talked about anything explicitly, but I'm happy with what it is for now. I think he is, too."

MJ nods. "He is. I can tell." We both look at her. "What? I have a sixth sense." She taps her temple with her nail, and I smile.

"I'm happy for you. As long as you're good, I don't care. Just make sure you talk about things, okay? Figure out what you want next after all this and what he wants. I just want the best for you, Sheyanne."

I gently kick his leg under the table this time, clearing my throat to avoid the emotions building in my chest. "Oh, shut up. Don't be all soft on me now."

He leans forward and flicks my forehead. "You're an ass."

"And you're a jerk."

MJ watches with amused eyes. "You two are something else."

The sound of my phone vibrating breaks the moment, and I look to see a text from Blake. It's about her next gig in Tuscan in about a week, the last one before Christmas, which is just two weeks away. She's extended the invite to Shane and Liam as well, and I respond instantly that we'll be there.

"You guys want to go to one of Blake's gigs? It's next week."

MJ grins. "Yeah, absolutely. Babe?"

Shane shakes his head playfully as he sits back, resigned to letting MJ call the shots. "If you're going, doesn't that include me?"

I look pointedly at MJ. "See? Jerk."

She laughs, a warm chuckle. "I'll be at the counter if you two need anything."

Shane watches her walk away before turning back to me. "I'm serious."

"I know that, Shane. And I meant it. I am . . . happy. It's just unexpected, okay? It's just a lot for me to wrap my head around."

"That someone cares about you?"

Alrighty, then.

I blink. "I guess."

"Lots of people care about you. My jerky-self included," he jokes, and I roll my eyes. "You shouldn't be surprised, is all I'm saying."

"It's not just that. I have to learn how to do it, too, Shane. It's different, and it's strange, and I don't know if I trust myself to not mess it up yet. I'm trying though, okay?" It's then I realize I'm talking to my *brother.* Disgusting. "And you can never hold this conversation over my head because if you do, I will ruin your life."

He blows out a quick huff of air and sighs, but I know he thinks it's funny. I throw a piece of muffin at him just to be sure he understands me. "I get it; Jesus." He tries to kick me again, but I avoid it and stick my tongue out at him. "You're lucky I love you because you are a shithead."

I just grin. I'm extremely grateful for my brother, even though I'll probably never say it.

We pile the pamphlets in order of which ones we prefer. Shane decides that if Dad gives indication of remembering, we'll discuss it with him, and if not, we'll make the executive decision when the time comes. Each of us have two more coffees before we leave, and I make sure to grab two pastries, one for Dad and one for Liam, before we head out. MJ joins us as the shift switches over.

The air is cold, and Christmas lights and decorations are strewn about the town square. Stores have garland and twinkle lights, some white and some blinking in different colors. A tree standing in the square has been decorated with ornaments made by local artists or from the elementary schools. The decorations shine against the gray sky on the way home. Houses and random parks are decorated, lights sparkling on almost every roof or strung around the trees in the front yards. Even though it's barely five, the sun is beginning to lower as we walk into the house.

I head straight to my room to get changed, only to find Liam sitting at my desk. He spins, holding polaroids in his hand. They're of me, I realize, from my senior year in high school. We had all skipped one day to have an impromptu photoshoot with Gaylee's camera. It was fall in the picture, the mountains not quite snowcapped behind us, and I had on a black tank with thin straps and an oversized gray linen shirt. I remember that day. We went to the diner and got breakfast. Mrs. Dune didn't say a thing and just gave us extra waffles to go. That day was worth every bit of trouble we got into, which actually wasn't that much.

I didn't even realize I still had those photos, hadn't seen them when I had looked. Keeping my door open only a smidge, I sit on the desk next to Liam, our legs brushing. The small touch zaps heat into my body, and I remember what it was like laying on top of him, being wrapped up in him. Despite how that night had begun, I can only remember the good.

I clear my throat. "You snooping?"

"Couldn't help myself." He waves the photos around, but holds one in his right hand, his eyes roaming over it and then back to me. "I'm keeping this."

"It's yours. Even though I'm not smiling in it?"

He stands up, pocketing the single polaroid, and steps closer to me. My lips quirk, my stoic façade starting to fall away. He reaches up and traces my lips with his thumb. "Either way. Just nice to have a piece of you."

"I'm not going anywhere."

Liam rolls his eyes. "I know that. You don't give yourself away easily, Sheyanne. I'm going to take as many pieces of you as I can, however I can."

My breath catches in my throat, my heart swelling, and I attempt to keep my composure at his intoxicating words, almost letting it slip that he doesn't have to take them because I'm willing to give them up if he asks me to.

Then, he shrugs. "And you're just as beautiful when you're not smiling."

I wrinkle my nose, feigning disgust, while inside, I'm turning to mush. "Gross."

"True." He leans closer, his lips a breath away from mine. "Just accept the compliment, Sheyanne." He pecks my cheek instead and leans back again.

My skin heats immediately, spreading from my toes to my head. A half smile forms on his face. I reach in my small bag and pull out his chocolate chip scone. "Here, got you this."

"Thank you. See how easy those words are?"

"I'll kick you out." I try to push him back with my hand.

"No, you won't," he responds with a smile. "But your dad told me to send you his way when you got back."

I nod and take my hand back. I haven't really spoken to Dad since the episode. "Okay. Where is he?"

"In the barn." I hop down, but Liam grabs my hand before I can leave. "You all right?"

I avoid his eyes at first, then meet them. "Yeah, I'll be fine. Thank you." He doesn't let go, instead pulls me into his chest. My body tenses before I relax into his touch and let it soothe the nerves rumbling through my body. I rest my forehead on his chest, feeling the movement as he breathes. "Thank you," I whisper, repeating myself.

His hand cups the back of my head, his fingers tugging the ends of my curls before letting go. "Of course. I'm going to go help Shane and MJ with dinner."

I nod, and we exit my room together. He strides to the kitchen as I head to the front door and back outside. As I walk through the cold air, I can still feel Liam on my skin. The same way snow sticks to the ground or the rays of sun stick to your skin in the summer, he lingers. And I realize that letting someone comfort me isn't as hard as I once thought.

At least, when it's Liam, it's not.

He doesn't give me a chance to avoid it—as if he's more in tune, more aware of what I need in the moment than I am. Whether that's a single hug, a distraction, a simple touch. He makes everything seem so simple.

Straightforward and no bullshit.

So different from myself and the way I used to talk down to myself when I was upset, telling myself it was stupid or wasn't worth my anger or frustration. Years of telling myself not to cry, not to feel, to just push it down because that was all I was ever told to do.

But Liam, he takes all that shit away and pulls every emotion out whether I want to feel them or not. Then he's there, cradling them and handling the ups and downs like it's easier than breathing. Each time he does, I feel the weight being lifted off my shoulders. Which is why I walk with my back straight and head held high as I enter the barn.

The familiar smell of hay and horses that I experience every morning envelops me. I'm surprised to see Rayne cross tied in the center of the stalls and my dad with a brush in his hands. Teddy pokes his head out of his stall, flicking his ear as I approach.

Dad looks up, eyes landing on me. "Hey."

I pat Rayne on the nose softly as I stop. "Hey, you wanted to see me?"

He runs the brush over Rayne's back, her tail flicking as he does. Her eyes are warm, staring into mine. I pat her cheek. "Yes. I know we've had this conversation before, about my episodes, but I want to say again how sorry I am that is who I become."

I shake my head, focusing on the smooth coat under my hand. "Dad, it's okay. You don't have to apologize again. I know it's not you anymore."

He shakes his head, and I see how alike we are in that moment. "I don't care, Sheyanne. I wish—I wish this wasn't happening. I wish this wasn't the reason you came home." His voice is rough, scratchy, and when I look at his face, every emotion is visible.

I'm scared to talk, so I don't.

"I should've tried harder—to make you come home, to give you a reason to come home before this shit. Now, it's like I'm losing you over and over again."

My eyes start watering, and I focus on the colors on Rayne's coat. "It's okay," I whisper, knowing that it's not okay, that I hate this, too—but unlike younger me, I don't want him to feel guilty because it isn't his fault.

None of this is his fault. Or my fault. Or anyone's fault.

It's just life.

"I pushed you away, you pushed me away, and the one time neither of us is fighting each other, is the one time life truly gets in the way." He steps across from me, patting Rayne's cheek opposite of me. "And knowing that it only gets worse from here is what's killing me. I've seen Shane fall in and out of love before MJ, had him come to me for advice and ask for help even. But I've never seen you like that, until right now, and it's going to slip away."

He smiles, sad. "I want to see you live life, Sheyanne. See you happy with whomever that is. Blake and Gaylee, MJ, Shane, Liam. I want to see you experience everything we're supposed to in life. I want to see you discover life with Liam." I open my mouth to interrupt. "Don't even try. I may not have been as present as I should've been, but I still know when something's going on. You don't need to fight. This isn't me telling you to stop. If Liam makes you happy, which I can see that he does, then please, for me, don't run away from it."

He sits down on a bale of hay resting against the stall, and I stay, pressing my hand into Rayne, feeling her steady heartbeat compared to my own that is careening. This is not a conversation I ever saw having with my dad.

"Dad, you're not missing it." I want to say more, but it's all I can manage.

He sighs, the silence louder than anything. "Maybe not right now. But I am; I will. I'm going to miss so much from the both of you, and I get that; I've accepted it, but I am angry."

Now, the tears are visible at his eyes. This is the first time he's admitted he's upset. It's not a surprise; anyone would be upset at being aware they're forgetting themselves. And soon, that awareness will disappear. But right now, he knows it, and he's upset.

"I'm angry that we will never fully repair our relationship. That I will never really know the person you are and will become simply because I'm destined to live in the past and take you with me."

I roll my lips into my mouth and try to breathe in, but the breath catches in my throat, scratchy and raw. He stands up and comes closer to me. He stands taller than me by a few inches, but it feels like miles. I feel like a little kid again, looking up at my dad, and this time, it's not weighed down by a specific feeling, like expectation or disappointment. It's just heavy because I know he's right.

At that, I let out my own tears, for the first time since I was a kid, in front of my dad. My shoulders shake, and my chest hurts from trying to hold in the heavy sobs attempting to break free. We've had a rough time, there is no doubt, but realizing that we could try and try to build the best relationship we could against the challenge and knowing it will still be bent and broken stings. Dad pulls me into a hug with no hesitation, wrapping his arms around my shaky shoulders like he should've when I was dying for his attention, but I don't care because he's doing it now. I don't hug him back, mostly because I'm crying too hard, and I just let him be my dad.

"I'm sorry," he whispers over and over again, his hand on my back. "I'm sorry, Sheyanne." I can't respond as I'm wracked by sobs, my chest rattling. The fact that I can hear the thickness of his words and feel his own tears only makes my chest cave in.

I sought after my dad for years, fought for his attention and craved affection from him by drawing attention to myself the only way I knew how. All I ever wanted was my dad to *want* to be my dad, to feel the love he so obviously felt for Shane for me.

Now that I have it, sooner than I probably think, I am going to miss it. Because it will be gone.

I pull back, wiping my cheeks with the back of my hand like a child. "We still have some time, Dad. I get it. I'm not angry at you for what happens. I'll just need space when it does."

Rayne nudges her head into my chest between us, which brings a fresh sob to the surface, and I really hope I never cry again because it's too fucking much. "Sheyanne, of course that's what I want, but I've hurt you for years, and if you want to walk away, I won't hold it against you."

My eyes widen at the easy out he's giving me. Telling me if I left right now, he wouldn't blink, wouldn't hold a grudge. Before, this would've lit a fire under my feet, and I wouldn't have hesitated, but now, it fills me with dread.

I don't want to leave. I don't want to run away.

From my dad, from Shane, from this place. I want to be here.

"I'm not leaving, Dad."

He wipes away his own tears, looking down at me with warmth in his eyes. "Okay. I'll do my best to be here; I promise." I nod repeatedly. "I love you. I hope you know that."

I start crying all over again.

I don't say it back because it terrifies me and because a younger, more immature part of myself relishes in it. I deserve to hear it from him, that he does love me. That he realizes I was always deserving of it. That I realize I was always deserving of it.

So, I let my dad's words sink in, and he doesn't say anything, just kisses the top of my head as he wraps me in another half hug. We stand like that in the quiet for a moment, in the warm barn until he steps back, clearing his throat. He blinks a few times, and I pretend not to see the tears he tries to hide as he picks up the brush.

"Wanna help? I still have to do Teddy."

I sniffle, my own tears slowing down. "Sure; I'd like that."

He turns on the old dusty speaker behind us, Sade's voice lolling through the speakers as I lead Teddy out of his stall. He, like Rayne, shoves his heavy head in my chest, and I kiss his nose as his big brown eyes meet mine. He blinks slowly and flicks his ear as I attach a line to his own halter.

Dad and I share a small smile as we co-exist peacefully in the same space. It hits me that this, at least, is a new memory, one I can carry in the future of my dad and me.

It's nice to know that even now, I can create new memories with the time I have left. That just because something is fleeting doesn't mean it's not worth taking a moment to enjoy it. No matter how short or small or insignificant this memory might be, it happened, and I was here, with my dad, enjoying it.

Maybe it's all the small moments, all the little details that create the big picture, that mean more in the end than anything else.

TWENTY-SIX

Liam

If someone had asked me when I first arrived that I would ever end up craving the presence of Sheyanne Shaw, I would've told them they had lost their goddamn minds. Now, I'm thinking I'm the one whose lost his mind because all I want is to be around Sheyanne.

The only thing that's taken my mind off her is the letter from my dad I'm holding in my hands. He sends them about three or four times a year, and my grandparents must have forwarded it here this time around. I lean against the pasture fence, watching Teddy and Rayne walk slowly over the cold winter ground, and turn the letter over in my hand. The messy but somehow regular scrawl of my dad sits front and center.

Gently, I thumb under the edge of the seal and pull the letter out. Handwritten like usual, it's at least three pages long. He always sends a letter this time of year, usually for my birthday and the holidays, so it starts with *Happy birthday, Liam* and then wishes me a merry Christmas and happy new year and asks me to pass the message along to my grandparents. He doesn't talk to them often, but it's mutual; my grandparents don't bring him up much anymore. I read about how the house he was finally able to buy has been coming along and how the job at the mechanic's shop is going. That's one way he took after his own dad. I smile while reading it, able to do that now that I've gotten older and I'm genuinely happy to know that he's doing well.

He struggled far more when I was a kid. I could see it in the letters and in the way the conversations about him were framed. I think it was severe depression amongst other things. He didn't talk about them much because he never wanted the time we did spend together to be focused on that. And my grandparents shied away from talking about it when I was young. They've never explicitly said why, though I think they felt they had failed him in a way. Raising a man who went on to suffer with mental health, I think they both struggled with that and with the stigma surrounding mental health in general. Not that the stigma has dissipated; it still very much exists, but as I got older, they started talking about it, checking in on me and explaining it more thoroughly. In no way do I blame my dad for it, not anymore at least, but it had created a desire to be nothing like him, to have as much control as I could over my life.

I'm thrilled that even from a distance, I've been able to see him get better and the proper help. The only real difference in the letter this time around is him asking me to come visit him. He wants me to come at the end of February, to see the house and what not, and it could work, since that's when my contract here ends. I make a note to call him in a day or two and talk over the details. But now, all I can think about is what happens when the contract ends.

Sheyanne's words come rushing back from when she told me she didn't want me to leave. It was the most vulnerable I'd ever seen her.

Until coming here, my plans had been simple. Keep freelancing, saving enough to help my grandparents, figure out my next steps. I'd worked for a traditional office before, but I hated working for someone else. What I did love at the time was the fast-paced work of it, always having something to do, a problem to solve. But lately, it's sounded less and less appealing. Doing jobs I have to instead of jobs I want. I didn't think I'd enjoy the freedom this much, and while this job is certainly a special instance, there were plenty of freelance opportunities when I'd been looking.

I'm in way more control here, doing this, than I thought I'd be.

The most surprising thing is that I don't miss the unending workdays and the speed of it all. This place has forced me to slow down and consider what my grandparents have always said. As much as they love that I want to take care of them, they're right. It is my life, and after taking a deeper look, things I wanted before—well, I'm not so sure they're the things I want now.

Obviously, Sheyanne has a lot to do with it. She's most of it, if I'm being real.

I like that she makes me want to do things other than work, other than just striding toward arbitrary goals. She makes me excited to live, to take the time to do so.

I'm not looking forward to leaving like I did at first. There are things to figure out, work wise, life wise, but I'd much rather figure those things out with her than on my own. Much rather figure them out here in this tiny mountain town than back in Vegas.

My phone vibrates in my pocket, and I pull it out to see my grandma calling. "Hi, Grandma."

"Liam, baby, how are you? Did you get the letter?" she asks, and I hear the clang of a pot in the background.

"I did; just read it. He wants me to come visit."

"Well, it's been a while, right?"

Hanging my arms over the fence, I watch as Teddy trots around while Rayne just watches him, completely unamused. "Yeah, almost two years. I'll probably go. It's after this contract ends."

"Do you know what you'll be doing next? Job wise?"

"No, I don't actually."

The silence from the other end makes me smile. I'm not sure I've never not had something lined up. "Why not? Is everything okay?"

I chuckle. "Yeah, I just have to figure some things out first."

In the background, I can hear her pacing in the kitchen. "Things? What things? Is there something you're not telling me, Liam Carter Landon?"

I grin. "Not necessarily."

"Spit it out."

"I like it here more than I thought." I stop myself from saying there's someone I'm not sure I want to leave. Knowing my grandma, she'll figure it out herself.

All the noise in the background stops. "In that small town?"

"It's not so bad."

She hums, and I can picture her taking a seat at the small dining room table she loves so much because Pop made it for her. "Did you meet someone?"

"I've met quite a few people. You'll have to be more specific."

"Don't be smart with me," she snarks, but I hear the smile. "You met a girl."

It's a statement. My grandma doesn't usually need to ask questions. Often, she catches up quicker than you'd like. Though I made it pretty easy this time because I'd like her advice. Sometimes, I just don't know to ask for it. "I did."

"And that's all you have to say? Tell me everything—she must be special considering you haven't mentioned a girl since that last incident."

I can't help but laugh at her referring to the last time I accidentally introduced them to someone. It was the only time they'd ever met anyone I dated—or really, had been sleeping with—and it was an accident. And a mistake.

"That was two years ago."

Grandma scoffs. "She was terrible. So much so, I still get nightmares over her."

To be fair, I haven't thought about it since it ended. It wasn't very substantial, and the girl was just not someone I ever wanted to bring around my family in the first place. That run-in only solidified it. I've always been good at cutting ties; when something is over, it's over. I don't dwell on it. Honestly, until she mentioned it, I had forgotten. Because that girl—no girl I've dated or slept with—is even close to Sheyanne. Not physically, not mentally, not in any capacity.

"Grandma," I sigh, running a hand over my face, even though she's right, "you have nothing to worry about. I wouldn't have mentioned it if that was the case."

"Well to be frank, you didn't mention it. Her. I did. Now tell me."

Checking my watch, I know I don't have a lot of time before we leave. I'm surprised Sheyanne hasn't come looking for me already, considering we're running ten minutes late because she was still getting ready when I came out here.

I rack my mind for how to put it in simple terms for my grandma, enough for her to understand until she gets to meet her. "Her name is Sheyanne," I pause, turning to lean my back on the fence, only to see Sheyanne exiting the front door heading straight towards me. "She's coming this way, and I'd rather her not hear me talking about her."

"Make it quick then. You're killing me here."

I watch her stride towards me. "She just makes me want to change my plans. I thought I had it all figured out, but I'm not sure that's true anymore."

"You sound like your grandfather when he fell in love with me." She says it with so much confidence, it makes me laugh. She sighs over the phone, not exasperated, just accepting. "Guess we ain't never gonna get around to unpacking your things in a new place then, huh?"

Before I came, I'd gotten out of my temporary lease and put everything I didn't need in boxes and stuffed them in the garage of their house. "I didn't say that."

"Baby, you didn't have to." A silence charged with acceptance on both ends fills the space as Sheyanne grows closer. "Well, go. I know you've got something to do, and I'll see you at Christmas. I love you, Liam, you know that?"

"Yes, Grandma, I know. I love you, too."

She hangs up just as Sheyanne pauses in front of me, tucking her hands into her pockets. Heat thrums through my blood at the sight of her, and I can't help but take in every inch of her beautiful body. Black ripped jeans mold to the curve of her hips, and a silky gray top is tied right above the waistline, leaving a sliver of brown skin visible. It dips low on her chest. Her usual necklace is accompanied with a longer one that dips down between the valley of her breasts, and her curls are in her favorite half-up, half-down look. A long black leather jacket covers her from the cold.

At my slow perusal, a small but breathtaking smile has formed on her full lips. "You ready?"

I take one more long look at her and nod, all the while knowing I'd be perfectly content to stare at her all night. She taps her wrist. "Let's go, slow poke. People to see and things to do."

Standing, I make my way to her side, sliding my finger around one of her belt loops and pulling her closer for a second. My fingers brush her hot skin despite the cold. Thoughts of memorizing every curve and crevice, learning every sound I could draw out or make her feel, come rushing in—something we do not have time for right now. Leaning down, I breathe in the familiar scent of rose water from her hair and brush my lips against her temple, down her cheek, and then onto the bare skin of her collarbone. When her breath hitches, I can't help but smile against her skin.

Despite the flush of her cheeks when I look up, she's glaring at me, trying to act completely unaffected. The pink flush behind her brown cheeks says otherwise.

Knowing exactly what button to press, I pinch her side. "We're gonna be late if you don't start walking, Shaw."

She huffs and turns, taking me with her. "Stupid," she mumbles under her breath, and I can't help but laugh.

I know my grandma is right. That I'll probably never unpack those boxes, at least not anywhere in Vegas. Looking at Sheyanne, following her toward the car, I can't think of a thing I'd rather do or a place I'd rather be. The only thing that would make me leave and stay away is if Sheyanne asked me to.

As much as I'm looking forward to meeting her two friends under better circumstances, the only person I need to see is right next to me, and the things I want to do only involve her. but I also like seeing her in different spaces, seeing what can pull a smile onto that face or make her cheeks flush from excitement.

I like seeing what makes her come to life.

TWENTY-SEVEN

Sheyanne

The bar is absolutely packed.

Everyone is seated at the high-tops or the booths in the back or the tables set sporadically around the small dance floor in front of the stage. Neon signs light up the room with lyrics from an array of popular songs from all different genres and years, and the chalk sign above the stage has Blake's name on it. There's a microphone, a drum set, a keyboard, and a stool, and the energy in the room is invigorating.

There's a booth off to the side with a great view that says *Reserved*, and we head straight toward it. Gaylee is already seated and waves when she sees the four of us.

"Hey, glad you guys could make it." She makes room for us, and we scoot into the circular booth, Shane and MJ first, followed by Liam and me. "So, obviously I know the siblings, but I'm Gaylee."

G reaches out a hand to MJ first. I could see them being friends with their warm, delicate energy, and spending hours talking about their favorite thrift stores and vintage pieces and the fact that they both get along with everyone. MJ smiles after introducing herself, leaning back into Shane's arm as Gaylee turns to Liam.

"Liam," he says, reaching out a hand. "It's nice to finally meet you." He gives her a small smile, and she grins back, her star drop earrings shining in the lights.

When his hand comes back down, it lands on my thigh, and instead of giving into my nerves, I gently run my finger over his knuckles and play with the ring on his pinky. He glances at me knowingly and doesn't say a word. Instead, he just moves an inch closer to me, killing any space between our legs. Heat travels outward from his palm on my thigh and crawls in slow inches up my body.

"It's nice to meet you both." Gaylee directs her next words to me. "She goes on in twenty. She'll be so excited you came, even though you said you would. She's just nervous. She missed you a lot. Not that she'll admit that."

"Sounds like someone else we know," Liam chimes in, tapping his fingers on the table with a smirk. Everyone at the table laughs while I pinch the inside of his palm, feeling betrayed. Again, he meets my gaze and just turns his hand over, covering mine and resting them both on my thigh.

The server arrives for our drink order, and along with that, Gaylee orders some easy apps for the table before making a quick break for the bar's popcorn machine, bringing back a few bowls.

"How many times has she been here?" I ask, looking at the crowd, most of their eyes on the stage. "Seems like she's got a decent following."

Gaylee sips her drink. "Yeah, she's played here a lot over the past few years. She started with a band that came often and did covers. I think it was last year she went on her own. And it's been insane. A bar in Phoenix is the same way; they love her."

I lean into Liam's shoulder. "That's awesome. She deserves it."

"She's been singing and playing as long as I've known that girl," Shane muses, glancing around the table. "When we were kids, she would come over with whatever new instrument she'd learned and play it until we hated it."

G and I laugh because it's true. Blake is beyond talented. She could powerhouse her voice like no other, belting out songs like it was easy. Then, she'd switch up, soften it, go lower and smoother, and then she'd dig into that rough, rock rasp. Her song writing, her range, her voice—it all makes sense when she starts to sing. The last time I heard her was over four years ago; I'm sure she's even better now.

"So true. Remember when she learned the flute?"

Gaylee groans, leaning back. "I hated that instrument for months because of her."

Shane tugs MJ closer. "Personally, my least favorite was the trumpet."

Liam looks surprised. "She plays the trumpet?"

"Yes." The three of us chime, all with smiles on our faces despite the torture she put us through. I lean towards Liam, and he dips his head to he can hear me. "She plays pretty much everything. And she truly used to torture us. It never took long for her to pick them up, but those first few days of each were not fun. I'm sure she's picked up a few more instruments over the years."

"Do you think she'd ever do more than this?"

I shrug, spinning the ring on his finger. "I hope so. If she ever got a chance to work with someone," I shake my head, "I think she'd take the world by storm." I smile when I finish, and Liam taps my thigh with a small nod.

MJ looks at us. "I'm excited to hear her play."

Gaylee tucks a piece of hair behind her ear. "I hope you like it. She puts her heart into all this."

I hum in agreement as I lean back into the seat. Liam's thumb brushes my thigh between one of the rips in my jeans, leaving tingles on my skin. The smooth back and forth motion is both calming and igniting at once.

When the lights dim and the stage brightens, loud claps and rowdy cheers burst from the crowd. Blake comes on stage with a huge smile. With her curls pulled into space buns that only she could rock, lipliner and gloss, ripped jeans, and her guitar in her hand, she looks every bit the part. A drummer slips in behind her with a wave, but all the attention is on her.

"Hi, everyone!" The crowed cheers even louder if possible, and I'm grinning. "My name's Blake. I see some familiar faces here and some new ones. Hopefully, I don't disappoint. If I do, you were never here." A wave of laughter passes before she looks briefly at our table and dips her head, her smile growing.

She takes a seat on the stool, resting one leg on the bar, and pulls the guitar over her lap. "All right, I'm gonna start with a cover so you don't completely rip my songwriting apart." Blake grins, and watching her sit up there under the tiny spotlight reflecting off her dark skin with that bright smile on her face—it's obvious that this is her entire world.

She looks back at the drummer with a nod. He begins, and I recognize the song instantly. Gaylee meets my eyes. "You'll love this mashup. She's been practicing it for weeks."

When her voice comes through the microphone, it's even better than I remember it. The mashup is incredible, starting with a pop song that begs the question of being ready for something, of being ready for love in the middle of the night, and knowing that person is the one instantly. Blake taps in time with the beat in front of the microphone on that stage like she owns it, and she does.

She closes the song by telling us to let the games begin, then pauses as the percussion changes almost completely. It's suggestive, and with the easy plucking of the guitar, it's like she's leading us somewhere, and we have no choice but to follow. Blake then croons about a boy who loves his friends even though he cuts them off, changing the original and distorting it with her vocals. The rasp comes through on this song, the love story of the first fading into questions of whether someone is the right person, a paradox to the big smile she keeps on her face, like it's all a game, and we're just pawns. The smile turns sly when she closes it with a soft, raspy note. It's so Blake. It's incredible.

Abruptly, the upbeat sound turns soft, melodic. The soft strums of her guitar and the occasional drum beat on the cymbal weave a mesmerizing atmosphere, but mostly, it's her voice as she leans into the microphone.

Liam leans down, his lips brushing against my ear, sending sparks down my spine in the crowded room. "She's amazing." I shift closer to him.

I lean back to look at him, the neon lights painting shadows over his beautiful dark skin. "She is. Better than I remember." His hand moves further up, squeezing tighter around my upper thigh, and I turn back to the stage as she starts singing.

It's clear this song is the finale of the other two, a breaking point that's obvious when the first word out of her mouth is *unloyal.* Blake sings about how she's not sticking around to have her time wasted. Throughout she lets the guitar hang and just . . . sings. Her lower register is like a fog over the crowd unable to avoid the pull.

Despite the tale she sings about, I can't help but smile.

This is her world, and she belongs in it.

The way she sang three different songs with three different stories and made them her own—she told her own story and did it beautifully. She belts out the last lines of the mashup with no other sound but her voice, and everyone, including us, is standing when she finishes.

Shane cups his hands and whoops loudly. Blake turns, and her smile grows as the crowd cheers her on. She leans into the mic. "Thank you. You guys are awesome."

Blake stays standing and begins strumming again, the notes echoing as the room quiets. She changes it up, switching the notes drastically, and sends a wink to the crowd as her voice comes through. An original this time. The chorus is hauntingly beautiful, and I watch in awe as she moves through each verse and closes out the song. The crowd cheers again, and that's how the rest of the night goes. Blake places the guitar down at some point and switches to the keyboard, singing a ballad before getting back up and hitting the harder, more acoustic, angsty songs, and each time, it's as beautiful as the last. When she closes out her set with another cover, she receives a standing ovation. Her curls stick out of the space buns, and under those lights, she looks happier than ever.

After, Blake makes her way over to us. When she arrives, Gaylee hands her a drink as loud music fills the speaker from the radio system.

"Thank you guys for coming." She grins, taking a long pull of her drink as we all stand at the edge of the booth. "And nice to meet you guys. I'm Blake." She reaches out her hand to MJ and Liam who give her a smile back as they shake her hand.

"You were brilliant," I say.

Her brown eyes meet mine, and her smile softens. She sets her drink down and surprises me by hugging me. It takes me a second to catch up, but after a brief pause, I wrap my arms around her back. "Thank you for coming."

We stay like that for a moment, and I'm fully aware of the eyes of the group on us, but I ignore them and hug my friend back, my best friend, savoring every second. "Wouldn't have missed it."

Emotion floods me, and I tap it down as we step back. Everything is making me emotional, like a broken dam, every conversation, every moment of repairing a relationship that was broken is ripping me up and renewing me all at once. When I step back, Liam is right there, and his arm snakes around my shoulders, pulling me to him. He says nothing, just hands me my drink, and I take it gratefully, letting the condensation sink into my skin.

We sit back down, and Blake orders a round for all of us as Liam's touch pulls me away from the emotional edge I seem to be teetering on at all times these days.

"You okay?" He leans down, his lips brushing my ear again.

"Am I that easy to read?" I turn so our lips are only an inch apart, if that.

His eyes light up, and his lip twitches like it always does before he smiles. "For me."

"You suck." My eyes flicker to his lips and back up. He notices and quickly kisses me on the lips. Brief, chaste, but with a promise that he'll do it again later.

I turn back, feeling like I'm on solid ground now and engage more, tapping my fingers along to the songs playing above. Shane's enjoying himself, and I'm happy he came out and was able to relax. He's been taking care of Dad all this time without me, and some of that guilt still rests within me, but I'm beyond grateful he came tonight. He asked an old friend of Dad's to stay at the house, and luckily, it's been a smooth night.

The shots arrive, and we tip our heads back. The taste of Jameson takes over my senses just as the song changes. "Oh, come on; we have to go dance," Blake exclaims, sliding out of the booth and taking Gaylee with her. "Sheyanne, come on. You, too."

I hesitate but tap Liam, so I can get up. He smiles as he stands, and I grab Blake's outstretched hand.

"Interesting that you'll willingly dance for them, but I had to force you," he whispers as he passes me. I don't bother responding. I just backhand his chest and let myself get dragged by my friends into the crowded dancefloor.

We're surrounded instantly, the neon lights strobing above us and the heavy bass reverberating through the floor and into my veins. Gaylee, Blake, and I fall into rhythm together like we used to do at our old bar when we snuck in, dancing around each other to the beat, weaving in and out of other stumbling drunks, with big smiles on our faces. It's just like old times, but it's better.

I look over to see Liam staring at me, and a thrill runs through me at the sight. His eyes watch every movement I make, and I revel in it. They latch onto my hips, trail up and over every inch of exposed skin, and even from a distance, when he drags them up to my face, I feel the heat of his gaze. The attention that's only on me, even as he takes another shot, his eyes never leaving mine.

Blake sways closer to me. "He's beautiful." I raise a brow, smiling because she's right. "And he can't take his eyes off you." She feigns disgust. "It's so fucking perfect."

Laughing, I push her. "Shut up."

We keep dancing together, Gaylee cutting in between us with a stupid move or two, causing us to laugh again. Blake leans closer. "I'm really happy you're back."

Lights flash above us, and I shrug a shoulder, pulling Gaylee closer. "I'm happy I'm home, too, you big sap." Blake flips me off, but she can't hide her smile.

Gaylee gently taps both our cheeks, her nose scrunched. "I'm getting us more shots."

Blake and I grin as she moves through the crowd like she always has, like a wave making her way through everyone like it's nothing. Before I know it, I've spent almost two hours dancing with the girls who used to—and still do—know me better than almost anyone. And vice versa. We practically crawl off the dance floor as the bar turns the lights on, signaling closing time. Shane's waiting with a huge but tired smile on his face and his arm around MJ as he swings the keys on his finger. Liam reaches out as he stands, stumbling slightly.

My eyebrows shoot up, my hands landing on his chest. "Are you drunk?"

He holds up his fingers and makes a little space. "Only a little." I smile as he grins, free and bright.

I glance to my brother. "You ready?" He nods, "Let's go. Do you two have a ride or do you need one?"

Blake, who is also tipsy, answers, "Keith, *the* Keith, the famous Keith! Is coming to pick us up." Gaylee turns so tomato red, I'm almost concerned. She attempts to push Blake, who has her arms around her neck hanging off her, away to no avail.

I hug them both. "Okay, well, text me when you guys get home." After saying goodbye, Liam and I follow Shane out of the bar and into the dark cold night towards the car. Liam makes exaggerated steps, holding my hand with each one and pulling me along with a big smile.

"All right, come on, in the car." I point to the back seat as Shane starts the car.

Liam exhales and leans down to look directly in my eyes. "Yes, ma'am."

My skin shouldn't heat, but it does, unable to help itself at the low tone of his voice, and my heart stumbles in my chest. "Don't call me that." I can see MJ grinning from the passenger seat as she watches.

"What would you like me to call you? I'm happy to do anything you ask." He tugs a curl, and I feel it all the way to my toes, heat and longing flooding my body.

"Anything?"

"Well, maybe not *anything*."

A sly smile forms on my lips as I attempt to push him towards the car. "Too late." Fervor flickers in his eyes. "Now, will you please get in the car?"

This time, he obliges, and I climb in after him. I grab one of the waters I put in the cupholders earlier and hand it to Liam. He settles it between his thighs, but seconds later, rests his head on my shoulder, melting me on the spot.

"You looked stunning tonight. You always do," he mumbles, resting his hand on my thigh again. I blush, heat pooling in my cheeks when his fingers dip between the rips. He turns me into someone I didn't even know I could be. Giddy, blushing like a fool at a drunken compliment. With Liam, I know he'd mean it even if he was sober.

I lean over. "You're drunk."

"Doesn't mean it's not true." He squeezes my leg, and I intertwine my arm with his after clicking our seatbelts as Shane begins to drive us home.

I think Liam falls asleep because his body gets heavier, and his breathing settles. We get home quickly since there's no traffic, and soon enough, the old *Shaw Ranch* sign signals our arrival home.

"You got him?" Shane asks as he turns the car off and opens my door. MJ stands next to him, holding his hand with a tired look on her face.

"Yeah, go 'head. Thanks for driving."

Shane grins, his eyes flickering between the two of us, then leans down and kisses me on the cheek before heading inside. I give Liam a little push. "Come on, wake up. You're too heavy for me to even attempt to carry, you big oaf."

He adjusts, but his eyes open, clearer than they were earlier. "An oaf?"

"That's what I said. Now come on. I'm tired, and I want to go to sleep," I whine and pull his arm, hoping to motivate him out of the car. He holds back with his lips twitching until he gives in and steps out next to me.

Judging by the fact that there's no other car in driveway, I assume whoever stayed with dad left a bit ago, so I lead Liam towards his room. He yawns as I find his sweats folded neatly on the edge of his bed. "Here." I hand him the pants. "I'm gonna get water and change."

He nods, his eyes roaming over me. I ignore how my body hums at the look and narrow my eyes playfully before going to get changed myself and get us water. When I come back, he's petting Nyx, sitting in only his sweatpants. I hand him a water, quickly gazing over the strong, lean planes of his chest.

He doesn't say anything, but I know he notices my perusal. And because I refuse to go to sleep without brushing my teeth, I drag him to the bathroom after he downs half his water. In the bathroom, I squeeze toothpaste onto his brush and hand it to him. I wrap the silk scarf around the edge of my curls. As exhaustion hits me, I pull myself up to sit on the counter as I wipe gently at my eyes, trying to get the mascara off my lashes. Liam leans against the wall only a short distance away as he watches.

He's definitely sobered up, but I still see some of that goofy brightness from earlier.

A smile comes over my face as I look at him. "I like it when you're a little tipsy."

"Why?"

I kick my feet. "You just seem more relaxed."

Liam takes two slow steps toward me and wedges himself between my legs. His hands slide up the bare skin of my thighs, stopping only when they meet the edge of my pajama shorts. With a single finger, he traces down my nose and over my lips, before resting his hand on my neck. The side of his mouth turns up, teasing me with a smile yet to come.

"I'm that way around you, Sheyanne."

Before I can even attempt to respond, he grabs a fresh makeup wipe and pulls my own hand away with a gentle tug. With a somehow steady hand, he gently wipes at the rest of the mascara that clings to my eyes. A movement that gentle shouldn't make me feel like I could walk on water, but it does. Liam doesn't only care about me in the moments when I need it, but even now, in the quiet. After all the music stops and the lights are off, he cares about me in dim bathroom lighting when it's just the two of us.

I struggle to ignore the voice telling me I'll never be able to do the same for him. That there's no way I can repay him, no matter how much I try to because I don't trust myself enough to do it well, don't trust myself to deeply care for someone without them seeing the parts of myself I struggle with seeing. Doing the best I can, I shove that voice down, somewhere where I can deal with it later.

"I'm supposed to be taking care of you," I joke, but it falls flat, too many emotions clogging my throat.

His lips quirk, a sleek smile on his lips. "No, I like it. I like doing this." Liam drags the wipe over my eyelashes and under my eye until he's satisfied with his work. "Tired?"

I nod, wiping under my eyes, trying to fight the urge to sleep right here. With strong hands, he lifts me off the counter, his palms burning against my waist, and starts leading me toward his room.

"Liam, we shouldn't."

He shuts off the bathroom light. "Just for a little bit. Since you're supposed to be taking care of me and all."

"Yes because me laying in your bed will cure you into sobriety," I respond, hoping he can't hear the smile in my voice as he keeps walking. Silently, he pulls the covers down. The hand still on my waist squeezes gently, drawing a squeak out of me as I try to step away.

In the dark, amusement sparks in his eyes. "Just get in."

I do as he says, and he climbs in next to me. The ceiling fan stays on a steady rotation, cooling us down despite the outside temperature, and he turns off the bedside table lamp, shrouding us in darkness. I curl my arms under my pillow as I lay on my stomach but turn my head to face Liam.

He scoots closer to me, his hand slipping under my loose T-shirt, and instantly starts tracing intoxicating patters on my skin. His fingertips feel like liquid gold on my skin. They move back and forth and all around, and it feels like I might just melt under his careful touch.

I sigh at the contentment that settles over me. "Did you have a good time?"

"'Course. She was brilliant."

I would close my eyes, but even in the dark, I want to see all of him that I can. "Yeah, she is. I used to be jealous of her. And Gaylee, too." I let out a small laugh at the thought, of how badly I used to wish I could be like them.

Liam halts his movements for just a moment before continuing.

"They had—have—talents, passions, you know? Big ones, real ones. Blake literally wouldn't go anywhere without an instrument or her notebook with her messy scrawl when she had a lyric and just had to write it down. She was always talented, and she always will be. And Gaylee, she was making clothes out of thrifted material and vintage crap by the time we were in middle school."

Under the cover, my foot brushes his calf. "It was hard, because you shouldn't be jealous of your friends, of their talent, of something they love and are good at. That's all we're taught, but I wanted to love something like they did. I wanted to know what it was like to touch something, and it turn into something special. Maybe jealously is the wrong word, but I longed for something like that. I don't know; it's stupid. I just didn't have anything. Just the stables."

His fingertips press into the sensitive skin of my back for a brief moment. "You may not think so, but you're happy there. With Nyx and the horses. I've seen you out in the greenhouse, too, taking care of the garden with Shane. Or in the shed, trying to build things for the house. Maybe that isn't a typical passion or an obvious talent, or something to long for, but it's unique to you." Simple. Easy. That's how he says it.

Like it is something special.

Like maybe, there are some of us that will leave an impact on others, with a talent so bright it's blinding, but that doesn't make anyone else less special or less important. Like being content, being happy in your life with what you love, is just as important as anything else.

"What about you?"

"I don't have one either, not like them. After I got injured, I wasn't sure what to do. Genuinely, I always loved numbers. How easily they're put together, the fact that there is always an answer. I had a lot of questions growing up about a lot of things, so I hated things that didn't have a definitive answer."

Through the dark, I listen as Liam develops full circle for me. It makes sense, him liking something he could control or that had a guaranteed solution.

"I get that, completely." I reach out and tap cheek. "We're pretty useless," I joke softly. He rolls his eyes as he curls closer, his hand covering more of my back.

"We're not useless," he says with a quiet laugh. "You like spending time with animals and books, which isn't surprising, and I like numbers. I think we might just be a little anti-social."

"If I were to ask you a math question right now, you'd come up with the answer? Like that?"

"Probably," he says with no hesitation. "But if you ask me one, I'll ask you one right back."

"Never mind then, I don't want you to ask me something hard, like twelve times eight or something."

Liam laughs, a big belly laugh in the dark, breaking the calm for a moment, but I can't help but smile into my pillow. "I should probably be concerned you think that's difficult, but I've got enough to worry about without taking on your lack of math skills."

"You're such a nerd." I reach out and push his arm, but he only draws closer, continuing the addictive tracing that is trying it's best to lull me to sleep. "Can I ask you something else then?"

"You can ask me anything."

"What's your dream? In life, I guess."

Silence falls, his finger still going around and around on my skin. "I'm not sure I have one. I want to take care of my grandparents for taking care of me. But I think that's more of a goal."

"For you, Liam."

Liam squeezes the skin on my back, sending a pulse of heat to an isolated spot. "I had an idea of what I wanted. Not a picket fence maybe, but a house, some type of stability, a good, steady income. I used to want to start a company, but I like freelancing. I want to be able to live my life, be happy. You?"

I like that his dream is that he wants to be happy. I feel like some people might scoff at that, the simplicity, but I think it's beautiful. I try not to dwell on the use of *had* instead of *has*. Hope blooms that I might be a part of his dreams; I know he's a part of mine. My dream, what I want, is vulnerable and makes me feel exposed. It's also a little dumb, but it's what I want.

I'm the reason it hasn't happened, but it's Liam asking, and he's never judged me for anything before. "It's stupid, so don't laugh."

"I'd never laugh at anything that was important to you."

Warmth blooms in my chest. "I just want to belong. Somewhere. I want a family, not in the traditional sense, necessarily, but a circle that's my family, and I'm theirs. If that makes sense."

He traces in circles up and down my spine. "It makes sense." He moves in closer to me, our legs brushing together now. "I don't think dreams need to be these big things all the time. I think that the small things are just as important as anything else. A dream can be as simple as making it through the day. So, everything you want makes sense. That dream is valid. Though, I do think you have that circle already. You can belong anywhere you want, Sheyanne. You just have to figure out where you want to be."

At that, at those words that sink to some place deeper than my heart, my breath hitches. Liam's hands move down my spine to find my waist, pushing me gently and pulling me closer. He kisses me softly, and the taste of whiskey and the safe energy he always has seeps into me in the dark as I kiss him back. It doesn't go any further than a slow, steady movement of our lips, but even so, every single second of it takes whatever breath I have left and gives me life all at once, sending shivers from head to toe.

"Thank you," I whisper against his lips, and he kisses me again.

"Stop thanking me all the time. I'm just being honest."

"Stop telling me what to do."

His throaty laugh reverberates against my lips, my skin, and when he pulls back, he brushes a kiss against my cheek. His hand lingers on my back, staying under my shirt, and I'm happy he doesn't take it away. I cuddle into him without a second thought, not caring that I should go back to my room, and let him surround me and start to fall asleep easier than I have in months.

I know that while I still have to figure out where I might want to be, here in Flagstaff, or somewhere else, I know a part of me, a piece of me, will always belong with Liam.

TWENTY-EIGHT

SHEYANNE

"**A**re you excited to go home?" I sit cross-legged on Liam's bed as I watch him fold a T-shirt.

The question is a doubled-edge sword. Of course, he's excited to go home and see his family, his friends. On the other end, I want him to not want to leave because of me. However, that is something I will not—or at least not in the foreseeable future—admit willingly. That touches a vulnerable place I've yet to fully accept, how much I want him around all the time, even though we are always around each other.

He turns to look at me, piercing me with his brown eyes. "I want to see my grandparents and Wyatt." Liam moves toward me, placing his hands on either side of my hips. "But I'll miss you."

My heart flutters stupidly in my chest, and my lips twitch, his only a breath away from mine. "That's good," he raises a brow, "that you're excited to see them, I mean. Not that you'll miss me; I'm not that self-centered," I ramble, my cheeks heating instantly.

I am a bumbling fool around this man.

Liam chuckles low and deep, and any part of my body that wasn't hot is now flooded with heat. He reaches up with one hand and cups my face, his thumb brushing over my cheekbone, sending chills down my spine. "It'd be okay if you were. You can be as selfish with me as you want."

Liam leans forward and kisses me softly, like he's trying to brand me. Little does he know he doesn't need to try. I lean forward into his palm, giving him everything I can in that kiss. There's a knock on the slightly open door, and a voice follows.

"Hey—ew, my eyes!"

Liam chuckles against my lips right before pulling away, and I peek around him to see my brother covering his eyes. "You are a drama queen."

He spreads his fingers barely an inch. "My fault I don't want to see my sister kissing. Ew, even the thought disgusts me." Shane feigns a shudder.

I stare at him as Liam continues packing. "What do you want, Shane?"

"I came to tell Liam that I packed some snacks for the plane, but I regret ever coming in here with every part of my being."

I cross my arms. "Well, then leave."

My brother mocks me. "Then leave." He leans against the door.

"Seriously, what else do you need?" I motion since he's just standing there.

Liam laughs, deeper this time. "You two are something else."

"It's not me!" Shane and I exclaim at the exact same time and then meet each other's eyes with a glare.

"Shane."

"Sheyanne."

Liam glances between us for a moment before a glimmer of mischief fills his gaze. I'm about to speak, but he beats me to it. "Shane, if you'd like to stick around, that's fine, but I'm probably going to kiss your sister again."

Shane motions like he's going to be sick. "Gross, I'm out. Bye."

I exhale now that I'm finally back alone with Liam. I look around the room that has been Liam's for the past few months. It smells like him in here, and his things are neatly strewn about on the surface of the desk and the nightstand—it just feels like *him* in here, like he fits. I mentioned wanting him to stay, but seeing him leave, if only briefly, makes me realize just how much I really don't want him to go.

I won't bring it up now, but I'm determined to make sure we have the conversation when he gets back.

Liam notices. "What's with the frown?"

"That's just my face," I lie.

"No, it's not. Your lips are poutier, and you have a wrinkle right here." He comes over and thumbs the wrinkle on my forehead until I stop.

Hearing that he knows my facial expressions just like that makes butterflies erupt in my stomach. I never thought someone would care so much about me. Never thought anyone would want to.

I also never thought I was capable of caring about someone like this. "It's nothing."

I just want him to kiss me again like he told Shane he would. I stretch my arms, trying to avoid the subject and move on. He grabs my hands and pulls me up, intertwining both of his fingers with my own. He holds my hands tightly down by his side, forcing my head back a bit so I can look up at him, his eyebrow raised as if he's waiting patiently for me to spit it out.

Instead of saying it, I just lean up on my tiptoes and kiss him myself. Just a quick press of my lips against his—though I do flick the seam of his lips teasingly with my tongue before pulling back.

I don't make it far. With a steady hand, he buries his fingers at the base of my neck, tugging my curls and pulls me back. "That wasn't nothing."

And then, Liam really, deeply kisses me. His lips move over mine with ease, like he's done it a thousand times and won't get sick of it. I smile over his lips until I feel the brush of his tongue, teasing me like I did him. The gentle flickers and nips of his teeth send heat to pool deeply in the bottom of my stomach, and my knees feel like jelly. I part my lips just enough, and Liam takes full advantage of it, a low groan building in his throat as he tugs me closer, slipping his tongue into my mouth. There isn't an inch of space between us, and my entire body is pulled taut, but neither of us takes it any further, though I can feel how much he wants to. I want to, badly. All I can think of are his fingers on me and how I want them to trace every inch of me when we have the time. How much I want to touch him in return and make him feel even an ounce of what he makes me feel. I want Liam in full capacity, in every single way possible, but now, as much as I wish it was, isn't the time for that.

I sigh, and he catches it, kissing me again. "You need to finish packing."

He moves his fingers against my neck, but it feels like he touches all of me. "I know."

Neither of us move. I smile again. I smile all the time now.

It's disgusting.

He pecks my lips twice before letting go and stepping back. Carefully and quickly, Liam adjusts himself in the sleek black sweatpants he has on before turning back to his bag. Heat pulses between my legs, and I swallow, trying to clear my head.

Liam looks over his shoulder. "I'm not so sure you're good for my health."

"Yeah, well, the feeling's mutual, Landon." I sit back, still feeling his skin on mine, almost positive the sensation is here to stay.

We descend into a comfortable silence as I watch him finish his single bag. Though the room is charged with a tension yet to be released. The entire time he packs, he throws me sly glances and smiles that quicken my heart, and I am powerless to it all. Thankfully, he's only going for a few days and will be back for New Year's, which has always been my favorite holiday. I'm excited to spend it with Liam, who is quickly becoming my favorite person.

I shouldn't be counting down to when he comes back since he hasn't left yet, but I can't help it.

Right now, it feels like I have my family back, and my friends, and I have Liam, and everything is falling into place.

The days before Christmas pass quickly. I deck out Teddy and Rayne in their Christmas jackets for the cold pastures and the occasional quick snowstorm. The entire time leading up to the holiday, the sky is that strangely comforting gray where everything is quiet and serene, allowing the Christmas lights hung up on the house and the barn to illuminate even brighter.

Christmas Eve, it looks like it really will snow, thick and heavy that would quiet the entire world for the holiday. The only thing I would love more is if Liam was here. White Christmases don't happen often, but they used to be one of my favorite things. Pot roast cooks all day on the twenty-fourth, while the three of us spend most of the day on the porch with the space heater and tins of Christmas cookies and chocolates those boarding with us gave as a gift. We spend it listening to old Christmas music and the evening watching our old favorite Christmas movies since Dad is lucid. We used to celebrate both Christmas Eve and Christmas equally. A big meal on the twenty-fourth, and then on Christmas, a big brunch and mostly desserts. I make banana pudding and cookies and Shane makes a pound cake and usually a pie. We had leftovers forever, but it was worth it. When I got older, it was less exciting because I wanted to leave, didn't want to be around, but this year—it feels brand new.

When I wake up on Christmas day, I feel like I used to when I was a little girl. Excited. By the time I finish my morning with the horses and give them a few extra treats and moments of love, I find and Shane waiting in front of the Christmas tree with coffee brewing and bacon cooking on the stove. Quickly, I shower and change before heading back out to the living room.

"Is MJ coming over later?"

Shane leans back against the couch. "After she has her family time, I'm going to pick her up and say hi and then bring her back here."

"Does her family like you?"

"They love me," he says confidently, sipping his coffee. "I mean, really, who doesn't?"

Blinking, I stare at him. "How does she put up with you? I'm genuinely asking because I do not get it."

Mischief glows in his eyes, and he leans towards me. "She's in love with me. Duh."

I reach over to pat his cheek. "I can't wait to give a speech at the wedding."

Dad laughs loudly at my statement, and I grin at Shane's face. Because he knows it will be the most embarrassing speech I can manage. Dad surprises me again when he hands me giftwrapped boxes. "It's not much, just things that made me think of you."

I swallow the huge lump in my throat. "Dad, you didn't have to," I mumble, keeping my voice quiet.

He leans into the couch, shaking his head and barely making eye contact with me. He's just as nervous as I am. "I wanted to, Sheyanne. You're home for Christmas. That's reason enough."

Even if I wanted to respond, I can't because my chest is heavy, and I really, really don't want to cry. Shane speaks, clearing the emotions. "What about me? Your favorite son?"

I laugh. It's a wet laugh, tears threatening to fall, but the joke makes me feel better, especially when Dad rolls his eyes and hands Shane a few boxes of his own. I pad toward the back of the tree and find their gifts, leaving only Liam's behind, and hand them out.

"Well, here. I got you both some things as well. Merry Christmas."

"On three?" Shane askes, and I nod. He counts down, and the sound of crinkling wrapping paper fills the space.

My heart constricts when I open the first one. It's a horse figurine, painted beautifully, just like the ones I used to collect when I was younger and shut away in a drawer before I left. This one is light purple, painted in hazy strokes with white accents depicting a storm brewing. The emotions that had just cleared come rushing back.

"Dad, it's—"

He clears his throat, not looking up from his gifts. "It's nothing."

It's not nothing. It's beautiful. In my palms I turn it over, feeling the grooves and ridges from the textured paint before I set it down. The next one is from Shane, and it's a small box of my favorite candy from in town and a knit hat that has a satin interior for curls. On top is a receipt with the titles of a few books from my Amazon Wishlist. At the same time I look up, he does, too, holding the gifts I got him: a new faux leather wallet from one of the local farmers markets—sustainable but simple, with cool, detailed cross stitching—and an entire collection of X-men comics. He used to be obsessed when we were younger. When he got older, he still was but felt guilty spending his money on them.

We both grin at each other, and he tosses wrapping paper at my forehead. "Yeah, love you, too." I toss some wrapping of my own back and a piece of tape sticks to his cheek. I look at Dad, who is turning his gift over in his hands, staring at it.

It's nothing big, just a photo album with our last name stitched on the top. On the inside are pictures of all of us. The very first is the same one I have in my room. The rest are from when I was younger, since that's when the majority of our pictures were taken, but there are even a few from when I got older and some recent ones Shane and I have taken. There are pictures of everyone in Dad's life. Old clients and animals he's worked with. Each photo has a small written out caption next to it. I left some blank at the end for the future to fill in.

When he looks up at me, his eyes are brimming with tears and emotions I don't have words for. Neither of us say anything, just share the smallest of teary-eyed smiles. He flips through it slowly, and I look away in fear that I'll start crying.

Shane catches my eyes and grins, leaning closer to whisper. "Aw, someone does have a soft side."

I whisper-yell back, "Leave me alone." My attempt to push him back fails because when I do, he pulls me in for a rough hug, and I mumble curses under my breathe. "You are so annoying."

"You're more annoying." My dad chuckles from his seat, still thumbing through the album when my phone starts ringing. It's a facetime from Liam, and Shane's eyes latch onto it. "Better get that."

I flip him off and pick up my phone. "I'll be right back."

Dad has a warm look on his face, his dark brown skin crinkling with a soft smile. "Take your time. We'll get breakfast ready." I dip my chin and head down to my room, softly closing the door behind me.

"Hi."

Liam smiles over the screen. "Hi. Merry Christmas."

"Merry Christmas." I roll onto my stomach, clutching a pillow. "How is Vegas? Your grandparents?"

He shrugs. "They're great. I missed them a shit ton. It's warmer than I remember." He gives me a sly look through the phone, and my heart flutters. "I wish I was there with you."

I maintain a semi cool façade, but my smile gives it away. "I wish you were too. But I'm happy you got to see them. What about Wyatt?"

As soon as I say that another voice enters the space. "Is that her? Is that Sheyenne?" And Wyatt practically pushes Liam out of the view and enters the screen. He glances from me to Liam with a slow growing smirk. "I forgot how pretty she was."

"Fuck outta here, man." Liam glares and shoulders his way back in, causing Wyatt to chuckle.

"Come on, I'm just messing with you. No need to get all jealous." Wyatt throws an arm around Liam, still smiling at me.

A laugh escapes my lips while Liam just shakes his head. "Hi, Wyatt." He attempts to sit next to Liam, but what follows is some type of testosterone battle that ends with Liam pushing him onto the floor with a smug grin. "Bye, Wyatt."

"God, you are such—"

"Language," Liam chides, and there is no explanation for why it causes heat to spread in waves over my body.

"A grouch," Wyatt finishes and pops his head back into the screen. "Hi, Sheyanne; Merry Christmas. I'll leave you guys to it before I end up knocked out."

When he's out of the room, Liam looks back to me with a shake of his head.

"That was unnecessary," I chime.

"He was taking up my time with you."

I let my head fall forward, my curls covering the warmth on my cheeks. "I guess I can't argue with that."

"But I do want you to meet my grandparents."

I swallow, my stomach dipping with nerves. "You don't have to, Liam." He doesn't acknowledge my response as he gets up and walks down what looks like a short hallway. I hear his voice quietly off screen before two more people join him in the camera.

"Grandma, Pop, this is Sheyanne."

They look just like him. His pop and him have the same beautiful deep dark skin, same nose. It's almost creepy how alike they look. But his grandma, they have the same eyes that crinkle a certain way when they smile and the same mole on their cheekbone.

"It's good to meet you, sweetie," his grandma says, and I smile.

"We've heard many, many things," Pop adds.

"I hope they're all good things. I've heard nothing but amazing things about the both of you."

I never thought I was the type that would be good with parents or grandparents or anything really. So, I'm really hoping they can't tell I'm terrified.

"Nothing to worry about," she smiles, and I adore her already. "One day, you'll have to join us. We'd love to meet you in person." My heart swells in my chest, and I look up to Liam who is grinning over them as he holds the phone.

"I'd love that."

We talk for almost thirty minutes. In that time, Shane silently enters my room, dropping off breakfast with a ruffle of my curls. Liam's grandparents are amazing. Liam sets up the phone, so he doesn't have to hold it, making it so they are all in the frame. We talk about Liam growing up, and they even pull out photos of him as a baby. Liam groans at the photos, but I can't stop smiling. My favorites are the ones where he is in an oversized track jersey with chubby cheeks. I also really loved his high school and college graduation pictures, the way his jaw shaped up and the sharpness in his brown eyes. He looked regal. His grandparents ask me about the stables and about my brother, dad, and how it became unexpectedly nice to be home. Then, his grandma and Pop tell me about what a suck up Liam was in middle school, how organized he was, and how all his teachers loved him before his attempt at a troublemaker phase in high school. I don't stop laughing the entire time.

After a while, his grandma says, "It was so nice to meet you, and I hope you have a Merry Christmas, sweetie. I'll let Liam take over again. I know he's probably tired of us taking up all his time with you." She leans forward and tries to whisper, "He's been looking forward to talking to you all day."

I grin.

"You ain't have to sell him out like that," his Pop chuckles, giving me a sly glance.

Liam shrugs in the back. "I don't mind. It's true." They smile at me and give Liam a kiss on the cheek before he leaves, heading back to what I assume is his room. I hear the click of the door behind him, and he sits down, leaning into a chair.

"I love them."

He shakes his head, looking at me with a warmth I feel through the camera. "I'm beyond lucky to have them. I'm glad you got to meet them. They love you." The words resonate deeply in my chest. I'm happy that I made a good impression. "My flight lands tomorrow night. Pick me up?"

"No, I'm going to leave you in Phoenix."

"Yeah, I miss you, too, princess," he deadpans but with warm eyes.

I do miss him. It's pathetic. "Yes, I will be there." I smile, knowing this is the best Christmas I've had in a while.

So different from the past ones that I spent alone or sitting at a bar or working a long shift. I haven't been alone today between Shane and my dad and Liam. I know that the entire day is going to filled with being around the people I missed and one extra addition. We stay on the phone for a little while longer, talking about everything and nothing, and I know then I'm walking into dangerous territory.

Really, I've *been* in dangerous territory and didn't know how to admit it, but I am falling down a hole that is filled with Liam and Liam only. I don't just miss him.

I'm falling in love with him.

Twenty-Nine

Sheyanne

The covering over the back of my Bronco keeps all the heat in like a little cocoon.

A bunch of old beat-up cushions line the bed where Liam and I are sitting with pillows for us to lean on. It's New Year's Eve, and I'm sure the town square is filled with its usual festivities and all the partygoers. It used to be one of the best nights when we were in high school—plenty of trouble to get into.

Tonight, I just wanted to do something with Liam.

Currently, he's tracing patterns on my thigh, my legs outstretched over his lap. Above, the covering of the trunk is see-through, the stars visible when I lean my head back, but I'm looking at Liam, whose head is leaned back with his eyes closed. I don't say anything. I'm content to watch him, to study him in the peaceful quiet.

"Why are you staring at me?"

I tug my lip into my mouth and wait. After a moment, his beautiful brown eyes blink open. "I felt like it."

He runs a hand up my calf, leaving sparks behind the steady touch when he trails it up my thigh, the flimsy leggings not acting like much of a barrier from his burning touch. "Am I up to your standards, Shaw?" His other hand rests dangerously on the top of my thigh, brushing back and forth over the bend of my hip.

"Are you fishing for a compliment?"

"Maybe. Maybe not. You certainly don't give them away freely." I'd think he was serious if it wasn't for the tug of his lips.

Still, I know I'm not the best with words. I'm content to just be around someone. But I can try for Liam. I figure everyone might need to hear things verbally sometimes.

"I know I don't tell you enough," I grab his hand and turn it over in both of mine. Placing my hand over his, I trace the difference with my other. The space between where my fingertips end and his stretch on. "But you knock every standard out of the park, Liam. I think you're quite beautiful."

My cheeks heat, but the answering smile on his face makes it all worth it. Watching his full lips part and his eyes brighten, turning molten when he looks at me, that smile—his smile—beats every single star that dots the night sky. It erases any awkwardness that lingers in my chest. His hand twines with mine, his larger hand shadowing my own, and I revel in the warmth of his palm.

Despite feeling exposed, I love that I can make him smile like that. It's a wonderfully fulfilling thing, making someone look that happy, making someone feel that happy.

"Got a pretty smile, too," I say, tapping his lips with my thumb. He presses a soft kiss to it in return.

"Giving those compliments away for free now?"

"Only to you." I blink, knowing Liam has gotten more of me than anyone else. And because he has always been so open with me, I figure I can try to do the same. "You are the only person who has seen so much of me."

He spreads my hand open, tracing up and down each finger and the sensitive spots in between. "And that scares you?"

I huff, humor infiltrating my next words. "Of course, that scares me. Have you met me?"

"What is that supposed to mean, Sheyanne?" Liam asks, expecting more, and I search for the words to give it to him.

The pillows cushion my head as I lean back. My eyes dance between the dark sky above me and his waiting but gentle eyes. The question rattles me and the tiny walls I still have left up. Tiny around Liam in comparison to everyone else.

I push them down, break them away piece by piece until I have the vulnerability he deserves from me.

"I haven't ever gotten close to anyone before because I am terrified that they'll see all the parts of me I don't like. You are the only person I have ever felt like this about, Liam. And I am still scared. Scared that you'll realize I'm more trouble than I'm worth. That one day you'll decide it just isn't what you want, that trying to figure me out, to deal with me, is a waste of your time." The painful honestly drips from my tongue. "I'm scared that one day, you won't want me."

At once, I realize two things. One, that is the scariest thing I ever said out loud. And two, there is no one on Earth I would've rather bare my soul to. The tension dissipates slowly, even with the fear running through my veins.

"As scared as I am, you don't make me feel like that. It's a contradicting statement, I know, but it—feeling these things doesn't feel scary with you. If we were stuck in the dark together, I feel like I'd be all right 'cause you'd be there." I sigh, not sure anything is coming out right. "What I'm trying to say is, you know me better than anyone else, and that scares me."

Gently, as he takes in the words, his hand grips my leg and pulls me fully over him. He settles my knees to straddle his hips like he's done before. It's strange, being put in a position of control when really, Liam is in control of everything. It's almost like he's trying to give me some leverage in the sharing of that vulnerability, giving me strength when I feel weak. I keep my hands in between us, waiting for him to speak.

"I'm not sure if you think you're alone in what you're feeling, but you're not. Whatever you feel, Sheyanne, I feel it, too. Whenever I'm not around you, I'm thinking about you, wishing you were with me." He leans forward, his lips brushing my cheek and his hands twining with mine. "And you're not trouble. You're human. Every part of you that you've showed me is incredible, Sheyanne. All the arbitrary things we all chase after—jobs, ambitions, money—I could spend my entire life chasing all those things, but why would I? None of them will ever amount to what *you* are worth."

My hands land on his neck, my thumbs rubbing the underside of his chin, feeling the slight stubble there. "Who are you?" I ask, my words muffled by the emotion, trying to figure out how this man stepped into my life.

His hands slide down my hips and around to my butt, pushing me fully to sit on his lap. "I'm whatever you want me to be."

I laugh, my eyes pricking with tears. "Can you stop being so nice to me? Please be mean."

Liam's eyes twinkle. "Fine. You were an asshole when I got here, determined to make everything difficult for everyone. You walked around trying to destroy all the control they had, and you didn't want to feel anything but angry. I didn't hate you, but I hated that. How easily you gave into those emotions, like you couldn't imagine feeling anything but angry. At some point, I decided I didn't want to fight with you, I just wanted to touch you, to make you come apart until that scowl on your face was erased by something good, something that made you feel. Then, I just wanted to see you smile. And when you finally did, it was the most beautiful thing I'd ever seen."

Any air I had left is gone. "That wasn't very mean."

"I tried."

He rolls my hips over his, and I feel the evidence that he's just as affected as I am, heat lighting me up at the hard feel of him. My chest is tight, desire crawling into every single crevice and taking over all my thoughts that aren't of Liam. I can't decide if I want to let him burn me or breathe more. He doesn't wait for me to make up my mind. Instead, his hand curls around the back of my neck, his fingers dig into my skin, and he pulls me to his lips.

He groans as soon as my tongue flicks out to touch the fullness of his lips, and the sound of him is like a match striking over gasoline. Red-hot heat blooms between my legs and travels over every inch of my body. One hand stays on his neck, holding him to me, keeping him against me, while the other presses against the back of the car that he leans on, rolling my hips over him roughly.

"Sheyanne." He grips my hips, and I look him straight in the eye, his brown eyes so dark and endlessly beautiful I could hide in them. But right now, I'm not above begging, not above tossing any pride I have left at his feet.

"Liam, touch me, kiss me, fuck me. I don't care. I just need you. All of you." I thumb over the sharp angle of his jaw.

He stares at me, intensity burning there. "You're going to be the death of me, Shaw."

My lips quirk, my hands never leaving his face. "It'd be a way to go out, huh?" Liam shakes his head, amusement mixing with the heat in his eyes as his grip grows tighter on my hips. "You don't have to, obviously—"

"I always want to touch you, Shey. You never need to doubt that."

My breath hitches. "Okay, well, you said you wanted to make me come apart. So, then make me."

Our eyes meet, filled with an intoxicating mix of longing and lust and emotions we haven't put words to yet.

With that, he kisses me, rough, skilled, branding himself on me. Then, he trails his lips over my neck, teeth nipping behind my ear, sharp and hot—addicting—when he sucks gently, chasing away the pain. His hands—those beautiful hands—are everywhere. In my hair tangling with my curls and crawling down my spine, brushing under my shirt, over the delicate skin of my ribs. I'm thankful for the heat that's trapped in the car and the blankets because he pulls my sweatshirt off with no remorse, leaving me only in a nude lace bra that doesn't leave much to the imagination. Liam groans at the display, leaning his head back with his eyes burning at the sight of me.

"You're not too much, Sheyanne. It's the opposite. I can't get enough of you." His hand trails over the swell of my breast, fingers tracing the delicate patterns of the lace that feel abrasive against my skin. A single thumb brushes back and forth until I'm a puddle.

"You have all of me, Liam," I sigh against his lips.

For some reason, the responsive press of his lips against mine and the combination of his words floating around in my head cause all my emotions to swell in my chest and threaten to make me spill out everything I haven't said. My eyes prick, and I will the tears back. I cried when he kissed me for the first time, and I really don't want to cry now. All I want is to be with Liam.

Swallowing my emotions down, I gain enough self-control to grip the bottom of his long sleeve and start tugging it up and over his head. My fingers trail over his hot skin, tracing the divots and dips of his abdomen, the smooth and strong planes of his chest, all the way up to his throat. He stops me in my tracks when he gently tugs and pinches my breast and the sensitive peak. My head falling forward to his shoulder, I release a heady moan, breathing him in on my next inhale. I spread my hands over his chest, gripping him tightly as he tortures me.

I am putty in his hands, and I don't care.

"Liam, please," I whine against his neck, my lips placing soft kisses there as my hips circle, searching for friction, for anything, for the touch of his fingers.

"I haven't even touched you yet; have I already reduced you to begging?" he whispers near my ear, a chill spreading from that spot and all the way down my spine. I lean back, looking him in the eye, and reach my hand past the band of his sweats, landing on the length of him and wrapping my fingers around to squeeze him.

His grip tightens on my waist as his breath hitches. "Don't push it, Landon," I breathe out, hovering over his lips, still clearly more affected in this moment.

"I like pushing you." He unwinds my hand, twines his fingers with mine, and tugs me forward. "And we're doing this my way."

Our lips meet again, and he grabs my leggings and tugs them down, carefully drawing each leg out, trailing his fingers on my skin as he does, leaving tingles in his wake. Eventually, all that remains is my bra and underwear. Liam wastes no time in slipping past the lacy underwear and touching my skin, pressing his fingers against the most sensitive part of me. His other hand holds both of mine behind my back. I try to roll my hips over the barely there touch, but as soon as I move, his beautiful torture comes to a halt. He pulls his lips and his hand away, pulling a groan from my lips as I fight how tightly my body is pulled.

"My way," he says again, and I blink my eyes open, glaring at him.

"Your way," I lean forward, my lips less than an inch away from his, "is stupid."

His fingers resume their movements, pressing against me, slowly, lightly, and my eyes flutter. It's a brief relief, immediately taken over by a pool of need. As I blink my eyes open so I can see him, Liam leans forward, kissing me deep before pulling away again.

"My way is all about you. Everything is about you. You can be selfless another time, but not right now. Just let me take care of you," he whispers against my lips, and I'm drowning in his words, in his touch. "For me, Sheyanne, it's all about you."

My head falls forward to the crook of his neck, straining against his hold as he discovers a rhythm that works for me, causing my breath to hitch, both at the feel of his fingers and the familiar smell of him. I'm helpless to keep in the small sound that escapes me as he circles, varying the tempo, teasing and flaming the ache and the need building so much, it's almost painful, but addictingly so. His lips brush my neck, my cheek, and he quietly instructs me to look at him.

"I like seeing you like this. Soft and searching and needy," he says against my lips, and I moan against his mouth as he circles his fingers. "I want you to need me." His tongue swipes my lips, owns my mouth. "It's selfish, but I want to be the only one who sees you like this from now on. Forever." His thumb presses down, and a finger easily slips into me. "I want to be the only person you need."

Another sound escapes from my throat as he works me up, pressing and circling and thrusting his fingers slowly until I feel boneless. He finally lets go of my hands, and my nails dig into his shoulder instantly, into the back of his neck as I hold on, the pressure building everywhere, like a bunch of little waves preparing for a big one. It's despicable how easily he knows my body already, how easily he can get me to the edge. My stomach tightens, and I squeeze his neck again, and right when I think I'm going to fall over and burn up into ashes, he stops all movement. I groan loudly into his neck, embarrassingly needy. Under my palm, his heart races in time with mine.

He takes his hand away and grips my chin, forcing me to look at him. "I want to feel you. Is that okay?"

I swallow, searching for words when my brain is hazy. "Yes." I kiss him. "Anything you want is okay."

His eyes are alight with so many things I can't keep track, and I don't have to when he kisses me again, harder, lighting me back up. Quickly, he slips his hands away and pulls his sweatpants and briefs down just enough. Pausing, he reaches for his wallet and pulls out a condom. I reach out to grip his wrist.

"I'm on birth control, and I haven't," I breathe, trying to find my words, "been with anyone since my last tests." I squeeze his wrist, feeling his pulse under my fingers increase. "I'm good if you are."

"I'm good." Lust takes over all the brown in his eyes as he swallows. "Are you sure?"

I smile as best I can even though I'm weighed down with need. Drowning in it. "Positive. I want to feel you, too."

My hands come up to rest on his lean muscled stomach and crawl their way up to his neck where I run my finger over the thin chain and the crook of his neck. Unable to stop myself from tasting him, tasting the cologne that clings to him, the smell of winter and sandalwood, the smell of Liam, I lean forward and kiss the dip in his throat. His head falls back as I go, searching for the spot that makes him tick. His breath hitches when I get to the curve of his neck, right under his jaw and I slip my tongue out, teasing the skin, kissing over it, taking as much as I can get.

Liam drops the condom and curls around my neck again, rubbing the spot behind my ear, driving me crazy and kisses me soft and tender, teasing me like always. He kisses down my neck again and places the sweetest kisses over my collarbone and down to my shoulder—parts I didn't even know would be sensitive until he touched them.

His hands move to my waist, and I use his shoulder for leverage as he lifts me, pulls my underwear to the side and slowly, so goddamn slowly, guides me to him. My lips find his neck again, my hand curling around his neck, feeling his textured hair under my fingertips, and a low moan escapes against his skin when he presses in fully, and I feel him everywhere. Liam snakes his arms around me, one tight on my lower back as I feel him pulse, his breath hitching in my ear, and the other up on my back, his hand tightly gripping the back of my neck, his fingers lost in my hair.

With a steady hand, he pulls my head out of his shoulder and back up to see him. He starts moving, starts driving the pressure back up, and it builds slowly but surely in the pit of my stomach, crawling up my spine, sensations rolling over all my skin. Burning a fire I'm not sure will ever go out. His arms are warm, and his eyes hazy as he looks at me, looks at me like no one ever has in my life. I circle my hips slowly, undulating until I find a rhythm that works for both of us. I reach for his cheek softly, bringing us together in a soft kiss. My heart beats quickly as every thought that isn't Liam and the way he moves, easily, smoothly, killing me each time, leaves my head.

"You are everything and more, Sheyanne," he whispers against my lips, and everything begins to swell. Every nerve ending fires madly as he touches me.

Liam kisses my cheek, behind my ear again, tongue teasing as he kisses down my neck and across my throat before finding my lips again. "And you are perfect."

I swallow roughly, trying to kiss him back as best I can when his hands tighten on my hips, and he thrusts slowly but deeply. Everything starts to happen at once. The slow burn, the slow, tortuous build starts to spread out. My entire body pulses with heat as a moan escapes my lips again, though Liam catches it with his lips and never stops kissing me. I tip over the edge, falling though it feels like I'm flying as the pressure burns through me, touching every part of me. Pleasure invades all my thoughts and hits every nerve ending I have as I dig my nails into his neck, trying to ground myself. But it just keeps going. The orgasm is long and possessive over my body. I'm not even kissing him so much as panting over his lips. But Liam doesn't stop. He keeps moving, keeps circling and thrusting and draws those waves of pleasure out for as long as he can until I finally inhale again.

When I can form a coherent thought, all I can think about is how good he feels against me, in me. Everywhere. I loosen my grip on his neck and blink my eyes open, my cheeks hot when he looks at me. I go to kiss him again when he thrusts harder, and I lose my breath again, unraveled and overly sensitive now. He smiles against my skin, placing kisses on my cheek, my neck, the line of my collarbone, knowing exactly what inexplicable torture he's putting me through. This thing with him isn't just physical. It's the intimacy that is burning underneath the strong touches and soft kisses that adds to it all, makes it feel a million times better than anything else in my life ever has.

Placing my hands on his chest, I push up, out of the warmth of his neck, searching for his lips again. When I open my eyes, I find him already looking at me.

Liam's lips turn up at the edges, pressing against mine. "One more, with me now."

He reaches down between us and adds his fingers to where we're connected and circles slowly, until I'm lost in him all over again. "Liam," I groan, "it's too much."

It's both not too much and it is. I don't want him to stop, but I might die if he doesn't.

"No, it's not. I've got you." He kisses me again, pulling at my lip, my stomach tightening tortuously. "Let it all go, Sheyanne."

Warm lips brush against my temple, his hands holding me in place as I try to push away from him and push closer to him at the same time, sensitive but in search of another high only he can bring me. I tighten almost immediately around him, squeezing him as I let him move us, completely at his mercy now. His groans only add to everything I'm feeling. They sink over my skin, and I want to memorize them, memorize the way he affects me and me him. His grip tightens in my hair again as his movements quicken, all my nerves firing sporadically once again, like someone flicks a million lighters over all my skin, the flame licking me, burning me higher and hotter than it did before. With a sure grip, he tugs my hair, exposing my neck to his lips, where he kisses and licks and bites, and the pressure explodes as my eyes squeeze shut, the stars above me disappearing. The feel of his own pleasure escaping him with a loud groan on my throat make my eyes flutter open, watching him feel everything I am.

His hips move slower, drawing it out for both of us, bringing us back to the ground on his terms until they still, and I practically slump forward on to him. I trace the marks my nails left in his dark skin, feeling the divots and kiss my way up, needy and loving until I'm at his lips. Liam's head is leaned back, his chest heaving under my palms as he catches his breath, and I've never seen a more beautiful sight.

A tired, post sex, hazy Liam might send me to my grave.

Unconsciously, I move my hips when I lean up, and he groans, his eyes blinking open. "Do you want me to die?" His hands grip my hips, stopping any accidental movement.

I smile, kissing him again, unable to help it. "No, because then we can't do that again."

He huffs out air in a weak laugh and squeezes the curves his hands rest on. My phone lights up in the dark, and I glance over to see the time, just a little past midnight. Turning back, I find his eyes on me, dark and amiable and—god damnit the prettiest brown eyes I've ever seen.

"Happy New Year." I kiss the edge of his jaw, and his hands finally leave my hips.

They trail up and down my spine, thumbing the edge of the lace bra and around, coming up to cup my cheeks, still flushed and hot. "Happy New Year, Sheyanne."

I grin, going back in for more kisses wherever he'll let me. His cheeks, his nose, his neck, and his lips, especially his lips. They move with mine, slowly, both of us taking our time and not needing anything more than to be kissing. I don't ever want to kiss anyone again. I know right now, right here, no one will ever look at me like he does or kiss me like he does. Or care about me the way that he does.

I have no idea if Liam loves me, is in love with me, though I hope he is. Because I am so in love with him that it hurts. Hurts to think about the years where I didn't even know him but didn't have him. Hurts because I know I will never love anyone like I love Liam in this lifetime or the next.

And then, all that delicious hurt is obliterated at the idea, the possibility, the hope, that the years to come will be filled with Liam. Filled with him doing crossword puzzles in the morning. Filled with the way he smiles around me, how he gives into it and lets that bright look take over his face. I want to spend my life learning about the man who doesn't let anyone else know about that mental bruise from his childhood or how his desire for control, for stability, comes from the unknown—I want to spend my life being worthy of knowing Liam like no one else does. Of loving him like no one else can.

Golden hour used to be my favorite thing in the world, the golden sky and all the stunning shades that followed, but Liam is my favorite thing to exist ever.

Liam makes me feel golden.

And realizing I love him is the most beautiful thing I have ever felt in my life. Loving Liam is the most beautiful thing I've ever *done* in my life. He reminds me that life should be lived in technicolor, not shades of gray or in muted tones, but in every beautiful shade imaginable.

Everything else ceases to matter to me except this. Except Liam.

Thirty

Sheyanne

I should be focusing on the book in my hand.

I'm not, not even close. Ever since New Year's last week, every time Liam is close to me, he's all I can focus on. Right now, the pages are blurred because Liam is right next to me, his fingers moving slowly over my ankles that rest over his legs. He's completely focused on the tablet in his hand. I'm not sure what's on it; I don't pay attention to it because he's right there.

The house is quiet. Shane and Dad are walking around the grounds before the sun sets since it's not absolutely freezing outside, and Nyx is sleeping peacefully on the floor below me. Turning my eyes back to my book, I try to focus on the words before me, but it's useless. As if he knows I'm thinking about him, he squeezes my foot, and I squeal, trying to pull it back at the sensation, but he holds it tightly.

He's grinning when I look over at him, held hostage by his hands. "Having some trouble focusing over there?"

I close my book. "Shut up." I kick against his leg, trying to get free, but he holds on.

For a moment, he studies me. "You look happy."

Liam cares about my happiness, my feelings, more than I feel I deserve some days.

Some days, I worry if his energy would be better spent on someone else, but the longer I spend with him, the less I feel like that. Knowing someone cares about me makes it easier to care about myself even if I still have things to work on.

I shrug, affecting nonchalance. "I am."

And I mean it. I mean, I'm not perfect, I'm not happy all the time, and there are days when the anxiety comes crashing back in when I think about what still needs to be discussed, but I'm trying to manage it.

Having everyone around helps, having my friends back and my brother back. Relearning my dad as best I can. Having Liam. Right now, nothing's happened to test that happiness, but I hope it stays that way.

I pop up onto my knees, escaping his hold, and crawl over to him, leaning back on my heels directly by his side. "I'm going to start dinner before MJ gets here. Do you want anything?" I ask, spinning his ring.

I like doing things for Liam, helping him when I can and spending as much time as we both can spare with one another. It's easier than openly expressing how I feel, hence why I still haven't told him I love him. But I love showing him in little ways like this. I just hope he knows that.

Liam reaches up and tugs a curl, watching when it bounces back into place. "Can you just hand me a beer? If you don't mind."

Leaning forward, I press my lips to his cheek. The stubble is gone, and his hair is freshly cut from yesterday. I find myself missing some of the roughness of the stubble, but I also enjoy how smooth his face is when it's not there. "Yup."

I hop up and head towards the kitchen. The sun falling in the sky paints the interior golden through the windows. It feels good right now, to feel like this. In the silence, I take a deep breath, enjoying how I feel like magic.

The dishwasher is loaded and running, the only sound besides the TV Dad has turned on. Everyone else still sits at the dining room table except Liam, who needed to run to his room for a call. When I return, Shane hits me with a look that makes me feel apprehensive.

Confused, I rest a knee on my chair. "What's that look for?"

My brother shares a look with MJ, and I swallow my nerves down.

"I have something to tell you. Dad already knows."

I sit down and bring my knees up. "Okay."

"I'm going back to school."

My eyebrows shoot up in surprise. I never knew he wanted to—I suppose I never asked—but I'm still surprised. His bachelor's was in psychology, I knew that, but this is a surprise.

"This week."

More surprise, but I shrug. "Shane, that's awesome. So why do you look like that?"

The hesitation scares me. Makes my heart drop a little. "I'm not going to NAU. I'm leaving; we're leaving." He holds up MJ's hand, which he's holding onto. "We're moving to Seattle."

I let it sink in for a moment, trying to dig through how I feel. Sadness is the first immediate emotion that begins to invade my brain. I was feeling good here, I was—but that's because I was with everyone again. Anxiety crawls in after, sneaking in through the door the sadness left open and settling into a corner in the shadows. Like it's waiting to attack.

Despite it, I force a smile onto my lips the best I can. "Shane, that's really great." My words are wobbly. "I'm happy for you. Why didn't you just tell me sooner?" I try and force a teasing tone, but it falls flat. No one addresses it.

Shane runs a hand over his curls. "I don't know. I should've. It's just, I didn't even know if I was gonna go at first. But it's a good opportunity, and they gave me a scholarship—"

"I'm not mad at you for deciding to go; you don't need to defend the decision, Shane," I interrupt. I'm not mad.

But I am fragile, and it would be a bold face lie if I said I wasn't.

It's like everything was going too well for just a little too long. Rationally, I know my brother isn't leaving *me*. Like I left him. But it doesn't feel like that right now. It doesn't feel like that at all.

"What about the stables?"

Dad speaks now. "Everything is still in my name. I told him we could figure it out over the phone soon, and we'll get help if you need it."

I nod, blinking back tears. I look to MJ. "And you're excited?"

MJ gives me a cautious smile, and guilt enters the door now, too, taking a seat next to the anxiety sinking deeper and deeper. I don't want them to feel guilty; they shouldn't. It's a great opportunity, and I should be happy for my brother, and I am. But I am also not.

"Yeah, I've always wanted to go." She smiles, resting her head on Shane's shoulder. "And I'm excited to go with you," she says, kissing him on the cheek.

If I was feeling better, I'd feign disgust, but all I can do is smile as my nails dig into my palms. I force a quick inhale. "When do you leave then?"

Shane pats MJ's hip and looks back to me. "Wednesday." In three days. My brother leaves in three days.

Dread takes a seat now, too, the door to my emotions not even hanging on anymore. It's wide open, letting all these sharp-edged feelings right on in.

"Man, now you really are gonna become a genius," I joke, swallowing hard.

Some of the nerves dissipate from Shane's shoulders. "I was always a genius. Now, I'll just had the creds to prove it."

I laugh, but it's weak and sounds wet instead of carefree like it should. I stand and go over to him. "Can I have a hug then?" My brother sticks out his lip like a kid, and I know he's teasing me now. "Asshole." I kick his chair, and he stands up finally.

MJ quietly moves to the couch as I wrap my arms around my big brother. When his arms come around me, it only makes me want to cry. I suck in a breath and squeeze. "I'm going to miss you."

"I'll miss you, too, shithead," he mumbles into my hair, and I pinch his back. "You know I'm not leaving you, Sheyanne. Not like that."

"No, I know." A tear creeps out, and I reach up and wipe it away.

But you are. I understand what he's saying, but it won't sink in.

The logic has no place in my head right now. It is nothing compared to everything else I'm feeling, though I know my feelings are irrational in comparison. It both makes sense and doesn't make any sense at all.

It hits me that this is what I did to my brother. And I did it without a goodbye. The guilt grows in my chest.

"You're gonna be great here, you know. I'm only a phone call away." Shane rocks back and forth like he used to when we were kids and he had trapped me in a hug.

I love him, but right now, I need to get away because everything he says makes me sadder. Makes the anxiety dig in a little deeper.

Patting his back, and wiping my cheeks again, making sure there are no visible signs of tears, I pull back. "Will you need help packing?"

He pockets his hands. "No, we're not taking much. Most of it, I've already started. We're driving my truck up to the apartment we found."

My heart cracks a little bit more. "Wow, you really are all grown up."

"I'm older than you." Shane rolls his eyes and flicks me on the forehead. Whether or not he can see the emotions on my face, he doesn't acknowledge them.

"Doesn't mean you act like it." I head towards the hallway, a slow escape before my brother sees me cry. "I'm just gonna go find Liam; I'll be right out."

Shane's face softens, but he's got a sly smile growing. "Love you."

I roll my eyes as I turn, but it does nothing to staunch the tears that fall. "Love you, too," I call and enter my room just as everything comes rushing in. The wood against my back does nothing to ground me, nothing to make me feel better.

Nothing to take away the fact that Shane is leaving.

I'm not upset about staying. I like being here. The day to day, the routine. It's not that. It's that I've never done it alone. The dark corner the anxiety tucked itself into unfolds as the tears fall, shrouding my thoughts in shadows and squeezing my chest. It works hand in hand with the dread, the sadness, the guilt, eating at me from the inside, telling me this is a bigger deal than I know it is.

Slowly, I walk through my room and towards the bathroom, where the door to Liam's room is ajar. His voice floats through, and I realize he's still on the phone.

I don't want to interrupt him with tears, so I sit on the edge of the tub and listen until he's done. But I end up hurting myself more.

"Nah, I'm just about finished up; there's nothing for me to do. Nothing left for me here," he mumbles, and my heart stops, and the shadows, if possible, grow even darker, blocking out all rational.

His voice travels into the room, hitting me with unreasonable pain. "I'll probably leave here soon and come home for a bit first."

Blood rushes past my ears as a wave of hurt touches every inch of me. My blood, my skin, everywhere. The words are not making any sense. I asked him to stay, didn't I? Or did I just tell him I wanted him to? It's different. It's so fucking different. I stand, not willing to sit through whatever else he's saying to whoever else he's talking to about him *not* staying. Behind me, I shut the bathroom door and lock it, striding for my bed, and let the tears fall.

Everything stops making sense as the anxiety swirls like a hurricane, going from a category one to a five instantaneously. I run it over and over in my mind, all the times I could've asked him to stay, all the times I just assumed he would. We never talked about it in detail; we said we would, but we didn't. We danced around the subject and never really figured it out. Maybe he's just realized he's better off away from this place. Better off away from me.

This on top of Shane and MJ leaving presses me deeper into the dark. I shut down bit by bit, just like I used to.

That old fight or flight instinct comes raging in. Caught in the eye of the storm I've created in my head, all I want to do is run away. Leave all the overpowering—unjustified—emotions behind and go.

Beneath the storm, resentment brews—all of which is directed at myself. Not for letting him in, not for falling in love with him, not for discovering how much I love it here.

No. I'm angry for not even being able to consider anything else.

I've latched onto the worst-case scenario, and I'm going to hold it like it's my lifeline. Like no other possibility exists. I'm trapped in the negative cycle my head has created, knowing this is wrong of me, knowing this isn't true, and unable to find the calm in the storm and get out. I want out, but I can't find the exit.

I wonder if this is how people felt when I left without a word? Is this how it feels to be left in general? Maybe it's all karma. For all the people I've left before. For all the mistakes I've made.

I love my brother, and he's leaving. I love Liam, and he says he's leaving, too.

It's ironic really. I have always been the one to leave, to run away. But I've never been left before.

And it hurts a million times more.

THIRTY-ONE

Sheyanne

The day Shane leaves is no better.

It feels like the whole world is quiet, but inside my head, it's loud with unspoken fears, unshed anxieties.

I stand next to MJ and the rented U-Haul attached to my brother's truck. He already said goodbye to Dad, who is inside, unable to watch his son physically leave. Right now, Shane is saying goodbye to Liam on the porch, easy smiles on both of their faces as they hug. I wait, intent on keeping my act up. I haven't really spoken to Liam since I heard him on the phone three days ago. The days were busy with Shane packing and finishing up the final touches Liam needed help with. Apparently, he was closer to being done than I had thought. And then, the days were busy with him packing, so if he noticed the silence, he didn't push.

We both know he's too smart to not have noticed though.

With a causal handshake, Shane steps away and strides towards me. MJ pulls me in for a quick hug. "I'm going to get in the car so you can say goodbye." She taps my nose. "If you need me, don't hesitate to call."

I give her the smallest smile I can manage and squeeze her back before she steps away. Shane kisses her on the cheek before stopping in front of me.

"What's your deal, Sheyanne?" he asks, done feigning ignorance about my silence.

"Nothing." My teeth pull at the skin on the inside of my lip. "Can I please just have a hug? Before you leave." My voice is steely, but I feel like I'm standing on the edge of falling apart. Especially with Liam watching from the porch.

He sighs and pulls me into his chest. "You're going to be okay. I promise," he whispers, rocking me back and forth. "Whatever happened, will you just talk to him? I don't want you to be alone here, so please, for me?" He squeezes. "Your brother's dying wish."

Despite my tight chest, I pinch his back. "You're not dying, asshole; you're just leaving."

Shane pulls back, his fluffy curls light brown in the winter sun. "Just do it."

"You need to get on the road."

"I need my sister to be okay more." Shane looks over his shoulder and sighs before looking back to me. He pulls me in again. "You are so happy here. I hope that you can see that for yourself soon. And I hope you let yourself be happy in other ways, too, Sheyanne. Just don't let the silence get too loud."

My eyes burn, and I hold him until it's time to let go. I blink back tears so he doesn't see and hope he can't see the anxiety and the sadness burning in my eyes. "I love you," I murmur. "Now go." I give him a gentle push to the truck, and he steps away with a classic Shane smile.

The ignition starts and dust kicks up from the gravel under the tires, and I'm left there watching.

I look over to Liam, knowing I'm in the wrong and not knowing how to man up and talk to him.

I feel unable to push past the barrier of fear that waits in the shadows, ready to crawl up my spine at any second. The words pound in my head, *nothing left here for me*, over and over and over again, feeding all my irrational worries. I trust Liam, even standing here apart from him. I know I'm missing something, because I do trust him, more than anything.

But I do *not* trust myself. Don't know which part of me to believe. The one that loves him or the one that is terrified. So instead of figuring it out, I climb the steps and go hide out in my room like I have been.

Hiding behind my locked doors in all the ways I possibly can.

THIRTY-TWO

Sheyanne

My silence stretches into the next day.

The past four days now have been a magic act of avoiding all things Liam. His gaze, his hand when he reaches out when I walk past him. I find a way to escape, some excuse to descend into hiding.

Shane's words linger about letting myself be happy for once. But not standing in your own way is a lot easier said than done. Especially when I'm terrified that when I do talk to him, he'll just tell me exactly what I don't want to hear. That he is leaving. In hiding behind the fear, at least I can avoid the hurt.

Dad and I have spent more time together in these past few days. I haven't said much to him either, but it's nice to have him around. He's been doing well, mostly lucid, only a few incidents early in the morning or late at night, but it only speaks to his steady decline. He told Shane and I before Shane left that he and Liam were officially finished, earlier than they'd thought.

Dad pats my arm as we circle towards the pasture, drawing me out of my thoughts. "You all right?"

I don't know the answer.

"Sheyanne, what's going on?"

We lean on the fence, our breaths forming little white clouds in the cold air, remnants of snow on the ground under our feet. He rubs my back. Every comforting touch he gives brings more emotions to the surface because he never gave them before.

Vulnerable words grip my throat, but I force them out anyway. I need them out; I want them out. "Liam said he was leaving. He said he wouldn't, but I heard him say he was going home."

"Is that why you've been ignoring him?"

I glance away, my eyes latching onto Rayne who lifts her head and chews slowly as she gazes in our direction. She saunters over, her tail swishing behind her. Teddy follows because he hates being left behind, and they stop a few feet away from us.

"I don't want to get hurt."

"Are you sure that's what he meant?" he asks gently, and I know it's a reasonable question, but reasonable is not how I'd describe myself.

I feel hurt and a little bit blindsided. "Dad, can you just be on my side right now?"

His face is calm and patient. Understanding swims in his eyes as he looks at me. This is as open as I've ever been with him.

"I'm always on your side. I have years to make up for, so I'm always on your side." He pulls his arm around my shoulder and tugs me closer. "I just—I see how much you care about him. How you two treat each other. And it seems like you're hurting now. I want you to be sure."

Swallowing, I search for the words, but I don't find them. I'm not sure; I don't know what to do. That's a lie. I know what to do, and it's to stop avoiding Liam.

Dad doesn't push any further. "Help me inside? Your old man is old and tired."

That brings a small smile from my lips. "You're not that old."

We walk back, feet crunching, my heart hesitant in my chest as we do. We approach the house, making our way down the small incline on the pathway. The creak of the old front door opening snaps me into awareness, and the sight of Liam walking out sends my heart plummeting to the ground. His eyes are dark and trained on me.

I drop my dad's arm without even thinking about it as we reach the porch. He eyes me and Liam but just kisses me on the cheek and makes his way inside. I meet Liam's eyes, hyper aware of the space between us. Physically and emotionally.

One that hasn't been there since he first arrived.

I don't want to, but I'm retreating, and have been for four days—strapping anything vulnerable I might say down since it doesn't matter.

I cross my arms and kick the gravel. "So, you're going home?"

His sigh is audible from here, the gray sky sitting over us like an omen, no sign of the sun now. "Sheyanne," he steps forward, but I step back, "what is going on?"

It's not anger that surges through my veins. It's hurt, it's uncertainty, it's fear.

"I heard you on the phone. You said there was nothing left for you here. That you were going home," I mumble, staring at the ground.

"That's why you've been avoiding me?" he asks, and I force my eyes up. Guarded. He starts to smile. "That's not—you didn't hear everything, Sheyanne. I said there's nothing left here for me to do, so—"

I interrupt. "Yes, I know. I heard that the first time. I don't need to hear it again." He frowns as the words hit me right in the chest, hard, knocking me breathless all over again. *Nothing left.*

Nothing.

Left.

I'm being unfair to both of us. But if I push him away before he can hurt me, maybe I'll save myself some pain. Maybe I'll be able to patch any hurt back together.

Confusion and understanding flicker in his eyes but also anger. Good, I want the fight. I want him to get angry, to yell at me and to leave because I pushed him away, not because he figured out I wasn't worth staying for.

He's been my sounding board when I've been upset, going through things, and I hate that instead of giving him that chance, I'm shutting him out. Since I can't run away, I figure I can force him to. A new version of my old self. How shitty it is that all my bad habits come back as soon as trouble strikes?

"That's not what I meant, and you know it."

Vulnerable words claw at my throat begging to get out. *I love you. Please fight back. Please don't hate me. Please stay.* They scratch, begging me to let him in.

The words sit on my tongue, and I want to scream them, throw that at him. But I don't, so I shove them down. I don't want him to stay because I begged him to.

"It's what I heard."

"So, this is how it's going to be? You overhear bits and pieces of a conversation not meant for you, so you ignore me and push me away?" He steps forward, closer to me, and I hold my ground. "That's what you're doing, isn't it? You're scared, so you're hurting me? You want me to run away?"

My heart beats quickly, and I flex and unflex my fingers, hating that he's right. Hating that even now, he can read me without even trying.

"I'm not scared. I get it. It was a contract; the contract ends. I was just a bonus."

Liam steps forward, closing the distance, only an arm's length away now. Physically, at least. I keep my face neutral as I study his beautiful face. The dark skin, the warm brown eyes. The lips that have imprinted themselves in my mind.

But my mind won't let me focus on anything good.

"If you think that, then you haven't heard a single word I've ever said to you." His voice is hard and firm, and it send chills down my spine.

"I heard them. Maybe I just believed them a little too much. Maybe you just knew the right thing to say." I see the hurt flash in his eyes, and I hate it.

Hate that I'm doing this. Hurting myself won't hurt as bad as being hurt though. I've hurt myself before; it's nothing new.

"You don't believe that."

I keep my eyes trained on his. "Doesn't matter, Landon." He flinches at the use of his last name. It used to be playful, but now, I just do it to separate us.

"Will you please hear me out?" he asks calmly, and I hate that he's so composed. He hasn't raised his voice one fucking time, and it's driving me insane.

He's meeting fire with indifference, and I am only burning myself.

"Nothing you say is going to make me unhear what you said. You want to go home? Then go."

He steps closer, invading my space fully. "Don't yell at me because you don't know how to deal with a scenario that you're creating. I'm not against you, Sheyanne. You're only fighting yourself."

Tears prick, and I don't know if it's because I'm angry or sad or both.

Liam's skin brushes mine, and it burns, but in a different way. I look away, trying to step back and put more space between us. I thought I was getting better, and I have in some ways, but maybe I was just distracted, and all my issues were still there, under the surface.

Liam shows up for me all the time, but I *still* don't know how to show up for myself. And now, I'm not sure I'll learn how if he stays.

"I'm not, that's not—it's what I heard," I argue weakly, not even able to lie. He steps closer again, invading my space, and it takes everything I have not to beg him to invade my entire life.

"Are you dense?" he exclaims. "I fucking love you, Sheyanne. Haven't I made that clear?"

Everything comes to a halt.

My entire body stops fighting, my hands unclench, and I just look at him. I don't know what he sees in my eyes, but he closes the distance, his hands immediately cupping my cheeks. "I have to go home, but not because I'm leaving you. You told me you wanted to stay, for me to stay, and I need you to understand that I would never have left you. Yes, I need to go home, but I was always going to come back to you, Sheyanne."

My entire body aches, and I feel like I've ripped myself apart. I always thought I never deserved him, and I don't. *I don't.* But I want him anyway, so I need to be better. For me. Because he just told me he loves me, and I can't say it back.

The only thing that breaks free are words I didn't know I believed so deeply until they escaped. "You deserve better."

A tear rolls free, and I look away from the only man that's ever made me feel like I deserved anything.

His thumbs brush my cheeks, pressing on the tear. "I can't deserve better because there is no one better for me than you." Liam steps closer, our entire bodies brushing.

"This can't be what you want." I swallow, feeling him against me, attempting to ground me.

Even now, the edge of his lips twitch, his eyes never leaving mine. "Sheyanne, I didn't even know what I wanted until I met you."

The words settle deep in my heart, there to stay.

More tears fall as a realization hits me. I found safety with Liam. A place I could go where I wasn't judged, I wasn't hated, I wasn't coddled. He was safe. But the problem with finding safety in another person is when left alone to your own devices, it's hard to find safety within yourself.

And if I can't trust myself to love him the way he loves me, if I can't stand on my own two feet, then all I am ever going to do is hurt him. With Liam holding my cheeks, I realize I am so fucking sick of hurting other people.

It is … overwhelmingly exhausting.

"Sheyanne," he murmurs my name softly, his fingers on my skin, trying to bring me back. But I hit the self-destruct button. I did this, and it's not fair to expect him to put me back together. I have to do it. "If you need space, I'll give it to you. I will give you whatever you need."

The sob rips itself out of my chest, and I look at the patience in his eyes. Liam has never, not once when I needed him, looked at me with anything but that patience. It is unwavering, and it is something I didn't know I needed until I met him.

With a shaky breath, I say it. "I need you to go.

He doesn't remove his hands from my face, but his eyes burn. "If that's what you want."

I take another look at him, the openness in his eyes. There's hurt there, too. In hurting myself and chasing an unnecessary fight, I realize I've poked an old bruise. I breathe, trying to hold in my tears. "I'm not leaving you. I don't ever want to leave you. But this can't happen in the future. I don't want to do this to you ever again."

I reach up, wrapping my fingers around his wrist, holding him to me. It isn't anything close to what I want. But if I want anything with him, a future, a love, anything—everything—I need to figure this out on my own. I'm not better. I haven't grown as much as I thought.

I've only slapped a band aid over old wounds and called myself healed.

"This is not what I want." A tear rolls down my face, and he wipes it away just as quickly. "But I need it. I can't expect you to be here every single time something goes wrong. I heard what I wanted to hear, and I tried to make a fight out of nothing because I don't trust myself. And I don't want to make you feel like this. I can't do that to you. Not ever again."

I love you. I love you. I love you.

But I don't say that. I do love him, profoundly, with my entire body and soul, but I don't want to manipulate him. I don't want him to hurt anymore at my hands. So, I'll hold it in and lock it away until I can fully love him.

I tighten my grip. "I'm sorry. I'm so sorry; it's just what I need. I need you to leave so I can figure out how to stand on my own two feet."

"You know if you asked me to stay, I'd be here for you every step of the way."

A sad smile interrupts the tears as I search for the right words. He lets me. I always hated that saying that you couldn't love someone until you loved yourself. I think it's bullshit because that isn't true. With him here, offering to stay if I needed it, I know that even if I hated myself, I'd still love him. And he would still love me. It's not a hate for myself that keeps me from asking him to stay; it's that I don't trust myself like he does.

He trusts me to love him no matter what, but I don't believe in myself. I am sure of Liam. It's me I'm not so sure of.

"I know that. But—" I exhale, "I have to be able to fall down and trust myself to be able to get back up. I'll always want you there after, to give me a hug." He smiles. "I've just gotta do that standing part on my own. I don't want you to be a crutch."

"Okay. I'll go because it's what you need. Just know you could push me away a thousand times, and I'd still find a way to come back."

I let my eyes close at the words, soaking them in. He's the most reassuring person I've ever had in my life, and it wasn't something I knew that was good for me until he came along. It was never something I got when I was younger, and he gives it so freely that I can't help but want to hold on tight to it.

I can't find the words to respond, so I just nod while his hands hold me gently.

Liam swallows and brushes another tear, the tenderness ripping me into more shreds, if possible. "You're not alone in this, alright? I love you, Sheyanne." He places a feather light kiss on my lips as his words sink in. "I love you."

Sobs wrack my body, and I rest my head on his chest, hating how weak I am when I thought I was stronger. He wraps his arms around my body, holding me tight.

The only thing I know without a single doubt is that Liam is it for me. That I'll never feel this way again in my life about anyone. It's knowing this that helps me rationalize the decision because he deserves better than half-assed love. He deserves someone that doesn't flame a small fire before understanding why it started.

Someone who can be there for him like he is for me.

Behind his back, I interlock my fingers, holding him, knowing I have to let him go, at least for what I hope is only a moment in our lives. All of this made me dig deeper, realize there's more that needs to be worked on, on my own. No depending on someone else, no hiding, no running, no more excuses. I love him so much that I have to let him go.

For now. Not forever.

But that doesn't quell the ache that I have to take the next few steps alone.

No Shane, no Liam. Dad needs me, not the other way around. I've known where I belong, but I haven't found myself.

That hurts just as much as letting Liam go.

He must sense my acceptance because he pulls back to look at me. With a quiet sigh, he brushes his lips near my temple and down my cheek. "You call me when you're ready, okay?"

Afraid to speak in case I start sobbing again, I pull him impossibly closer to me, taking one last hug, feeling the touch of his skin, the steady breaths he takes, and hoping it'll get me through. He believes in me. I just have to believe in myself.

Thirty-Three

Liam

The city lights of Vegas don't excite me like they used to.

When I arrived almost a week ago, the lights that greeted me weren't a welcome home. They just reminded me that I left my home back in Arizona.

I grew up here; part of me will always love it. It's full of memories of stumbling about the strip with Wyatt, watching the immense number of bodies trying to crowd themselves into a party, wasting money we didn't have back then all over the street or in the casinos.

But no part of it feels like home anymore.

My home is tucked between snowcapped mountains, a girl with long curls and deep brown eyes that light up when they see me. Even now, picturing Sheyanne comes easily to me. The way her hips curve into her smooth thick thighs, the freckle she has on the tip of her nose and the ones that follow the curve of her eyebrow. Or how, whenever she reads, she sinks into the couch as if she's hoping it'll swallow her up and put her inside the book. I can also picture her watery eyes when she asked me to leave, the sadness but also the determination swimming in them.

Leaving Sheyanne was the last thing I wanted to do.

Not when she was struggling even though she tried to hide it at every turn. Not when she is going to have to help her dad on her own. I admire the strength she had in asking me to go. But fuck, after being around her in such proximity constantly, I can't stop thinking about her—and missing her.

Wyatt chuckles from the passenger seat. "God, it's painfully obvious how much you don't want to be here."

The stoplight turns green as we head towards my grandparents. "That's not true. I missed y'all."

He snorts. "Stop lying. I'm not mad at you, I'm just pointing out the obvious." The warm air enters the car through the open windows, the sun traveling between clouds in the otherwise blue sky. "When you going to see your dad?"

"A week or two." I slow, approaching my childhood home.

The old Camaro Pop is always working on is out in the sand-colored driveway with the hood open instead of covered in the garage. It's deep blue color contrasts to the neutral tones around it, the sun glimmering off the paint.

"And when are you going back?"

Putting the car in park, I run a hand towards my forehead and down over my eyes. "Whenever she's ready."

"Is she all right?" Wyatt asks.

"For the most part. I can't speak for her, but I think when she came home, it was a lot to deal with. She's anxious often, and she said she wanted to work on it on her own." I leave out the details because as much as Wyatt is a brother to me, some things are better left private.

"Almost like how you were when you dealt with your dad."

"Sort of. I wanted everyone around when I dealt with all that," I chuckle, remembering how I almost never wanted to be alone because I didn't want to be stuck inside my own head. "She wants space, which is fine—just different."

Even though I wish I could be there, we had—have—very different relationships with our dads. Mine was distanced growing up. His mental health never directly affected me. It was more about the adolescent me getting old enough to wrap my head around him not being around. Sheyanne's dad was always around, but not in the way that she needed him. And then she grew up and left, only to come back and get to know him. If she wasn't struggling, I'd be more surprised. But the fact that she could ask me to leave means she's grown more than she thought.

Wyatt and I climb out and head toward the beige, single-level home. The door is painted a vibrant green, courtesy of my grandma, along with the window frames to match.

"Good for her, knowing what she needed to do." Wyatt pats me on the shoulder, adjusting the bag of groceries we picked up for Grandma on his shoulder. "They know you're not staying?"

"Grandma does. I told her about Sheyanne for all of five minutes, and she responded like she'd never see me again, made me feel like I was eighteen instead of pushing thirty," I say, Wyatt letting out a deep laugh in response. "I'm sure she told Pop, but I'll see."

Wyatt shakes his head, the single stud in his ear that we both went and got the moment we were able, glinting in the sun. "Can't say I saw it coming."

Pop sticks his head out from the hood of the car, wiping his hands on the rag he pulls from his pocket. Wyatt grins and strides towards him, reaching a hand out until he's pulled in with a pat on his back.

"Hi, Pop, how you doing, sir?" Wyatt greets him. My grandparents are practically his third pair.

Pop shrugs, leaning on the car after adjusting the ballcap protecting his bald head. His hair started turning gray a few years back, and I swore the world ended when he walked into the kitchen where Grandma and I sat and practically shouted, *Look at this*. We just raised our eyes, and five minutes later, he came out with no hair at all. I think it was because Grandma's hair had yet to even suggest graying, and the man couldn't stand the idea of graying alone. I wasn't sure I'd ever seen my grandma laugh so hard in her life.

"Doing all right, son. Glad to see you both again. It's been a while since you were here together."

He rubs a hand over the coarse dark hair growing around his chin, still untouched by the gray, and crosses his arms. The sleeves of his shirt are rolled up, exposing his dark brown skin in the sun. Luckily, I spot a streak of sunscreen he failed to rub in on his arms, so I don't bother asking if he has it on, knowing how much he hates when I harp on him.

"Just like old times, aside from all the trouble," Wyatt chimes, pulling something out of the grocery bag. A sugary pink lemonade and a pack of Twizzlers, my Pop's favorites, though he's not supposed to be drinking or eating them as much. "For you."

"Bless you, Wyatt. You never try to restrict me."

The front door opens, Grandma appearing with her hands on her crossed arms. Her braids are tied back away from her face. "What was that?"

A laugh builds in my throat, and I cough to cover it up as Grandma raises a brow at her husband, who has too slowly moved the contraband food behind his back. He just smiles charmingly at her, and Wyatt bumps my shoulder with his own as we move towards the house.

"Nothing, Tara. You know I love you," Pop murmurs, striding past us and kissing her on the cheek. The straight line of her lips twitch, and she turns her eyes to us.

She turns her stare to Wyatt, who just turns on the sheepish, amiable smile that has gotten him out of trouble with almost everyone on this planet. His parents and grandparents, my grandparents, teachers, everyone, and anyone. He leans in and kisses my grandma on her cheek.

"Hi, Grandma T. I couldn't say no; the man begged me." He blinks, and I watch my grandma soften, like everyone else. It'd be incorrigible if that face hadn't also gotten me out of trouble in the past as well.

She pats his cheek. "Go on in. Lunch is finished. And set those things on the counter for me please."

"Yes, ma'am," Wyatt responds and strides into the house, the hallways decorated with pictures on every wall.

Finally, I have the chance to greet her myself and kiss her on the cheek as well. "Hi, Grandma."

She gives me a full smile, unlike the other two—not that it's a competition—but I always liked winning. "Hi, baby; come on in."

I step inside beside her, standing almost a foot taller than her as she rests her palm on my back and leads me in. The past week I've been home, I've either been here or at Wyatt's, but every time she greets me like it's been three months all over again. The photos on the walls are filled with me and my grandparents, my graduation shots from high school and college, my grandparent's wedding photos. There are a few of Dad as well and even Wyatt occasionally tossed in. The beige frames contrast the various colored walls. Deep green like the front door in the living room, light blue in the entry way, and in the kitchen, a tan wall with warm orange detailing—something the three of us had done when I was younger to brighten up the inside.

Being back makes me reluctant about my original plans. I can't buy them a new house and expect them to drop this one and go. They love it here. I love it here. They made this place a home not just for themselves but for me, for Wyatt.

A home isn't something you buy; it's something you find, something you make. All the money in the world couldn't buy that.

In the kitchen, I find Pop carefully spooning pulled pork into the homemade rolls on the sheet pan. There's pico de gallo, shredded cheese, raw and fried onions off to the side. When he's finished, he sets the plate down on the table and leads my grandma to the chair. Finally, she smiles at him. The lines near her eyes crinkle when she does. The sun peeks in through the detailed windowpanes, shrouding them both as he pushes her chair in with a parting kiss on her cheek.

"That's how you do it, gentlemen, if you were wondering," Pop murmurs quietly to both of us as he begins to make his own sandwich, bumping us out of the way.

"I can hear you, Charlie."

Laughter racks through Wyatt and myself and echoes around the kitchen. Pop doesn't deny anything, just continues making his sandwich with an unashamed grin before taking his own seat. We follow shortly after, sliding in around the small eat-in section of the kitchen. The sun descends as we talk, time passing without me even being aware of it.

Wyatt talks about the art gallery he works at and the new collection he has coming in a few weeks, the one that for the first time, he gets to run on his own, to which my grandparents practically explode with excitement. They've always loved the gallery and have gone there plenty of times, and I am thrilled to know the years Wyatt has been working there are paying off. Pop mentions finally cutting back on his hours, which earns him a pleased smile from my grandma, and she excitedly tells us about a new business opening she is catering.

When dessert sits in front of us, Pop's famous banana pudding, Grandma directs a look towards me. "You sure about visiting your dad?"

"Yeah. He sounds good, seems like he's doing well." I take a bite, glancing at my grandparents. "Is that okay with you both?" They've never objected to me seeing him, but they are my parents, even if I don't call them mom and dad. So, I always double check with them since they haven't seen him in years.

Grandma waves her hand. "Of course, it is, Liam. I just wanted to check."

Pop follows up, "Every time you ask, my answer is the same, son. I support whatever you do. You're grown." Wyatt chuckles beside me, and I grin. "What about work?"

"I'm taking some time off while I visit." I've got enough saved up that I could take off longer if I wished. "And I wanted to talk to you both about the house."

They cut their eyes to me, apprehensive, knowing how much I've talked about wanting them in a better space, but being here, walking through that hallway since I've been home, it's obvious I was delusional.

"I was wrong for thinking you'd want to leave. But will you at least let me pay someone to help fix it up? To make the adjustments you've always wanted?" I ask instead of just stating what I want them to do, hoping this is the middle ground we can both agree on.

Pop studies me for a second, glancing at Grandma, who just looks at me like she always had. Proud, even with the littlest things. "I think we can make that work."

I lean back and exhale, letting go of the control I felt I needed to do what was best for everyone. Pop pats me on the back as I do. Grandma eyes with me a knowing look now, like she can see that I just want them taken care of since I don't think I'll be around to do it. Even though they always chastised me for worrying and picking at them, it'll make me feel better that the house isn't falling apart when I'm not here. I'm grateful for this place, for where I grew up, and for the people that raised me, but I'm also ready for the next steps.

And those steps don't involve being here anymore.

My dad's house is more than I'd imagined. It's a small ranch style, but it's his. There aren't many pictures. One of us when I was younger and the few we've taken over the years. The years in between are easy to see because we both look older in each one. We're seated in the tiny living room, occupying the two chairs that are in front of the TV. I've been here for a week already. I expected it to be awkward, I guess, but it hasn't been. Taking time off work and spending it with him instead has been nice. As we've both gotten older, it's gotten easier each time I visit.

"I'm happy you were able to come this week," he says, taking a sip of his water.

I thumb through the condensation on my own glass. "Me, too." I glance over. "I was thinking I don't need to go back to work right away. I could stay and help with the few things left you have to do around the house if you want."

"You sure? I know you like to keep your schedule busy from what you've said."

The TV flashes with highlights and re-runs of the current basketball season in front of us. Before, I probably wouldn't have extended my trip. I'm not sure if it's been watching Sheyanne reconnect with her dad or just getting older, but I'd like to stay while I can.

"I'm determined to enjoy my time off this round. I don't have to if you have things going on."

Dad smiles, and it looks exactly like his father's. "No, no. Just working at the shop. I'd like if you stayed longer."

We eat dinner as we watch TV together. Every now and then, we'll comment on the teams, on a bad play or a good play. He eventually turns it into his own story about when he used to play in high school and college. I knew he had a scholarship to play in college and then tore both ACL's and got put on pain medication for months in the year and a half before my birth. We don't dive into that. I know the full story, and I'm not going to waste my time here reopening old wounds.

On his tenth or twentieth commentary of the night, I chuckle. "You should've been a sports commenter."

Dad grins, nodding in agreement. "If I had been able to dive back into sports, I would've. I just knew that wasn't an avenue I could take. It was a boundary I'd made." I worry for a second that I unintentionally opened a lane of conversation that he won't want, but he just keeps talking. "I love it. I'll always love it, but I love it more from the outside now. And I like the shop."

I dip my head. Over the week, I got to see the mechanic shop he worked at and some of the projects he had going on. Just like Pop.

"Enough about me. What's going on with you? Any new plans?"

"Hopefully planning a move," I say with a shrug.

He cuts his eyes to me, sharp and knowing. "Out of Vegas?"

"Out of Nevada." He waits for an explanation. "I took a job in Arizona for a few months. Met a girl."

Dad exhales with a grin. "And it all makes sense. Why 'hopefully'?"

The TV flashes in front of us, and I pause. I'm in no way mad at Sheyanne for what she did, even after everything. It takes a lot to ask someone to walk away. That doesn't mean it didn't hurt when she tried to push me away again. And I know that often, I don't worry about myself when there's a situation because it's easier to focus on the other person. That's something I can't do when I go back. We're going to have to prioritize communication even when we don't want to.

"She's got some stuff to work through, and she asked that I leave to do it," I start. "It's not 'hopefully.' I do plan on moving there at some point. I just sometimes worry I'm not the right person. She asked me to go, but should I have fought to stay? I was there all that time." I take a sip of water. "I guess I just wonder if there was something else I could've done."

Across from me, Dad leans back in his chair, looking so much like Pop it's uncanny. We may not be the closest family members on the block, but I'm grateful to have him, too. "You did what she asked, Liam. That's more respectful than doing the romantic version," he says, cracking a smile before it fades into a more contemplative look.

"Maybe . . . maybe there is always more we can do. I think that's part of life though. Knowing or regretting a decision we did or didn't make, a conversation we did or didn't have." He swallows, and I glance away, knowing we're talking about a lot of things in one. "But I think the fact that she was able to ask that of you says something in and of itself. There's a level of trust in that, in being able to request something that isn't easy or expected. She didn't give up, but she's gotta figure out some things on her own so she can show up for you. I'm not sure if that helped at all, but I'm not the most versed in all this."

"No . . . that was great. For the most part, I just want her to be all right."

A slow, sentimental smile takes over my dad's face. "That's all we ever want for the people we love, right? As long as you both try, I think you'll be just fine, Liam."

It's strikes me as strange that I chose to have the conversation with Dad instead of Wyatt or my grandparents. Maybe it's because I think he might understand Sheyanne if they ever met. He's dealt with this on a personal level. Maybe it's because there is a certain level of distance between us that makes it easier, to be honest. Whatever the case, I am grateful for him and the relationship we have now—and the sincerity in which he approached the situation.

Sheyanne did the difficult thing in recognizing she was wrong, recognizing what she needed to do for herself and for us in the future. I gave her space because that's what she needed.

Life isn't going to giftwrap perfect choices and perfect people and hand them over.

Sometimes, we have to do things we don't want to in order to get to where we want to be. I know that I don't want to go through life without Sheyanne, so we'll do what needs to be done.

I don't need perfect. I just need Sheyanne. And we'll get there together.

THiRTY-FOUR

SHeYanNe

I've decided that self-growth is overrated.

Okay, not really, but yeah. It fucking hurts. And it's hard. And it's hard doing it alone.

I know it's what I need, but some days, the loneliness, the weight of it all, just gets so goddamn heavy.

Like every single day in the past two weeks, I stare at myself in the mirror and inhale.

It's been over a month since Shane and Liam left. Right now, in this moment, everything feels like an uphill battle. The first week, I couldn't look at myself for longer than thirty seconds before finding something wrong, something to be angry with, annoyed by—not necessarily externally, though I picked on those things, too, like the frizzy ends of my hair or the stretch marks on my hips—but with me. With myself. I struggle with why I insisted on pushing people away, why I ever ran away in the first place, why I couldn't just *breathe* somedays. Things I thought

I'd buried but haven't.

However, this week, I've made it to a full minute with the deep breathing and the mirror before regret starts to surface in my eyes, and my body tenses. Shutting off the lights, I leave the room, Nyx waiting for me like always. He shoves his head into my hands, and I bury my fingers in his fur, thankful to have him. And Teddy. And Rayne. I've only called Shane once since he left to update him and tell him that Liam was gone for now. He wanted more information; I could practically sense the questions waiting, but I don't want to burden him while he's in school and adjusting to a new place.

I told him I'm handling things, and I am.

Before Liam left, he sent me all the files he'd created: an excel sheet with the budget and monetary details, a zip file with the work he and my dad did together, along with all the medical records and notes from Shane. He gave me a manila folder of the same things, so I had two copies, one digital and one physical. They're tucked away safely in my desk, and I back up my laptop every other day.

I'm handling things.

Since they've left, I wasn't sure if attempting to manage what I thought was anxiety entirely on my own was smart. So, I've been seeing a psychiatrist who dabbles in cognitive therapy, and after she diagnosed me with moderate generalized anxiety disorder, we've been waiting to see how I do with the tasks she's given to me to measure our next steps. It wasn't Shane leaving or overhearing Liam and asking him to leave that led to my decision to seek help.

It was a culmination of everything I've held onto for years—the negative emotions from my adolescence, the self-pity I drowned in, the forgiveness and kindness I couldn't give to myself—it was all of it. I'm not scared of the next steps, whatever they may be, and honestly, it was a relief to be told I wasn't crazy. That I struggled but that there are ways to deal with it. Healthy ways.

The tasks so far have been more challenging than I thought. The mirror is one of them, and I hate it. Hate every second of it. But it is getting easier. The other is journaling, which I haven't decided how I feel about yet. It's only been about two weeks of the tasks, but I hope they get easier with time. My most recent journal entry sits on my bed, a letter detailing everything that scares me, makes me want to run away. It was not easy to write.

I pad down the hallway to find Dad sitting at the dining table with the in-home care nurse that started last week. Cecilia smiles at me over a cup of coffee. She comes every other day to monitor him since we knew he wanted to stay home as long as possible. He's struggling more than he'll admit to me. Some nights, I sleep on the couch in case he wakes up in the middle of the night. All the keys are hidden away in my room. It's exhausting.

But I'm handling it.

"Morning, Cee. Morning, Dad," I mumble, heading for my third cup of coffee despite it being close to lunch time. Cee greets me before she continues reading the paper. Warmth from the ceramic mug sinks into my skin as I take a deep breath.

I lean against the countertop, staring outside at the gray sky. Shortly, I'll need to go exercise a few of the horses in the stables and check on the greenhouse. "Sheyanne, will you sit?" Dad calls, and I tug the satin scrunchie out of my hair, nodding. I hear him quietly ask Cee if she'll give us a moment.

Pulling out the chair, I sit next to him, taking a sip. He wraps his hands around his own mug. "You doing all right?"

"I think I should be asking you that."

Dad pats my hand like it's second nature. We've gotten closer despite everything, being it's only the two of us now. "We know my answer. I don't know yours."

"I'm doing okay." My throat burns as I say it, hoping if I repeat it enough times, it'll become true.

"I know I wasn't there like I should've been before, but I'm here now. I'm here to listen if you need it." He keeps his voice low, but the words hit their target.

Tears prick my eyes, and it feels like I cry all the time now. Whenever my dad does something like this. Whenever he offers a kind word or a pat on the back. Whenever there's an episode. At night, I cry when Nyx curls into my side and my mind won't stop running. In a way, though, it feels nice to just let it all out. For the most part, I try to save my tears for when I'm alone.

"I'm okay. I miss them, but I'm okay."

He studies me for a moment. The intense perusal sets me on edge, but I'm trying to be comfortable with the uncomfortable now. So, I wait. "I know that what you did wasn't easy. Asking him to leave when you wanted him to stay. I just want you to know that I'm proud of you for knowing what you needed to do and following through."

I look down, watching the creamer swirl on the surface of my coffee. "I only did it because seconds before, I had a breakdown." I force my lips up into a fake smile, hoping he doesn't see through it.

He does.

Dad raises a brow like he used to when he would catch me getting into trouble or before yelling at me. But the feelings I have now compared to before feel normal. Like he's my dad now. "People make mistakes, Sheyanne. All of us do. But you did what you needed to do for you. It's not something a lot of people could do. I certainly don't know if I would've been able to tell the person I love to leave."

Nervously, my eyes flicker around at the *L* word. "I never said that. I care about him, but—"

"I might be old, but I'm not blind." He gives me a small smile, crinkling the brown skin of his face.

I won't say it out loud to anyone but Liam for the first time.

My throat closes up, so I stand and kiss my dad on the cheek. With a parting nod, I slip out the front door with my coffee in hand and jacket tugged on. The smell of evergreen trees and fresh winter air center me as I head towards the small greenhouse first. I water everything Shane has planted, all the fresh herbs we use, the smell of basil and mint filtering in.

I think of Liam all the time. Every single day.

I wish he was still here. Wish I could touch his soft skin or just have that steady, calm presence of his around me, enveloping me like always. Wish I could play with the ring on his finger or feel the softness with which he always touched me.

But he isn't. Not yet, at least.

I haven't called him since he left. Not because I don't want to talk to him, but because I'm scared I'll beg him to come back before I'm ready, and then one day, I'll destroy us for good. Aside from a few texts, I keep my phone away from me most times or on do not disturb, forcing myself to have some control.

The smell of the stables invades my senses as I enter the barn. Hay is stacked on the side, ready to be strewn about where it's needed. Some of the horses are still slowly chomping on their feed from the morning as I stroll through. This is the one place that I thrive.

Here, I let myself just be.

Sweat cools against my skin as I dismount Teddy. He was my last of the day, so we went out on the trail, sat under the trees, and took some time in the cool air. I remove the saddle and his reigns before brushing him down. When his tail swishes my butt, I smile at him, and he dips his big head.

I pat his haunches, running my hand over his tall back before leading him into his stall. "Thanks, buddy, I needed that today." Teddy dips his head again, and I kiss his nose before finishing up and heading back to the house under the setting sun.

The colors are muted behind the gray like they have been the past few weeks. No golden hour, no painted sky, just gray. For now. I know it'll come back soon. At least, I hope it does.

I walk past Cecelia's car and check the mailbox, surprised to see a package inside addressed to me. I make my way to my room and place the package on my bed. It's a small box, no bigger than a book, and when I see the name on the return address, my heart swells.

Carefully, I pull it open. It's a book, one I had been waiting for, with a small note inside.

Sheyanne Meli Shaw,

I always wanted to use your full name, and I finally got my chance. I know you want space, and I'm not sending this to intrude. But I remember how excited you were for this book to release, and I just wanted to be the one to get it for you. Shane seems like he's settled well, and I've talked to your dad once or twice. The in-home care was a good call, but I know you're capable of making smart decisions, so I'm not surprised. By the time you get this, I'll probably be visiting my dad. He asked me to come in his last letter, and I never got the chance to tell you. If you want to write back, I attached the address, or you can text me. And if you don't, that's okay, too. I just wanted to let you know I was thinking of you and that I miss you, but

I am so incredibly proud of you.

Liam

Tears fall from my eyes without my permission at the handwritten note. He's still there. He's still here for me. But I don't feel like I'm doing amazing at all. I feel like I'm struggling intensely. I've never spent this much time with myself. When I left the first time, throughout college, I worked, and I drank, and I partied with people who weren't friends. They were a distraction. This is different. It has to be, but it's so much harder than I thought. I read the note over and over again, and I can't believe I ever said that he only told me what I wanted to hear. He was always honest with me. Always open, and he still is.

I send him a quick text, letting him know I miss him, too.

With a deep inhale, I hold the letter gently, thumbing the words like they might transfer to my skin. They've already wrapped around my heart, just like Liam has, and they settle into the cracks that have formed over time. Tears fall in slow trails, and I wipe them away when I can catch my breath. With a roll of my shoulders, I tuck the letter in my nightstand, and I let myself feel what both my dad and Liam have told me they feel. Proud. I am proud of myself, in just the slightest, smallest amount.

Because I am handling this.

Thirty-Five

Sheyanne

Time has a funny way of passing quickly when you don't want it to and slowly when you do.

Some days here feel like moments, and some feel so long, I swear they never end. It's the last Friday in February, and I've officially been here a whole month and a half by myself. Maybe it's not anything big to some, but I'm proud of the fact that I've done it.

These days, I'm up to a minute and a half of looking in the mirror in the mornings. The deep breathing is something I've come to enjoy, learning how to center myself on good days and on bad ones when the anxiety breaks the surface. At first, I thought it was stupid, cheesy. It still sort of is, but it *is* teaching me how to be comfortable with myself in all aspects and all mindsets, no matter what. It's still hard, but it's not as painful as it once was.

The smell of spaghetti sauce, basil, and meatballs permeate the space when I hear a knock on the door. I've become a full stable-hand, an aspiring chef, and a girl who's close—well closer—with her dad than she'd ever thought she'd be. Wiping my hands, I head to the door, surprised to see Blake and Gaylee outside.

"Hey, sorry to bombard you." Blake tucks a long braid behind her ear. "We wanted to come over. Surprise," she mumbles, and my cheek twitches. I step back, widening the entrance so they can step inside.

Gaylee grabs me in a hug, arms wrapping around my waist. Before I can move, Blake joins, hugging me from the side. I curl my arms around them both. "Well, this isn't suspicious at all."

Their answering chuckles shake my whole body as I melt into the embrace, not really caring why they're here but happy they are. I usher them in, and when I turn, Dad and Cecelia are standing in the hallway, surprising flickering over Dad's clear eyes.

He's having a good day today.

"Mr. Shaw, it's been a long time," Blake speaks first, nervous now. I smile.

Dad looks over her and Gaylee for a moment before smiling in return, a sight I never thought I'd see. The three of us in a room and my dad smiling. "You've both grown up. I know that's what happens, but it's been a while."

"I want to apologize—"

Dad holds up his hand, stopping Blake in her tracks. "Please, you don't need to apologize. Are you staying for dinner?" Surprise fills her eyes and Gaylee's, though she hides it better.

"If you'll have us, we'd love to stay."

He waves them in, and when he's not looking, Blake gives me such a drastically confused side-eye, it makes me chuckle. I introduce them to Cecelia who moves to help in the kitchen, pulling out a salad I made a few moments ago.

Blake clears her throat, taking a sip of the water I hand her, and

Gaylee eyes me from where they sit at the dining table with my dad. "So, Mr. Shaw, how have you been? I know about everything, but I wanted to ask." She takes another sip to stop from rambling, her nervous habit.

"I've been better than I deserve." He meets my eyes.

"Dad, stop," I mutter. "He's been good. Cecelia is here every weekday now, and things are going all right. Today's a good day."

My two friends stare at me for a moment, and I shrug.

I don't know how to explain how Dad and I got to this place. It's not anyone's business but mine about the apologies we made. I don't need to tell them that every day, he takes a walk with me to see the stables where he can say hi to the horses or help water the plants. While not every day is a good day, they don't need to know about how night is usually when we revert to the dad and daughter relationship of my high school days—which wasn't much of a relationship at all. But during the day, even when he's not lucid, which is often, most times he tells me I look like his daughter, placing me as someone from a past life. Other times, he thinks I'm a kid again, which isn't so bad. It's the days he doesn't remember who I am at all and asks where Shane is that rip my heart into tiny little pieces. That's when I asked Cecelia to come every day, no matter the cost.

For the most part, we have a relationship, something we haven't had in years, so I'm thankful for that in any capacity.

Gaylee breaks the silence. "Well, I'm glad to hear that. Happy you're having good days. If there is anything we can do," she looks at me, "for either of you, please let us know."

Cecelia comes up next to me. "Okay?" She rubs my back, and I nod.

"Thank you, Cee. I know I say it every day, but I really do mean it." She smiles, her fair skin crinkling when she does, and I pull her into a quick hug because no words can fully express how thankful I am to have her here.

I watch from the kitchen, Cecelia and I working in sync as my dad and my two friends fall into a semi-easy conversation. He asks about what they're doing, Blake's music, and Gaylee's designs. He's attentive and smiling, and the more he listens, the more they talk, opening up.

When we eat, it's much of the same. Dad even tells a few jokes, and we all sit around and laugh. Again, listening to him ask about their plans, their dreams, is not a conversation I ever saw us having. And Dad takes it all in stride, returns their excitement with genuine enthusiasm and encouragement. Hearing him do that, watching it, stiches up a wound I wasn't even aware of. While the absence of my brother and Liam doesn't escape me, it's easier with Blake and Gaylee here.

And maybe while I'm doing this, learning how to be me, I can have them at least.

When the plates are cleared, Dad insists on cleaning up with the help of Cecelia and practically shoos us out of the kitchen. On his good days, he likes to do as much as possible, and I don't take that away from him.

We head to my room like old times and settle in. They take my bed while I spin back and forth in my desk chair. My letters are still visible, so I slip them in the drawer until I decide what I want to do with them. Blake splays out on her stomach, grabbing a pillow to rest on as Gaylee plays with the lace on her sleeves.

"Can I ask you a question?" Gaylee's gray eyes meet mine. When I dip my head, she continues, "I know Shane left, but where is Liam?"

You will not *cry, Shaw.*

I swallow, but at this point, avoiding tears may be impossible.

"I asked him to leave," I sigh. Nyx places his head in my lap, and I tug his floppy ear, exhaling.

"I'm confused," Gaylee murmurs.

Blake glances at me. "What's going on, Sheyanne?"

"I freaked out on him. I overheard something and took it out of context and made it a huge deal. Instead of giving him a chance, I ignored him and tried to start a fight so he'd leave." With a shrug of my shoulders, I glance away. "I thought I was getting better. Handling things more maturely or whatever, but every time something went wrong, Liam was there."

My breath hitches as I try to continue. "He means a lot to me, and I don't want him to be just a crutch. He deserves better than that, and I was never going to learn, never gonna be able to go through life if I didn't learn how to do it on my own. So, I asked him to leave so I could do this. But it's fucking hard." My throat squeezes, and I do what I do every morning—pull in a deep breath and blow it out—until the anxious feelings subside.

Nyx whines and attempts to snuggle closer to me as I finally look up to see my friends' eyes swimming with empathy. Not sympathy, but empathy, which makes a world of difference.

"Sheyanne, that's not an easy thing to do. I don't think I would have done it." Blake sits up, her braids cascading over her shoulders.

I draw my legs up. "It feels like I'm taking the easy way out."

"Nothing about what is going on is easy. Shane left to go to school, your dad is suffering from Alzheimer's, which you're now dealing with alone. You're also running a stable with no help. And you told the guy you—" Gaylee meets my eyes, her lips tugging, but she straightens them, "—the guy who you like very much to leave. All so you could do what you needed to do for yourself? I don't know if we're back to where we once were, but I'm so proud of you."

Emotions swell, and I stand up, making a beeline for the tight space between the two and sitting between them, squishing us together. "We're back. I hope we're back." Blake fully wraps her arms around my shoulders, and Gaylee squeezes my waist.

My eyes flicker to the desk where their letters sit. The first letters I wrote. "Hold on, I have something for you." I pull myself out of my embrace and grab them. My handwriting is scratchy, and I remember struggling to keep up with my thoughts. Carefully, I hold out the papers. "I wrote these in the past month. I've been writing out my thoughts in letters to people I thought deserved them."

For my own sake, I leave out the part about my psychiatrist. They aren't apology letters like I thought when the task was given to me; they became me having the space to write what I needed to say and never did, or never could. It was cathartic, and I hope it is for them, too.

Blake's light brown eyes widen in surprise. "You don't have to give us these if you don't want."

With the slightest smile, I nod. "I want to. You don't have to read them here or ever. I just want you to have them."

As soon as the papers are out of my hands, a small weight is lifted off my shoulders, pride surging. Because I did this. No one else.

They each fold them up carefully, and I retake my seat between the two. "Now, what did you need to tell me?"

Blake turns over on her back and places her hand over her eyes. "How do you always know?"

"Whenever you used to come over unannounced, it was because you had something to say," I say, resting my chin on my knee, leaning into Gaylee's shoulder. She smells like daffodils—sunshine even in the winter. One of the silver cuffs on the end of Blake's braid is coming undone, so I reach over and fix it, patiently waiting.

Blake sticks her tongue out at me but sits up again, hugging my pillow to her chest. "It's really shitty timing." I wait, knowing she'll spit it out eventually. She glances between me and Gaylee, and then Nyx reaches up his head and sniffs her palm, causing her to smile. "Fine, fine. I'm moving. To Chicago."

I blink.

Oh.

Blake rambles on, taking my silence for something else. "It's for music. A friend of a friend at the spot you came to knows a producer. He set us up to work together. And I got a gig at this local spot, a consistent one. It pays shit, but it's for music."

Silence stretches again. I wait for the crash to land heavily on my shoulders and crush me again. The same one that sunk in when Shane told me. But it doesn't, at least not like before. Sadness fills my chest and skates over my skin, but I breathe deep a few times, knowing it's normal to be sad at change, even upset, as long as I can manage it.

I smile, my eyes pricking and tears falling as usual now. Instead of retreating, I lean forward and hug Blake tightly, wrapping my arms around her back. The tension falls away as she hugs me back. "I was so worried you'd be upset, especially after all that you said."

Shaking my head, I swallow. "Blake, I would never be upset. That opportunity is everything." I pull back. "I'd probably have punched you if you didn't take it." Pulling Gaylee into the embrace, I meet her eyes. "Are you going, too?"

"Only for a week or two. Just to help get her moved in and settled." A little extra sadness settles, but mostly, I'm excited. For Blake. This is all she's ever wanted, all we have all ever wanted for her. "Then, I'll be back to bug you." Gaylee pats my cheek, and I laugh.

It's wet and tearful, but it's a laugh full of an array of emotions all leaving my body at once. "I'm really happy for you, Blake."

My fingers spread out on her back, and she holds on tightly, Gaylee wedged somehow between us. The three of us again. I never imagined we'd be like this after everything. There's a lot to unpack. I'm incredibly happy for her but also incredibly sad that my life is changing again. But life without change isn't really a life, is it? Without change, I would've never met Liam, never rekindled my relationship with my dad, with Shane, with my two best friends on the entire planet. I never would've realized how much I belonged here.

It's then I figure out you can be happy and sad at the same time.

And that it isn't so bad.

THIRTY-SIX

SHEYANNE

A crashing sound jolts me awake.

I sit up, back sore from the couch I was sleeping on, and blink, adjusting to the darkness. It falls quiet, and I wait. Then, the sound of a door opening, hard footsteps over the creaky hardwood floors and angry grumbles erase the silence. My stomach dips as I place my feet on the ground, moving toward the hallway to intercept my dad.

Nights have become a warzone. Almost every night, he has an episode or wakes up confused and disoriented. Blinking away the three hours of sleep I had gotten, I see Dad appear in front of me. Confusion flickers in his eyes, his mouth set angrily. He stops in his tracks when he sees me. Some nights, he knows me, though a younger me. Some nights, he doesn't know why I'm home, and some nights, he doesn't know me at all.

I wait to see which tonight will be.

"Who are you? Why are you in my house?" he growls, and my heart drops. Sadness floats through my blood, pulling me down, but I try not to let it sink in.

Steeling myself, I say, "It's me, Dad, Sheyanne."

He hesitates. "I don't know you. Who are you?"

"I'm your nurse. I'm here to help you," I respond, taking on the roll I usually do when he forgets. He barely remembers Cecelia anyway, and it doesn't matter what name I give. I step forward calmly, and he lets me wrap an arm around his shoulder. "You've just been in an accident and needed some extra help."

Dad nods, going along with it, even though his eyes stare cautiously at my face.

"I'll get you some tea, and we'll get you back to sleep. Is that all right, Mr. Shaw?"

He relaxes a bit, and I begin to lead him until something changes. Dad starts pulling away. "No, no. I don't know you, and I haven't been in an accident. What is going on?"

I swallow. "It's okay. Here, just sit."

He pulls back, pushing my chest, and my arm tugs, ripping my shoulder back awkwardly. I bite my lip to keep from cursing at the sting of pain. "No. Something is wrong. Where is Shane? Sheyanne? Where are my kids? They're young. Where are they?"

My throat is dry, and every part of me aches as I come up with a lie. "They're at a sleepover, Mr. Shaw. Only for the night. They'll be back tomorrow."

I hope it's enough, that my lie will placate him enough to let me get him back to bed. He glares at me. I cross my arms. After a moment, his shoulders fall, and I exhale, trying again to lead him to the table. He lets me help him sit.

Nyx pads over to him, gently resting his head on his leg, and after a moment Dad begins to pet him with a shaky hand. The sadness sinks deeper. I bite the inside of my cheek and start making the chamomile tea that usually helps, but I can't help but wonder. Does Dad he know he isn't himself? Or does it just feel . . . normal?

A large part of me wants to call Shane and unload. Of course, I'll update him like I always do, but he doesn't need the nitty gritty. He lived with Dad before I came home for four years. Even without the diagnosis, it couldn't have been easy. But doing it on my own gives me a tiny amount of strength. One that makes me feel proud.

Not to say leaning on people is bad—it isn't. But for me, it allows me to avoid things, and I can't do that any longer. I haven't been.

I place the warm cup of tea in front of my dad and sit, trying to stop my hands from tapping on the table. "Thank you," he says gruffly, and I purse my lips in a half smile, nodding, taking what I can get. This was an easier night, and for that, I'm thankful.

"Will you tell me more about your kids?"

His brown eyes find mine. The wrinkles of his face warm as he smiles, and the confusion in his eyes fades for a moment. "Shane is thirteen, so I've got my work cut out for me soon. But he's a good kid. He's smart, smarter than I was. And a hard worker. Funny, too, for a kid."

I grin at that because Shane was always telling jokes and making people laugh. Hell, he still does. But then, I remember myself. My heart falls because this time those years ago, I was eleven going on twelve and fighting for attention. I have no idea what might come out of his mouth.

"Sheyanne," he begins, contemplative, "she's hard. Harder than I expected. She's spirited and always asking questions, not afraid to push anyone's buttons. And she's only eleven. But it's obvious she's my daughter. Sometimes, I think the reason we fight is because we're so similar. She's strong, and I know she'll stay that way; I just hope I don't hinder the process trying to figure out how to be what she needs. I don't think I'm doing a great job at being her dad, but I'm trying." He chuckles then. "She doesn't know, and its years away, but I hope one day she takes over the stables. Shane loves it, but not like her. I just don't know if she wants it."

Immediately, I have to look away so he doesn't see the tears in my eyes. Someone he thinks is a stranger and not his daughter, twenty-two instead of eleven, and still growing up. The idea that he always wanted me here, wanted me to take over, hooks into my chest and sits there like an anchor. Heavy but comforting.

I clear my throat. "They sound great. And I'm sure you're doing the best you can. They'll be okay." Reaching over, I pat his hand and finally work up the courage to give him a small smile.

"Yeah, I'm sure you're right." He finishes the tea. "Thank you for helping. Even if I'm not sure why." Nodding, I help him up and slowly lead him back to his room. He doesn't like when I help him, as he's told me every time I do this at night, so I stop at the door.

"Have a nice night, Mr. Shaw. I'll see you in the morning."

Without a word, he heads toward the bed, and I pull the door closed behind me, leaving it ajar. Nyx waits for me on the couch, and I grab my knitted blanket, shut off the lights, and pull it back over me as I sit down next to him. Before I do anything else, I grab the package from the mail earlier that I've yet to open from Liam.

It's another book, one I haven't heard of, and on the inside, there's another note from him. I hold onto it like it's my lifeline.

Sheyanne Meli Shaw,

I saw this book at the store, and it made me think of you. You'd be surprised at how many things I see throughout the day that remind me of you. Every time someone frowns, I think of you. Every time someone is sarcastic, I think of how much better it would've sounded from your lips. Then, I end up thinking of your smile, the way you try to fight it off every time, but you end up giving in anyway. I also think of you when it's quiet, and I wish you were there to fill the silence with me. Especially the hours before the sun sets when the sky turns gold. I know you see it, too, and it's almost like we're in the golden hour together, even while we're apart. I got your note, and I'm happy you're doing well, doing what you need to do. Since you asked, Dad is good, better than I thought. I hope you know I'm always cheering you on from the sidelines, and I'll be there whenever you decide to reach the finish line.

Liam

P.S. You're doing amazing, probably more than you think you are.

Holding the little note to my chest, I lay down, resting my head on Nyx's haunches, and pull my blanket up to my chin, tucking the note close in the dark. In that cocoon, the safety I created, the emotions bubble up and overflow. Today, I'm not sure what the tipping point was, my dad's words about young Sheyanne or Liam's kind words in writing that I'll keep forever.

There is no stopping the tears when they do finally decide to fall, so I let them.

Crying isn't a weakness like I used to believe it was. Even though it's not my favorite thing because it leaves my eyes puffy and my throat dry, it is the only way I find I'm able to get all the weight off my chest, to let myself drain so I can make room for other things. I've cried at night more than I'd like to admit instead of pushing the tears down like before. So many times, I thought I'd cried enough to last me for days, only to find a whole new reservoir of tears less than twenty-four hours later.

Lying there with tears leaking from my eyes, I accept that I am both alone and not alone. Physically, truly, I only have Dad and Cecelia on a constant basis, but beyond them, Shane texts me almost every day—MJ, too. Liam sends his notes that I keep in my nightstand and locked away in my heart. I know that if I needed them, I could call Gaylee and Blake. Any one of them would have my back if I needed them.

I'm alone, but I am not lonely.

This is the first time in my entire life where I have understood what that means and how enjoying my own company makes a world of difference when things get hard and the burden deepens. I know that every morning, I can get up and make it through the day, which is exactly what I'll do tomorrow and the day after that.

Except tomorrow, like every tomorrow, I'll be the slightest bit stronger than I was today. And every day, I trust myself—my decisions, my choices, my actions—just a little bit more.

Thirty-Seven

Sheyanne

The pill bottle stares me in the face.

Orange with a white label and completely unassuming in the soft, bathroom light.

I'm not scared of the medication, not like I was when it was first brought up. I was apprehensive when my psychiatrist suggested it, and behind that, the feeling of failure creeped in. As if I wasn't strong enough to do this, to handle these waves of emotions on my own. I know that's not true, that it's just another change. It helps that she's hopeful it could be short-term, to help me progress as I learn and adapt to the feelings and emotions that build in my head. It's a low dosage, an easy place to start.

I can do this.

With a quick exhale, I take the little pill before commencing my daily mirror ritual. In the two weeks since Blake left, I've gotten up to two minutes. As much as I may have dreaded this before, it's incredible to feel how much easier it's gotten, how I don't pick apart myself, inside or out, detail by detail. I've come to realize there's a vast difference in pushing along, pushing yourself through, than actively trying to *be* better. I know I grew a little when Liam was around, in the ways I let him in and let him see parts of myself I was scared of, that might scare him. But this is the first time that I have felt and seen that growth in myself. And done it by myself. Some days are still harder than others, but it's become … nice to have this time dedicated exclusively to myself.

No longer do I feel the need to run away from her; instead, I've learned to enjoy embracing her.

When I exit the bathroom, Cecelia sits at the dining table with a newspaper in her hands. She glances up and smiles as I enter. I assume Dad is still sleeping after last night. Before anything else, I check my tasks for the week in my journal. This week, after almost two months, the task is to write a letter to myself. About everything—my childhood, why I left, how it felt coming back, and how I felt undeserving of everything for a while. About what I want and what I'm scared of. The idea pumps fear through my fingertips. The single sentence written just stares me in the eye, so I turn away, not quite ready to face it head on.

"Did he have an episode last night?" Cecelia asks as I pour coffee into my to-go container.

Exhaling, I answer. "Yeah, he did. It wasn't terrible, but it's practically every night now." Glancing up, I catch her looking at me, a sad, knowing glimmer in her eyes. My shoulders drop. "You think it's time."

"I know you want him here, and I know he wants to be here." She leans back to rest on the counter, tucking her reddish hair behind her ear. "But you're tired. And I know you sleep on the couch every night. I know you don't want to hear it, but the number of lucid days he has are dwindling. It'd be better to get him acclimated to a new place sooner rather than later."

"Okay. I'll call Shane, and when Dad is up, I'll talk to him." I dig my fingertips into the roots of my curls, already tangled from a sleepless night. "I'm going to head to the barn if you need me."

Cold air seeps through my layers as I stride under the gray sky. Nyx trots next to me, his paws crunching over the dead grass. Pushing open the large barn doors with a creak, I smile for the first time in a few hours. The horses' noses peek over the stalls, and their ears prick. There are six in total now, including my own two, and more people want to board with us. I know I'll have to hire help soon. One by one, I work through the horses—Alexia, Roha, Fiona, Bolt. Each one has their own personalities, makes sure life is never dull. As usual, I save Rayne for last, running my hand through her mane and letting her press her nose into my chest. Every time she does that, it's like she takes away all the stress, the weight, the work, the ache of the pressure of doing all of this. In thanks, I hold out a sugar cube, making sure to take one to Teddy, too, since he waits for me—and Rayne—with his head over the fence.

After a moment's hesitation, I take out my phone and call Shane. After two rings, he answers. "Hey, what's up?"

"Hi, Shaney, how are you?"

A laugh comes through the speaker. Light. Happy. "It's been good. MJ says hi and that she misses you."

"God, tell her I miss her, too." I trace my fingers over the rough wooden grooves in the fence.

"What about me?"

"You're all right."

"Being related to you is like having the plague."

At that, I laugh, unable to hold it in. "I miss you, too, dickhead." I sigh, but I mean it. I really mean it.

"I know; I'm awesome." There's a small smacking sound, and I'm hoping it's MJ, keeping him in check for all of us. "How have things been?

You don't tell me much when I text you."

"I don't want to bug you." In front of me, Teddy and Rayne trot around the large pasture, dipping into the back where the bare trees overhang the fence before reappearing into the open air.

"You're not bugging me. Did something happen?"

I take a sip of the coffee, barely even aware of the cold anymore as I tell Shane everything. All the nights Dad wakes up disoriented, how Cecelia is full time now. "I have to pick a facility. It's time. I've been sleeping on the couch, and I can't—it's too much, and Cecelia thinks it would be good to get him acclimated now."

"Why didn't you tell me earlier?"

"Shane, there's no use in that. I didn't want to worry you."

Footsteps in the background let me know he's pacing. "That's not how this works, Sheyanne. I don't care how much it worries me. I want to know how both of you are doing. Please tell me from now on."

Leaning over the fence, I let the wood dig into me through my coat. My eyes flit over the green of the winter pine trees, the snowcapped peaks in the distance, and Nyx walking through the pasture like he's one of the horses, Alexia even gives him a little chase, at which he barks excitedly.

"All right, I will. I was thinking of the facility here or the one in Phoenix. Ideally, if we can get it, I want him to be closer."

"Sounds good to me. I trust your decision."

Those words resonate all the way to my bones, filling some of the fractures I have from breaking and attempting to heal and filling those empty, unhealed spaces.

I can't help the sniffle, and my brother notices instantly. "Are you crying?"

"No," I argue, but the sound is choked, and frustratedly, I wipe a stray tear away. "Yes."

Shane sighs. "I know you want to do this on your own. I know that's why you asked Liam to leave, but you don't have to, Sheyanne. It doesn't make you weak to ask for help."

Another tear falls, but I smile, rubbing my sleeve over my wet cheeks. "No, I know it doesn't. But I'm not alone. You text me all the time, and Liam, well, he sends me notes. I'm not alone, Shane. I'm just figuring things out. I don't think I'm doing too bad."

The smile is clear in his voice now. "I think you're doing just fine."

More tears track down my face at the kind, reassuring words, but I don't make a sound, just let them fall as the emotions shutter in and out. After another moment, we hang up. With a decision to be made, I stand up straight, hoping Dad is awake so we can get this over with. Even with the problems, the disorientation, I'll miss him in the house. Dad is seated at the table when I enter, an old, patterned sweater covering him, and I grab the pamphlets out of the kitchen drawer before taking up a spot next to him, Cecelia across from me. He leans back. His eyes are a bit clouded but land directly on me. Afternoon, we've noticed, is when he's most lucid at all now, if we're lucky. After a moment, he rubs his temples, sighing.

"It happened again last night?"

I give him a weak smile. "Dad, it happens almost every night."

Without even saying anything, he gently grabs the pamphlets out of my hands. "What's all this?"

Even when he's lucid sometimes, he doesn't remember things. Some days, he remembers the disease, and some days, he doesn't. Some days, he remembers certain details and not others. Cecelia said that's how it can be in this stage, but it eventually all dwindles down.

"I can't give you what you need here anymore. It's too much. I'm scared you'll hurt yourself, and—" I crack my neck, fighting the lump in my throat. "It's just time, Dad."

Dad looks between Cecelia and me before he nods. "Okay, whatever you think is best."

I take the pamphlets back and show him the one in town. "This is where I'm going to call first. You're close, and I'll be able to visit more. I'm going to do my best to get you here." I pull out the second option. "And if not, it'll have to be Phoenix. That's the second-best option."

Reaching over I pat his hand, hesitant at first before becoming surer of myself. "Okay."

Cecelia clears her throat. "I may still have a connection at the Flagstaff facility, so I'll see what I can do." She grabs her phone and makes a call, leaving us alone.

"I'm sorry, Sheyanne."

I shake my head. "No, there's nothing to be sorry for. It's not your fault."

"You're exhausted. I can see that." Wetness pools in his eyes when he looks at me, the sight shocking me like it does every time he shows open emotion. "I just wish we had more time."

I anxiously place my hands between my thighs because it makes me vividly upset. Two things I can't control are my dad's disease and time. I can't turn back time, and neither can he. I can fight it all I want, hold on and pull as hard as I can, and still, these two things are unchangeable. They are not dynamic; they will not do what I ask.

They are fixed. Set in stone without a care for who they knock down.

Internally, I struggle. Resentment bubbles up, bitter and hot, fighting with the uncomfortable coolness of acceptance that contests to find its place. I can't change these things, but accepting it doesn't dissipate the other unruly emotions I experience.

"Well, you're still here, and I'm not leaving. We'll just make the best of it, like we have been." My voice is a little shaky, but the words finally crawl out. In my dad's eyes, I find glimmers of surprise and sadness, but most genuine, most clear, is pride. He stands, and before I know it, I am pulled into a hug. He squeezes me, strong and steady in this moment, and I don't hesitate to wrap my arms around him.

"I'm proud of you," he mumbles into my hair.

For the first time, I say something to him I haven't said in years. "I love you, Dad."

He cups the back of my head, and if he feels the small tremors that run through my body or feels the tears land on his chest, he doesn't acknowledge them. "I love you, too, kid."

No matter how hard being here alone has been, I wouldn't trade it for the world.

Wouldn't trade this moment for the world.

For the next week, we spend every free moment together. Luckily for us, Cecelia is able to use her connections and get us a spot at the Flagstaff facility, only a short drive a way. We spend our time doing simple things most days. He gets tired, and every day is a mystery. Some are worse than others, but for the most part, the week before his admittance date is far better than I could've wished for.

Whenever he's able, I bring him outside to the stables. Nyx barely leaves his side, and the horses greet him every time with a nudge of their nose or a swish of their tail. He helps where he can, sprinkling hay down, helping with the stalls, brushing the horses down, and picking their hooves. Often, we spend the time laughing, telling stories when he is lucid and me listening to his when he isn't, taking on whatever role is necessary.

There is only one moment where he reverts into the dad of my teen years and knows me only as the daughter who can't stay out of trouble. It's around dinner. I just put the horses in the stalls, and when I enter, he thinks it is years before, and that I am sneaking in. These days don't really phase me much anymore. They hurt, yes, but I don't simmer in it. I let it happen, and then I move on as best I can, knowing that's not the dad I have anymore. I do my best to just appease him, say sorry, and promise to do better until the anger ebbs away, and it's just my dad and me, even though he thinks I'm six years younger.

Today, the Sunday before he goes into the care facility, has been one of the best days I've had with him. Ever. Chili is simmering on the stovetop, cornbread cooks in the oven, and we're almost three hours deep in a game of monopoly.

He's been fully lucid since earlier this afternoon, and it hasn't faded yet.

"Can I ask you something?" He shakes and rolls the dice. I nod as he moves six spaces, avoiding a hotel on my property.

"Yeah."

"Will you tell me how you see your life going?" Dad looks up, and I furrow my brows, taken aback. "I just want to know, while I can, what you want your life to be like."

My heart stings and stretches in conflicting emotions as I ponder the question. What do I want? It's harder than it should be. I never allowed myself to want much past getting away from this place. But that backfired in a way I'm thankful for.

I know I want to expand the stables. It's been an idea in the back of my mind for a while, and I know it's what I want. To hire more people, expand what we do. Especially in the summers, maybe a program for troubled kids, or those suffering from anxiety or other mental health struggles. I've seen what animals can do for me, and I wonder if they can help others. There's a ton of research to be done, of course, but I would like that. A lot.

At the very least, I want to board more horses, just because I can.

I know I want Liam back.

His brown skin that glows under the sun, his eyes that see every inch of me even when I try to hide, his hands that were so sure of themselves when he touched me. Whether that was a drag of his finger along my neck or my shoulder, or his hand with mine, or a claiming, comprehensive touch, he was always so sure of every movement. I want his reassurance back. Now I know that's not a bad thing and just something that makes me, me. He did it best. Always knew I needed it before I did. I want the teasing back. The playfulness we both had with each other, the snarky smiles, and teasing pinches.

I want the way he simply held my hand, like it was the easiest thing in the world having me by his side.

Beyond Liam, I know I want a lot of things. Another dog, to fix up the house a bit, fix some of its broken parts. Expand the pasture and the garden. They're simple things, but that's all my heart wants right now.

I tell him so. He smiles at my list. "That all sounds great. When are you going to ask Liam to come back?"

I roll the dice, unsure. It's not like growth or change has an end date. Everything takes time, and I still have ups and downs, but I don't feel like I would let a moment or a misunderstanding destroy me anymore. The letter to myself sits unwritten on my desk, and I know, at least, that must be done first. Who knows how long that will take.

"Soon, but not yet," I say, keeping it vague. I move my game piece eight spaces, landing on one of my own properties. "What's your favorite color?"

Dad lets out a big belly laugh at my question, and I smile at it. The rest of that Sunday, while he's still here, physically and mentally, I get to know my dad better than I ever have.

Even if he forgets what I told him today in a day or a week, it doesn't matter.

He knows me.

Thirty-Eight

Sheyanne

The drive to the assisted living facility, Mountain Side, is only fifteen minutes long. Yet it feels like so much more than just driving down a road; it's a whole new chapter, one that floods my senses with heavy grief.

Silence has been the norm today. At breakfast, we barely spoke, me with a weight on my shoulders and Dad with cloudy brown eyes. Even now, the radio is off, and the silence remains in the car. I park, shutting off the car, and exhale. He thinks I'm seventeen today, a year filled with the silent treatment, snide remarks, and a craving for attention. Since I haven't said anything, neither has he. The lucid dad of yesterday is nowhere to be found. I've done my best, trying to find a gentle way to explain what's going on, but I don't want to confuse him more. I'm never sure I'm doing this right.

Without a word, I exit the car, and he meets me at the front. As we step forward, I wrap my arm through his and walk him towards the door. His eyebrows furrow, though he doesn't say anything at what he thinks is odd behavior for me. We're greeted, checked in, and every required form is signed or filed away, and then we're being led to the room. Some of the nurses come in and introduce themselves, offering to take him on a tour while I bring in the sparse boxes of stuff from the car.

Every time I pick one up and carry it in, a piece of me goes with it. A piece that never got the father I know now. One by one, I let them go. Loosening my grip on them and on the pain those memories bring. I know the ache from those years will never completely fade, but they aren't useful here. Maybe in my letters or when I need to talk them out, but there is no need to carry them today, to be weighed down by the past when this is hard enough.

Once everything is moved in, I begin to unbox. Dad helps a bit, but confusion still rests on his familiar features, and I don't want to overwhelm him. I wipe my hands on my leggings, sweaty and nervous. "I'll leave the rest for you. Is that okay?"

He stills me with a look but nods. "Yes, that's—that's fine." There is a nurse in the room, I suppose to help with anything after I leave. The longer I stay, the harder this will be.

The tightness in my chest pulls taut. An ache saturates my body. "Okay, I'm going to go then." Quiet words, but he nods. After a brief hesitation, I step forward and hug him. He tenses, then wraps his arms around me, unsure of himself. My head spins with emotion at having to leave him here. Dad's hands find my back and hold me to him, rocking us ever so slightly back and forth.

"Love you, Dad," I whisper, not caring if he hears it or not. It's more for me anyway.

I think he does because he squeezes me tighter before I pull back. The familiar sensation of tears builds without warning, but I push them back. No one needs to see me cry here. I don't need to make it any harder.

Lingering in the doorway, I watch as he looks around from where he sits on the edge of the bed, rubbing his hands on his pants, and I can't help but feeling like I'm failing, betraying him by leaving him here.

I know it's not true, that he needs more help than I can give him, but guilt comes rushing in, engulfing my head with second thoughts, weighing down my heart. Forcing myself to take deep breaths, I turn and leave. I hand the final forms to the front desk and head back to my car with a heavy soul. The tears come pouring out as soon as I shut the door.

Ugly sobs wrack my body, shaking me to the core. Tears pool in my palms as I press my hands to my eyes, trying to stop them to no avail. The heat comes through the vents, fogging up the windows, and I pull my knees up, leaning my forehead on them to let the tears fall. There is no use in trying to fight the heaviness in my chest, in my throat, or the helplessness growing at my fingertips. It takes me a long while to catch my breath. Moments until every time I try to breathe, it isn't accompanied with tightness in my throat.

With still wet eyes, I pick up my phone, heading to the top of my favorites. I only hesitate for a moment before clicking on Liam's name, officially calling for the first time since he left.

The tone rings in my ears, louder than usual to my oversensitive nerves. He picks up after the fourth ring. "Sheyanne?"

My name on his tongue breaks my heart even more while simultaneously filling the space between the cracks like liquid gold on broken pottery.

I can't find any words, and he exhales. "Can you just let me know if you're okay? Please. Just a word."

Finding my breath, ignoring the hiccups making an appearance with my tears, I manage one word. "Yes."

He doesn't say another word after that, and I just cry, holding the phone to my ear. There is no sound besides the occasional hiccup that leaves my throat. I shiver despite the heat coming from the vents and sink into my seat, letting everything run its course. It's different than the other times I've cried to him. This time, it doesn't feel like I'm an endless well with no relief in sight. At some point, I hit a wall. My eyes sting, but my tears dry up, and I'm able to find the space to breathe. As much as calling Liam and his steady silence helped, he wasn't the fix. He didn't drag me out of the dark against my will.

I let it happen, and it ended, and it's not the end of the world.

"You still there?" I say softly.

"Wouldn't be anywhere else." His voice is stable, but I can sense the little tilt to his lips in the tone of his voice. "Talk to me, Shey."

"The house is empty now." A hiccup escapes as I wipe a stray tear away. "I put Dad in a home today, in assisted living. He's been getting worse, and it was too much for both of us at home. It was time, but now, the house is empty."

"It sounds like you did the right thing then."

A few more tears fall as the guilt creeps back in, just an inch. "It doesn't feel like I did. It feels like I'm leaving him."

Liam is quiet for a moment. There's a rustle in the back, and in my mind, I picture him sitting down and settling in somewhere. If he was here, I know he'd find a way to touch me, a hand on my ankle or brief touch down my leg. My chest eases a fraction.

"Hard decisions hurt more than the easy ones, baby. They always do. Sometimes, that's how you know it's the right one," he murmurs softly, and something in me swarms full of warmth at the word *baby*.

He's still Liam. Despite the difference and the time and the space that I asked for, he's still my Liam.

I knew I made the right decision before I called, but he helps me solidify it. My gut isn't twisted, telling me I'm making a mistake, and my thoughts aren't screaming at me. It's just my heart that aches and tears, but I know this is the right thing in the long run.

"It is; I know that." I sit back, leaning on the headrest. "I miss you."

This time, the smile is loud and clear. "I miss you, too."

"How have you been?"

He adjusts in the background, and I realize I could facetime him. He wouldn't hesitate if I did, and he wouldn't blink twice at the tears. But for now, a simple call is enough.

"I've been reading a lot, mostly the books you had on your shelves."

A sound similar to a snort escapes me. "Why?"

"I want to know what you like."

I smile finally. "Well, I'll have you know I've been playing Cool Math Games in my free time."

Liam lets out big, husky laugh that sends a thrill down my spine. I missed that sound. "Becoming a math genius for me?"

I would do pretty much anything for you, Liam. The thought pounds my brain, but I keep it to myself. "Well, I figure you'll be in charge of all that, but at least I won't have to ask you what two plus two is."

"You thinking about the future, Shaw?"

I sniff, my fingers finding purchase in my hair as I close my eyes. "I am always thinking about the future with you."

Through the phone, he inhales. "I like reading the books you love. I remember watching you read them, seeing the bookmarked pages and the underlined quotes when I'd sneak a look. Figured I buy them for myself, learn everything that you love."

If I ever doubted this man loved me, I was obviously delusional. "You think about me, too?"

"I think about you all the time, Sheyanne," he murmurs. "When I wake up and when I go to sleep. Every moment in between." Tears begin pooling again against my will. "I think about the way you lick your lips right before you smile, like you're trying to stop it. And the way you always stick your feet under my leg when we sit together. The way your eyes turn soft in the sun or when you look at me. How you trust me with your feelings. I think about you all the time."

It's nice to know I am just as imprinted on him as he is on me. Just as in love. Just as seen.

"Stop making me cry, Liam." I rub my hand across my face, taking the wetness with me.

"That wasn't my intention. I wanted to make you smile. Or laugh."

I sniffle but smile anyway. "You're doing a terrible job."

He clears his throat. "Let me try again. There was this one scene in this one book; it was quite detailed. I remember you had put a mark by it. It involved a fantasy about something. Let me see if I remember—"

I choke out a laugh at the word fantasy, my cheeks flaming. "Shut up, shut up, shut up."

"It got you to laugh, didn't it? I missed that sound."

Tears keep falling, but the laughter spills out all the same. If this were anyone else, the vulnerability, the intimacy in going from one topic to another would feel feigned, manufactured. With Liam, everything comes naturally.

"Thank you."

"For what?"

"Being you," I say.

He's silent for a second, and I realize I probably don't tell him enough. Not that he strikes me as someone who needs reassurance, at least not like I do, but I should tell him more. I make it a mission to do so, especially when he's back.

"You ready?"

I know what he's asking. As much as I want to be, as close as I am, I know I'm not. Not yet. Not quite. But I'm so close I can almost taste it.

"Not yet. I'm sorry."

The tone of his voice lets me know he's rolling his eyes. "No apologies."

"Fine. But soon. I promise. There's just a few more things I want to do and figure out on my own, okay?

Liam chuckles again. "Shut up, Shaw. Take as long as you need. I'm not going anywhere." I sigh and go to speak, but he continues. "I'm proud of you."

That shuts me up real quick.

Everyone else keeps saying how proud they are, but from him, it feels different. Profound. He's written it to me, but hearing him say it strikes deep. Liam has seen me at my very worst, more so than anyone else, and while I wavered, he never did. He is a foundation, and at times, I worried I'd overwhelm him with everything I'd done. Not once though has he moved, and that statement is the most beautiful thing I've ever heard.

"Okay." I struggle to find anything else to say. It's a meager response that does not encompass my feelings, but Liam knows me and loves me anyway.

"All right, well, I've gotta run. I'm late for dinner with Wyatt. Are you okay?"

"Yeah, I am. I didn't mean to make you late." I bite my lip to keep from saying I'm sorry again since I'm sure he'll tell me not to anyway.

"You didn't make me do anything I didn't want to do. Call me whenever you need, all right?" Liam's voice is quiet and confident, like it always is.

"All right. Tell Wyatt I said hi."

He agrees, and we hang up on three together. The silence comes back, but I don't need it anymore, and I turn on my music. Glancing up, I take in the building where my dad will be living and force myself to inhale three times before finally putting the car in drive.

And I head home, to my home, alone, for the first time in my life.

The house is quiet. It's always quiet, except for the low hum of music or whenever the TV plays in the background, but there is a silence now that comes from the lack of residents. It's just me and Nyx now, who kindly greeted me as soon as I came in the door and let me hug him till I felt I could stand on my own two feet. I take my second pill of the day before I set out to make dinner by myself and for myself. I pad around, my sweatshirt covering my entire body, and take in the rooms. My renovation plans are still on the dining table, where dad and I talked about them all week when he could. He gave me the go-ahead to do whatever I wanted. One of his jackets is still hung on the back of a chair, and a few hats are strewn about.

I pour myself a glass of water, feeling a headache coming on, and take out whatever I can manage to make for dinner. It's then I notice the envelope and folder on the counter, leaning against the coffee maker with my name on it in Dad's permanent half cursive. I pick up the envelope first to find a letter addressed to me.

Sheyanne,

I'll keep it short and sweet. I wanted to write to both you and your brother. Cecelia had to help me mail his, but I did it ⊠. I wanted you to have in writing how proud of you I am and how happy I am to have you as a daughter. I don't know what the future will bring, but I know it will be tough on you and Shane. This is my reminder to lean on each other like you always did. And lean on the people you love. I've talked to your brother, and he was fully on board, but in the folder, you'll find your name on everything. The deed to the house, the ownership of the stables, all accounts, courtesy of Liam, are in your name. Everything is yours if you want it. When you were a kid, it was easy to see how much you loved it here despite the challenges. And now, it's easy to see how that love came back. I'm happy I was able to witness it. I'm happier I got to know you. Keep doing what you're doing.

I love you,

Dad.

When I look up with blurry eyes, I realize that this is now my house. Everything is mine. I have no idea when he even discussed this with Shane, and Liam must've helped, but everything is mine now. I'm the only one left with a firm hold on this place. It feels . . . peaceful.

They could all see how happy I was here, despite the anxiety that ran through me, the conflicting emotions I felt every day. They all knew it before I did. Even Dad saying "if" I want it, leaving it open for me to walk away or to sell, leaving me the option, is a trust I've never been granted. It feels so goddamn good. And I know deep in my heart I won't walk away. This is my home.

Wiping away the tears, I continue dinner, the old stereo spinning with a CD. Nyx lounges, and when dinner is done and on a plate, and I sit down at the dining table, I realize this isn't the first time I've been alone in my life, but it's the first time I don't hate it.

The circumstances suck, but it doesn't feel like something I can't handle.

Even though everyone is gone, I know I have them in my corner. I know that I'm in theirs.

I might be on my own now, but I'm not alone in all the ways that count.

Thirty-Nine

Sheyanne

My birthday arrives sooner than I would like.

The rest of February and entirety of March passed without a thought because I dove into my plans, not wanting to put anything off. The guest room, Liam's room, is being turned into the master, my dad's into the guest room. My room is being converted to a library and office, while I leave Shane's room alone. As happy as I was to have the house, sometimes walking through it, I felt the old ghosts of the past, and I wanted a change—needed it. Every time I went to see Dad, at least twice a week and often more, I gave him updates. He hadn't been lucid much, but he went with it. A caregiver was always a few steps away.

Three more horses have come to board with me, and I've got a volunteer, a young college student who is pre-vet, Tiana. I've hired a stable hand—Jamie, who is around Keith's age and grew up on a farm and wanted to get back into the life—and I'm looking for another. They love the work and the animals, and that's all I can ask for. I ride every other day, if not every day, on the trails in the woods behind our property, bundled up and the cold pinching my cheeks, but it's always the highlight of my day.

Today, on the start of my birthday, I'm staring at the still blank letter to myself after taking my medicine. I've moved up slowly, and while it's not a huge dose, it helps. With coffee steam floating under my nose on the screened in porch, I sigh.

I want to move on.

I've moved on and forgiven, been forgiven by some, and written to everyone else. I haven't given the letters to everyone because they're more for me anyway. It's the way that my psychiatrist found worked for me, so we've continued with it. Whether I share the letters, like I did with Gaylee and Blake, is up to me. I've written to Shane and to Liam. Also to Chief Banner and his wife, and everyone else I could think of to whom I needed to get out everything on paper. It's a freedom, being able to express my thoughts to them.

Everyone except myself.

So as a gift to myself, for turning twenty-three, I force myself to do it and find the words to say to myself, even if I don't want to.

"Sheyanne, open up!" Keith's voice delivers shock to my veins. I close the book and set it on the coffee table, heading toward the door.

Then Gaylee shouts, and it all makes sense. "Excuse me, open up! It's your birthday, and we're here to celebrate." I can't help but grin at the surprise.

Spring has started to make her appearance as she does every year around my birthday in the early days of April. Some of the trees are filling out in the distance, and the flower bushes that line the front of our—my—house are beginning to show signs of blooming. The fresh coat of paint on the barn and greenhouse stands out brightly in the warm, blue sky. It smells like spring, so fully, so completely.

"Well, hi." Gaylee grins as I open the door and lean on the frame.

"Hi, nice to see you two." I glance between the two of them, and Gaylee flushes, but I don't push. "Come in. I can't kick you out now, can I?"

The flower drop earrings she wears jingle when she shakes her head, patting my chest as she enters. Keith follows, leaning down and giving me a quick side hug as he does. My soul heats up at their arrival.

"Are you making something?" Gaylee asks, finding her seat on one of the new stools I bought for the countertop. The dining table is currently in the garage since I'm freshly staining it. "Oh, Keith give her the flowers."

Before I can register my shock, Keith pulls his hand from behind his back, and hands a bouquet of flowers to me with a smile. "From the both of us. Happy birthday."

I take them with a shaky hand that I try to hide, and the smell of lily and jasmine permeate my senses. After a vase is filled, I gently cut the bottom of the stems at an angle and place them in the water. My throat is tight, and I have to cough to clear it. "And yes, I'm making a cake."

"For yourself?"

Playfully, I narrow my eyes. "Yes. I didn't want to bug anyone, and I wasn't sure if you were even home."

"You're not bugging me; we're friends," Gaylee says, and I shrug, sheepish.

"No, I know. I just—I was okay being alone. But I'm happy you're here."

Keith interrupts. "Well, let's not go forgetting about me. I'm also your friend." He bumps my shoulder, drawing out a laugh before going to sit beside her. Gaylee pats his shoulder, amused.

"I'm happy you're both here," I mumble, meeting his eyes. "Better?"

He grins. "Much, thank you. You may continue." Nyx barks, and I rest my forearms on the countertop.

"Blake wants to call me so we can all be here," Gaylee says. "If that's okay?"

My heart swells at least three sizes in my chest at the people I have in my life again. Shane called bright and early this morning before class and talked to me while I did my usual routine, jokingly singing with MJ and cracking stupid jokes about me getting old. Dad, while he wasn't lucid, at least knew who I was today, just younger. But it was nice that he was at least partly with me today.

"Yes, of course."

Blake answers her call with her signature grin, her long braids blowing behind her. The city of Chicago passes behind her in the frame until she's seated around some greenery. "Happy birthday! I wish I was home, but I'm glad I could call at least."

There's tension in her face, but she hides it with a smile. I don't bring it up. When Blake doesn't want to talk about something, she won't. I capture us all in the frame by setting up the phone on the countertop and getting the frosting ready. We talk about everything.

My dad going into the care facility. We talk about Chicago a bit. She loves the city, even though it's colder than she could've imagined, even in April. We talk about Keith and his plans, which we discover are that he now wants to open his own bar. He doesn't say where, and I have a feeling if Gaylee's opportunity with this designer she's working with remotely takes off, he'd go where she went. But I won't be pushing for information about that either. I'm happy to watch things unfold on their own.

Them being there, talking with me as I decorate the cake and we order pizza and sip on the wine I have bought for myself, it hits me that it's the best birthday I've had in years. My cheeks hurt from smiling so much, my stomach is full, and my eyes even sting from laughing so hard I cried. I haven't had a day like this in forever. Surrounded happily by people I love and not minding so much that I'm getting older. Blake hangs up sometime between the cake frosting and the cake eating, off to another gig, she said. Gaylee and Keith stay longer into the night after the sun had descended in the sky.

"Before we go, I have something for you," Gaylee exclaims, clapping her hands together, Keith watching with an overly casual look to disguise something else in his eyes as she searches through her bag. He looks up, meeting my gaze, and I simply raise a brow. He grins.

"Gaylee, you didn't need to get me anything, really."

She waves her hand at me. "It's not just for you. It's for me and Blake, too, you'll see." After a moment or two, she pulls out a small box and with it, a dainty gold chain with small numbers connected by a fine chain. She holds it up. "I made the bracelet, but I got these numbers added."

She places it in my hand. "You made this?" My eyes flick from her to the jewelry. "Gaylee, this is beautiful. What are these numbers—a coordinate?"

With a grin, she nods. "Yeah. It's where we met as kids, on the playground off the trail in my neighborhood." She holds up her wrist, her own chain glinting in the kitchen lights. "Blake has hers, too."

Without hesitation, I pull her into a hug. "Thank you. I love it." Tears fall without my permission.

Gaylee pulls back, amused. "You crying is always going to be strange."

I wipe a tear and joke, "I'm not crying."

She smiles and pats my cheek. "Whatever you say. We'll leave you to it. I love you." She pulls me back, squeezing me tight before letting go. At the front door, where the air has turned cold again, Keith hugs me, too, wishing me a happy birthday again.

"Thank you, guys," I say as they leave.

The silence greets me when I shut the door, candles burning throughout the room behind me. I grab my phone and settle in on the couch next to Nyx just as it rings with a facetime. Liam.

"Happy birthday, Shaw," he hums, smiling. "How's it feel being old?"

I pull the blanket up higher around my chin. "Coming from you?"

He's on his bed, shirtless, and he stretches an arm behind his head, his lips quirking. "I'm not old; I'm aging well."

My eyes latch onto his dark skin. Not even the screen distorts how smooth it is and how sharp his jaw is. His earring shimmers under the light when he moves, just like the thin chain on his neck. I barely remember what his skin feels like. It's been almost three months since I've touched him, been around him. I miss him deeply. All the love I feel for him, that sits on my chest like a weighted blanket, is bursting to get out.

"Are you saying I'm not aging well?"

"Not at all. You're the most beautiful girl I've ever seen. I have no doubt you're going to stay that way." The words are so casual from his mouth that it takes me a second to register them. When it does, I blush deeply, and I'm sure he can see it. "How was your day?"

I turn, curling into the couch and leaning my phone against it as Nyx rests his head on my calf. "It was good, simple but good. Dad was better than I thought he'd be, and Gaylee came over."

"I'm glad to hear about your dad. Let me see what Gaylee got you."

My brows furrow. "How did you know she got me anything?"

He studies me through the phone, his look settling deeply in my bones. "She wanted to make sure you'd like it. I knew she was coming over; that's why I waited to call."

Liam talks to my friends about me. The thought turns my insides to mush.

I hold up my wrist where the bracelet rests. "Here; it's pretty. She did a brilliant job." After a second, I pull my wrist back down under the blankets. So many words sit on the tip of my tongue that I have to let silence fill the space for a moment so I can properly form them.

My eyes flicker between Liam on the screen and the letter I wrote earlier, sitting on the coffee table, complete.

We speak at the same time.

"So, tell me about the changes—"

"Will you come back? I'm ready if you still want to-"

We both stop at the same time. My heart pounds, my biggest want fully out in the open. Liam's brown eyes brighten through the screen. His lips begin to curl, waiting.

"Repeat that?"

"I'd like you to come back. If you still want to, if you still want me. I want you here." I grip the blanket in my hands, willing myself to stay calm and ignoring how my heart has dipped into my stomach.

"Of course, I do."

Exhaling, I pull the blanket over my mouth, hiding my disgusting smile. "You're sure?"

He rolls his eyes, his muscles moving under the low light of his room as he adjusts, sending heat through my entire body even through the phone. "I am. Are you?" He turns it back to me.

"I've never been so sure of something in my life. Please come home."

Home to me.

When he smiles, I wish nothing more that he was already here, so I could touch him, hug him to me, and run my fingers over his skin, retracing every dip, every muscle, every scar, and everything I've already memorized. He looks at me like I gave him the stars and all the constellations in the sky. Makes it feel like he isn't so far away. It's as if he's right next to me, cuddled up on the couch, and in that instance, I can see it. The mundane tasks we'll get to do together, the routine we'll hopefully have.

This time apart made me realize it doesn't matter where we are or how much space is between us. We've always been under the same sky, and I know nothing else matters as long as we find our way back again.

Forty

Liam

Like I thought, no one was surprised when I said I wasn't staying in Vegas.

The day after Sheyanne asked me to come back, I told them I'd be leaving. They all just looked at me as if they'd expected it; I never led them to believe otherwise. I was never going to stay. It took my grandma the entire three weeks between the call and now to remember the name of the town, but she got it. Her and Pop reminded me that I was still expected to visit and to bring Sheyanne with me. That was an easy promise to make. I thought it might be harder to leave, but it wasn't.

I was leaving one home and going to another.

Now, I watch as Sheyanne works on a table in the driveway. She hasn't noticed me, and I see the headphones in her ears as she moves. Nyx watches from his seat on the porch, wagging his tail excitedly, but I held up a palm, willing him to stay, which he did. I assume she never got my texts that I was close, but I don't rush.

I just take her in.

It's been almost four months since I saw her in entirety. Her leggings mold to the curve of her legs, the softness of her thighs, and cup her waist. The cropped shirt leaves a sliver of skin open between the two in the spring air, just warm enough to paint a flush on her soft brown cheeks as she works, her curls held back loosely away from her face. I missed the softness of her skin, the valleys and curves of her body pressed against mine and the way it feels like she compliments me in every single way. Missed talking to her every day, about how she felt, the way she trusted me to listen. The way she always wanted to spend time with me or do things for me to check in.

It was never unclear that she cared about me. As much as I hated leaving, I'm glad she was able to care enough about herself to do what was good for her. I understand that healing and dealing with things like anxiety isn't a straight line. It's jagged, accompanied with ups and downs and twists and turns. I've worked through it before. I've been the person on the other end with my dad. We got through it day by day, step by step. It was scary then. It has never been scary with Sheyanne. My time here before, I tried to make sure she understood that, that I'd love her through it all.

I was never scared of loving Sheyanne.

Not when she attempted to push me away, not when she retreated, not when she did what she needed to do. I have loved her every day for months. More. I've loved her every day for a long time, and I don't plan on stopping.

Standing there, I watch as she works over the table with some kind of paint, moving in a slow circle until finally, she lifts her head. She doesn't see me right away. Her eyes are closed, and her hand goes to the back of her neck as she twists it back and forth, inhaling and exhaling. After a moment, her head dips forward, and when her eyes open, surprise flickers, taking over her features before it falls away. Kicking off the car,

I stride toward her until we're only inches away. I take time to study her face, easily reading the nerves she's feeling.

Sheyanne tugs her earphones out. "Hi."

My lips twitch, and I pocket my hands. "Hi."

"You're here," she exhales, and I nod, her hesitation confirming she didn't get my messages from earlier. As I stand in front of her, letting her run through her thoughts, her shoulders loosen. "Thought you might've changed your mind for a second there."

It's a joke. I can hear the playfulness in her tone, but I can hear the nerves, too, the honesty in her words.

I shake my head, letting a small smile form. "I'm never going to change my mind about anything regarding you, Shaw. Not in this lifetime or any other."

Her cheeks flush, and she moves forward, killing the distance in a split second and wrapping her arms around my waist. There is no hesitation as I wrap my arms around her, fitting her against my body in the spaces that belong to her, tightly so she understands I have no plans of ever letting her go, trying to get her to understand that I'd fuse us together if I could. Her head falls into the crook of my neck, and with a gentle tug, I untangle the scrunchie from her hair and bury my fingers into her curls, holding her to me. We don't rock, we don't move, we barely even breath as we hold onto one another. I can feel her heartbeat, moving in time with my own, not frantic, but steady and sure.

There's no place I'd rather be than right here.

Sheyanne feels like home. She is home.

She leans into me from where she sits on my lap in the rocking chair.

The porch is painted, fresh compared to when I left, but that's a minor detail compared to her. I rest my hand on her thighs, tugging her closer, roaming over the curve of her hip.

"Tell me what's changed," I ask, my other hand finding purchase on her bare waist, feeling the heat of her skin seep into mine.

The fullness of lips upturn, and her fingers trace the chain around my neck. "The house is different. That's what I did between moving Dad to the home and now. I wanted it to be perfect for you, for us." Her eyes find mine. "I mean, I assume you'll just move in, since we kind of already did that."

A small laugh breaks through. "You'd have to drag me away if you didn't want me here."

Her smile widens, and she nods, going on to tell me about the house, how she made my room into our room and her dad's into the guest room. New paint, new furniture. She tells me about her new employees as the stables grew, and she tells me about her dad, how he's rarely been lucid the past month, how she cried every time in the car after she visited. Then, she tells me how Shane is almost done with his first semester and looking forward to a summer in Seattle while getting an entry level job in the psych wing of the small hospital while he gets his degree. My favorite is when she talks about the stables, how she's enjoyed the work, the horses, like we all knew she would.

"You're happy, right?" I ask, just to confirm.

Sheyanne nods, grabbing my left hand from her thigh and intertwining our fingers. "I am, so much more than I thought I'd be." This time, she studies me, brown eyes trailing over my face. "And are you? Happy?"

Once, I might've hesitated, thought the slowness, the quietness of the town wouldn't be what I wanted. Instead, it's turned into everything I didn't know I needed. Given me the ability to slow down, to enjoy things and do jobs as I like them. And her.

"More than you know." I reach up, tugging a curl and twirling a stray one around my finger. Looking up, I meet her deep brown eyes. "In the future, though, I'm not leaving. I can't walk away again, okay?"

I mean it. I hated being apart from her. It's a vulnerability I wouldn't usually admit. I know why she did it, and I enjoyed being with my family, but it doesn't compare to being with her. She is a part of my life now, a part of me.

Her thumb brushes over my jaw. "You beat me to it." She smiles. "I'm sorry for doing that, Liam. For reacting that way, for pushing you away, for hurting you. I'm never gonna ask you to leave again, all right?"

Relief loosens my shoulders. Whatever she sees when she looks at me, whatever vulnerability she catches, she softens, and she smiles. She curls around me, burying her head in my neck and allowing me to feel the gentle press of her lips on my skin. I revel in the touch.

"I know that things won't be perfect, and I'm still scared about a lot, but I don't want to do any of it without you." She sinks into me, picking her head back up. "I read your letters every day once you started sending them. I'm pretty sure I have them memorized at this point. I can't describe how they made me feel or how you being proud of me made me feel. You were the best part of my days, even though you weren't here. So, whatever happens, we'll deal with it together from now on."

Sheyanne hasn't said it yet, that she loves me, but it's easy to see in the depth of her brown eyes. I'd be fine if she never said it at this point, knowing that she'd show me in her own way, like she is now, by trusting me with things I know she's never said to anyone else.

"You know I'm still proud of you, right?" I ask, and she nods. "And you know I'm in love with every version of you, right?"

Pink breaks through the warm brown of her cheeks, her fingers twining with mine. "You've never let me forget it."

"Never will."

Her hand tightens on mine, her other steady on my neck. "I'm happy you're home. I hope you know that."

I reach up, tugging a soft curl, loving the warmth and the trust I see reflected in her eyes. Savoring the fact that she views this as my home now, too. "I do."

"I'm even happier you're gonna stay."

I squeeze her waist in response, unable to do anything else but sit there and enjoy the way Sheyanne loves me.

Which is the only way on Earth I want to be loved.

"I'm all yours, Shaw."

Forty-One

Sheyanne

After an hour, everything from Liam's car is moved into the house.

It's not neat, it's not put together, but it's inside. Multiple duffle bags, a large suitcase, and a few boxes. He didn't bring any furniture since I had it, and we could always buy new stuff. But everything he needs is here.

I wipe my hands on my leggings. "Want me to show you the updates?" He nods, and I take a long sip of water from my glass first. He picks it up, taking one after me, and I roll my eyes. "It's different, almost like a brand-new place. At least back there," I say, pointing towards the hallway.

I told him briefly when we were sitting on the porch about what I changed, but not in detail and without mentioning how I was nervous about showing him two certain spaces: the office space and our bedroom. Liam just motions for me to show him. I still feel him on me from our hug in the driveway, from him holding me on the porch, the lingering feel of his skin on mine that stirred a low burning flame under my skin. I pass Shane's room since nothing is changed, and I show him the first space, my old room, all for us now. For me when I want to read, hence the shelves that line the entire back wall, and an office for him, marked by the desk in the middle of the room, still covered with tarp since I need to finish painting. I'm painting it a soft yellow since that's Liam's favorite color, and I'm going to add accents of deep green for Dad.

"It's your favorite color, or will be when it's done," I point out first. "The desk is for you. I wasn't sure if you were going to freelance and do contracts or get an office job, but I wanted you to have a space that you could come to for work or for anything really." I lean in the doorframe as he sticks his head in, surveying the room.

Liam leans back, a soft smile on his face as he grabs my hand, squeezing it in his larger one. The heated tension between us grows, pulling us closer and closer with every passing second. Unable to stop myself, my eyes flicker between his lips and his eyes, which have been on me since he arrived, swimming with an endless and unreadable swell of emotions in the deep beautiful brown.

"It's perfect. Thank you."

I hum my response, keeping his hand in mine, and show him Dad's old room, now a guest room. It hasn't been painted yet, so everything is covered, but all the furniture is here and ready to go. Liam looks on in his thoughtful silence as always.

Finally, I reach our room, his old room. All the hard work paid off. The bathroom has been refreshed with simple fixes unconnected from the office. The right side of the counter is bare, all my toiletries situated on the left. Now, the bedroom is painted beige with light green accents and the deep brown furniture from my old room, with a few new thrifted pieces. I found stained glass lamps and placed them on the nightstands, and when the light hits them, they paint the room in a kaleidoscope of colors. It's my favorite place in the house, and I can't wait to share it with Liam.

"This is ours." I squeeze his hand. "You're really stuck with me now; hope that's okay."

Instead of answering, he wraps his arms around my front and pulls my back to him. "And if it wasn't?" His lips brush against my neck, my cheek, smiling against my skin.

I reach back to pat his hip. "You're shit out of luck, but you're welcome to sleep on the couch."

He laughs, the sound echoing against me, heat flooding every pore on my body. "Even better."

Liam reaches down, keeping an arm around me, and grabs the hand that rests on his hip. With sureness, he brings it up to kiss the palm, brushing each fingertip with his lips before intertwining them, leaving me in his grasp, breathless.

When I can finally form words, I lead him further in and show him the closet space that's his and the empty nightstand on his side of the bed, the drawers that were saved for him in the dresser. Trying my best— and failing—to ignore the heat that pulses at his proximity. I step away, making me aware of the air at my back since he isn't there anymore as he takes it all in. When he turns to me, I see appreciation glimmering in his eyes. Pride blooms in my chest at the sight.

The need to kiss him hits me instantly, latching on to his full lips that are pulled into the smallest of smirks as he watches me. Sometimes, I hate that he reads me so easily, but I know no one else can, and that makes me love it more.

I jump up to sit on the edge of the bed, watching him impatiently. I'm waiting for him to make the move, that's obvious, but he's taking his sweet damn time, and I'm sick of it.

"Looks like you got something on your mind." He leans against the dresser opposite of me. We're just in time for the afternoon lights to hit the stained lamps, and colors begin to paint the walls. "What is it?"

I cross my arms. "Are you gonna kiss me or not?" I finally bite out, and he laughs, his eyes softening as he looks at me. The sound travels over me like his fingertips have before, following a path only he knows.

"Come here."

I stay put. "You come to me."

He shakes again with laughter, throwing his head back for a moment before looking at me with a small shake of his head. "Oh, I did miss this."

My cheeks warm as I bite the inside of my cheek to hide my smile. He pushes off the dresser and strides toward me, hands landing on my thighs. The touch travels over my body like a chill, following his hands. Without a word, he slides his hands up the sides of my thighs, over my waist and up my arms, until resting them on my neck, his thumbs on my jaw. Every inch of me he has touched is alight with life.

His eyes darken as we face off, breaths apart. "This what you wanted?" The movement of his thumb steals my words for a second.

"I want a lot of things."

Liam smiles with the warmth of summer. "Give me the whole list."

Inching forward, our lips barely touch as the energy between us teems with life and lust and longing all at once. "Start with this one please."

Not another word leaves his mouth as he finally melds our lips together. Tension evaporates from my shoulders as I sigh into the soft kiss. Callouses on his palms scratch my skin, and I love it. The kiss is slow, and it stays slow. Instead of a claiming, it is assured, poised. Liam is telling me he's here, that we got through it, and that neither of us is going anywhere. Aside from a teasing touch from his tongue which makes my heart skip, a gentle nip from my teeth which makes his grip tighten, we don't take it any further. We don't need to. There is a connection between both of us in this kiss that I am addicted to. The gentle push and pull, the softness, the understanding, it's all just as invigorating as our other kisses, our needy ones.

It's everything I needed and more.

Liam is so much more than I ever would've thought to dream of for myself. Now I can't imagine a life without him in it. There is no dream I have that doesn't involve him.

He pulls back an inch, as the colors from the lamp shroud us in a stunningly, muted rainbow as golden hour begins outside.

Liam places dessert in front us at the counter. An array of things his grandparents made for us. An almond poundcake, lemon bars, double chocolate chip cookies, and fresh granola bars. I take it all in, leaning back, still slightly full from dinner.

"I think they miss you." I place a small plate in front of each of us. The smell of dinner is replaced with the candles I have burning.

He shrugs with a warm look on his face as he begins to cut the desserts. After placing a piece of each on our plates, he holds up a finger, instructing me to wait. I watch as he ruffles through his bag before coming back to me with two small packages in his hand.

"I know it's late—very late—but I got it for you. I was going to send them but then you asked me to come back," he says, sliding them over with a smile.

"You didn't have to."

"Just open them," he instructs with an eyeroll, and I kick his foot with my own. I tear the first open gently. It's a polaroid camera. "I still have that one of you, and I remember how many you had, and it seemed like something you enjoyed. Figured it would be fun for us to do together."

Instantly, I'm overwhelmed in the best way at the things we will get to do together now.

The second is a book, a custom scrapbook. It has prompts, spaces to write, spaces to add pictures and memories. The opening page has a letter from him.

"You can read that later." He points to it, but part of me wants to read it just to see him sweat. I also want to tuck it away, to keep it safe and precious like the others he sent me that I've hidden away and memorized.

I place both gifts gently on the counter and stand, forcing myself between his seated legs to hug him tight. "Thank you," I say into his chest, breathing him in. He squeezes my side and brushes my hair out of my face with his other hand.

"You're welcome." He leans forward, pressing a kiss to my forehead and then to both my cheeks.

I look up at him, my hands under his sweatshirt. "I'm so glad you're here."

Liam smiles at my words, brushing a thumb down my nose. "Not more than me."

He reaches around me and grabs the camera, already filled with film, and holds it out. He spins me so I'm facing forward and leaning into him instead of trying to bury myself in his chest. Either way is fine since he's still surrounding me. Liam leans down, placing his cheek closer to mine, our skin brushing as he does. His free hand lands on my waist, pulling me back as he situates the camera to capture a photo of us.

Our first picture together.

"Oh, I forgot." I untangle myself from his arms and drag him with me toward the living room. There are two cases on either side of the TV now, new with glass windows to see in. All the DVD collections of his favorite shows line the shelves. "I know a lot of these have been taken off streaming services, and some I just wanted you to have. I got you *Fringe* and your favorite seasons of *Law and Order*."

There are others in there, too, intermixed with DVDs and movies I had and ones I know he likes as well. It's not big, but I wanted him to feel at home.

"There's room for you to add whatever you want in there." Twisting my lips to the side, I find him smiling next to me. "It's your house, too. I want you to feel like it's your home as much as it is mine."

This time, he pulls me in playfully with an arm around my shoulders and places a bunch of loud, random kisses on my face until I'm laughing, trying to escape his strong hold. Nyx barks, running around our legs and trying to join in.

God, it's so cheesy, but if this is what love is, if this is what being loved and loving someone is, I'd give everything else up in a heartbeat just to feel this with Liam for the rest of my life.

"It already feels like home. This is all more than I could've asked for." He finally stops to let me breathe.

I shake my head, overwhelmed with the vast array of emotions he always makes me feel. But the warmth in his eyes reminds me he feels it, too, and we are in this together. We make our way back to the dessert we abandoned and spend time eating and wasting film on the camera. I grab a Sharpie to make little notes on them and tape so he can help me add a few to the scrapbook. He may have gotten it for me, but I'm going to treat it like ours.

It's ours. All of this is just ours.

The rest of the night is spent taking turns updating each other. I tell him more about Dad, how things before he left were good between the two of us with the help Cecelia gave. I tell him about the walks we took at least once a day and about the stories I asked him to tell since I never got them growing up. I told Dad about my own life, the decisions I made while away, and how much of a blessing in disguise him asking me to come back was. After, I tell Liam about the medication and the psychiatrist and even the letters, a bit scared he'll look at me differently, but he doesn't.

It makes me feel like a million bucks.

In between, we brush our teeth side by side, wash our faces side by side, smiling at each other in the mirror as he sets up his stuff on his side of the counter, placing it neatly compared to my organized chaos. I watch from the bed, draped in his T-shirt, as he puts a few items away in the drawers, saving the rest for later.

When we climb into bed with Nyx at our feet, Liam tells me about seeing his dad for the first time in two years. How he enjoyed visiting him so much, he stayed for a month, taking on a freelance project in the meantime. They got to do mundane things like breakfast and dinner, talk about his dad's house and Liam's decision to stick with freelance. He tells me he wishes he got to see him more and would make more of an effort to do so moving forward—and that his grandparents and his father want to meet me. I tell him I'd be honored.

At some point, in the darkness of the room where we are sharing *our* bed for the first time, he pulls me over, practically draped on top of him. I rest my arms across his chest as he traces up and down my spine in an addictive, beautiful pattern. Everything is easy, falling back into step with one another, talking about things we didn't necessarily enjoy but that don't seem as bad when they're told to each other. It's so easy. That's the exact position we fall asleep in, my hand resting on the space where his neck and shoulder meet, his splayed on my back. My leg is against his with the sheet drawn up around us.

It's how we fall asleep, but a few hours later, I lay here on my side, unable to find sleep again.

I stare at the wall opposite of me, at the shadows painted on it from the light of the moon that creeps past the blinds. There's a little space between us, but his hand rests on my hip.

I don't know why I'm awake, not really. I just know I missed him so much that I want to tell him over and over again in every possible way I can. But I won't wake him up for that. Maybe a tiny part of me is scared this is the dream, and if I close my eyes, I'll wake up in reality.

"Sheyanne," he mumbles, his voice gravelly from sleep, taking me by surprise, "I know you're awake. And have been awake. What's wrong?"

For a moment, I go still before exhaling.

He slips his hand up around my waist, palming my stomach to pull me back into him, eliminating the space. Liam's warmth crawls into all the spaces that belong to him, pulsing over my skin like a living thing. A gentle touch of his lips on my neck sends a chill down my spine, claiming me, causing me to turn over to face him. He blinks his eyes open, trailing his hand from the top of my spine to my lower back, over my butt. He grips right below it, tugging me even closer.

"Nothing, really." I find him in the dark, studying the shape of him.

He looks on like he doesn't believe me.

My lips tug up. "Really, it's nothing. It just feels like a dream that you're here."

His hand tightens, and his leg, already semi intertwined with mine, pushes fully between my own, as if he's touching me everywhere he can to show me that it is real.

An amused look fills his eyes in the dark. "I'm here." He squeezes below my butt to emphasize his words. "You're here." He leans up, keeping his leg between mine as he pushes me onto my back. "And I assure you, this is not a dream. Anything else you need me to tell you?"

I swallow hard, my body awake and very aware of him. Everywhere. The way he breathes, the way he feels. My hands grip his forearms as he holds himself above me, barely, so I can feel his body on mine. "You are such a fucking smartass," I mumble, breathless, more focused on his muscles under my palms than anything.

He nuzzles my neck, placing little kisses there as he does, stealing my air with each one. I let go of his arms, trailing my hands up his bare stomach, over the smooth skin and the planes of muscle until I find his face, pulling it back to look at him. My chest is on the verge of bursting as I do.

It feels like I'm drowning, and the only one with any air is Liam. Looking at him watch me, I see all the things I feel reflected back at me. The ache, the longing for another person even though they are right in front of you. The feeling that no amount of time on Earth could be enough with them, but that every single second will be spent loving them.

"I love you, Liam Landon." A low sound begins in his chest as he takes me in. Any uncertainty or fear that this isn't real dies because no dream could feel this good. He looks at me like I'm the only person he's ever seen.

"I have never loved anyone the way I love you. Never wanted anyone to ever see all of me until you came along. Then you saw me, and I saw you. It all feels like a dream, but you are better than any dream I have ever had in my life. You make life feel like magic, Liam." My eyes burn with pressure, but all I feel is bliss. "I am so in love with you. Sometimes so much so, that I forget how to do anything else."

I run a thumb over his soft lips, tracing the shape, not caring that a few tears creep out and slide down my temples. "I'm not always vocal enough, but I just," I exhale, "I just want you to know that I won't ever let you go. Even when I have bad days or we fight or whatever, I'll love you through every single one. You are stuck with me forever."

The words sink into the air, land around us like snowflakes in the winter, soft and quiet. Liam looks at me, really looks at me, like he always does. His face transforms with emotions, his hand coming up to my face, wiping away a tear on my skin. And I just watch him love me. He doesn't have to say anything. I know how much he loves me. I needed to make sure he knew how much I love him.

He presses his lips against mine, and I feel everything he feels in that single touch. It's soft and fleeting because he pulls back to look at me again.

"Who's speechless now?" I murmur with a wet voice when he doesn't kiss me again, blinking up at him, wanting him and needing him. Desire and love for him pulsate in my veins. He sits back, his hands finding the end of my T-shirt.

"Take this off," he commands.

"Don't start something you won't finish."

"Me getting you naked is the first step on a long list of things I plan to finish right now." My blood heats at his words. "Off."

Swallowing, I sit up, coming face to face with him. I lift my arms and wait patiently as he slides the shirt up and over my head, leaving my upper body bare. His fingertips trail back down my bare sides, over the curve of my breast, his eyes never leaving mine. Leaning forward, I place a kiss at the center of his chest, trailing my lips up along one side of his neck before reaching his mouth.

"What's next, Landon?" My lips brush his, and his breathing deepens.

Silently, he pushes me back, trailing his hands up my legs, leaving fire in his wake as he finds the band of my underwear and wastes no time in pulling them down, tossing them wherever he tossed my shirt. In response, I lift my foot and place it on his sweats, telling him what I want.

He presses his finger in the center of it, sending an unexpected tingle up my leg that settles in my core before placing it on the side of his hips. He removes his sweats slowly, like he's trying to torture me until we're both completely naked.

Even in the dark, I can see every beautiful inch of him. All of him long, hard, and lean above me, blocking out the darkness around us. He settles in between my legs, and I feel him instantly there, and a strange sound leaves my throat. A steady hand finds my neck, his thumb brushing the curve of my throat.

He smirks. "Any other comments you'd like to make?"

My chest heaves with the effort of breathing as he begins to slowly move against me, torturing me with little movements, setting each of my nerves on fire. "I'm sure I'll think of something soon," I get out, my heart beating erratically in my chest.

Liam leans down and kisses me, licking the seam of my lips and dipping his tongue in my mouth when I sigh. My hands find his bare waist, pulling him closer to me, not caring if it makes it harder to breathe. I'll survive off Liam if I have to.

He trails a hand down my left leg, cupping under my knee and pulling it up as he continues to circle himself against my core, not doing anything but making my head spin. That same hand dips between us, feeling all of me, and he presses his thumb against me as my nails dig into him in response. He sucks my tongue briefly before giving me a searing kiss and then slowing it down. I reach down and feel him in my own hand, wanting to give him the torture he's giving me. I squeeze the length of him tightly, catching the puffs of air in our kisses when I do, and twirl my thumb at the very tip of him before dragging it back down, ever so slowly.

Before, we were in a rush, like we couldn't get close enough to each other fast enough. This time, we both know neither of us is going anywhere. He moves his lips down my cheek, towards my ear, onto my neck. Torturously, he nips and kisses that spot until I'm begging him to come back to my lips. I pant as he uncurls my hand and holds it near my head. He starts and stops his movements repeatedly, tightening my stomach and teetering me off the edge before pulling me back at the perfect second. I can't help the groan that escapes me when he leaves me there, wanting more, again.

"Is teasing me on your list?"

He nips my neck, tugs on the skin behind my ear and around my jaw. "That is always on my list."

"All right, well, you've succeeded. What's next?"

His answering chuckle makes me smile—at the ease between us, even now, in an intimate moment. "Getting you to smile, so that's crossed off, too." He meets my eyes, slowing his movements against me. "Just so you know, if it wasn't clear, there's been no one else."

I kiss him, confirming my own answer. Nothing's changed since the last time.

Liam pulls back, eyes deep and brown. "There will never be anyone else."

I blush, adding to the heat that's already wrapped around my body. In answer, I lean up and kiss him again, searching him out, finding the spot that pulls a moan out of his throat, a sound I want to record and keep on loop forever.

My hand finds the back of his neck, damp with sweat just like mine is, and I pull him down to me, kissing each side of his mouth as my body erupts with heat before kissing him again, deeply. He reaches down and lines himself up before leisurely pushing himself into me, pulling a long quiet moan out of my chest that he swallows with our kiss.

He forces my other knee up, sliding deeper, and I don't feel anything that isn't him. Not the sheets at my back or even my own skin. All I know is Liam and the taunting thrust he gives me, all the while kissing me. My hands won't stop moving, trying to touch as much of him as I can. His skin burns with mine as we settle into an addictive rhythm.

His lips trail over to my ear. "You're mine forever, Sheyanne," he breathes, never stopping. "I'm not stuck anywhere. I'm exactly where I want to be." His eyes find mine. "With you."

I turn my head, brushing our lips together, and force myself to soak in the words. He presses his lips, his entire body against me. Liam's lips find my neck, giving us a moment to breath but giving me no reprieve. He nips and tugs at my sensitive skin, picking up his rhythm and dragging me closer and closer. With a steady hand, he grabs my leg, attaching it to his hip, our chests brushing, his simple chain cool against the hot skin of my neck. Liam tugs the skin of my neck, his tongue on my skin, twisting his hips, and everything reaches a peak. A peak I'm helpless to do anything but fall over, digging my finger into his back as I pulse around him with his name on my lips. He continues moving beautifully, drawing every bit of pleasure out of me that he can. I feel the smile against my neck as one of his hands trails over my stomach, caressing the skin underneath my breast, giving me almost no time to recover.

Every nerve ending becomes a thousand times more sensitive, every brush of his skin, every touch of his lips, slow circle of his hips, or steady thrust brings a helpless sound out of my chest. I'm both overwhelmed and craving more of him, trying to get away and trying to get closer any way I can. My hand curls against his neck, digging into his skin, feeling the tenseness in his shoulders, in his back, as he tries to prolong everything.

"Sheyanne," he murmurs, my name like a prayer on his lips, his head buried in my neck, his exhales sending chills over my skin.

I find his skin with my lips again, kissing his neck as everything in my body rebuilds at his command. Fast, sure, irresistible. His hand tightens in my hair, pulling my chin back, whispering my name against my skin, muscles moving in rhythm under my hands. I moan softly against his cheek as it becomes unbearably hot, and that does it.

A low groan escapes him, in time with my own, with a few quicker movements hitting a spot that feels euphoric as he pushes us both over the edge. The hand that's not keeping him pressed off me is buried in my hair, tugging just enough as we finish together. The pleasure rolls through me slower this time, like a slow catching fire as he twitches inside of me, all his tight muscles finally relaxing in the darkness. Stars burst behind my eyelids, heat burning over my skin, as I hold him to me.

My head is light, airy, and my entire body is weightless, unable to feel anything but the remnants of pleasure floating around it. Liam rests further on me, not bothering to hold himself up anymore. I'm too tired and too in love to care if he crushes me, fitting in the spaces between us, forcing us even closer.

I love it. I love him. I never want him to move.

After a few moments, minutes, hours, I feel his hand leave my hair, and he drags it down my neck, tickling me, until he lifts his head. My cheeks are hot, and my entire body still tingles, but I smile when I see his eyes again. With a soft look, he leans down, a gentle kiss between us, and I sigh into it.

After a moment, he reaches over and drags my tired body closer to him. Our skin is hot as he pulls the sheet up, tucking us together and tucking me into him. My arms drape tiredly over his chest, my head tucked into his neck, which I can't help but kiss.

Liam intertwines our hands, moving to glance at me.

"I love you, Sheyanne, so much more than you can imagine." I stare at him, at the love in his eyes, and relax into his hand that rests on my thigh. "There is no one else in the world for me. It was and is always going to be you. You're my best friend; you're the love of my life."

I'm lost in everything about him, the words he hums in the soft darkness, the smooth stroke of his free hand on my bare hip, over the heat of my skin. Our eyes meet in the dark.

"You know, ever since my birthday, that sunset, that golden hour, I haven't looked at it the same, not once. Every time I think about it, I think about you."

His hand squeezes me, his lips find my forehead, and I try not crawl over him, try not to just fully settle myself on top of him.

"Every golden hour to come belongs to you and me."

I brush my thumb over his cheek, resting my palm on his skin, and kiss him again. When I do, I feel the warmth of the sun during sunset, the early rays that warm the cool morning sky and the ever-changing colors of the sky. I say everything with that kiss. He's the colors in my favorite sunset, a painting I never imagined seeing, a person I never imagined I'd ever have the opportunity to love. He is all my favorite things in the world, and he is better than every single one. Secretly, I wouldn't care if the world was cast into perpetual darkness from this moment on as long as I had him.

Liam is my golden hour now, and I don't need anything else.

FORTY-TWO

Sheyanne

Liam and I fit together better than I could've imagined.

In only a little over a month, we've fallen into a routine that combines both of us now. The two of us in one house, together, permanently. Fortunately, over that time, the work around the house has calmed down. The office library is finished, and most often while he's working, he's in there. If he's not, he's at the dining table with me. Like he said he would, he's stuck with freelancing, both in advising and in graphic design, which so far is working out, though I know he keeps his eyes on a few salary options in town just in case.

Often, my favorite parts of the days are when we're both at the table together in silence. A silence that doesn't need to be interrupted with words, just a silence in which both of us exist with one another.

During the week, we take turns cooking and share chores. Some weeks, he does most of it if I am overwhelmed or my anxiety gets the best of me. Sometimes, I take the larger share when Liam is working overtime or wrapped up in a project he can't bear to look away from. We don't keep score, and we don't pick at each other because we always get it done, either together or for one another. Once a week, we make it a point to do something together—go riding, go on a hike, go to the diner and get milkshakes, aside from our usual sunset watches out at the old spot that's become ours or on the screened-in porch.

Today's Friday, the day when I, or we, usually visit my dad, which we did earlier. Since Liam's been back, Dad hasn't been lucid at all. The upside is that he hasn't yelled in a while, and I'll happily take what I can get. Today though, Liam came, his second visit. I was sixteen again and pretended he was my boyfriend to which my dad tried and failed to hide his shock and told me I wasn't old enough. We laughed it off and appeased him the best we could. I don't care how hard it gets sometimes as long as he is still here. And today was a good day.

A few hours later, I've just returned from getting groceries and smoothies for the two of us. Strawberry banana for me and raspberry for Liam. When I left, Liam was bent over the computer doing some work, and that's exactly where I find him as I enter with bags on my arms, with Nyx asleep at his feet. Setting the groceries down, I take a moment to watch him, to let it sink in that he lives here with me. I do this more than I care to admit—almost to remind myself this is our home now, our life in a place I never thought I'd return to.

I once thought I would've handed all my broken puzzle pieces to Liam. While I would have, I didn't—don't—need to. I'm not broken, and he's not someone that would've allowed me to give myself up like that.

Instead, I put myself back together, rounded out the edges, and took control to the best of my ability. I'm still learning, still adapting. But this way, I don't have to give tiny broken pieces of myself to anyone. Besides, Liam is a piece of the puzzle that makes me. I don't have to give myself up because he's already a part of me. And the best part is, I know I'm just as much a part of him. He never lets me think any differently.

There's no way I could ever string together the words to express how thankful I am for him, how I fall more in love with him every day we live together.

On soft feet, I pad over to him. "What're you doing now?" He's so focused, he doesn't answer. With a smile, I shake my head, placing his smoothie down. "Crunching numbers and taking names?" I try again. This time, I hear the quick inhale of his breath in a small laugh.

He leans back in the chair, tipping his chin up to look at me. "Sorry," he says, his hand curling around his smoothie as he takes a long sip. I place my hands on his shoulders, running over the cotton of his shirt, and bend down to give him a kiss on the cheek.

"All good; just making sure you were still in there." Smiling at him softly, I go to move away, but he grabs my hand, pulling me over his shoulder to intertwine his fingers with mine.

"Thank you," he murmurs, pulling me closer to kiss me deeply, tasting like raspberries. He pulls back and traces my smile with his thumb, setting my blood on fire, a low hum under my skin. I love when he does that, and he knows it. "I'll help you put everything away."

"You don't have to. You can keep working." I attempt to pull away, but he just stands with me, twirling our intertwined hands over my head so I'm not twisted.

"No, work can wait," he says. Just like that. Like helping me is now the number one task.

Liam never fails to make me feel loved. I tug his hand and rock up on my tiptoes, kissing him for it. Knowing he understands my silent thank you, my silent appreciation, and putting all my love into that simple touch of our lips. His eyes warm as he takes me in, following me to the kitchen.

Everything gets put away except for the pizza dough he made earlier for our usual pizza night. The entire time, Nyx pads back and forth between us, searching for anything stray, hitting our legs with his tail. Liam gives in, bending down to give him a treat and petting his floppy ears.

I take a long sip of my smoothie, amused at the sight. When Liam stands, he fixes his focused gaze on me. "Are you hungry?"

My lips form a smile around my straw. "Are you?"

Anytime he's hungry but is worried it's too early for dinner, he just asks to see if *I'm* hungry. Today though, I think he asks because he usually cooks on Fridays. Since visiting my dad can go one of two ways and I'm not always in the best headspace, he's always offered. But today, I feel good.

He shrugs, looking away sheepishly, and I shake my head, charmed by him. "I can start dinner if you want to finish work."

"You sure?"

I slide towards him, my smoothie left behind. "Nope. I'll probably die if you don't cook, but I'll try to figure it out." That pulls a smile from his lips. "Yes, I'm sure." I pat his cheek, "You can ask me, you know, to cook or do things more than you do. I like doing things for you. You know that."

I try to tell him more these days, so he can hear it, too, the way I always hear from him.

Liam bends down to my exposed shoulder, my cardigan falling off my arms, and brushes a kiss there. Fleeting but substantial. He moves, hovering above my lips. "Whatever you say, boss." He cements his words with a quick kiss before pulling back.

I roll my eyes at his words, poking his chest. "Go finish your work."

"I'll come help in a bit. I just want to get it done before the weekend." He pats my hip twice before retreating to the table.

I find my headphones and place them in so I don't distract him as

I move around. With music playing in my ear, I find the flour and the rolling pin first, discarding my cardigan on the counter stool. Outside, the late afternoon dwindles into the evening, the sky turning orange through the windows and the air seeping in through the screens we've left open. In between endless kneading and rolling, we empty our smoothies, and I find his empty cup, tossing it with mine, only to replace them with a small glass of whiskey for both of us, putting Liam's on a coaster in front of him. When the dough is flat enough, I decorate it with pizza sauce and shred the array of cheeses we use every Friday, and the barbeque chicken pizza we planned on comes to life as the oven preheats. It goes in at exactly seven, and I'm in the middle of wiping the counter when my earphone is plucked out of my ear.

I turn to see Liam place it in his with a smile. He moves around me, grabbing the fresh vegetables from the fridge and lettuce to make a quick salad, all while I'm wondering if he'll recognize the song. It's the one we danced to in the barn so many months ago, one I've listened to on repeat since.

It takes him a moment. I sip my whiskey and sit on the side of the clean counter while he cuts. He glances up when he does, recognition in his eyes. "Good choice," he says, smiling.

I pluck a tomato from the pile. "I listen to it all the time." When the song ends, I hold my hand out and put the earphones away. "Get everything done?"

He nods, sliding all the cut vegetables into the bowl with the lettuce, and washes his hands. "Wanna do anything special this weekend?" Liam moves in front of me, hands landing on my thighs. I rest my arms on his shoulders now that we're almost eye level.

My fingers roam over the back of his neck. "Not really. Can we just watch movies? A marathon maybe?"

"Good with me. You gonna build that fort again?" he asks, raising a brow, completely amused at the idea that two weeks ago, I was dead set on building a pillow fort, and that's just what I did.

"You'll have to wait and see. I like to keep it interesting."

"Who knew that when you finally showed me your idea of fun, it'd be building forts to have movie marathons." Liam grins as I narrow my eyes.

I reach out with my foot, attempting to kick him, but he moves out of the way. "Jerk." He just grabs my leg and trails his fingers up, squeezing the ticklish spot behind my knee.

Luckily, the beeping oven saves me. With a careful hand, he pulls the pizza out to let it cool. I take the time to admire him, like always, as he moves around the kitchen. Grabbing two plates and two bowls, he scoops the salad into them. It shouldn't be so hot watching him serve food and set it on plates. I'm sure it's the way he's just as assured in his actions here as everywhere else. Either way, I try to ignore the heat's familiar travel over my skin.

Liam cuts the pizza, putting three slices on both plates and taking the time to salt the ones on my plate because he knows I like it. All that budding heat turns into soft, glittering affection.

He's back in front of me before I can blink, his hands on mine. "Come on," he says as he tugs me down, lifting me off the counter and depositing me on my feet. With full plates and glasses of whiskey, we make our way to the porch.

I added a bench on the side opposite the rocking chairs, lined with cushions with lights flicking on the posts where we take our seat. We settle in, the stars starting to light up the sky above us. It's stupid, but I feel giddy over the simple conversation I know we're about to have. Every Friday night, no matter how we're feeling, how I'm feeling, we go over the rest of our week. It's mostly just me listening to him talk about work or show me what he's working on since the stables is more consistent, but I like hearing it all from him.

"Spill it, Landon," I say, like I've won a prize.

It's almost like I do though, watching his eyes light up, turning molten at my simple request.

We sit there under the stars with our Friday night pizza, with my feet tucked under his thigh like always. I'm not sure what I imagined my life would be when I was younger or when I left, not sure what I thought it would turn into or what shape it might take. Deep down, I know none of them would've been as beautiful as this. None of them would've ever compared to this.

And I never thought I'd think that something as simple as this, as sitting here with the love of my life, doing our simple routine, would become one of the most beautiful things in my life. But I am so glad it did.

The next morning, I wake Liam up by laying entirely on top of him, waiting for him to notice he's got a whole other person's weight on him. It doesn't take long before one eye blinks open. Early morning sunlight reflects off the stained-glass lamps, diluted rainbows appearing on the ceiling. His hand roams up my bare legs, over the dip behind my knee, toying with the edge of his shirt I have on, to eventually settle themselves over my back. The heat from his body combines with mine, our skin brushing against each other in the quiet morning.

"Morning, Shey," he murmurs, his eyes closing again.

Smiling, I turn my head to rest it on his chest. If I didn't have things to do, I'd be content to stay here all day. Nyx is curled up at the foot of the bed, all of us fine with having a lazy and late—for me—start to the weekend.

Below me, Liam breathes deep and consistent, and I turn to watch the light creep through the windows and reach its rays onto him. His brown skin turns golden as it does, and he barely even notices. He's probably halfway on his way back to sleep. Most days, he's more willing to wake up than I am, but on the weekends, it's like a switch flips for us. I take slow, cautious movements not to wake him as I climb off. As soon as I land on the soft rug near the bed, his hand shoots out, catching my wrist.

He squeezes it twice and heat climbs up my neck even though his eyes aren't open to watch. I lean over like I always do when he does this to kiss his cheek and then his lips. "I'll be outside, and then I'll make breakfast, okay?"

Liam just hums his response against my lips, pulling a smile from my own as we share one more soft kiss, as simple and as beautiful as this morning is. Only then does his hand uncurl from my wrist. I head into the bathroom as Nyx takes my spot, curling into Liam's side on the bed. Part of me is jealous at Nyx staying in bed with Liam instead of following me, and part of me completely understands because I'd like to be doing the same damn thing.

It only takes me an hour to get everything done in the stables, Teddy and Rayne greeting me like always but enjoying the warm air and the bright green pastures. Liam is still fast asleep when I head back in for a quick shower and is still that way when I come out. I chuckle as I head into the kitchen, this time with Nyx on my heels, and start the coffee. The speaker plays music at a low volume, enticing me to hum along to the songs as I pull out fruit, eggs, and bacon, setting each on the counter. Halfway through, Liam makes his grand appearance in the hallway. I pour him a cup of coffee and slide it over to him as he shuffles into the kitchen.

"Morning, sleeping beauty," I chime, amused. He rolls his eyes, his own smile pulling at his lips. He cups the mug in his hands and leans to press a kiss to my temple. The smell of his bodywash lingers and intwines itself in the air around me, distracting me momentarily.

"Thank you," he says, placing a kiss under my hair on my neck.

A shiver crawls down my spine, and I shoot him a look. "You're dangerous. Get away from me."

A laugh escapes his lips as he takes his seat at the counter across from me. "Wanna take a walk after we eat?"

"Sure."

As the food finishes, I plate it up, sliding his over and taking my seat next to him. The music still croons in the background as we eat in comfortable silence, my feet resting on the levels of his stool until we're finished. Liam is done before I am, and like always when I cook, he takes care of the dishes and cleans up the countertop. I hop down, ready to go when he grabs my hand, tugging me closer to him as we head outside.

It's already warmed up from this morning, the sun passing between thick white clouds. The horses are scattered around their various pastures, munching on grass or lazily sleeping in the warmth. I pull myself up on the fence once we're closer, resting my feet on the level below. Liam places his hands on either side of my hips on the rough wooden fence. Teddy and Rayne rest a few feet away, having moved closer when they saw us approaching. Rayne has taken a liking to Liam, which always makes me smile, knowing her affection is hard won. She comes closer, pressing her nose into my back before hanging it over the fence to sniff Liam.

"So, I have a stupid question," I start off, and he turns to me, his eyes still filled with amusement from Rayne's antics as his hand rests on my thigh.

"Shoot."

"Someone asked me what we were. I know it's stupid considering we live together, but I guess I never really thought about what to tell people.

We never really talked about it. I'm not worried; I just thought I'd ask." My words tumble out as I twist a curl around my finger.

Liam smiles, his eyes bright. "Boyfriend is fine."

"Fine?"

He chuckles. "It doesn't matter to me what you say because I know I want to spend the rest of my life with you." My heart stops in my chest. "But I don't think there is a causal word for that. For knowing that when the times right, I'll ask you to marry me, and if you don't want to get married, that's fine. I'll make it so you understand that I mean it."

Liam steps between my legs, and my hands land on his shoulders, shaking with God knows what. We've talked about the future. I told him when I think too hard about marriage, the idea scares me. It seems like most times people are happier before, but maybe that's just because they aren't willing to make it work or maybe because they forget that things might get hard. We've both agreed we don't ever want to be apart, no matter what. To me, it doesn't matter if we're married or not. It doesn't mean we love each other any less.

I don't know much, but I do know that the idea of marrying Liam doesn't scare me. Not one bit.

So," he snakes his hands under my oversized T-shirt, warm palms on my waist. "Boyfriend is fine. Boyfriend is perfect. Even though I think it's too simple a word, it does the job. Does that answer your question, Shaw?"

My heart flutters; my brain has gone hazy as my eyes land on his lips. Swallowing, I nod. "Yes."

Liam smirks, knowing the effect he has. "Do you think you might want to spend the rest of your life with me?"

I don't hesitate this time, tracing my fingers up his shoulders until one of my thumbs presses on his bottom lip. "I told you, I don't see my future without you in it. So, yes."

His smile deepens as he playfully nips my thumb before I take it away. His brown skin warms in the golden light of the sun. Those stupid, beautiful brown eyes soften when he takes me in. "You're the only girl I've ever loved and will ever love. You know that right?"

I swear to God, it feels like my heart falls out of my body. "Yes," I breathe, tracing his skin.

"Then we know what this is. It doesn't matter what we tell people. We'll always be us."

There's barely any air left in my body, but I still bite out a typical response. "This was a lengthy explanation."

He rolls his eyes with a smile. "Did it answer your question?"

"I suppose." I narrow my eyes playfully.

Liam pinches my side, drawing out a squeal as he attacks my sides until he's pulling me off the fence. The sun shines down on us between the clouds as he catches me, like he always does even though I've learned how to catch myself, too. A laugh escapes me, my skin burning under his touch, a permanent collection of butterflies in my stomach. In an instant, his hand is intertwined with mine, and I glance up to meet his eyes.

"You're lucky I like you, Shaw."

I shrug, grinning. "The luckiest." I tug him closer. "But I'm luckier you love me. And because I get to love you." An adoring smile forms on his lips as he wraps me up in his arms.

And I know that no matter what happens, it'll always be us against the world. We'll always be on each other's side, no matter what life may throw at us along the way.

I squeeze his hand so he knows everything else I can't properly say, and he squeezes mine back. When he leans down to kiss me, an appreciation for this place and for him floods my body, fills me with a pure unfiltered joy. There's no place I love more than Flagstaff, Arizona and no one I love more than him.

Liam Landon is the only person I want holding my hand in this walk of life and the ones after. No matter what color the sky is, whether it's a rainbow of colors and bright sunshine or a midnight sky dotted with stars and uncertainty, I know we'll make it to the next sky, whatever it may be, because we'll be doing it like we do everything else.

Together.

Epilogue

Liam

It never takes me very long to find Sheyanne.

If she's not with me, she's in one of three places: the library, the screened in porch, or the barn, usually with Nyx by her side. I stride over the brown grass towards the barn, tugging my hood up around my head as the cold of November settles in.

Peeking in, I see her exactly where I expected. Teddy is cross-tied between the stalls as she brushes him. She reaches up on her tiptoes to get the top of his back before falling back to her heels. I slip inside and head straight towards her. Nyx's tail starts wagging from where he sits on a bale of hay, and Teddy flicks his ear at me.

Before Sheyanne realizes I'm there, I sneak up behind her, wrapping an arm around her warm waist. The brush drops, and I chuckle, my left hand finding hers and immediately going for the metal that circles her ring finger, brushing over the tiny gold, jeweled band.

"I hate when you do that," she mumbles, but leans her head back on my chest anyway. Her brown eyes shoot up to mine, alight with warmth, as I tuck my chin into the curve of her neck and sneak a kiss there.

"No, you don't," I murmur against her skin before looking down at her.

Sheyanne sticks her tongue out at me, right before I lean down and capture her lips in a kiss, nipping on her full bottom lip as she intertwines her left hand with mine. My thumb never leaves her wedding band, a compliment to my own. I'd thought of getting married before, the idea of it, but it never fully came into picture until I fell in love with Sheyanne. I never visualized anyone until it was her. Getting married at the courthouse in secret, with only Cecelia and Sheyanne's dad as witnesses, was the best thing I've ever done with the best person in the world. Or at least the best person in the world in my eyes.

Sheyanne spins, her curls bouncing around her face. "What can I do for you, Landon? Didn't you see I was bonding?"

There's something better about her referring to me with my last name, knowing it's hers now, too.

I roll my eyes, still spinning her rings. "I have a surprise for you in the house and need you there. If that's all right with you."

Her brown eyes sparkle, her lips fighting a smile. "I guess I can make that work." She leans up and presses her lips against my cheek, sending my blood rushing. "Give me a second."

I step back and lean against Rayne's stall door. Her nose comes over the edge and nudges my face. Reaching up a hand, I pet her neck to appease her, a soft whinny filling the space. Sheyanne goes about the usual motions, unclipping Teddy and leading him into the stall. She's completely oblivious that I told everyone we got married a month ago and have been planning a small party for her. The timing was perfect. It's the weekend before Thanksgiving, so everyone was already off work or able to get off. Shane and MJ landed last night, Gaylee should have picked Blake up an hour ago with Keith, and Wyatt was already in town at a motel. Within an hour and a half, they should all be here.

The only person not coming is her dad. It's too hard on him and on her, despite her protests. He's never lucid anymore and is visibly getting worse. That's why we made it a point to have him at the wedding. He wasn't fully aware, but he knew who she was, and I know, even though she couldn't say it, that it meant the world to her that he was there.

I have just enough time to get her ready and give her gift number one, even though it's late. And it's not really a gift yet, but she'll understand. The second one will be made today, after we take pictures and add them to a photo album I had made specifically for this. For our wedding party. Sheyanne slips her hand into mine after turning off the music, and we head towards the house. Instantly, I drag her toward our bathroom.

"Go shower and then get dressed in what's on the bed when you come out."

Her eyes narrow. "Liam."

When I lean down and press my lips to hers, she sighs, and her shoulders relax. "Just trust me. Also, wait here one second."

She pulls back just enough, smiling against my lips. "Fine." I slip into the bedroom quickly, grabbing the piece of paper made to look like a certificate, and head back. She stands when I enter again.

"What's that?"

I hold it out. "A late wedding gift."

On the paper is a local stable, not far from here where one of the mares is having a foal. Sheyanne's been talking about getting another horse, just for herself to add to Teddy and Rayne, but she never quite bites the bullet. I'd been calling around for a while when I finally heard back and didn't hesitate to put a deposit down. If she doesn't want it, since they're local and know her, they promised me my money back, but it makes no difference to me as long as she's happy.

"Liam, you can't be serious? A foal?"

I shrug, my eyes trailing over hers, shock and love lighting up in her eyes like fireflies. "I mean, we still have to wait seven months, but yes. If you want it." Before I can say another word, she practically jumps on me, her arms wound tightly around my neck, and I circle her waist with my arms, holding her up.

"You are the best. I can't believe you did that," she mumbles into my neck, her nails digging in just a bit.

"I know it's what you wanted. I just wanted to make it happen." Squeezing her to me, I exhale, feeling infinitely lighter when she's around. "But now you really do need to get ready."

Her body shakes with a small, silent laugh, and she kisses my neck before unwrapping her arms. She steps back with a bright grin and warm red cheeks and lifts up her arms. I chuckle, understanding her wordless request. It's not like undressing her is ever a chore. Gripping the end of her crewneck in my palms, I slide it up and over her body, trailing my fingertips over her skin as I do.

"I don't have time to get in with you, so this won't work," I point out, tossing the sweatshirt in the hamper, my eyes lingering on her bare skin and the simple bra that covers her breasts. Sheyanne tugs her curls into a messy bun on top of her head with a sly grin. I step around her, turning on the hot water.

"If I have time, you have time." She shimmies her leggings down her legs, and my chest tightens despite myself. "Come on, please. Don't make me shower alone."

I trail my eyes down her figure, unable to help appreciating the curve of her body even though I have it memorized. The smooth light brown skin, the curve of her shoulders into her waist, speckled with a few sporadic freckles, and the curve of her hips around the skimpy lace she wears.

"You say that like you don't usually." I step closer, unable to stop myself, and reach behind her back, unsnapping her bra and letting it fall to the ground. She presses herself against me, and my hands instantly find her hips.

"I do, but I don't want to now. Come on, baby, for me?"

She forces a pout, though her lips fight her, dying to curve into a smile, and I shake my head, knowing she has me wrapped around her fingers. My hand finds the back of her neck, and I lean down, pressing my lips to hers. Her warm palms land on my chest, and I feel the heat through my layers. I press my fingers against her warm skin and hold her lips to mine. It's clear I've lost this fight.

"We have to be quick, and then you have to get ready without one single question or a word of protest," I murmur against her lips, now fully curving into a smile. We both know she won't follow that instruction, but I say it anyway.

My wife's hands find the end of my shirt, and I'm helpless to deny her anything.

"Whatever you say," she says, kissing me again before lifting my shirt. Steam fills the space, already clogging the mirrors.

When she steps into the shower and smiles at me, with an outstretched hand, I know without a doubt I'm looking at the rest of my life. And I hope it's always like this. Her pushing me and me giving in and vice versa. Sheyanne fighting smiles and me dragging them out of her anyway. I hope we never lose all the little things that make up the two of us.

Because I can't imagine life any other way.

"Liam, where did you even get this? Why am I wearing white? What is going on? Why are you dressed up?" The string of questions escapes the bedroom door and reaches me to where I lean against the wall next to it.

Nyx looks up at me with a wagging tail, and I pat his head and lean down. "You know your mom is crazy, right?"

"Stop shit talking me to my own dog, Landon."

I can't help the chuckle that escapes me as I tuck my hands into the pockets of my dress pants. Sheyanne pulls open the door, her curls falling down in beautiful coils over her still bare skin, only covered by her towel. Thankfully, from here, she can't see the people that are waiting off to the side in the living room.

"Liam please, tell me," she whines, reaching for my hand. I let her take it and squeeze.

I step toward her, leaning down in the door frame. "No. Just put it on, okay? Gaylee made it for you."

Surprise fills her eyes, and she turns to glance back at the dress laid out on the bed. It's ivory satin, and it's off the shoulder, as Gaylee described it, designed perfectly for Sheyanne. She didn't wear a wedding dress when we got married, which was fine, but we also didn't get any pictures. That's something we'll be fixing today, with all her friends and most of her family here.

"I promise it's worth it. Now go."

After a kiss on her forehead, she quiets and turns back into the room, closing the door behind her. I exhale and wait. Almost twenty minutes later, she steps out. The long satin dress crinkles, her shoes I placed out dangling in her hands. When she steps into the hall next to me, I see her feet peek out from under the long dress. Her deep brown curls are left natural and hanging around her face and over her shoulders. The only jewelry she wears are the rings on her fingers and the tiniest amount of make up around her eyes. Her cheeks warm when she notices me staring.

"You're beautiful." I take her hand in mine.

Sheyanne's eyes light up, nose scrunching. "Gross." I chuckle, squeezing her hand again before stepping forward. She stands, pulling me back. "You're beautiful, too, you know." She runs her thumb over my knuckles until I give her a smile.

"Come on," I say, and lead her down the hall, Nyx trotting on her other side.

Just as she opens her mouth to ask another question, our guests make their appearance known, shouting "Surprise!" as they do. I watch with unconcealed amusement as her jaw drops a little. Her eyes flick around, landing on everyone—Shane, MJ, Gaylee, Blake, Keith, and Wyatt, who she's become very close with. With a small clatter, her shoes fall to the ground.

"What are you guys doing here?" Sheyanne doesn't know where to look. Her eyes flick around at all her friends, equally as dressed up, and back to me.

Blake grins and rubs her hands together. "Your *husband* invited us. Wanted you to have a celebration."

MJ waves around her camera. "You're getting pictures. That's why you're dressed up."

Gaylee dances on the balls of her feet. "Oh, the dress is perfect. You look perfect, Shey."

It's silent for a moment. Sheyanne is completely speechless, and then, she turns to look at me, like for a moment, it's just us two. "You did this for us?" she whispers.

"For us. For you." I run my hand up her back, over the soft skin and back down her arm until I'm holding her hand again. "There isn't a thing I wouldn't do for you." Her blush deepens as no more words escape her.

For a moment, her grip tightens before she releases my hand all together, only to wrap her arms around my waist. I breathe her in as she does, the familiar rose water and light floral scent invading my senses. After a moment, she lets go with a smile, rushing towards her girlfriends, casting off the men for the time being.

I move toward her brother, Keith, and my best friend. "Thanks for coming."

"I can't believe you got married," Wyatt speaks first, drawing me into a hug, patting my back a few times. "It looks good on you. You look happy, brother."

Happy is a perfect word to describe what I am.

Shane grins over at me. "Guess me and you are brothers now, huh?"

"I was destined to be stuck with this family, it seems," I say drily, but we laugh, and he pats me on the back.

"We're happy to be stuck with you, too. Well, at least she is," Shane responds and reaches down, handing us each a beer from the cooler he brought.

Keith, someone I've grown close with over time, shakes his head, the same smile on his face as the rest of them, though his time is divided between talking to us and staring at Gaylee. "You make her very happy, and you fell into this place easily. It's no surprise to me. I'm happy for you guys."

I turn to look at Sheyanne, currently being fawned over by her three girlfriends with a bright smile on her face. They complement the dress and the ring, laughing as they spin Sheyanne around in circles. As if she can sense me looking, she turns, looking over her shoulder, and her smoldering brown eyes meet mine. No feeling on this earth could beat the feeling I get when she looks at me like that.

It's like the world stops turning to give us a moment to just exist in the same time and space together.

After a few more moments, we all come together. I give each of the girls a hug, grateful they could come. Gaylee and Keith have become regulars at the house, Blake is visiting from Chicago, a few new tattoos stenciling her dark brown skin, and MJ looks just as in love with Shane as she does every time. As we stand there, I'm deeply thankful for them and what great of friends they are, not just to Sheyanne but to me. I turn to watch as Sheyanne embraces each of the boys with a bright smile, even when she threatens to kill her brother if he messes up her hair.

Our own little family, all here together.

When all the hugs and "I love you's" are said and done, she gravitates back to my side. She wraps her arm around me and rests her head on my bicep as we wait for MJ and Gaylee to get the digital and polaroid cameras ready. The sky is gray outside, the quiet promise of snow on the horizon, but the mountains and winter pines are visible in the background, and I imagine they'll be perfect for the pictures. There are string lights hung up in the living room and kitchen—Shane's job when he first arrived. It all looks beautiful, just like the girl standing next to me.

Gaylee gives us the thumbs up when she's ready, and everyone cheers, excited to watch.

I brush my thumb over the inside of her arm. "You ready?"

Sheyanne looks up at me with a warm smile. "I'm ready for everything that involves you. Are you ready?"

I lean down, pressing a kiss on her cheek and then quickly over her lips. "For everything."

SHEYANNE

Hours later, everything is quiet in the house.

Liam and I are leaning against the headboard with a plate of cake between us and the polaroids from today. He told me once Gaylee got the digital ones ready, he's putting them in a photo album for us, which only made me more emotional than I already was. Then, they explained the use of the polaroids—so we could have some to look at today. The photo album he designed sits between us. It's black with a space on the front for photos, and it has our last name embroidered on the front. On the first page is our wedding certificate marked with our signatures and the date we got married.

Getting married in the courthouse was the best thing we could've done, and I don't and never will regret it. But him doing this for us, having everyone over in a late celebration of our wedding, was something I didn't even know I wanted until it happened. There was cake and drinks and the people that make up my family, aside from Dad. Even that doesn't sting as much as it could, since he was there at the courthouse with us, and even though he was a little lost, he walked me down the hallway like it was an aisle.

Everyone stayed over and is spread about the house, since we all drank and danced and laughed in between pictures. Wyatt is passed out on the couch, Shane and MJ in his room, Blake and Gaylee in the guest room, and Keith on the recliner in the living room. It's nice having them all here. While I see Shane and MJ for holidays, they've decided to stay in Seattle even after he graduates. I don't see Blake that much, haven't since she left for Chicago. Wyatt comes down every so often, but I know Liam misses him, so I'm so happy he could come as well.

Taking a bite of cake and ignoring Liam's eyes on me, I pick up the square pictures.

There's one of me and Nyx on the floor, and a second of the same image, except Liam is bent down between us, and I'm looking up at him.

Another with just me and the simple flowers Blake had brought just for this moment. Another with me and the makeshift certificate for the foal coming in the spring, with Liam behind me making a thumbs up, twinkling lights illuminated in the background.

There's one with my girls. Blake holds my hand tightly as she looks at me, her curls fashioned into braids that hang long down her back, while Gaylee curls her arms around us both, peeking her head out as she does. Then there's one with the four of us girls, my arm around MJ when she jumped in with us. We then forced Liam into one, and then I took a picture of him with all the girls he's come to look at as family.

And then I have one with my brother—who just couldn't resist tugging my curls, so in response I fluffed his up. I smiled anyway. There's one with Keith and I grinning as we clinked shot glasses together. And one of Wyatt and I doing some stupid pose and making fun of Liam.

Then, there's a few of Liam and the boys, each dressed up in suits and dress shirts in various shots around the kitchen or on the porch.

I love all those, all the ones that document our family and friends.

But the ones of Liam and I capture us in a light I never even imagined.

There are so many of us now; I can't wait to see the digital ones. There's one of him kissing my cheek from behind with cake in my hand. And one where he's seated and I'm leaning on his shoulder, looking away, but it's perfect. Another of us dancing, with smiles on our faces as he pulled me closer. There's one of us simply kissing, like we're each other's lifelines.

My favorite is the one where neither of us are looking at the camera. We're on the porch, and I'm leaned up on my tiptoes, arms tight around his neck and his tight around my back, both of us buried in each other with the snowcapped mountains in the background.

Liam adjusts next to me and plucks the image out of my hand. His fingers brush mine, and the feeling of them lingers like every time he touches me. I look over to him. "Are you happy?" he asks.

The question is pointless. I've been happy since the day he came back.

I turn towards him, my feet tucked under his legs, my shoulders draped in his T-shirt. "Happier than ever, Landon."

He smirks, his eyes warming when he looks at me. "You know, I'm not sure if calling me Landon has the desired effect since you are now also a Landon."

My heart flutters at that. It's not like it's new; we've been married for seven months, but today made it all feel a bit more real.

"Not going to stop me."

He grabs the plate of cake and takes a bite. Before putting it down, he feeds me one as well. "Nothing stops you, Sheyanne." Liam grabs a few of the pictures. He holds up the one where we're both standing behind the cake, looking up at each other. "I'm keeping this one."

I raise a brow. "They're ours. You can keep them all."

Liam reaches out and pinches me, drawing out a squeal. "I know that, smartass, but I want this one specifically."

"What are you gonna do? Put in your wallet?"

He shrugs. "Either there, the office, or my car."

My entire body flutters. "Liam, we barely leave the house."

He chuckles, his hand curling around my ankle. "Well, when I do, I get to have this with me. That all right with you?"

The idea of Liam keeping a part of us in his pocket at all times pretty much destroys my heart in the most beautiful of ways. I lean in, jokingly. "As long as you keep it forever."

His grip on my ankle tightens. "I have no plans to do anything else with it."

I lean forward like I'm going to kiss him but fake out and go for the plate on his nightstand. I don't get far. Liam's free hand reaches up and grips my chin gently, bringing my lips to his, burning me from the inside out in the gentle action.

With a sigh, I tuck closer, his warm skin against mine as his arm curls around my back and his hand lands on the bare skin of my leg. Somehow, he twists us and has us laying down flat and the covers pulled over our heads, so quickly I can't help the squeal that escapes me, my head light with laughter. I slide down and into our little cocoon of the covers as he places his leg over mine and his arm over my waist, trapping me in place.

"Wait, can you reach into your nightstand?" I ask, blinking innocently.

He kept today a secret; that is a fact. I had no idea until I walked into the living room, but when he told me to get dressed earlier, I figured it was the perfect time to hide his late gift. I was going to save it for Christmas, but then he started being all secretive and bossy.

Liam narrows his eyes but uncovers himself just long enough to do so. When he comes back, there's a box in his hand. Our wedding bands don't match. Maybe it's stupid of me, picky, but I want them to match. Mine was made to compliment the engagement ring, simple gold with a few baguettes inlaid in the thin band. Liam's was plain gold, which was fine, but I wanted him to have something as nice as what he got me.

"Open it." I squeeze his wrist before he lays down next to me. Curling into his side, I tuck my arm around his, resting my head on the pillow to watch him in the dark.

He flips open the box to see the gold band with a singular diamond to match the style of mine. "I was going to save it for Christmas, but then today, when you wouldn't tell me, I figured I'd give it to you now." Liam turns it over in his fingers, rubbing his thumb over the outside. I press my lips to his arm. "It's also engraved."

Finally, he turns to look at me. "Sheyanne," he says roughly, the sound traveling over my skin. I'm not sure why I feel like crying, but I do. Maybe it's everything from earlier; maybe it's him looking at me like

I gave him the whole world. Maybe both.

"Would you just look before I start crying, please?"

His lips quirk, and he turns back to the ring, using his phone for a flashlight. I can see the delicate words when the light hits them, and he stops turning it, so I know he sees it too. Next to me, he stiffens, and I look over at him to see emotion written plainly on his features.

I nudge him, clearing my throat. "Hey, I'm the crybaby of the relationship, not you." A tear streaks out and slides down my cheek that I wipe away.

"*You're my dream.*" He holds the ring tightly in his hands. The only time I've seen Liam cry was right after we signed the marriage certificate, and that practically destroyed me, so if he cries now, I know with certainty I won't survive.

In the shadows of our covers, he slips off his old ring and slips on the new one. When he returns, he wastes no time in burying his hand in my curls and tugging my lips to his. In that singular press of his lips, I feel everything he doesn't say. After I pull away, I reach over and grab his left hand, twirling the ring like I always do.

Liam adjusts us so he can look down at me, leaning up on one elbow and positioning himself above me in the dark warmth of the covers. Smiling with watery eyes, I squeeze his wrist. "It's true; you are."

He swallows with a small shake of his head and bends down, sticking his head in the crook of my neck. I can feel the little puffs of air he lets out, and I just run my nails up and down his back. Usually, I am the one struggling to find words, but the tables have turned tonight. In the quiet, I give him a moment, trying not to cry myself.

When he picks his head back up, I change the subject. "Thank you for today." He nods, brown eyes swimming with emotions. "Are you happy?"

He bends down, kissing the hollow of my throat, his simple chain brushing against my skin, cooling me with the contrast. I feel his hand bury itself in my hair, his fingers gently caressing my head like he does when I'm anxious. He kisses up my jaw until he's fully hovering above my lips.

Liam's lips curl gently, just brushing mine, my body so aware of his. "No one is happier than me."

"I am." I sneak my thumb in between us, pressing on his full bottom lip.

He kisses it, and my entire body flushes. "No, you're not."

"You're going to fight me on this? Can't we both be happy?"

Liam chuckles against my lips, the sound resonating all the way to my bones. "You started the fight, but I'm going to finish it."

"How?" My brows furrow, and I wrap my hand around his arm, holding him to me.

He kisses my cheek, then my other, then the bridge of my nose, and then back to my lips. The heavy weight of him resting on top of me under the covers relaxes me to no end. "By making you the happiest girl alive for the rest of your life." His lips move against my own with his words in a teasing kiss.

"That sounds a lot like losing," I say, a wide smile spreading on my face.

"It's not really losing if you smile at me like that."

And with that, he takes any air and any argument I have left. I rest my head back. "Fine, you win." His head falls to my neck as he laughs again. "But I have one condition."

He lifts his head, meeting my eyes in the dark. "What's that?"

"You said my life. It's our life."

Liam is quiet, his left hand coming out of my hair, and he traces his fingers down the side of my face before pressing them against my skin. I feel the cool metal of his new wedding band on my cheek. He smiles at me, a soft one, but it settles in my heart, anchoring me to him.

"Your life is my life, Sheyanne." His lips brush mine, eyes never leaving my own. "So, I suppose that's a condition I can accept."

With that, he kisses me deeply, solidifying how our lives have come together. It might not make sense to some, but it makes perfect sense to me. Obviously, we have our own lives, and we can both stand on our own two feet, but I understand what he means completely.

Our lives have melded together so seamlessly that it sometimes does feel like we're on the same lifeline. That our lifelines were designed to twist and turn and meld together. That even if the world tried, they couldn't untangle us from one another.

So, he kisses me like I'm his lifeline, and I kiss him like he is mine.

Acknowledgements

I wrote this book for anyone like myself—for anyone of color, for anyone who has ever been made fun of for liking something that was deemed "uncool" or "not for you." It is for you. It has always been for you, and it always will be for you. This was born out of wishing to see myself, to see girls who looked like me or my friends or my family, in spaces that they never got to see themselves in. Whatever space you find yourself wishing was for you, it is out there, and I hope you make it your own. This is also, unexpectedly, probably the most personal book I will write. Bits and pieces of myself ended up within the pages, within Sheyanne, within the things I love, the things I hope for, and the dreams I have. And also in my struggles. This process has been hard, opening myself up to publishing this book and this story but getting here, to this point, I know that it is all worth it. Even if just one of you finds a piece of yourself here, I am eternally grateful. I know authors shouldn't have favorites, but this book, this story, will always have its own special space in my heart.

To my mom—for being my mom and for always being kind to me when I was not kind to myself or to you. Thank you for always accepting me as I was and encouraging me to be whoever I desired. To Dad, again, hoping you'll never read these, but thank you for always wanting more for me and pushing me to follow my dreams.

To Kennedy—you love this book more than I could've hoped for. You kept loving this book even when I felt lost with it; you have loved this book all along. At times when I wanted to stop, you always encouraged me to keep going. You are such an amazing soul, and I'm so grateful for you and your friendship. You are deserving of the entire world. I can't wait to search high and low for your own personal Liam Landon (who I will find if it kills me; it is the least I can do.) More seriously, I'm, as always, thankful to have you in my life.

To Liya—my love. The way you love *Golden Hour* and the way you unfailingly were there to help whenever I needed, thank you. I hope this story in its final version still holds the same place in your heart as before, just like you will always have a spot in my own.

To Est—the love and the comments and the feedback you gave to *Golden Hour* made me smile when I wanted to cry; they made me love my characters again from the outside. You are a shining star in this world, a loving friend, and an amazing person. The type of person I hope everyone gets to have in their life—I'm beyond grateful for you in mine.

To Sab—you were again, the first person I ever told about *Golden Hour*, a random text about me visualizing two people on horseback in Arizona. You are my horse girl bestie for life, the SpongeBob to my Patrick—we are the chaos sisters (!) and I am so, so grateful for you in my life. For the friendship we have, the facetimes where we are endlessly nosy, the jokes, and a shared love for a million things. Thank you for being you. I love you forever!

To Kay, Maria, Steph—your comments on the story were everything in its early stages. Your support through everything, I am forever thankful. I wouldn't be here without you guys.

To Mia—happy birthday! I love you!

To Steph M. and Jordan—sad girl libra squad forever. Life would be infinitely boring without you both. I love you.

To Jenni, Emaan, Foo, E, Nirvair, Jordyn, Emery, Carm, Asli, Jules, Jay, Shan, Cate, Pome, Nicole P., Alexis, Miya, Zoe, Ivanna, Kelsey, Hope, and to all my other friends—there are too many of you to name at this point (which is insane; I am crazy, so thank you for interacting with me anyway). Thank you for your love. You guys are all brilliant. Those of you who are writing, I cannot wait to read your words in their finished form. To you, who are always excited, who are always swooning over books with me and crying over them, too, I love you all so, so much. If you think I'm talking to you, I am.

To Nakia, Taliyah, Lia, Elan, Lex, Katelyn, Sahara, Jess, Avery, Daisy, Carol, Chloe, Yami, Bia, Rose, Karina, Carly, Catia and so many others—your kind words, your edits, your videos, your posts about *Mine Would Be You*, truly are something I am so grateful for. Thank you all for doing what you love so authentically and including a book of mine.

To April—thank you for editing this second book with me! You are amazing, and I'm so grateful to work with you. To Tiffany for proofreading, Sarah for the lovely formatting, and to Acacia—the cover is more than I could have imagined.

To my dogs—yes, I had to. They (and all my pets) have been there in the darkest times. The unconditional love can never be repaid, but I will love all of them forever.

To the reader—this story terrified me. I was scared to put it out there, but thank you for welcoming it with open arms and excited hearts. Not sure what I would be doing without all of you, but it wouldn't be this. So, thank you for existing, thank you for being you.

ALSO BY K. JAMILA

Mine Would Be You

CONNECT WITH K. JAMILA

Website

Instagram

Spotify

Facebook Group

Newsletter

Goodreads

Twitter

Pinterest

www.ingramcontent.com/pod-product-compliance
Lightning Source LLC
Chambersburg PA
CBHW060604300726
48975CB00005B/1444